To Linda

Anne Goodwin

Thanks for reading

Matilda Windsor is
Coming Home

A C S

Inspired
Quill

Published by Inspired Quill: May 2021

First Edition

TW: This book contains mentions of rape and themes of mental trauma.

Chief Editor: Sara-Jayne Slack
Cover Design: Valeria Aguilera
Typeset in Adobe Garamond Pro

Paperback ISBN: 978-1-913117-05-4
eBook ISBN: 978-1-913117-06-1
Print Edition

Printed in the United Kingdom
1 2 3 4 5 6 7 8 9 10

Inspired Quill Publishing, UK
Business Reg. No. 7592847
www.inspired-quill.com

Praise for *Sugar & Snails*

An absorbing, clever and heartening debut novel.

– Alison Moore,
author of Booker-shortlisted *The Lighthouse*

Fiction delivered by a writer who knows not only how to craft her words but also what those words should be communicating.

– Dr Suzanne Conboy-Hill in *The Psychologist*

I loved this book. Sugar and Snails is beautifully written and a truly impressive debut by Anne Goodwin. It reminded me a little of Claire Messud's The Woman Upstairs. The character of Di, at first frustrating, grows more endearing as you begin to understand her. Her friend Venus and lover Simon are well-drawn; there as foils to Di's story. A beautiful and gripping read.

– Fleur Smithwick,
author of *How to make a Friend*

Sugar and Snails is a brave and bold emotional roller-coaster of a read. Anne Goodwin's prose is at once sensitive, invigorating and inspired. I was hooked from the start and in bits by the end. Very much to be recommended.

– Rebecca Root,
'The Queen's Gambit' actor

Praise for *Underneath*

A dark and disturbing tale of a man who appears ordinary on the surface, but is deeply damaged. Clever and chilling; [Underneath] is a story that will stay with you long after you've finished reading.

– Sanjida Kay,
author of *Bone by Bone*

[Underneath] is a compelling, insightful and brave novel of doomed, twisted romance driven by a sustained and unsettling voice.

– Ashley Stokes,
author of *The Syllabus of Errors*

It's a quiet novel that gradually unpicks the past to discover what lies behind the protagonist's façade. Obviously drawing on her experience as a clinical psychologist, Anne Goodwin takes what could have been a dry case study and builds it into a compelling read.

– Mary Mayfield,
Our Book Reviews

Intelligent, insightful writing which takes you beneath the surface of life in many, many ways.

– Pamela Robertson,
Books, Life and Everything

Praise for *Becoming Someone*

This is a varied collection which shows you different aspects of identity and what gives an individual a sense of self. You can dip into it or pick a story to read and can be sure that there will be a thought-provoking look at what it is to 'be'. In short: Powerful writing which examines what makes a person.

— Books, Life and Everything

Anne Goodwin has such an observant eye for human motivation and behaviour.

— Literary Flits

I loved the way the author was willing to play around and try different techniques, including one story in second person. Highly recommended.

— Dorothy Winsor, bestselling author of *The Wysman*

To call these stories 'psychological studies' might not be quite accurate, but it's close … All of them share Anne Goodwin's perceptive, sympathetic insights.

— Our Book Reviews Online

For the survivors, and those who
provide support along the way.

WHEN YOU FIND me, you will want to hear my story. Or the part of my story that tells of you. Until then, I turn it around in my mind to prevent it fading. When we meet, it will sing.

As a lass, I was full of stories. They kept Mother entertained after we snuffed out the light. Stories of a dazzling future with no thought of fathers, husbands, brothers or sons.

Yours begins one night when Mother's betrayal stole my appetite for fiction. "I'm sorry, Matilda, but I can't come with you on Saturday. Mr Windsor needs me at the shop."

"You should have said you had a *prior engagement.*" That's what she'd tell *me* if I was tempted to break *my* word when something nicer came along. But what could be nicer than hearing me recite? The shiny buttons and spools of thread and silken ribbon in Windsor's Haberdashery would seem drab against her daughter's red rosette.

"Grow up, Matilda. A child half your age would accept that if *I* don't work, *you* don't eat."

I turned my back on her. She reached for my hand, but

I slid it between my pillow and my cheek. She didn't try a second time. Didn't shepherd me through "The Lady of Shalott". Didn't beg for the next instalment of the saga of the girl from The Marsh who becomes a famous doctor. Soon, soft whistling signalled she'd dropped off.

Awake in the dark, while Mother slept, a hollow feeling swept over me. As if Mother preferred Mr Windsor's dreams to mine.

Chapter 1

October 1989

THE CUSHION SIGHS, squashed by a body sinking into the seat beside her. Matty scrunches her already-closed eyes. She does not care for distractions when she has a recital to prepare. And, never able to anticipate *when* she might be called on to deliver her lines, her day spools out as one continuous rehearsal. Matty's burden weighs heavily upon her, but she bears it with grace.

A whiff of lavender, but this is not her mother. Matty has been deceived before. The breath is too loud, too erratic. A smoker's lungs. Matty tilts her head away. Unmoored from the monologue, she is obliged to return, silently, to the start.

Hands folded in her lap, she conjures her mother behind closed eyelids. Mouthing the words from alongside the orchestra pit, her features contorted to magnify the shapes of the vowels. Matty smiles inwardly, as confidence courses through her bloodstream. Although she can reel off the words as readily as her name, her mother's prompting spells the difference between fourth place with nothing to show for it and a silken rosette.

"Matty!"

It cannot be anything important: her stomach signals it is too soon after luncheon for afternoon tea. Poetry pattering in her brain, she clenches her lips as if forming knots in party balloons.

"Matty, they'll be here shortly!"

Swallowing her vexation, Matty opens her eyes. A maid has a cardboard box in her arms and a small brown suitcase by her feet. "Are you leaving us, dear?"

The maid laughs, baring her teeth, which are in tiptop condition, remarkably so given the lack of affordable dentistry for the lower ranks. "No, but you are. They'll be coming any minute from Tuke House."

"Tuke House?" Matty knows of the Palladium and the Royal Albert Hall. She knows of the Folies Bergère, despite its salacious reputation. She has never heard of Tuke House. "Thank you, dear, but the current arrangements are tickety-boo."

As the maid flashes her teeth again, Matty studies her maw for a wink of precious metal. The prince gave her mother a pair of gold molars to match her wedding band, but when Matty's were due for renewal she'd made do with plastic.

"We packed your things this morning, remember?" Dipping into the box, the maid parades the bric-a-brac piece by piece: a chunky book with a crucifix on the cover; a crumpled brown-paper bag of chewies; a conker; a poorly-composed photograph of a boy balancing the Eiffel Tower on his head. Is this one of her mother's parlour games?

"You're going up in the world, Matty Osborne." Intent on memorising the contents of the box, Matty failed to notice the housekeeper encroaching. "Seems you're too good for us now."

I am? The housekeeper is never uncertain. Never wrong. If *she* thinks Matty is leaving, it would be unwise to contradict her.

Fishing in her pocket, Matty produces a palmful of coins. "Will this do for the taxicab?"

"Save your coppers for jelly babies," says the housekeeper. "It's a five-minute hop to Tuke House. You know, the annexe where the sanatorium used to be?"

"We went for a visit yesterday," says the maid. "Found your bed in the dormitory and had a cuppa in the lounge."

The memory roasts her cheeks. The butler, whose coarse accent and casual apparel led her to mistake him for a hall boy or porter, addled her further by asking how she took her tea. As if there were any alternative to *the way it comes*! Yet beneath that unfortunate incident lies a pleasanter proposition, if she can locate it. Matty shuts her eyes.

When she opens them, the answer appears before her. "Good afternoon, Ms Osborne," says the circus girl. "May I escort you to your new abode?"

From her plume of pink hair to her patterned harem pants, the circus girl is as cheery as a rainbow scuttling a storm. How was this bohemian character recruited to a country house? Matty will shower her with honours to prevent Bertram Mills and his cronies luring her back to the Big Top. She springs to her feet.

"Hi there, Matty." Even here, in the ladies' quarters, the butler is informally attired, in a handyman's blue jeans and a school gym shirt. "Haven't you any outdoor shoes?"

Matty checks her feet, colourfully shod in tartan slippers with a red faux-fur trim. What need has *she* for outdoor shoes? The man must be a communist, bent on bamboozling her with his rhetoric.

"Shoes?" says the housekeeper. "She's not scaling Scafell Pike." Nevertheless, she urges Matty to resume her seat. Then, after directing the maid to open the suitcase, she kneels on the floor to exchange Matty's slippers for leather shoes the colour of the conker, albeit with less of a shine. Matty *must* have been promoted for the housekeeper to fasten her shoelaces like a shop-girl in Browne's.

Helping her to her feet, the housekeeper whispers a warning, "Don't get too comfy, mind. You'll be back in two shakes of a cuddy's tail."

Matty feels something stir below her breastbone as her gaze flits between the housekeeper and the circus girl. A snip of rebellion wizened with neglect. As the feeling blooms, it comes through to Matty that her mother would not appoint this person to the position of housekeeper. She has been duped by her imperial bearing and midnight-blue dress. She should have detected something foxy in the thickly pancaked makeup. One cannot trust a person who prepares her face for the stage but never deigns to recite.

Matty links arms with the circus girl. She is leaving for a

more appreciative audience. No, she will not be coming back.

———————

LUMBERING DOWN THE tiled corridor with a batty septuagenarian on one side and a hefty bag on the other, Janice's muscles zinged. Neither the pallor of the barley-water walls nor the pong of industrial-strength cleaning fluid could diminish her delight, barely a month into the job, at having made a difference. While outwardly a sober – if flamboyantly clad – professional regulating her pace to the patient's crawl, inside Janice was a child skipping hand-in-hand with her playmate.

Shuffling along the spine of the Victorian building, Matty displayed no interest in the landmarks Janice was still learning to navigate. To the left, the doors to the continuing-care wards, rescued from anonymity by signboards strung from the ceiling; to the right, entrances to departments supporting, or parasitic upon, the business of warehousing society's estranged. Farther along, Market Square, with the patients' bank and small shop where they could spend their pittance, was a pauper's theme park, tarted up like an olde worlde confectioner's. Then the corridor leading to the boardroom and the main entrance, with the switchboard operator's cubicle in the teak-panelled lobby and the staircase to the offices of those who came to work in suits. They passed the primped-up canteen where, on the other side of reinforced glass, domestics in mustard-coloured tunics ministered to an ashtray in the centre of a table.

A few steps ahead, Clive Musgrove, the nurse in charge

of Tuke House, stopped at a door immediately beyond the stairway to the sewing room, and set down Matty's case and cardboard box to grasp the handle. Since the door opened outwards, he exited first, holding it for the women to go through. He nodded to Matty, "You'll be glad you wore your shoes."

Across the cobbled courtyard, Tuke's rear windows glowed. As the door to the main building crashed behind them, Matty stalled, joggling Janice's arm. "Okay, Matty?"

"Come on," said Clive. "You must be dying for a cup of tea."

Matty wouldn't budge. Although mild for October, the late afternoon sun couldn't stretch beyond the middle of the courtyard and Matty shivered in her flimsy dress and cardigan. Clive should've insisted she wear a coat. If she possessed one. "What's bothering you, Matty?" asked Janice.

"Will he find me?"

Despite her shabby presentation, she spoke like the Queen Mother, with clipped vowels and a tone scraped clean of opinion or capacity to offend. They didn't know enough about her to guess who *he* might be, and whether she *wanted* or *feared* being found. When Janice delved further, Matty simply smiled.

"Have you got a fancy man?" said Clive.

Janice bristled, but his teasing roused Matty from her torpor. With a girlish giggle, she shambled forward.

While proceeding at the pace of a tortoise, Janice's expectations hared ahead. *He* might be the crux of Matty's rehabilitation. The bridge to who she would have been if the institution hadn't squandered five decades of her life.

Chapter 2

A NO MAN'S land between the poles of summer and winter, Henry's birthday month brought no excuse for celebration. Nature, never his ally at the best of times, was especially villainous in October, when weather conspired with trees to make the pavements a combat zone. Fallen leaves, wrenched from the wood by the wind, were bashed by rain and hail to a slippery sludge, causing Henry to hobble. Returning from work in the fading light, canine filth lay in ambush, camouflaged by leaf mould. The hostilities weren't solely underfoot: misted glasses stole his sight and his trilby proved a poor deterrent to conkers bombing from horse-chestnuts.

From as far off as number 38, he could tell his garden gate had been left open. Not unlatched or ajar but pushed back to align with next door's fence. Any old Toto, Duke or Lassie could mooch in and relieve itself amid the shrubs.

The spaniel from number 51 was a prime offender, although when Henry had managed to catch its owner, the chap had the temerity to accuse *him* of negligence on account of a few un-nuked weeds.

After settling the gate between the posts, Henry approached The Willows. At least autumn brought reprieve from Irene's nagging to repair the concrete path. Or to sand and gloss the front door.

Stepping over the threshold, he retrieved his post from the doormat: the solution to the riddle of the unclosed gate. Three brown business envelopes, the addresses typed, unlikely to harbour news of his sister. Yet Henry's hopes could make a banquet out of crumbs.

Henry shed his hat and coat in the hallway and made for the kitchen. Dumping the letters temporarily on the draining board, he'd snapped the heads off three matches before his hand was sufficiently steady to ignite the gas beneath the kettle.

The first letter was an anti-climax: *his* address, some neighbour's name. Henry was damned if he'd hammer on doors to convenience a postman too idle to secure a gate. Grabbing a biro from the drawer, he pulled down the kitchen cabinet's hinged shelf as a makeshift desk, scored two bold lines across the envelope and printed NOT KNOWN AT THIS ADDRESS in between. That dealt with, he ripped into the other two envelopes. Even as he winced at the typewritten *Dear Mr Windsor*, he had to scan to the bottom to ensure neither carried the signature he'd waited fifty years to see.

A missive from Somerset House confirmed, *further to*

MATILDA WINDSOR IS COMING HOME

your recent enquiry, there was no record of a marriage or death attached to the name Tilly Windsor. The correspondence shuttling to and fro at roughly six-monthly intervals was akin to having a pen-pal; Henry envisioned a homely secretary in cats-eye spectacles who would fret if he left too long a gap. Scooping dried leaves from the caddy to the Brown Betty, he caught himself humming. Once he'd eaten, he'd rattle off a batch of queries to provincial papers. Henry fancied tackling the Scottish islands, and South Rhodesia if time allowed.

Henry couldn't fathom the other letter. Linda Quinn could have walked to his desk sooner than dictate a memo. He re-read it while the tea brewed.

He'd been stunned to be passed over on the previous head's retirement. Robbed of the position by an outsider, and a woman at that. But, fair's fair, apart from her reverence for computers – a source of banter between them – she'd done a decent job. Rumour had it she wouldn't stick at head of payroll, either hopping up a rung to head of personnel or sheering sideways for the same title with a bigger budget at County Hall. Linda was conscientious; she wouldn't move on without nominating a successor. If she wanted to gauge Henry's interest, she was wise to do so discreetly.

At fifty-seven, he had three years to make his mark before collecting his retirement clock. Despite the darkness gathering beyond his kitchen window, Henry's prospects gleamed. Good things come in threes: he'd gain his promotion; Irene would ditch her husband; Tilly would come home.

Were their father alive he'd reproach Henry for counting his chickens. Yet *he* also followed his faith, bowing to the Great Architect of the Universe, along with his fellow masons at the Lodge.

Henry chuckled as he identified the tune he'd been humming: *White Christmas* in October! If *one* of his three wishes were granted, The Willows would host its merriest Christmas since his mother's day. Since before the war. Before the Depression. Before Henry was born.

Chapter 3

Four months earlier

A WHITE P against a blue background: Janice was almost level with the sign when she swung the wheel to the left and shunted into the lay-by. A horn blared as a livestock lorry loaded with lambs sped past. Janice swore, but only the Snoopy swinging from the rear-view mirror heard her.

Silencing the engine, she scuffled into the passenger seat and stomped out onto the verge. Fisting the air, she dropped her jaw and screamed.

Traffic roared by, indifferent. The slate hillside wore the frown that had served it for millennia. A small brown butterfly danced from daisy to dandelion, oblivious. Throat tingling, Janice clambered back into the driving seat, grabbing a water bottle from her bag in the passenger foot-well on the way.

By the dashboard clock she had less than an hour to get

to her appointment. Or to find a phone box to tell David Pargeter she'd changed her mind. She could scoff scones spread with Cumberland rum butter in a twee teashop, fuel for the drive home. Or skip the scones and take a detour via Huddersfield and ask her dad to fix the car door.

Was it really over with Stuart? Could love perish between the first and second slice of toast? She'd imagined a cottage on a dirt track, a couple of Labradors to fill the gap before babies. On summer evenings they'd walk the dogs after work, up to the fells or down to the shore. (Janice oscillated between a coastal idyll and one inland.) Senseless pitching up in the middle of nowhere without him. She'd be better staying in Nottingham among familiar faces, and with a wider selection of post-qualification jobs.

The last year of snatched phone calls and hours on the M6 was bound to be stressful. Juggling essays, lectures and placements while Stuart grappled two hundred miles away with his first grown-up job. But it wasn't only geographical separation that strained the relationship. Feet in different counties, their politics had drifted continents apart.

Janice wriggled in her seat, peeling her cotton trousers from her thighs. It wasn't the weather making her sweat: officially summer, the sun was a mere phantom in the clouds. Nevertheless, she'd have felt more fragrant if she'd followed Stuart's advice and worn a skirt.

But how dare he challenge her choices? *You're not my mother*, she'd said, although Janice's mother would never ridicule her for *dressing like a student*. Ten months of ironing a clean white shirt every morning had consolidated Stuart's conservatism. And to think she'd defended *him*. When he'd got the job at Sellafield, Sheena would have come to the booze-up in a T-shirt proclaiming *Pigs Can Fly, the Earth Is Flat and Nuclear Power Is Safe* if Janice hadn't caught her.

With a shrug, Janice secured her seatbelt and drove off. She would decide at the next roundabout whether to continue on to the interview or head south.

LEAVING THE CAR park, the clock tower confirmed she'd made it with five minutes to spare. Despite being home to several hundred people, and workplace for as many staff, there wasn't another soul in sight. An aura of subterfuge enveloped Ghyllside – of deadness – as if behind the majestic facade lurked a yawning sinkhole, as if the roses in the turning circle were made of wax. Mounting the stone steps, Janice imagined mingling with the hapless new arrivals in the hospital's heyday a century before. The ache of rejection. The fear of never seeing a friendly face again.

Janice pushed through the revolving door to traverse the tiled floor of the vestibule to a window in the teak-clad wall. In a room barely bigger than a broom cupboard, the receptionist plugged and unplugged cables on the switchboard. "You take a seat, Miss Lowry," she said, when Janice stated her business. "Mr Pargeter will be with you in a jiffy."

A stab of nervousness took Janice by surprise. After all, she'd only come out of politeness. Or apathy. She didn't *want* the bloody job now. But interview practice was gold dust whatever the circumstances. Glancing around, she couldn't spot any rival candidates. Unless the frail woman mumbling into a paper bag was also about to qualify as a social worker. Janice watched her pluck a jelly baby from the packet, bite off its head, and add its body to the tail of a procession snaking the bench.

Engrossed in the etiquette of a parallel universe, she seemed unaware of Janice, too self-absorbed to shimmy along for her to sit or deposit her bag. Yet the woman raised her gaze. "Did you run away from the circus?"

"Pardon me?" Janice would have been less shocked if the walls had addressed her. And, had she credited the patient with a voice stronger than a whisper, and the will to use it, she'd never have imagined her speaking like royalty.

The woman inspected a yellow jelly baby and stuffed it up her cardigan sleeve.

Could this be part of her assessment? Was the telephonist-cum-receptionist observing from her cubbyhole, scoring her for empathy, warmth and genuineness on a Xeroxed sheet? "The circus?"

She was still awaiting a response when a tall man emerged from a door opposite the entrance. Janice drank in his casual get-up – open-necked shirt, mud-coloured cords and Jesus sandals with socks – and sensed him appraising hers. But he didn't blink at her pink hair, T-shirt and harlequin harem pants. If all the patients were as wacky as this woman, and the staff similarly offbeat, working at Ghyllside might be fun, with or without a boyfriend to go home to at night.

"THANK YOU, MS Lowry. Is there anything you'd like to ask *us*?"

When David Pargeter showed up dressed as a

stereotypical social worker, Janice had expected her interview to be equally relaxed. Yet five people faced her across the table in the walnut-panelled boardroom. Either they couldn't trust David to recruit someone half-decent or this junior social work position punched above its weight. Luckily she hadn't let on that she wouldn't have applied if the Society section of the *Guardian* had advertised a wider range of entry-level posts.

David, as immediate manager, had grilled her on institutionalisation and stigma; Yvonne Conway, *his* manager and head of social work throughout the hospital, tested her knowledge of The Community Care Act; Graham Scott, manager of the health staff within the rehabilitation sector, elicited her views on social role valorisation, sounding as if he scarcely understood it himself; Parveen Shakir, consultant psychiatrist, enquired how she'd respond to a patient who believed the TV broadcasted their private thoughts; while Clive Musgrove, nursing manager for Tuke House, asked what, if anything, should be done about a patient who didn't rise from his bed until four in the afternoon. Even without the dismal start to her day, she'd have found their questions draining.

But not so much she hadn't the energy to pose a few of her own. "Can I check I've got the role absolutely straight?" Janice had studied the job description, of course, and discussed it with David by phone. But then she'd wanted a job – *any* job – within commuting distance of Sellafield. To uproot herself to Cumbria, she'd better know *why*. "The social worker would be a generic team member ..."

Five heads nodded. (Actually, four. Dr Shakir's rocked

from side to side.)

"With specific responsibility for liaising with the patients' relatives prior to discharge," said David.

"If they have any," said Clive. "Some have been here so long, they've lost touch."

"So there'd be some detective work?" The chandelier blazed brighter. "Would I have other clients?"

"Beyond the twelve from Tuke House?" said David. "Some, but not many."

Social work luxury.

"The commissioners want the project well resourced." Graham Scott brushed back his heavy fringe. "The press will eat us alive if we slip up."

Janice was on the brink of protesting that the slipup lay in the previous regime of divorcing people from their communities, not in reinstating them, when Parveen Shakir flicked her wrist to consult her watch. There'd be ample opportunity to argue with Graham if she got the job. And it made sense to gradually augment her minimal mental health experience beginning with the easy cases. "I suppose Tuke takes the least disabled patients?" Creaming off, like the old grammar schools.

"Not quite." Graham explained a different team would resettle those assessed as having potential to live independently, while Tuke House would take the next level down, preparing them to leave as a group with twenty-four hour support.

"And the same nurses will move with them," said Clive.

The lights dimmed. A mini institution beyond the asylum walls. Yet it might house the quirkier characters.

Such as the old dear lining up jelly babies on the bench. Janice directed her query to David. "I wondered about the woman in the reception area."

"Matty Osborne?"

"Maybe. She didn't introduce herself." Janice regretted not introducing *herself* first. "Is she in the resettlement group?"

Graham laughed. "I'm afraid *she'll* be going feet first."

"I thought everyone would be discharged. Isn't the hospital closing down?"

"Not in Matty's lifetime," said Graham. "She must be seventy if she's a day."

Janice resisted challenging the ageism; it was enough that David looked embarrassed. The more she delved into this job, the more complicated it seemed. And the more intriguing.

Chapter 4

October 1989

D ESPITE HER DILIGENCE in tidying her thoughts on retiring to bed, Matty awakes to disarray. Who has put her mind in a muddle and how did they penetrate her skull? It is as if a kitten has whiskered its way into a sewing box and woven a cat's cradle with the thread.

When she dares open her eyes, it is obvious something larger and fiercer than a baby cat is responsible. A team of workmen have shifted the walls, shrinking the room to half its normal size and trimming the beds to four, all but hers unoccupied. How could they have accomplished such a feat without waking her? Matty has to concede it feels cosier, but they should have consulted her first. *Buck up*, says her mother. *All will become clear in due course.* Indeed, the moment she curbs her curiosity, it comes through to her that *she* has moved, and to a more congenial section of the house.

"Morning, Matty. Ready for breakfast?" The person addressing her from the foot of the bed looks too jolly to be a guest. But why would a maid wear a sweater and *slacks* instead of the standard blue dress? "I'm Karen, your primary nurse. We met yesterday."

"Mine?" Matty *has* gone up in the world if she has been allotted a lady in waiting. A pity she is so sloppily turned out. "Did my mother not provide you a uniform?" A dark frock flatters the fuller figure.

The maid laughs. "I don't know about your mother, but Tuke House went into mufti to break down barriers between residents and staff."

She cannot consent to staff exchanging their tidy uniforms for androgynous leisurewear; the distinctions reassure both servants and guests of their place. But the lower orders can be tetchy when confronted. With youth on her side, her maid – Karen, or is it Kitty? – will adapt. Although obese, she has a perfect peachy complexion. It would be amusing to seek to improve her. Under Matty's tutelage, the girl might progress to one of the grander houses, Dalemain or Levens Hall.

———————

"SO, FOLKS, SHOULD we discuss the new lady?"

The consultant's question was rhetorical, but Janice had to stifle an instinctive *Yes, please* like a kid granted a second helping of ice cream. The weekly gathering of the multidisciplinary team – the two psychiatrists, the clinical psychologist, the occupational therapist, the charge nurse, a staff nurse and Janice for social services – was where, in theory, different perspectives on the residents' difficulties were aired, debated and solutions agreed. Thus far, Janice had struggled to carve an opening through the dizzying diagnoses, the unfamiliar acronyms and the medications with their multiple aliases. But Matty Osborne reduced the entire team to novices. In fact, Janice was ahead of her colleagues, having met Matty on Ward 24 before the transfer was mooted. She'd even chaperoned her to Tuke House, demonstrating a commendable team spirit and a flexible interpretation of the social work role.

Parveen Shakir turned to the doctor at her side, a scrawny man with a tweed jacket, a buzz cut and prominent ears. "What have you gleaned from the notes, Mervyn?"

Dr Mervyn Yates selected a buff-coloured file from the stack on the table at his shins and read: "Matty Osborne, seventy-year-old single Caucasian lady with a diagnosis of chronic schizophrenia …"

"Sorry, Parveen, Mervyn," said Clive Musgrove, the charge nurse, "but could we hang on for Karen? I'm encouraging the primary nurses to get involved in the clinical meetings. She shouldn't be long."

Parveen gestured her assent with a sideways tilt of the head. As the consultant conferred with the junior doctor about an alteration to another patient's medication, Janice felt like a sprinter who had jumped the gun. "Has anyone asked her if she'd prefer Matilda?"

Janice's contribution went unacknowledged, as Karen Gilmour bustled into the room, a black ring binder under her elbow. "Apologies everybody. I had to write Jimmy Ryan a chit."

Parveen twitched the arm of her glasses, signalling Mervyn to return to the notes. "Matty Osborne, seventy-year-old single Caucasian lady with a diagnosis of chronic schizophrenia, medication biweekly intramuscular fluphenazine, first admission in nineteen thirty-nine aged twenty. No previous psychiatric history, family history of psychosis on her father's side ..."

"Excuse me," said Norman Willis, the psychologist, "could you clarify that?"

"Which bit?"

"Family history of psychosis."

Mervyn rifled through the file. "There's nothing specific, but it's mentioned in every report."

"That's because everyone copies out the history from the last one," said Norman. "There isn't any *evidence* it's real."

"There's no evidence it *isn't*," grumbled Mervyn. "You have to take it on trust."

"Even if it's *inaccurate*?" snapped Norman. "So myths become dogma, psychiatrists regurgitate what fits the medical model and edit out the rest."

"Once Matty's settled in *she* can give us the gen on her father," said Clive.

"And how *is* she settling in?" asked Parveen.

Karen opened the nursing file. "She's really sweet and everything, but I have to say ..." She paused, continuing after a nod from Clive. "It's early days but I'm staggered they rated her as having community potential. I'd have put her down for a nursing home with round-the-clock obs."

Janice noticed Norman stiffen. Overseeing the assessment of the long-stay population on everything from table manners to verbal aggression represented the zenith of his career. Although impressed by the mammoth undertaking, Janice was sceptical about prognostic tools employed to ration opportunity. Crystal-ball gazing, like the old Eleven Plus exam, which branded kids as failures before they reached their teens.

"I don't want to cast aspersions on my colleagues," Karen went on, "but the assessment's so subjective …"

"It would be easy to rate someone *too* positively," Clive added.

"Did you sleep through the training sessions?" said Norman. "The scale didn't come out of thin air. It's got *excellent* interrater reliability. Stronger than for psychiatric diagnosis." His face – at least the upper half not masked by his moustache and beard – was flushed.

Janice feared hers was an equivalent shade of scarlet. She lifted her mug from the table. And replaced it. She'd finished her tea during Effie Atkinson's review. "Speaking hypothetically, what would happen if someone's scores *were* artificially inflated?"

"They'd be out of their depth in the current affairs group," said Heather Cooper, the occupational therapist. "Like a child starting school in nappies."

"Or a manager promoted to his level of incompetence," mumbled Clive.

"Let's see how she gets on, no?" said Parveen. "We'll review her in four weeks."

"Four weeks?" If Matty *was* a year behind, she couldn't catch up in *forty* weeks.

"Sister Henderson's keeping her bed open," said Clive.

"In case it doesn't work out."

"Isn't that a tad pessimistic?" No-one had contradicted Janice at interview when she burbled about high hopes and second chances.

"Realistic," said Clive.

Janice had to accept there was little *she* could do to prevent Matty being relegated to Ward 24. Most of the aptitudes required fell within the nurses' and occupational therapists' remit. Like a candidate afforded a preferential interview by dint of disability, it was now up to Matty to prove herself.

"Is there any family contact at all?" asked Parveen.

Janice sat straighter in her seat. "Not according to Sister Henderson. But I'll write to the people at her last address."

"Last address as in fifty years ago?" said Mervyn.

"I've got to start somewhere." She didn't let on she'd sent the letter already. Before Matty was officially on her caseload.

"Absolutely," said Parveen. "Keep us updated on any developments."

Janice didn't know what she'd have said if the team had advised her not to. Would Matty's plaintive *Will he find me?* have convinced them she should try?

Chapter 5

HENRY STRODE INTO Linda Quinn's office as the church bells chimed two. Exactly on time for their meeting. A minute later would have been disrespectful; a minute earlier, unduly keen. Enthroned behind the hardwood desk that would soon be Henry's, his boss stared past him to the door. "Don't you have a union representative, Mr Windsor?"

Henry peeked over his shoulder. The letter had referred to his *right* to bring someone, not his *obligation*. His father dubbed unions a gang of hooligans blocking decent folk from doing their jobs. "We'll sort it sharper without an umpire." He didn't need a union chap to choose an executive toy to replace the Newton's cradle on Linda's desk. He didn't need a union chap to access the budget to repaint Linda's lilac walls.

"Your prerogative." She gestured for him to avail himself

of one of the two vacant office chairs. "I've got good news and bad news. The latter shouldn't come as a shock."

Henry smothered a smile. "It was on the cards." Would *he* be tasked with arranging her send-off? Or would her personal secretary – *his* when she'd gone – organise the whole caboodle? "You'll be sorely missed."

Ruby-cheeked from his compliment, Linda Quinn shuffled her papers. "I've worked my socks off to accommodate you, Henry. But this refusal to move with the times …"

Computers! Why dredge up *that* fiddle-faddle now? Squinting against the glare from the window behind her desk, Henry couldn't read Ms Quinn's expression. The light lent her face a saintly halo, but her tone was neither pious nor playful. He tethered his gaze to the silvery balls of the Newton's cradle as he fumbled in his jacket pockets for his lucky conker, but all he found was grit-infected fluff that vexed his fingernails, and a nut of hardened gum. "If it ain't broke …" Henry was proud of the payroll system he'd introduced in the seventies. Had he lived long enough, his father would have been proud too.

"Every other council in the country has switched to computers."

Henry squeezed a finger between his shirt and his neck. His collar hadn't felt so tight that morning. "A passing fad." What could a computer achieve that a typist with a Selectric couldn't? Or a smart schoolkid with a scientific calculator?

"The antidote to business drudgery. Which you'd have discovered for yourself if you'd agreed to go on a course."

Henry glanced at the empty chair beside him. A union

chap might have defended his decision to veto residential training.

"You leave me no choice, Henry. You've failed to meet the demands of the job."

A cloud snuffed out the sun, affording Henry an uninterrupted view of the car park and, beyond it, the graveyard of St Mark the Evangelist's church. At least with his father dead and buried Henry couldn't disappoint him. "And the good news?"

"It wasn't easy, but we've figured a way to keep you on." Scrabbling in her desk drawer, Linda brandished an ID badge on a phlegm-coloured cord. "Up to three years' protected salary. Your pension's secure."

Henry clasped his hands in his lap. He'd be deputy head of payroll until he accepted the badge. But he'd have to take it eventually: it bore his mugshot, in his heavy glasses and a striped shirt with a white collar Irene bought him one Christmas. "What does a Senior Assistant Clerical Officer without Portfolio *do*?"

Linda ratched through her papers and slid him a sheet of A4. It didn't say much: the title took up half the page. "You're familiar with the clause at the end of job descriptions regarding *any other duties required by the post*? In this case, that's the *core*."

"A general dogsbody?"

"With a desk in the multi-use office and up to three years' protected salary."

"What would I actually *do*, Linda?"

Ms Quinn waved her arms expansively. "You'll embrace a broad spectrum of projects across multiple sectors. The mayor's office, planning, electoral services." She beamed. "Don't they say variety's the spice of life?"

Henry stuffed the badge into his pocket to cosy up to the fluff and the unchewable chuddy. "I suppose I'd better clear my bits and bobs out of payroll."

He'd almost reached the door when Linda called him back, her arm outstretched. "Your old badge, please, Henry. It's no use to you now."

NONE OF HIS colleagues witnessed Henry collecting his belongings from the desk he'd occupied for nearly forty years. He hadn't a deal to show for it: his fountain pen; his slide rule, and the scientific calculator that had rendered it redundant; half a dozen packets of chuddy and as many plastic cigarette lighters; the mug Irene had brought him from Benidorm; a strew of pre-decimal coins. They barely covered the bottom of the cardboard box he'd emptied of photocopying paper to transport his effects down the corridor. Unlike the other desks, his hosted no photographs of friends or family: the risk too great of Irene being recognised; his sole picture of Tilly too precious for public display.

Initially, he felt detached, as if playing the part of an honourable but temporarily disgraced bank manager who would be exonerated before the credits of a Hollywood classic. It wasn't until he'd scoured the drawers several times over that his frustration at mislaying his conker filtered through.

Of course he could get another. The pavements were littered with them. But this was *Tilly's* conker, entrusted to him when she left. He'd cherished it through boarding school and national service, proof that, despite not knowing his mother, he'd known maternal love. It symbolised their mutual loyalty: *her* pledge to return; *his* willingness to wait.

Henry lifted the box and put it down again. He couldn't start a new job without ballast. Scooping up pencils, staplers, erasers, Post-it notes and highlighter pens from his colleagues' desks, he dumped them in the box. He opened drawers and extracted spiral-bound notebooks, pads of squared paper and transit envelopes the colour of tangerines. Only when his box was full did Henry find the strength to leave.

AT THE END of his first day as Senior Assistant Clerical Officer without Portfolio, Henry popped into the corner shop to pick up a frozen cottage-pie-for-one. Although he'd scarcely done a stroke of work, he felt exhausted, unable to envisage embarking on anything more taxing that evening than sitting by the fire with Radio Four.

Turning into Sheepwash Lane, he noticed, in the light of a streetlamp, a young woman at his garden gate. Deducing, from her bulging bag, she'd be delivering free newspapers, Henry slowed his pace to avoid colliding on the path. Her dusky complexion and gaudy guise made him think of gypsies, or a hippy or a punk or whatever the current craze might be. Or a layabout from the Tech, with her spiky pink haircut and harlequin trousers tucked into black pixie boots. An influx of students would pollute the neighbourhood with all-night parties, loud music and drugs.

When she loitered at the gate, gazing up towards the

attic, Henry had to confront her. "Can I be of any assistance?" Had *she*, and not the postman, left the gate open the previous week?

"Thanks, I'm looking for the Osbornes."

Henry shook his head. "There are new people at The Laurels." The street was swamped with strangers; no-one remained from his father's day.

"I'm chasing up the family from number forty-four."

"Did Tilly send you?" In his mind, he'd watched more versions of their reunion than repeats of *It's a Wonderful Life*. As he'd grown older – and his sister older still – he'd imagined her daughter making contact. Recently, he'd graduated to grandchildren, but he'd never imagined being accosted by a pink-haired clown in jazzy jeans.

"No-one sent me. I'm from social services and one of our clients has this as her last address."

An administrative error, a computer glitch. Or a prank. "There's no call for social work here. I suggest you try The Laurels."

"I'll do that." Yet she stayed put. "You can't tell me about the Osbornes who used to live here?"

On any other afternoon, Henry might have been more hospitable. Her air of entitlement notwithstanding, she was just doing her job. But he'd had his hopes raised and dashed enough for one day. "I don't, and if they ever *were* here it must be a long time ago. I've lived here my entire life."

HENRY SPOTTED HIS conker in the hallway's gloom immediately on opening the door. It sat on the hall stand, brown shell melding with brown wood. He wasn't so superstitious as to believe it could have altered Linda Quinn's opinion but it might have encouraged him to *try* to convince her of his worth. He'd thought, by controlling his emotions, he was taking it like a man. Perhaps he'd taken it like a schoolboy who, summoned to the headmaster's study, bends over instantly and drops his shorts.

After hanging up his coat, Henry lingered in the hall, rolling the conker between finger and thumb. Hard as diamond, and to Henry as valuable: the very kernel of his self. His image of the day he'd received it was, like most early memories, part reality, part wishful thinking and part scene from a sentimental film. When truth proved elusive, Tilly would ground him, anchor him to the facts. She was the fulcrum, the heart, the bull's eye, the star around which the disparate fragments circled. Tilly had given him the conker moments before she left.

Henry had been five or six; his glamorous sister and surrogate mother roughly nineteen. Setting down her suitcase, she'd crouched until her face was level with his. In his memory, she was doing up the buttons of his coat, which was bizarre when *she* was leaving, not him. Perhaps she'd squatted to kiss his cheeks or wipe away a tear. "You'll be a brave little soldier, won't you, Henry? I'll not be gone for long. Will you look after this till I come back?"

Now he clenched the conker so tightly it threatened to sear through his palm. Then, as if his arm acted independently of his intentions, he bowled it down the hall, where it skimmed the tiles like a bouncing bomb. His sister had broken her word. But, although kidding himself otherwise, so had he. With so little to remember her by, he couldn't shrug his shoulders when her conker went AWOL. He'd done his best, but the law of the school dormitory, ditto the military barracks, held that the more treasured the possession the greater the probability of it going astray. Yet only the portion of his mind that was stuck in single digits could equate *his* betrayal in replacing the original conker to *hers* in reneging on her promise to return.

Trudging upstairs, Henry ruminated on his resistance to residential training. If he'd succumbed to Linda's pressure, might he be deputy head of payroll instead of senior assistant in nothing at all? But since his father's death he'd never stayed away at night lest Tilly come knocking. He might have chanced it if a computer could magically locate his sister. But a glorified calculator-cum-typewriter couldn't succeed where letters to editors in five continents had failed.

Passing the doors to his bedroom, the bathroom and the bedroom that had been his father's, Henry mounted the steps to the attic. Irene tolerated his keeping a sanctuary for Tilly; not so his father's room. *You're not expecting* him *to rise from the dead too?* Sometimes she nagged so relentlessly, or protested so pitifully that his smaller room triggered her migraine, he acquiesced to bonking on the bed he was conceived in. It always left him feeling grubby: George Windsor would never have coveted another man's wife.

As a child, he'd been enchanted by Tilly's room, with the sloping ceiling and patchwork quilt. He'd spent hours staring over the rooftops, but he hadn't come upstairs today for the view. Opening the middle drawer of the vanity table, he exhumed a black-and-white photograph: his sister holding onto her hat with one hand and *his* hand with the other, and their father standing slightly aloof. When he was small, because of his name, he truly believed his father was the monarch. In the photo he seemed stern and regal, whereas Tilly looked generous and down-to-earth. Now the real king's daughter had worn the crown for practically as long as Henry had been at the council, while *his* father's daughter remained out of reach. *Who were you, Tilly Windsor? And where are you now?*

On turning fifty, Henry was confident he'd fulfil his three ambitions prior to retirement. Seven years on, his faith in the first, his sister's homecoming, was fading. The second, to head a department at the council, had toppled that day. But the third, to share his home with a woman, remained viable. Undeterred by the age difference, Irene's commitment to their clandestine meetings hadn't wavered. Now her twins were grown, she might divorce Eric and settle down with him.

Chapter 6

"HE SAID HE'D never heard of any Osbornes, and he's lived there all his life."

"And how long was that?" said David.

"You mean, how old was he?" said Janice. "I didn't ask."

As if abruptly conscious of his feet drifting into the gap between them, David drew them back into line with the chair legs and rested his hands on his knees. He conducted his supervision sessions in a windowless room more cupboard than office. Anyone would feel cramped, even without the sink and kitchen unit where the social workers made coffee and forgot to wash their cups, but David was a beanpole. "It can be awkward, can't it?"

Janice had struck lucky with David Pargeter as her manager, an unflappable bloke who pounced on the positives in an imperfectly executed task. But Janice didn't *want* to provide a second-best service. When her letter rebounded marked *Return to sender*, should she have discussed it with David before dashing to Sheepwash Lane? "Late fifties? Early to mid sixties?" Older than her parents and younger than her grandparents.

"And Matty's been here …?"

"Half a century." Silently inserting *fucking* between *half a* and *century*.

"He'd have known her if the address was accurate."

"How could it be wrong?" She'd tried the houses either side, but maybe she should have visited all the forties, the whole street.

"It was a long time ago, Janice." David chuckled. "Before even I was around. And they wouldn't have been so rigorous about records. Not with war imminent."

"It's no big deal to write out an address."

David stretched his legs, studiously positioning them away from Janice's. "One of the hardest aspects of this job is letting go."

"You think I should drop it?" A manager could be *too* chilled.

"If her parents were alive, they'd be too decrepit to take on someone like Matty."

"But she's fabulous."

"I bet her relatives wouldn't find her so endearing. Untreated psychosis is no joke."

Janice recalled a conversation with Ronnie Bloomsburg's sister that made her shiver. But Matty's case was different. "She should never have been admitted."

"You do come across some tragic stories." David shuffled his legs. "But you can't fix the past. You've given it your best shot. Let's focus on the future, supporting her transition to the community if that's what's in the offing. How's she doing on Tuke? She's not too freaked by the demands?"

WHEN SUBJECTED TO the indignities of female biology, Matty's mother advocates pegging her mind to a more agreeable location. So, lying on the couch as her maid prepares to poke a needle into her posterior, Matty rehearses "The Lion and Albert". Although the monologue is rather coarse, she has read it to the boy until her voice turns to gravel.

She is nearing the climax – where, the lion having devoured their child, the Ramsbottoms are in a frazzle – when the medicine seeps into her muscle. No matter how many times she submits to it, Matty finds the sensation peculiar, as if her derrière is swallowing concentrated castor oil. It is a blessed relief when Kitty slides out the needle and rubs the spot with cotton wool. "That's it for another fortnight."

Matty presses her toes into the couch to pull up her panties. "Toodle-oo, babies." She wriggles onto her side.

Kitty helps her to her feet. "You do know what your injection's *for*?"

Is *she* familiar with that malarkey? Can Kitty be so worldly-wise? "For protection."

"That's one way of putting it. Protection from nasty thoughts."

MATTY IS SOMEWHAT peeved when Kitty asks her to adjourn to the lounge to await a journalist. In her current condition, she will struggle to summon her customary zest. Her injection can dim the lights upstairs as well as *down below*.

On the threshold, she pauses. There are *men* in this section of the house. Matty will extend the hand of friendship to anyone, but bass notes do drum on her ears. Fortunately, she has encountered only ladies in her bedroom, but the fellow who sat opposite her at breakfast slurped his tea in an exceptionally galling fashion.

She scans the felt-topped table where she has seen them clack coloured balls back and forth, but the green is deserted. She scans the television where they sometimes track herds of hyperactive horses, but *it* shows a maid sprinkling scouring powder in a bathtub. The men have either become invisible, or they are out at work.

Indeed, the room is unoccupied except for one person, rocking on a chair beside the fish tank. Regrettably, *she* is more irksome than the men. Slight, with a long tapered nose and cheeks the hue of a mandarin orange, she seems oblivious to the athletics of the fish, despite sharing their marine heritage. She gawps at the baby she cradles as Matty swans past to sit in the bay window.

It is most irregular for a guest to breeze in with a baby in her baggage. Matty cannot comprehend how this one has slipped through. She ought to pity the shrimp-woman – her maid too slovenly to attend to *her* injection – but the feeling she evokes is contempt.

It is not difficult to avert her gaze. Straining her neck,

she revels in the view of the estate chapel across the tarmac. The fiercer challenge is preventing the creature invading her mind. To defend against this, Matty prepares her thoughts for the forthcoming meeting. What should she tell the journalist about Tuke House?

The guests are too eccentric and the staff too spirited to be restful but – men, shrimp and baby notwithstanding – her new quarters are superior to those she left. Significant enough to have a name, not a number, while the regime is reminiscent of an Alpine spa: morning soaks in a private bathroom, nourishing meals and hikes in the grounds with her maid.

Kitty – or is it Kathy? Karen? – is shaping up. In contrast to some previous assistants, she does not shirk her duties and is eager to learn. Nevertheless, her poverty of education is manifest in some peculiar obsessions. For example, she has developed a fixation on a picture she found among Matty's belongings. It had a jagged edge, as if ripped from a magazine, although Matty cannot imagine how it has passed the editor's scrutiny when the child has the Eiffel Tower sprouting from his head. She thought Kitty forward in asking who he was. While acquainted with several VIPs, Matty cannot keep tabs on *everyone*, informing Kitty that, if she was so interested, she could *have* the blasted picture. To her credit, the maid refused to take what was not hers, which confirmed the girl's character, and Matty's discernment in appointing her. Matty has had maids who have purloined her possessions, as unpleasant as it was impossible to prove.

Wrapped in thought, Matty has forgotten the interview when Kitty comes to collect her. She is tempted to say she has had a change of heart – whether from *Vogue* or the local rag, journalists can be tiresome – but feels compelled to comply when the maid asks so nicely. She also derives some gratification from the shrimp-woman's envy as Kitty escorts her to the door.

It is testament to the magnificence of the house that her mother has allotted a room to press conferences. Roughly the size of a scullery maid's garret, it is furnished with two leatherette armchairs at a low table, upon which are two cups of tea. Kitty has thought of everything, short of introducing her to the gentleman seated there, a fountain pen in his fingers and a fat folder on his lap. But Matty will not bore her brain with superfluous names and the journalist must know who she is or he would not have come. He is a dreary specimen: a rake of a man with elephant ears and a convict's haircut, albeit redeemed by shiny shoes. Settling into her seat as Kitty leaves the room, she nods encouragement.

His preliminary queries lack initiative but Matty responds with her natural charm. *Does she know what place this is?* "My home, obviously." *How long has she lived here?* "I have never lived anywhere else." *Can she remember what brought her here?* "You do not need me to tell you about the birds and bees." *Does she know what year it is?* "I do, my dear, do you?"

She takes a sip of tea. The journalist follows suit. *Does she hear voices when no-one is there?* "Never." She hears the boy singing nursery rhymes, but that is a *single* voice. Unless she joins in.

Does she experience odd sensations? Modestly, Matty drops

her gaze. *Does she feel as if someone has taken control of her body or mind?* Clucking at the impertinence, Matty brushes her skirt. "My mother married a prince."

"Your father was a prince, was he? Did *he* have strange experiences?"

Matty weighs the question meticulously. His war would have been an exceedingly strange experience, living in a muddy trench under attack from General von Bulow's men. Could the young journalist conceive of the horror?

How gaunt he is. How pale. It is not only The Great War that makes men martyrs. Not only in battle that they suffer. From her skirt pocket, she produces two jelly babies and offers them to the journalist. Does he decline because they are headless, or because he is not partial to red? Popping them into her mouth, she wonders what *would* amuse him. Having neglected her practice of late, a recital would be inapt. Even an exasperating journalist deserves better than "The Lion and Albert". "Do you come here often?" she asks.

"Indeed I do." He could pass for human when he smiles.

"Isn't it spiffing?"

"Which aspect especially?"

"All sorts." It comes through to Matty that male guests create a festive atmosphere. Such is the modern manner. How to convey this to the young man with due decorum? Stroking her sleeves, she notices she is wearing a cashmere twinset in a cheery primrose. "Shopping and so-forth."

The journalist perks up in an instant. "How do you cope with money?"

"Fortunately, I have sufficient reserves in the bank."

"Then you withdraw some to go shopping, I suppose?

Does it get complicated? Keeping it safe? Checking your change?"

How to explain the etiquette to an outsider? Ordinarily, she visits the butler in his office who writes a chit which she takes to the estate bank, if she can find it. Then she takes the cash to the shop for four ounces of jelly babies. But one day, spurred on by Kitty, she emerged from the bank with a fistful of five-pound notes. "I put them in my purse and my purse in my handbag." Then they marched past the sweet shop to the main door where a limousine received them, as if they were stars of the silver screen. They entered a department store and ascended to the second floor (in the lift, as Matty did not trust the moving staircase). Kitty plucked garments from the rails and, when Matty tried them on, declared which were the most fetching. "She has exquisite taste."

"I'm glad to hear it." The journalist's countenance has improved, no jelly babies required. "And are you ready to move to the community?"

His meaning obscure, Matty smiles, but she cannot entertain the notion of relocating so soon. "I'm quite content here …" Conscious of the journalist's raised eyebrow, Matty alters course. "Although I could live elsewhere if I had my maid."

Chapter 7

THE TEAM GATHERED at the boardroom table as Graham Scott, the general manger, unfurled the architect's plans. Navy lines on glossy grey paper, spindly lettering as if etched with a single hair. Janice thought of Escher's mathematically-inspired drawings, yet this artwork wasn't an optical illusion but the launch pad for a revolution in psychiatric care.

Graham talked the team through the setup: a row of three houses, each with a kitchen, toilet and lounge-diner on the ground floor, an attached garage, and four bedrooms and a bathroom above. The team psychiatrist, Parveen Shakir, lifted her glasses and lowered them again. "I can't see the treatment room."

"We agreed not to have one," said the charge nurse, Clive Musgrove. "These are people's *homes*."

"But they're still our patients, no? They won't stop

needing injections and so forth because they've moved a few miles up the road."

"They'll have their bedrooms for that," said Clive.

Parveen appealed to the psychologist, Norman Willis. "Don't tell me you'd conduct counselling sessions in a bedroom?"

"*Psychotherapy* would be inconceivable in a bedroom."

"I assumed you'd see them in outpatients?" said Graham.

Norman scratched his beard. "It's a Herculean task coaxing them to trek from Tuke House. Can you imagine Effie Atkinson getting a bus back to the hospital?"

"Not at the moment," said Heather Cooper, the occupational therapist. "But we're working on their community skills."

"Any news on *where* they're going to put us?" asked Clive. "If we're out in the sticks there might not *be* a bus service."

"It's not official," said Graham, "but Estates have got their eyes on the Briarwood baby clinic."

"I know it," said Heather. "That derelict building on Corporation Road."

Yet to construct a mental map of the area, Janice made a mental note to consult her A-Z.

"A monstrous carbuncle," said Graham. "The neighbours will be chuffed to see it knocked down and replaced with three shiny new homes."

Parveen continued glowering at the plans. "There's not even a staff room. Where will you store the notes? Take your breaks?"

Clive snorted. "Remember the mission statement? *Ordinary valued lives.* None of *us* have a staff room in *our* homes."

"There'll be a locked cupboard for the nursing notes in the kitchens," said Graham.

Janice didn't mention that a locked drawer in an unlocked room wouldn't pass muster in social services, but resolved to discuss case-note security with David Pargeter in her next supervision.

Parveen turned to the occupational therapist. "Heather, have you thought where you'll run your groups?"

Graham tapped a rectangle on the blueprint. "You could use one of the lounges."

"That wouldn't be fair on the residents who opt out," said Norman. "They'd be trapped in their bedrooms until it was over."

"They'll be *discharged*," said Clive. "Why would they *want* occupational therapy?"

Heather blushed. "You might ask why nurses. Why a psychologist."

Norman swept a hand across the plans. "What's the *purpose* of these buildings?"

Clive groaned. "We went through all that last year."

"So why are we arguing now?" said Norman.

"I wouldn't call it arguing," said Graham. "Debating the fine detail."

"We'll keep going round in circles," said Norman, "until we clarify whether the priority's what the site *looks* like or giving vulnerable people the support they need."

His logic didn't defuse the tension. Janice had come to

the meeting bubbling with anticipation but her colleagues' bickering had flattened her mood. She was irritated with herself as much as with them; her novice status no excuse for staying mute.

The boardroom's opulence oppressed her; its elegance obscene. The hospital's Victorian patrons hadn't seen fit to extend the panelled walls, moulded cornices or chandeliers to the wards.

At her interview in this room, Janice had been asked about the pros and cons of multidisciplinary teamwork. Now she realised what she *should've* said. They had to set aside their professional differences to defeat the common enemy of discrimination. "Remind me why we've got garages. None of the residents can drive."

"I hoped the staff could use them," said Clive. "It's no fun hacking ice off your windscreen after a nine-hour shift."

"The board insisted," said Norman. "If the project fails, houses with garages would be easier to sell."

"Could we convert them?" asked Parveen.

"The garages or the board members?" said Graham.

"To create another room?" said Heather.

"A staffroom?" said Clive.

"Or a clinic room," said Parveen.

"Or a group-cum-interview room," said Norman.

"Or all three," said Heather. "Three garages, three extra rooms."

"Brilliant," said Clive.

"Makes sense," said Graham. "Although it might strain the budget."

"I'm sure *you* could make a case for a top-up," said

Parveen. "Given what we'll save by closing a ward."

Janice should've been glad she'd nudged the group to a compromise by querying the point of the garages, but were they short-changing the residents in playing safe? There was nothing *normal* about a house with hospital baggage stowed in the garage.

Chapter 8

F ISTING THE PINKING shears, Janice trimmed a sheet of shiny red paper and slid it across the dining table to her mother. "For the last time, I don't mind."

"Thanks, love, but there must be more exciting things you could do on your birthday."

A cardboard box dripped tinsel snakes onto the carving chair. One of her mum's many toolkits, it housed the ingredients for thirty individualised crackers, a few hundred seasonal cut-outs for tiny hands to decorate and thousands of links for paper-chain streamers. "I'd forgotten how hectic your job gets in the run-up to Christmas. I'm happy to muck in." Her dad would've been helping also if her mother hadn't insisted he replace the brake pads on Janice's Polo.

"We *were* surprised when you rang. It's fabulous to see you but you haven't spent your birthday with us since your teens."

"You didn't *have* to bake a cake."

"Didn't you like it?"

"It was yummy. Once you'd scraped the burnt bit off." Janice laughed. "But I shouldn't have put you to the trouble."

"*Nothing* I do for you is *ever* any trouble. Not one single thing." Her mum arose from the table, wrapped her arms around her and pulled her in. "Do you want to tell me what's wrong?"

They'd hugged when she'd arrived, shoulders tense from hunching over the steering wheel, but this was different. This made her want to melt into her mother's body, seeking a physical fusion they'd never had. "Who said there was anything wrong?"

"No-one. Nor would you have to tell me if there was. But you're here when you could be with your friends in Nottingham. Or making new ones in Cumbria. You can't have come for my baking. Could it be the job's a bit of a let-down?"

"No, it's fantastic!"

"But you've been there two months and haven't discharged everyone? I was an idealist once."

"Oh, Mum, the injustice! The waste of so many lives! There's a woman who's been incarcerated for half a century. For no reason at all."

"Let's mash a brew and you can tell me her story. I don't know about you, but I could murder another slice of burnt cake."

———

ALTHOUGH NOT TIMETABLED into her induction, the wards for Ghyllside's most severely disabled patients weren't out of bounds. With a gap in her diary, Janice invited herself to the women's continuing-care ward.

Ward 24 was on the first floor, above a similar facility for men. Plodding up the stairs, Janice pondered whether they were intended as a disincentive to the men from visiting the women or to the women from leaving the ward at all.

A corridor led to a large lounge bordered by stiff-backed chairs where old ladies sat in splendid isolation while, beyond their reach, a television chatted to itself. The afternoon sun spilling through the high windows could not dispel the gloom. Hunched figures paced the carpet while others, seated, snored or muttered witchy incantations. Some rocked and others contorted their lips and jaws like gurners at Crab Fair, except that these women didn't twist their faces for a prestigious prize, but as a side-effect of antipsychotic medication.

In contrast to the rehabilitation wards, the staff wore the traditional nurse uniform, in deepening shades of blue spanning the hierarchy from nursing assistant to sister. Although the residents had no official uniform, they all wore shapeless floral dresses in non-iron nylon with thin cardigans, and slippers.

In a blue so dark it was a hair's breadth from black, Sister Henderson occupied a desk in an office with an observation window into the lounge. As Janice took a seat by the open door, one of the pale-blue minions set down a tea tray with matching teapot, milk jug, and china cups and saucers, a lidded bowl of sugar cubes with filigree tongs. In addition to tea, Sister Henderson dispensed a slew of demographics: who was the oldest; who had been resident the longest; who had been subjected to the most courses of ECT. Her monologue was punctuated by a procession of old ladies to the door, whom Sister Henderson studiously ignored. Janice was becoming accustomed to the ritual when the nurse cut short her soliloquy on insulin coma therapy. "Matty Osborne! Away and meet the new social worker."

Who should shuffle forward but the delightful eccentric who'd asked if she'd fled the circus? Janice extended her hand. Instead of taking it, the patient curtsied.

"Tell our visitor about your mother," said Sister Henderson.

"My mother married a prince," chimed the old woman.

"What else can you tell our visitor, Matty?"

"Matilda told such dreadful lies it made one gasp and stretch one's eyes …"

Janice recognised Hilaire Belloc's humorous poem about the girl who cried wolf. When her father read it to her and her sister – pausing after *Fire, fire!* so they could shout *Little liar!* – the child's death provoked fits of giggles. Now, prattled by the victim's namesake, it seemed obscene. As Matty fixed her gaze on a smudged whiteboard and Sister Henderson looked on devotedly, Janice couldn't decide which woman was battier. The poster in the social work office, of which she'd initially disapproved, struck her now as painfully pertinent: the passage from *Alice in Wonderland* where Alice tells the Cheshire cat, *I don't want to go among mad people.* In her youth, Matty might have felt the same.

Her monologue complete, Matty bowed and left. Sister

51

Henderson asked Janice to guess her original diagnosis.

"Mmm, I leave that to the health staff."

The nurse leant forward, revealing fissures in her thickly plastered makeup. "Moral decrepitude!"

Janice perused her mental filing cabinet for her psychiatry lecture notes. She found a reference to moral *treatment* from the early days of the asylum movement, but moral plus diagnosis had her flummoxed. Had Sister Henderson made it up? "Moral …?"

"Decrepitude! Frightful, isn't it, but this was the tail end of the thirties. Less tolerant times."

Janice had studied labelling and stigma. She knew terms now deemed offensive had had their glory hours: *lunatic; cretin*; even *mental handicap* had recently been superseded by *learning difficulty*. *Psychiatry* was morphing into *mental health*, *chronic patients* into *residents*. "Was that another word for schizophrenia?" An advance on *dementia praecox*.

"They say you have to be deranged to have children."

"Puerperal psychosis?" The ease with which the jargon tripped off her tongue would have pleased her tutors.

"Not necessarily. Imagine a lass, not much younger than yourself, drilled by parents and church to save herself for marriage. She's stepping out with a local lad, thinks he's the bee's knees. With war on the horizon, she lets him go all the way. When the inevitable happens, her chap scarpers."

"That can't have been uncommon. If every unmarried woman who fell pregnant was diagnosed with moral-whatever the wards would be chock-a-block."

"Most would've been packed off to the country," said the Sister. "Once the child's adopted, they'd slot back in at home."

One woman's loss another's gain. "And Matty Osborne?"

"Mebbe her father smelt a whiff of scandal. Mebbe she'd been a bother and he wanted shot of her."

"The family could determine the diagnosis?"

"I wouldn't say *determine*, but they could influence. Especially if they had some clout and were pally with the medical superintendent."

"But this was fifty years ago! In all that time no-one noticed she was sane?"

"Well, after a while, she wasn't. When I met her forty years since she was as you see her today, only ten times as volatile. Mad as a hatter and supremely institutionalised."

"And *did* her mother marry a prince?"

"Absolute codswallop. Or, if you want the technical term, delusions of grandeur."

"So what's next for her?"

"What do you think?" The Sister nodded towards the day room where Matty brushed imaginary dust from her lap. "She'd stick out like a sore thumb in the community."

Out in the lounge, as if at the flick of a switch, the patients became animated, spines straightening and heads turning to the corridor beyond Janice's view. She heard an orchestra of clinking crockery as a nursing assistant ferried an aluminium trolley into the centre of the room. "Is it okay for me to go and have a chat with her?"

"If you want, although it won't be terribly illuminating. Our Matty's no conversationalist."

But a more congenial one than you! Janice humped her

bag to a wipe-clean chair beside Matty. "Hello again."

Matty didn't speak until the nursing assistant brought her tea. "Thank you, dear, and one for my guest."

"I don't think our visitor would want this."

The stumpy blue-green cups and saucers were the poor relation to Sister Henderson's fine china. Janice felt outraged on the patients' behalf. "I'd love a cuppa."

The nursing assistant did some weird acrobatics with her eyebrows.

Matty drank. "Nothing beats a nice cup of tea."

"I so agree."

Stomping back to her trolley, the nursing assistant began to pour. Janice didn't twig she hadn't been asked how she liked it. At the first sip, she gagged.

The trolley was laden with cups and saucers and a gargantuan aluminium teapot, but no sugar bowl or milk jug. Not even a bottle. Had they set her up?

If so, Eyebrows seemed loath to participate. Janice refused to turn to check whether Sister Henderson watched from the window. She swallowed another sip, pretending it was Indian chai without the spices. If the patients stomached it, so would she.

Draining her cup, Matty broke the silence. Despite addressing the carpet, her enunciation was clear, her accent refined. "My mother takes Lapsang souchong with a slice of lemon."

Under that unflattering outfit, beneath that crinkled-crepe skin, a young heart blazed. The hospital had stolen her home, her boyfriend, her baby. Her life. But fifty years' segregation hadn't erased everything. A spark of personality endured. It was down to Janice to blow on that spark and rekindle her fire.

Why shouldn't Matty drink Lapsang souchong, orange pekoe or Earl Grey? Served with a sliver of lemon, a wedge of lime or a feast of seasonal fruit. Sweetened with honey, if she fancied it; coloured with Cornish clotted cream.

———————

"YOU CERTAINLY RISE to a challenge."

"I'm not on my own with it, Mum. There's a full multidisciplinary team." With a dampened fingertip, Janice gleaned the crumbs from her plate. "But no-one cares the way I do. Cares like it's personal."

"Are you making it *too* personal?"

"Didn't you tell me the personal is political?"

"I probably did, but I wouldn't have told you to run yourself ragged over it. It's a lot to deal with on top of moving house, a new area, splitting up with Stuart … You didn't take the job hoping you'd get back together?"

"I took it because I wanted to make a difference."

"You could make a difference in Nottingham with your friends."

"I can't jack it in. I've hardly begun."

Her mother uncoiled herself from the sofa, opened a drawer in the sideboard and brandished a newspaper clipping. "I saved this from Wednesday's *Guardian*."

Skimming the advert, Janice's toes tingled. Some other social worker's opportunity to innovate. To live in Nottingham.

"I said to your dad, that job's got Jan's name on it."

"I can't mess Ghyllside about."

"There's no harm in ringing up for a job description."

"I can't quit before I've *achieved* anything." Janice didn't dwell on what she *had* achieved. Or *how*. The risk would be in vain if Matty could be returned, like shoddy goods to a shop, to be Sister Henderson's performing monkey. "I'm supposed to reunite the residents with their long-lost relatives. But I've flunked with Matty."

"Have you tried the local paper?"

"Advertising? That's breaking confidentiality."

"You needn't say *why* you wanted people to get in touch."

Should she try it? Place one newspaper ad and reply to another?

"When you think adoption and fostering publish kids' *photos* …"

"Is that how you found me and Roz?"

Chapter 9

HIS FATHER DECREED that a job worth doing was worth doing well. From the men who emptied the bins right up to the mayor, each cog in the system had to pull its weight. Although George Windsor had never envisaged his son being demoted to Senior Assistant Clerical Officer without Portfolio, the edict remained. Henry carried out his responsibilities assiduously.

Those allocating his tasks conceived his role as more onerous than he did. To avoid him standing idle, they found him work they could have done themselves in the time it took to explain. That morning, Arthur from Procurement had spent half an hour briefing him on requisitioning the municipal Christmas tree, a procedure that took Henry under ten minutes.

Afterwards, he'd been commissioned to monitor playground activity at the park; a tally of tiddlers on the roundabouts and slides. When Henry pointed out most were at school, Arthur shrugged. "Pity you're allergic to computers," he said, a non sequitur if ever there was one.

Aside from manipulating his frozen fingers to record the figures in his notebook, and the guarded glances from mothers pushing infants on the swings, Henry didn't mind the work. It wasn't as futile as he'd anticipated: amongst the toddlers trussed up in their snow suits like teddy bears, he spotted a number of older children. Henry had to turn a blind eye to the truants: his assignment to the attendance officer wasn't for another week.

Espousing the school kids' disdain for authority, Henry took the long way to the Town Hall. Despite having lived here his entire life – apart from exile to boarding school and national service – he often felt disorientated in the shopping centre. He'd expect some *shops* to have changed hands, and function, since his childhood, but how had the *buildings* shifted? He couldn't even suss out where Windsor's Haberdashery had stood, with its ribbons and buttons and bales of cloth, and the overhead network of pneumatic tubes conveying the cash from the counters to the office he should've inherited when his father retired.

Now he persevered through the ugly 1960s arcade, pausing at the jewellers'. He planned to ask Irene to marry him and only a cheapskate would propose without a ring. But the constellations of diamonds and rubies arrayed in the window diminished him as dramatically as those in the sky. What jewel could persuade her to plight her troth with a chap on the downward track to retirement? Was a solitaire stingy or sophisticated? Was a giant gem vulgar or symbolic of her preciousness? He should've got this done and dusted when he was young.

When home on leave he'd stayed there, with Mozart on the gramophone, rather than braving the ballroom where his peers jitterbugged and jived. In his dreams he had the pick of pretty girls, his cordy spilling seed on the sheets. But in the flesh they put the frighteners on him. They'd take the mickey if he asked for a dance.

People were chary of single men gone thirty. Afraid they might be one of *them*. At school, such goings-on were standard if you were small and unheroic on the rugby pitch. The purpose of education being to build character, there was no firmer underpinning than knowing life could never be so dreadful again. The boy begets the man by enduring without blubbing: if school were based on kindness, they'd all be Peter Pan. When Henry began boarding at his father's alma mater, older boys were packing their kitbags to fire-bomb Germany. Buggery was the perfect preparation for the butchery of the battlefield. A cold wet bed for the beaches of Dunkirk.

School gave him the forbearance to wait for Tilly, the humility to adapt to his truncated role at work. His father had exhibited a similar stoicism, never succumbing to despair at losing both his daughter and his wife. Rarely mentioning either, his example was so powerful, it did not occur to Henry to search for Tilly until after his father's death.

Irene was different. Whether via a new diet, a new style or a new skill, Irene was on a continual quest for self-improvement. It didn't matter that she'd abandoned her

French class by February; she'd enrol for Italian with high hopes the following year. But her "evening class" in local government was a constant, the alibi for Thursday evenings in Henry's bed. Was she ready to study with him full-time?

Henry's brooding brought no clarity. He couldn't venture through the jeweller's door. While a ring would demonstrate his commitment, what use was an ornament she couldn't flaunt before her friends? Perhaps she'd prefer something practical. She'd hankered after her own salon since she was a junior at the barber's. Henry's loan had enabled her to buy a van and go solo, cutting and curling in people's homes. But that was only halfway to what she really wanted. Now, with a set of sinks and associated plumbing to convert the front room into a salon, he'd give her the real McCoy.

HIS MISTRESS COCOONED in his arms, the aroma of tomato and continental herbs wafting up the stairs, it should have been romantic. But Irene laughed.

He'd been acquainted with her whinnying laugh since she was a cocky teenager sweeping up at the barber's. He'd thought she'd grow out of it but she'd been coming to The Willows once a week for a defrosted ready-meal and a bit of slap and tickle since her twins were in primary school, and she hadn't yet. She told her husband she had a night class, but Eric must have been unusually thick or unusually detached not to have grown suspicious in over a decade. Sometimes Henry imagined Eric was in on the arrangement, sending his wife for a weekly service. Sometimes he doubted the husband existed.

The bed springs squeaked as Henry fumbled on the bedside table for his spectacles. "I'll buy you a ring if that's what's bothering you. After you've divorced Eric."

"Did I *say* I was putting in for divorce?"

"Not exactly. But with the twins grown up …" Henry polished his glasses with the edge of the candy-striped sheet. "If you're not keen on tying the knot again we could live together."

"Living in sin? What would your father think?"

"I'm serious, Irene."

Irene's breasts wobbled as she hauled herself up the bed. "Did you have anywhere in mind for us to *live together*?"

Sometimes he wondered if Irene's brain was wired properly. Or if the chemicals that lightened her hair clogged the vital pathways. "Where do you think?"

"Darling, I'd sooner live in a garden shed." She pursed her lips for a kiss.

Henry couldn't reciprocate. "What's wrong with it?"

"Honeybun, it's a mausoleum. All this Victorian furniture. Wallpaper from out of the ark."

"We could decorate."

"It needs more than a lick of paint."

"We'll get central heating." Henry wielded his trump card. "Turn the sitting room into a salon."

"What? *Tilly's for Fillies?*" Irene punched his arm. "If we ever *did* get hitched, I'd only be your wife on paper. In your heart, you'd be wedded to *her*."

Chapter 10

H AVING WAITED IN vain for her five-minute call, Matty laces her shoes and cuts across the courtyard to the main corridor. Stowing the chit in her cardigan sleeve, she turns not left towards the bank and shop but right, pursuing the passageway uphill past the ginnel shunting off to the laundry. A little puffed on reaching the theatre, she makes straight for the steps to the stage, scarcely pausing to catch her breath or to admire the gilded frescoes. Dispensing with an introduction, she delivers a faultless rendition of "Escape at Bedtime". Not a soul applauds.

Has she been sent to the wrong establishment? Or the correct place, at the wrong o'clock? Looking down, she sees what previously skipped her notice. Instead of rows of upholstered seats facing the stage, the auditorium is a jumble of trestle tables where guests are fashioning rosettes from reels of ribbon and cardboard discs.

As she descends the stairs, a man approaches, garbed in a grocer's cotton coat. Belatedly, and grudgingly, he claps. "That was excellent, Matty. But the theatre was decommissioned yonks ago."

"It would make a beautiful ballroom." Now the seats have been removed, the grocer might ask her to dance. Even a shopkeeper should have the grace to steer a lady between the tables.

"Those were the days, eh? It's Industrial Therapy now. Have a word with your charge nurse if you fancy earning yourself some extra pocket money."

Deary me! Some of the guests must *work* for a living. And at so mundane a task. Ought she to get back on stage to divert them with a cheery monologue? Given their lacklustre reception thus far, her words might go a-begging. As with crab in aspic and *foie gras*, a degree of sophistication is required to appreciate the arts.

Retracing the route to her quarters, Matty resolves to recite for her own amusement henceforth. Why stand in a draughty theatre when she can build a bespoke stage in her mind? She prays her mother will not think her remiss.

ENTERTAINING HERSELF IN the bay window of the lounge, Matty smells coffee as bodies flop onto the seats at either side of her. Abandoning Kipling's "If", she opens her eyes to her two favourite girls.

"We've come from the MDT meeting," says Kitty.

"With some exciting news," the circus girl adds.

"Do I have a visitor? Is it him?"

Some of the shine leaves Kitty's face. "Was he your

boyfriend?"

The circus girl steals a glance at the shrimp-woman over by the fish tank. "Your baby?"

Matty has no answer, but the boy adored guessing games. "My mother married a prince."

Kitty clears her throat. "Anyroad, we came to tell you they've decided you can stay."

"Of course," says Matty.

"You've settled in marvellously." Kitty lowers her voice to avoid arousing the shrimp's envy. "Much better than expected."

"Thank you." Is there a rosette for *settling in*?

"So you'll be here for Christmas," says Kitty.

"And out in the community in another year or so," says the circus girl.

Kitty pats her arm. "And I'll be there with you."

"And they all lived happily ever after."

"Speaking of the community, Matty," says the circus girl, "I've asked you before, but does Sheepwash Lane mean anything to you?"

Matty's eyelids droop as she tunes in to her mother. *How sweet is the shepherd's sweet lot!* Although not partial to Blake's poetry, it will pass a pleasant hour.

ALONE IN THE admin office, Janice twirled on the secretary's chair. Then she removed the plastic dust cover from the Selectric, aligned the application form with the roller and turned the knob to feed it through.

She wasn't being deliberately deceitful: the secretaries

couldn't spare a typewriter during office hours, and it was pure coincidence she'd stayed late on the day David Pargeter left early for a dental appointment. Crazy upsetting people when there was no guarantee she'd make the shortlist. She'd save her apologies for when, or if, she required a reference.

Her mum had been right about the attraction of the AIDS post: the combination of social stigma and terminal illness triggered her inner Mother Theresa. But despite championing the downtrodden since childhood, Janice was no self-sacrificing saint. Wary of burnout, she balanced her benevolence with personal ambition. She'd make her name at the cutting edge.

There had been a point, midway through her training, when she'd considered jacking it in. It wasn't the depth of deprivation, or the limitations of the resources available to meet unlimited demand. It wasn't the Kafkaesque complications of the benefits system, or the sheer volume of stuff to learn. Janice's enthusiasm had dipped when it dawned on her the rough ground had been broken, the era of innovation past. Nothing new could be unearthed regarding the dissatisfactions of the role of housewife, the politics of disablement, social justice in underprivileged communities or parent-child attachment. Adoption, which had incited her interest in the profession, had been commandeered by a social worker in the city where Janice trained and there'd never be a bigger scandal than the children told they were orphans and shipped to Australia without their parents' knowledge or consent.

Matty Osborne had revived her sense of purpose. Nowhere better to battle discrimination than an asylum, or so she'd thought, until her mother drew her attention to the medical wards where young men's vitality leached away.

Their predicament mirrored Matty's: shunned by society; robbed of their futures; punished for having sex. Were AIDS patients hit harder because they died physically, in addition to socially and psychologically? Unable to judge where best to deploy her skills, Janice would let fate decide. If she applied and didn't get an interview, she'd dedicate herself to psychiatry with renewed zeal.

Yet she hesitated to put her fingers to the keyboard. Having drafted her application at the weekend, she already had the words. But that was prior to Matty passing her probationary period at Tuke House. Why strive for a greater challenge now?

Because she couldn't publicly take credit for Matty's placement, while making no progress where she could. The *Times and Star* had published her appeal for family or friends to make contact. So far, no-one had.

Wheeling back the chair, Janice sprang to her feet. Her mind full of the Nottingham job, she hadn't bothered to check her pigeonhole on entering the room. Now, as if she'd wished it into being, she found a folded sheet of purple A5. The call must have come in as the secretaries grabbed their coats, after Janice had left *her* office but before reaching theirs.

Resuming her perch on the swivel chair, she spun around, and around again. Then she released the application form from the typewriter, tore it into confetti and threw it in the bin. Taking a breath of professionalism to temper her exuberance, she picked up the phone.

Chapter 11

FATHER CHRISTMAS FLIES in with gifts for the children. But Matty cannot find the boy. She has searched under the beds and in the lavatory cubicles. She has even tried the kitchen and the butler's pantry, but both doors were locked. Hal has toys and sweeties aplenty, but she cannot permit the shrimp-woman's baby to monopolise the treats.

She is heading for the lounge – in case he sneaked back there while she was peering into cupboards and rummaging through drawers – when the circus girl comes lolloping lopsided down the corridor. Although Matty can scarcely afford to loiter, she grants her a moment of her time. Yet she struggles to make out the words above the jamboree in the lounge. The circus girl has lost her dear sister? Can Matty boost her morale?

A picture comes through of two pink-haired girls in sequinned bodysuits, swinging on the high trapeze.

Departing the bars in synchrony, they cross mid-air to rapturous applause. Without her sister, the act is doomed.

Tears nettle Matty's eyes as a second image materialises. The girls are twins, fused from hip to shoulder, sharing three legs and one pair of arms. Circus freaks, but treasured by their mother and fellow performers. Unnatural, but never lonely. Tragically, one sister is dead: her legs, head and torso surgically removed, leaving her twin with a sense of longing and a cockeyed gait. Contemplating how to soothe her, Matty perceives her mother prompting from beside the orchestra pit. *T'was the night before Christmas …* Ah, yes! "Christmas is for families."

"You're right, Matty," says the circus girl. "I'll try her number now."

———————

WHEN JANICE GRUMBLED to Norman Willis that it was infantilising to schedule an adult Christmas party for a mid-December mid-week afternoon, his rebuke stung. "Give it a rest, Janice. Not everything's a political crusade." She was gobsmacked, stunned speechless that the most curmudgeonly of her colleagues considered *her* a killjoy. That she could be accused of militancy by the man who rendered sparring with psychiatrists an Olympic sport. So she restrained herself with Heather Cooper, as they sipped from plastic tumblers of low-alcohol fruit punch. She didn't criticise the nearby church for patronising the residents with impersonal gifts. Didn't comment that the hospital chaplain dressing up as Santa to dole out gaudily-packaged socks and bath salts was both belittling, and confusing by merging the secular and Christian seasonal myths. Pushing her paper hat up from her forehead, Janice focused on the positives: a break from routine for residents and nurses; a rationale for the relatives' visits.

Gazing around the room, Janice's professional inadequacies boomeranged back at her. Less than half the residents had visitors, although Vicky Logan's numerous aunts could compensate for others' deficiency. While those *with* guests were no chirpier than those without, Janice vowed to do better next year.

Matty Osborne scuttled from the room. "God love her," said Heather. "She hates crowds."

"Or she's missing her family."

"I imagine she's forgotten she ever had one."

Should she tell Heather that was about to change? The occupational therapist would be as thrilled as she was, but Janice hadn't yet managed to catch Violet on the phone. She hadn't even told David, reluctant to let slip she'd placed the advert without consulting him. But the secret felt bigger than she was; had the punch been stronger she'd have blurted it out.

Heather forestalled such indiscretion. "I suppose we'd better mingle."

Chatting with Ronnie Bloomsburg's sister, Janice feigned interest in her Christmas pudding recipe, while counting the minutes until she could leave to try Matty Osborne's sister's number again.

The secretary's scribble on a piece of purple paper: *Phone Violet Osborne re your ad in the T and S.* But when Janice had tried, no-one had picked up. She tried the next morning, and every morning and afternoon since. No answer. Either it was a hoax or the secretary had copied down the digits incorrectly. But wouldn't a sister, estranged for fifty years, ring again if she thought Janice had neglected her call?

Violet seemed as exasperating as her own sister. Roz also kept sporadic contact, yet nothing could sever the tender bond between them. Matty deserved that too.

Abandoning the festivities, Janice found Matty in the corridor, looking uncharacteristically glum. She'd put a smile on her face if she told her about Violet. "Going back to the party, Matty? Wouldn't it be fabulous if your sister was here?" Janice held her breath, anxious the slender hint may destabilise her.

Matty appeared unable to take it in initially. But she didn't spit it back with *My mother married a prince.* When it came, Matty's response was completely lucid. "Christmas is for families." Were those tears in her eyes?

As Matty scuffled off, Janice remembered visiting a hill tribe in Thailand. How moved she'd felt, how honoured, to sit with the women, communicating by gesture. Stripped of the commonalities of language, wealth and culture, their shared humanity shone through. The same thread tied her to Matty and the other long-stay patients. It *wasn't* compassion, or not only. It wasn't being at the leading edge. Her fundamental motivation was more basic: defying the divisions of client and professional, the disturbed and the supposedly sane. She had been drawn to Matty from the first but, until now, she couldn't tell whether Matty noticed. But Janice had tossed her a rope, and Matty had caught it.

Christmas is for families: Matty had revealed the shadow of her sorrow.

If that had been her sole success that day, Janice would have gone home satisfied. But when she returned to her desk and dialled Violet Osborne's number, after four rings, there was an audible shift. Not, unfortunately, a living breathing person, but the promise of one. A recorded voice – sounding so like Matty's that Janice's spine tingled – inviting the caller to leave a message after the tone.

Chapter 12

ANOTHER CHRISTMAS MINUS Tilly. Another year insisting he was inured to it. Another year conceding he was not.

If anything, it got harder with maturity, as if, like his employment, his patience had a shelf-life shortly to expire. He couldn't envisage what there'd be when he reached his limit. Was it, like death, an absence, a no-thing? Henry felt unprepared. Half a century of endurance left him ill-equipped for much else.

Some years he'd treat Christmas as an ordinary day, turn off the television and eat beans on toast for lunch. Some years he'd put up a tree, wrap presents and roast a chicken, set an extra place for Tilly and another for his dad. However he approached Christmas day, the final hour found him seated by the fire with enough whisky to engender a headache but not enough to assuage his grief. And his shame on acknowledging he'd spent the day in frenzied anticipation of the greatest gift imaginable: his sister's knock upon the door.

He didn't begrudge Irene Christmas with her family. But this year's loneliness cut deep. No promotion. No Tilly. Would he lose Irene too?

Henry fingered the horse chestnut in his pocket. Solid as stone, as his loyalty to Tilly. But, unlike the game in the schoolyard, he'd waited for Tilly alone. It wasn't until their father's funeral that Henry wondered about other siblings.

Pouring another three fingers of whisky into his tumbler, Henry contemplated the prospect of a similar scenario at New Year. Could he ward off despair with a resolution? But what he wanted was outside his control.

Henry jumped to his feet, forgetting the drink in his hand until the liquid soaked through his trouser leg. No matter. He set down the glass on the fireplace and panted upstairs to Tilly's bedroom window. Stars pricked the night sky while, down below, a lozenge of light seeped from the dining room into the yard.

Across the backstreet stood a derelict single-story building that had once served as a clinic for mothers and babies. He didn't need to see it to know it was there. Although larger than strictly necessary, the location would be perfect for Irene's salon. Not so close he'd cramp her style but near enough to The Willows to nip through the backdoor for lunch. Time and again he'd considered enquiring whether the health authority still owned it and if they'd be willing to sell. Whether he could remortgage the house to cover the cost.

Fuzzy from drink or excitement, Henry flopped onto his sister's bed. This coming year he'd do more than consider it. He'd make it *happen*, and Irene could call her salon whatever she liked.

Chapter 13

A S SHE JOINED the ring road at the roundabout, Janice had to guess where the white lines divided the lanes. The streetlights had clocked off already but Janice had to take the sunrise on trust. She wasn't alone in taking to the road when the New Year – the new decade – had barely begun. Were the others also on the hunt for an open pharmacy, or for a bargain in the sales?

The wipers battered the windscreen, but the road remained a blur. Futile blasting it with hot air from the demister, unless she leaned to the left to squint through an unfogged patch in the middle. But her head throbbed with the slightest deviation from the horizontal, making her gullet spasm and her eyes stream. Did the wiper mechanism need adjustment or was it due a new blade? If she'd noticed at Christmas, her dad would have fixed it in a flash. What if it wasn't the car, but her eyes? She'd never had a hangover affect her vision before. But then she'd never had to find a pharmacy after four hours' kip.

She'd *so* looked forward to shedding her professional persona on a long weekend with her friends. But there was a border between playfulness and recklessness, and Janice had breached it. Steeling herself as a police car overtook her, she could have cried, if tears wouldn't have further distorted her view of the road. Last night's alcohol swam in her veins; if she lost her licence, she'd lose her job.

At the next roundabout, the police car signalled right towards the city centre. Janice signalled left. Four months since moving to Cumbria, had she forgotten how to navigate the city she'd made her home for four years? A notice in the window at the Beechdale Road pharmacy indicated that the nearest alternative open on the bank holiday was on Russell Drive. In her haste, she'd driven off in the opposite direction. Having no key, she'd left the door on the snib, expecting to be back in ten minutes.

In Nottingham, she reverted into a younger, calmer, happy-go-lucky version of herself. The same shared house, the same room, with the mural of the tropical beach she'd painted herself. She couldn't help feeling smug at having carved out a more mature and independent existence, but oh so grateful that her friends had kept a space for her to regress.

Janice had been as keen to attend the party as anyone: she hadn't had a decent night out in months. Sheena might wake up with a pounding head and blame Janice for leading *her* astray. Unfortunately, a headache was the least of it.

She'd mastered the concept of contraception before she

started her periods. Not until beginning social work training did she grasp the extent of her mother's achievement in preaching caution while celebrating the carelessness which brought *their* family into being. While acknowledging sex was fun. She'd be doubly disappointed if she found out Janice had not only got so smashed she'd had sex without protection, she'd done it against the cold tile of a bathroom wall. Which might have suited Stuart but was bloody uncomfortable for her.

No contact in four months of living and working within an hour's drive of each other and then pitching up at the same party two hundred miles away? Daunted initially, Janice took his presence as a challenge, an opportunity to prove that Janice-and-Stuart was a 1980s relic. Her body believed otherwise, her juices on standby from the moment his laughter pealed out above the hubbub in the crowded kitchen, bypassing her brain.

Was Stuart waking up on someone's sofa with a head hammering with regret? Or in a soft bed with a warm body at his side? Wherever he was, whatever his mood, he wouldn't be racing around Nottingham on a drug run.

If Janice was panicked, with the safety net of the morning-after pill, women in a similar quandary must have been shitting themselves fifty years ago. She'd wanted Matty's story to be romantic, like the tragic heroine in one of those operas her mother enjoyed. But there was nothing romantic in singing solo when the situation called for a duet.

Janice braked sharply. Another thought struck her as she clocked the green neon cross. There were more serious consequences than pregnancy to consider. Ought she take an

AIDS test or insist Stuart get one? The complications mangled her mind.

Parking the car, her head reeled as she dived under the seat for an umbrella. Sheena would know: she'd been swotting up for the job Janice had almost applied for.

The pharmacy door yielded to her touch, and the aroma of cotton wool, TCP and nail varnish reassured her that last night was a hiccup. She'd get herself sorted and back to the house with the makings of a breakfast fry-up before anyone realised she'd left.

Chapter 14

"**Y**OU'LL NEVER GUESS the crack I heard today from one of my ladies." Irene's smile bloomed and withered as Henry failed to react. "Go on, then," she said.

Sex had been hurried, although not unsatisfactory. They'd dressed quickly and dashed downstairs to the only room with a fire in the grate. Henry would have been hard pressed to say whether their rush to evacuate the bedroom was owing to January's frosty weather or its association with his rejected marriage proposal towards the end of the previous year. After wolfing down the chicken tikka masala ready-meal at the table, they sat at either side of the fire, nursing mugs of tea. "Go on, what?" said Henry.

"Guess!"

"You said I'd *never* guess."

"You could try, but." She sounded surprisingly aggrieved.

Could it be that, despite her protests, she *wanted* an engagement ring? Her fingers, clasping the mug, could take more than her wedding band. His attention on her hands, it snagged on her skin's raw mottling. "That rash is back."

"Don't change the subject! You never take an interest in my work."

Didn't he? But there wasn't a deal to discuss. Hairdressing didn't invite debate. And besides. "Isn't that rash about your work, from the colours?"

"Yes, but I was telling you summat important. There's more to relationships than a bit of nooky. We have to *talk*."

"We *do* talk." Obviously Henry hadn't mentioned his demotion. And he wouldn't bring up the baby clinic until he had word it was for sale. "You know about Tilly."

"I know you've piddled more years than I've been on this earth watching for someone who's not coming."

"You don't know that." Henry's eyes itched as he stared into the flames. "She was everything to me."

"Well, you weren't everything to her or she'd have been back by now."

"That's a cruel thing to say."

Irene leant forward to touch his knee. "Haven't you served your sentence?"

"I gave her my word."

"You're like that dog in that filum, *Greyfriars Bobby*. Except you're a human being with the right to his own life, what's left of it. You realise, don't you, she'll be an old woman? She'll need you more than you need her."

"Exactly! She sacrificed her youth for me. Thirteen when our mother died. I want to repay that debt." He and

Irene would care for Tilly together.

"You've checked the old folks' homes and whatnot?"

Henry nodded. "The local ones, anyroad."

"Ghyllside too?"

"YOUR CLASS WOULD'VE finished ten minutes ago," said Henry.

Irene had donned her coat when she'd shifted a few paces from the fire, but she wasn't leaving without the letter to post on her way home. "The teacher's invited me for a drink. We're meeting his sister in the Commercial."

Seated at the table, Henry fed the typewriter a sheet of off-white Basildon Bond. "It's a waste of twenty-two pence for the stamp."

"And now the teacher's come back from the bar with half a lager and lime," said Irene. "Too mingy to buy me a rum and Coke."

Henry said nothing. She'd eat humble pie when she discovered he'd already written to the Health Authority. About the baby clinic. *Too mean?* He jabbed at the keyboard until the letters traffic-jammed within an inch of the ribbon.

"Now I'm telling Tilly her brother would never have found her if it hadn't been for one of my ladies. Even then I had to chain him to the chair before he'd write to the hospital."

After separating the typebars, Henry wiped his inky fingers on his hankie. He typed as fast as he dared, trying to drown the whine of Irene's monologue in the ticking of the keys.

Irene continued to address herself to an imaginary Tilly,

hovering beside the grate. "*George Windsor's daughter would never go barmy*, he said. Imagine if my lady thought the same when she came home from holiday to find her answer machine clogged with messages from a mental patient?"

Pulling the lever to the left of the roller, Henry heard a satisfying ping as the carriage repositioned itself at the start of a new line. "They wouldn't let patients use a phone."

"Mebbe I didn't catch each itsy-bitsy detail. I was listening with one half of me and timing her colour with the other. Hairdressing's dead technical, Tilly, as you're aware. Mebbe it was her doctor on the blower. My lady stressed it was vital to the treatment."

"I don't know why you'd think *your lady*'s friend's case would have any bearing on Tilly's. Not if the lass has been locked up since she was twelve."

"Don't patronise me, Henry. I get enough of that from Eric and the twins."

Warned by the quiver in her voice, Henry relented. "I suppose there's no harm asking." But it was exhausting, sometimes, to be dragged into the slipstream of her flights of fancy. And if Tilly *were* confined in the funny farm, their reunion wouldn't match Irene's fantasy of a quiet drink in the pub. Tilly a raving lunatic? He couldn't bear it. But he wouldn't have to. His serene and sophisticated sister never crossed Ghyllside's threshold. Unless as a visitor. Or a member of staff.

Chapter 15

1931

WHEN YOU FIND me, you will want to hear my story. Or the part of my story that tells of you. Until then, I turn it around in my mind to prevent it fading. When we meet, it will sing.

As a lass, I was full of stories. They kept Mother amused after we snuffed out the light. Stories of a dazzling future with no thought of fathers, husbands, brothers or sons.

Yours begins one night when Mother's betrayal stole my appetite for fiction. When she announced she'd be working at Windsor's Haberdashery on the Saturday, instead of coming to hear me recite. I felt sad for her missing out on the entertainment and then mad that she didn't seem to care. She seemed to think I could trot along merrily with Violet and Mrs Braithwaite. As if she didn't know a girl needs her mother's help to shine.

I WAS THE first to congratulate Violet after the adjudicator pinned the rosette to her bodice. It might have been only green, but she took home more than I did. As I hugged her, I didn't mind losing to prove a lass won't win unless her mother's watching.

My smile kept its shape to our side of the viaduct. When we got down from the bus, Violet wanted to link arms and skip to the door. But she was stopped short at the Steam Packet. We would have taken a tumble if Mrs Braithwaite hadn't grabbed Violet's arm. "Heavens to Murgatroyd! There's a motor outside the house."

She dragged us into the pub doorway, where beer and cigarettes overwhelmed the homely tang of seagulls and gutted herring. "Can't let the rent man catch us. Not today."

Violet fingered the lace at her neck. Mrs Braithwaite smacked her hand away but I'd guessed where she'd got the money for it. It wouldn't be the first time Mother's payment for our room had gone on trimmings for Violet. I tightened the bow in my hair. If Mother had kept the cash to stitch *me* a new collar, *I'd* have had a rosette.

"The rent man doesn't drive a motor, Mother." Violet's everyday voice migrated closer to her performance voice with every contest. "The rent man rides a bicycle."

Even so, we loitered, as, down the street, barefoot bairns left star-fish handprints on the motor's paintwork. When the driver's door opened, the older lads and lasses, or the brighter ones, sprang back to escape a tongue-lashing. They might have been ghosts for all the notice the gentleman took of them. Nose in the air, he sauntered around the motor to the passenger door.

Before he got there, a woman stepped out onto the kerb. "Strewth," said Mrs Braithwaite, and no wonder. The woman was Mother. With rouge on both cheeks.

My own cheeks flushed. Mrs Braithwaite and Violet dashed forward, but if they were after an introduction they were thwarted, Mother shaking the man's hand and hurrying him back into the car. By the time I caught up with them, he'd driven off.

Mother stood there, befuddled, as if she'd forgotten the contest. As if she'd forgotten me. When her face softened, I burst into tears.

MOTHER BEGAN ACTING peculiar after that. If I were generous, I'd say guilt was at the bottom of it but I suspected jealousy. Not a pleasant thing to say of one's mother but I couldn't ignore the fact that Mrs Braithwaite's daughter won a prize and hers didn't. Mother, who preached there was no shame in losing as long as you'd done your best.

As we undressed for bed, she asked me if I'd like to go to Stainburn School. Didn't she know the uniform was mustard and maroon?

"I'm quite content at Lawrence Street," I said, reaching under my nightgown to lower my drawers.

Mother climbed into bed, holding back the covers for me. "Half the teachers are illiterate. It's no place for a brain like yours."

"Let's send my brain to Stainburn and leave my body at Lawrence Street." I enjoyed making Mother laugh. "We haven't the brass for the whole of me."

"There might be a way," she said.

"In a story!" Curling up beside her, I related the adventures of the clever girl from The Marsh who becomes a lady doctor, her skills in demand worldwide. Every summer and every Christmas she comes home to run a free clinic in honour of her happy childhood.

Mother lay beside me, rigid, although she squeezed my hand at the end. Later, as I drifted off, I fancied I heard her sobbing. Perhaps she'd rather I didn't become a doctor. Perhaps she'd rather I was a missionary bringing the gospel to the heathens in Africa. Or I didn't go away at all. If I became a teacher at Lawrence Street, I'd never have to leave The Marsh.

WHEN WE GOT back from church, and I made to change out of my frock, Mother stopped me. "I've a surprise for you, Matilda. Mr Windsor's invited us for tea."

"Mr Windsor from the shop? Why?" I'd planned to go to the shore with Hilda that afternoon – or anyone else who wasn't fussed about recitals and rosettes.

Mother laughed. "Because he wants to meet you. To see what a charming young lady you are."

"Why should he give a hoot?"

"Why, why, why – you sound like a three-year-old not a young lady going on thirteen."

"In seven months." *I* was generally the one to amplify my age.

"However old you are, Mr Windsor has asked us both to tea, and I have accepted. And I'd appreciate a little hush until we go."

"Will he collect us in the motor?"

"We'll take the bus." Mother's face relinquished its sternness. "But he might drive us home."

I took advantage of the thaw to ask if I could call on Hilda first, but Mother was adamant I stay indoors. "You could use the time profitably studying your Bible." I stared, mouth agape, but she was pulling my leg. "Or you could read Mrs Christie's new whodunnit. I borrowed it from the Carnegie yesterday."

I REFUSED TO be intimidated by a street so grand the houses had names chiselled on the gateposts. Like gravestones. As at the cemetery, trees lined our route, pushing through the pavement at intervals, as if Briarwood was so healthy, vegetation reigned over stone. Each house had an individual front garden, but I sniggered at the absence of willows. The Willows might be palatial compared to our room at Mrs B's, but it was a far cry from Windsor Castle.

Violet would ask if I'd spilt tea down my frock, but I embarrassed myself in an altogether different way. I did not slurp from the saucer or forget to extend my pinkie as I raised my cup. I did not smear jam on the Chesterfield or gobble up the dainty sandwiches in one bite. But it was a terrible gaffe to say "Thank you, Mrs Windsor" to the lady who offered me the plate. I *had* thought it curious she wasn't introduced and, whereas Mother wore a handsome lemon costume, *she* wore black.

Mother had neglected to tell me there hadn't been a Mrs Windsor since the current Mr Windsor's mother died. I blushed at my blunder and didn't regain my appetite until the daily woman had cleared away the food.

When Violet preferred play to chores, we ordered make-believe servants to do them. (If I tried this with Hilda, she laughed, saying we'd less chance of *hiring* a servant than becoming one. Which proved she hadn't a romantic bone in her body. Even if her mother sent her to elocution, she'd never win a rosette.) Now I could tell Violet that having someone wait on you wasn't as amusing as we'd imagined. Yes, it would be heavenly to have someone to hoick in the coal, scrub the doorstep and black-lead the range. But a maid teetering at your elbow when you're trying to impress your mother's employer? I'd have sooner poured my own tea than worry where I should put my face when an adult did it for me.

Before she left, the daily woman brought Mother a fresh pot of tea, with a saucer of lemon slices instead of milk. I wrinkled my nose at the smoky bouquet, so I was relieved when Mr Windsor invited me to tour the house. At last, something positive to tell Violet: she would have loved the attic room with sloping walls in the pitched roof. From the front window, we could see right across town to The Marsh, and there was another window over the rooves at the back. Mr Windsor explained to me that other householders used the attic for a live-in maid, but it would be unseemly for a bachelor to share a house with a young female who wasn't kin.

There was also a bathroom and separate flushing lavatory with paper that didn't leave newsprint on your bum. (Violet hated sharing the outdoor privy, so I investigated this as a priority. Twice). In addition, there were two grand receptions on the ground floor and two large bedrooms and a box room above. As Mr Windsor admitted, it was a lot of house for one man.

I tried to warm to Mr Windsor. Mother being so gay in his company, he must be a gentleman. But how could I tell when I had no-one to measure him against? He *looked* no different to men I'd glimpsed on the bus or in the queue outside the Oxford Picture House, with his clipped moustache and his three-piece suit. But Violet would want to know whether there was more to him than an indoor bathroom.

Snug in bed that evening, I prayed Mother would be back to normal. But the idea of Mr Windsor rattling about in that enormous house had stoked the green-eyed monster in her.

"Don't you wish you had a bed to yourself, Matilda?"

"A bed to myself? It's cramped in here with *one*."

"I was thinking if we lived somewhere different. With a room of your own."

That *somewhere different* set me off on a tale of a girl who marries a prince and moves her mother into the palace. When the prince dies, there are so many rooms mother and daughter sleep in a different bed each night of the week.

WHAT HAPPENED NEXT made me fear for Mother's sanity. She had to be tapped for the course she'd set us on. She *said* she thought I'd guessed, but if I'd had the slightest inkling I wouldn't have troubled myself with minding my manners on Sunday. I'd have swigged tea from my saucer and sucked jam straight from the spoon. I'd have pushed my legs apart and let my frock ride above my knees.

I crossed my fingers when I promised to keep quiet until it was official. I needed to confide in someone. I couldn't talk her out of it myself.

I could tell Violet. But she'd advise something reckless, like running away. I couldn't tell a teacher: Mother would be mortified if I took our private affairs to school. I *could* tell Mrs Braithwaite if I could get her alone, but it would take more than a couple of minutes while Violet was at the netty or fetching a bucket of coal.

It would be awkward, but *someone* had to make Mother see sense.

Chapter 16

January 1990

IT IS MOST irregular to find the office locked so soon after breakfast. Matty raps on the door. She has known them to cower behind it, calming their nerves with a cigarette, especially in the evenings when the guests are particularly perplexing. She presses her head to the paper-thin cleft between the door and its frame, but hears nothing beyond the drumming of her ear. She knocks again and rattles the handle. Not a sausage.

Resting her back against the door, she slides down, knees crunching, down until the carpet scrapes her fingertips. Shifting her weight onto her palms, she eases her rump onto the floor and stretches her legs, pointing her feet to the ceiling. Her left slipper is beginning to fray above her big toe. Has Kitty thought to purchase a new pair?

It is cooler at ground level and the flooring chafes her

thighs, but the corridor will be her custodian until the situation alters. Until the staff unlock the office or an utterly unanticipated solution presents itself.

She does not stir at the sound of the doorbell. No-one of importance uses it; they all have keys. Not the guests, of course, but that does not pose a problem: in the daytime the outside door remains unlocked and, if not, the staff would be standing by to open it. *Where are they?*

"What are you doing down there, Matty?"

The circus girl, lopsided as always, unbalanced by her leather bag. With her clown-shaped trousers and eccentric hair, she never fails to brighten Matty's day. When she first clapped eyes on that rose-tinted streak, she took pity on her, presuming it a birth defect, and invited her for afternoon tea. Her complexion, however, was normal, if somewhat swarthy. Matty harbours no hostility towards gypsies, as long as they can scrub floors and make beds and what have you.

This morning, the circus girl's cheeks are as pink as her hair as she deposits a clutch of keys in her bag. "Come on, we'll be late for the meeting."

Although she ought to wait for a chit, Matty permits the girl to help her to her feet and escort her to the lounge.

The room is hushed, despite the crowd arranged in a ring, with stiff seats borrowed from the dining room to supplement the easy chairs and sofas. It would be fun to circle the room patting the heads up and down at different levels. She recognises several of the guests, plus the butler in blue jeans and a gym shirt, inexplicably rejecting the black tie, wing-collar shirt and morning coat befitting his role. Matty would be prepared to let that pass for now in exchange for a chit and is poised to tell him so when the circus girl ushers her to a sofa.

A man clears his throat and thanks everyone for coming. He is seated aloft on a dining chair directly in front of the television, its blank face explaining the quiet. Buoyed by a sense of occasion, Matty battles the sagging cushions to hold herself erect.

The fellow has a child's haircut, with a thick fringe buttressed by his eyebrows. Fortunately, he is wearing a man's suit, albeit a brown one. A Belgian, no doubt. An associate of Mrs Christie, a woman blessed with a capacity to solve the most intractable riddles.

The detective has a peculiar speech impediment, as if his words are larger than his maw. Brought up to be civil to everyone, even foreigners, Matty nods encouragement when he falters. With the circus girl radiant at his side, it is not unpleasant to watch him. Far superior to the television. Yet she is distracted by the shrimp-woman rocking her baby, back and forth, back and forth so violently Matty fears it will regurgitate its milk. Whenever the shrimp-woman's elbow encroaches onto her share of the sofa, she has to resist digging her in the ribs.

Reaching between the seat cushions for evidence to assist the detective, Matty is met by a sodden paper hanky and a five-pence piece. The coin reminds her of her quest for jelly babies, obliging her to hasten to the office to collect a chit. She tries to rise but her derrière cannot push against candy floss. The edge of her hand sweeps her lap.

The circus girl translates for the Belgian: "This is the start of a very long process. There'll be ample time to prepare."

Matty transfers her attention to the diamond pattern of the girl's pantaloons. In such glorious apparel she could be anyone: a pirate, a sultan's favourite or the genie from Aladdin's lamp.

"The nurses are leaving with you," the butler adds. "All that's changing is our base."

"What if I don't want to move?" says one of the guests. "I've been here since England beat West Germany in the World Cup in nineteen sixty-six."

"Everyone's going eventually," says the Belgian. "Not just Tuke House – the whole hospital's shutting down."

"And we're being turfed out to live on the streets in cardboard boxes?" says a man with artwork on his arms.

Excitement surges inside her like the dawn of a baby. Could it happen, or is it a fairy-tale? Amy Johnson soaring so high she could chisel a chunk of cheese from the moon.

"You'll be well looked after," says the circus girl.

"Who decided the hospital had to close?" A woman with witchy hair jabs a gnarled finger at the Belgian. "Was it you?"

Rather than solving a mystery, the detective has whipped up a new one. But, Mrs Christie having summoned him for a reason, Matty cannot show him the door. She racks her brain for a solution that would appease her guests without offending the foreigner. What did he say? Mr Chamberlain needs the house for a field hospital? Naturally, they must comply with the government's plans. "Buck up, everyone!" she says. "We must all forgo some comforts in wartime. Even our dear King George."

AFTER SETTLING MATTY onto the sofa between Effie Atkinson and a care assistant, Janice scanned the room for another vacant seat. She was on the verge of fetching an extra chair from the dining room when Graham Scott indicated the one to his right.

"Isn't that for Dr Shakir?"

"Double booked. Her secretary's just rung."

Janice sat, easing her bag off her shoulder and kicking it under the seat. "So what do we do? Reschedule?"

Graham swiped his shaggy fringe from his eyes. "I don't mind stepping into the breach."

Janice smiled thinly. Unlike Graham, Parveen put the patients at ease. She tried to make eye contact with the other members of the resettlement team but – checking diaries, turning off bleeps – they were otherwise engaged. Clive was advising Billy Dewhirst to flick the ash from his cigarette into the ashtray at his elbow instead of stretching beyond to drop it on the floor.

As Graham launched into his spiel, Janice assumed a veneer of optimism. Yet the residents appeared increasingly bewildered as he babbled about The Community Care Act, social role valorisation and quality of life. Crucial factors, as she'd argued at her recruitment interview; sadly incomprehensible to those directly affected. Dr Shakir might not have made it any clearer but the rhythms of her speech would've banished their concerns.

As the residents' expressions morphed from indifference to alarm, Janice caught Clive's gaze. If anyone was to stop the runaway mouth beside her, it would be the charge nurse.

Annoyingly, Clive raised his eyebrows and shrugged.

Effie Atkinson rocked her doll ever more vigorously. Matty Osborne brushed imaginary crumbs from her lap. Interrupting the general manager midsentence, Janice wished she could have risen above the platitudes she'd scorned at university. Her intervention sparked a volley of questions. *How would they get their medication in the new place? Would the newspaper lady still visit? Was the hospital to be dismantled and rebuilt elsewhere? Could they come back for Industrial Therapy?* Each speaker fanned the fears of their neighbour, as if they'd counted on a hospital bed to the grave and beyond.

Matty Osborne's plummy vowels broke through the gloom. "Duty calls. This house will be requisitioned as a field hospital. We can make do with a modest billet until Mr Hitler learns some manners."

Graham mumbled that today's villain was Saddam Hussein, but Clive spoke above him. "Well said, Matty. Let's pull together and make the best of what's ahead."

"THANK YOU, DEAR, that was delicious."

Au contraire, the food is barely palatable but that is no fault of the maid, or the cook, given the challenges of producing an appetising menu in wartime. Indeed, it would be perverse to eat cordon bleu when the men suffer so dreadfully at the front. Besides, flattering the staff pays dividends. If *they* are happy, so are the guests.

"Could you manage some jam roly-poly and custard?"

Matty nods. The sweet stodge is nursery food, but her

guests wolf it down. *She* lingers over *her* meals, masticating thoroughly before swallowing, while they scurry off.

Now, is the jam strawberry or cherry? It cannot be raspberry: there are no seeds to torment her dentures. The puzzle brings to mind the Belgian detective. The meeting was tremendous fun, with no-one dragged off in shackles, but it diverted her from a more pressing matter.

The boy's jelly babies! Shoving her bowl aside, she scrapes back her chair. Where is her maid when she needs her? Matty will have to collect a chit from the butler and take it to the bank herself.

The sign on the office door reads HANDOVER IN PROCESS. DO NOT DISTURB. Matty peels it off to sniff the blue plasticine that serves as an adhesive, then affixes the notice to the opposite wall. Now the door is unadorned, she is at liberty to knock.

It opens immediately to the width of the butler's head. "Can you give us two minutes, Matty? We're in handover."

Matty is loath to lower herself to the scratchy carpet. What would the detective advise? Why faff with a chit when she can get cash in a snap from the man with the hairy arms? Leaving the butler to his deliberations, Matty sets off for the secret stairs.

Chapter 17

"SHOULDN'T YOU BE taking notes?"

Judging by the ormolu clock among the gewgaws on the mantelpiece, the woman had nattered on for the past half hour about the achievements of her multifarious grandchildren and her flower arranging demonstrations for the WI. At uni, Janice had been commended for her interviewing skills, but that was before she'd met Violet Osborne. "Well, I'm not sure …"

"Write it down, dear, and Matilda's consultant can decide what's relevant!"

Ouch! All that stood between Janice and a petulant protest that *she* was an autonomous professional was the indignity of aping Norman Willis, even if her colleagues weren't here to witness it. Rooting in her bag for a spiral-bound notebook, she rebuked herself for failing to gauge the situation from Violet's perspective. Violet was as entitled to feel frustrated her visitor wasn't a sharp-suited psychiatrist with an attaché case as Janice was that Violet's surname came from her deceased husband. But, although not sisters, the girls had been inseparable in their school days, or so Violet had insisted when Janice finally got through on the phone.

"We'd *all* be grateful if you could shed some light on Matty's background." The psychiatrists would interrogate her report for early indicators of mental illness; the nurses for a stronger sense of the person behind the diagnosis with which to lure her into the *real* world. Matty's primary nurse, Karen Gilmour, had intended to join her but she was on sick leave due to a late miscarriage. "And *I'm* keen to trace any remaining relatives."

"I have to disappoint you there. Matilda was an only child. We both were. That was what drew us together. And that our mothers were war widows."

According to the medical notes, Matty's father had experienced psychosis. According to Sister Henderson, he'd had her committed. Now Violet offered a third version of the family history: a Matty fatherless from birth. "That must've been difficult."

"It wasn't uncommon. Half our class had lost *someone* in the war. If it wasn't a father it would be an uncle or brother. But we were lucky. *Our* fathers were heroes."

Janice envisioned sepia photographs of solemn men in military jackets buttoned to the chin. A child might plug an aching gap by making hers a prince. "Your mothers didn't remarry?"

"My dear, if it wasn't the war, it was Spanish flu. There

wasn't an eligible bachelor in Cumberland."

Janice's ears still marked Violet as Matty's double, their accents interchangeable, like continuity announcers on Radio Four. But her eyes put them on different planets. Whereas Violet's petite frame hinted at a calorie-controlled diet, Matty seemed shrunken and starved. While Matty looked washed-out even in the brighter outfits Karen had guided her towards, Violet, perfectly packaged in a cream silk blouse and pressed jeans, could have been Butlin's Glamorous Granny. Her sleek cap of ash-blonde hair flowed in concert with the slightest inclination of her head, dyed so alluringly Janice wished she could have enquired about her hairdresser. "Did Matty have anyone?"

"Good gracious! What are you asking?"

Had she misread her? Wrongly equated youthful presentation with a youthful attitude? Violet would be around the age of Janice's grandparents: neither her black-clad Italian Nonna nor her blanched Irish Granny could be described as progressive. She should have read the clue in the Thatcher-style pussy-bow blouse. Should she back off to avoid antagonising her further? Sod it, Violet might know the father of Matty's child. "Did she have a boyfriend? A sweetheart?" How had Sister Henderson phrased it? "Was she stepping out with a young man?"

"I'm sorry, but your advert didn't mention boyfriends."

Janice stared at the blank page in her notebook. "And *I'm* sorry this is so difficult." She couldn't mention Matty's pregnancy unless Violet did: patient confidentiality was infrangible. "Whatever you know would help."

"I don't know anything!" Mrs Osborne buffed her

wedding band with her fingertips. "I haven't seen her since I left home at thirteen."

"Oh." Janice confessed her disillusionment to her notebook: *friends up to age 13*. "You left for boarding school?"

"I left for *work*."

Both her grandmothers had worked from a young age; not at a *job* but as an extension of ordinary chores. Nonna clearing up, not only from meals consumed at the family table, but at her parents' café; Granny tending animals, not domestic pets, but cattle on the family farm. "At thirteen?"

"I was a scullery maid at Holker Hall."

"From your accent, and Matty's too, I imagined you *having* servants, not *being* one."

"Matilda didn't tell you?" Mrs Osborne's gaze fluttered from the leatherette sofas to the nest of tables to the stone-effect fireplace with alcoves housing Murano-glass figurines. As if to reassure herself of their solidity. "We grew up on The Marsh. Tiny cottages with no running water. Outside loos. Smashed to smithereens in the sixties and not before time."

"But your accents …"

"Elocution lessons. My mother was friendly with a tutor who took us for free. Had to scrimp and save for our stage frocks."

"You used to perform?"

"Public speaking contests. Very *la de da* for girls from our neck of the woods." For a moment, Mrs Osborne softened. "Mind you, Matilda had a competitive streak. That could be where her illness began."

Chapter 18

M ATTY SHUFFLES DOWN the driveway in her slippers, a shiny fifty-pence piece in her skirt pocket. Half asleep by the time the man with hairy arms stomped up the stairs, she was nevertheless alert enough to insist he show her the money before lifting her skirt.

In the past, the stairs led somewhere: a storeroom, a garret for a governess or the engine of some antiquated heating system. But no-one goes there now, apart from the man with hairy arms and ladies short of cash. The servants never venture near them; unaware the stairs exist, tucked away at the back of the building.

Matty did not mind waiting, although the uncarpeted floor was hard on her posterior and the secluded corner cold and dim. But she was disenchanted when, after the man climbed off her, she carried her coin down the corridor to find the shop in darkness. She pummelled the door and rattled the handle to no avail.

Buck up! There are other shops, bigger and better, beyond the estate. Visiting them with Kitty, they travelled by taxi. Today, low on funds, she walks.

The throbbing between her legs prevents her proceeding in the ladylike fashion in which her mother coached her. The end of the drive is not in sight when Matty begins to flag. Moisture penetrates her slippers and a wind slams her skirt about her knees. Glancing back, the house is too distant to return for a coat and stouter shoes. She presses on, cheering herself with thoughts of the boy's delight on receiving his sweeties.

Pleasant musings accompany her to the estate boundary. The gates are long gone, melted down for ammunition; the towering gateposts vestige of their grandeur. She cannot recollect whether, in her mother's heyday, someone was employed to open and close them. Or did visitors bring a liveried driver who managed this on their behalf?

Traffic whooshes by. Does the town lie to the left or to the right? Her recent escapade has scrambled her faculties. Nothing is familiar, as if a magic carpet has flown her to Arabian lands.

Despair is a sin, says her mother. Stasis a luxury. You must choose. Chancing on the right, her spirit surges as houses come into view. Some kind soul will offer her tea. Her mouth, she discovers, is somewhat tart.

A lavender bush tumbles over a garden wall. Although the flowers are pale and dry, Matty snaps off a sprig and holds it to her nose. She cannot approach a stranger's door with that man's stink upon her. Regrettably the fragrance is so frail it will take armfuls to neutralise his residue.

How sore her feet. How fierce her thirst. How chill the breeze. Yet it whispers redemption as it buffets her ears: she will save herself by *selling* the lavender house-to-house. At a pound a bunch, she would soon have the taxi fare. Although, being of such inferior quality, she might charge fifty pence.

Chapter 19

Henry was chuffed when the planning department sent him to put up notices in Briarwood. On home turf in the daytime, anonymised by a high-vis vest; such sanctioned truancy emboldened him to loosen his tie. It made him lightheaded in a manner both agreeable and unnerving, as if, unanchored, he would sail away. Henry told himself not to be so bloody pretentious and knuckle down to the job.

The Health Authority had ignored his enquiry; now he knew why. The old baby clinic, abandoned for years to rats and vandals, was to be demolished and a terrace of three houses erected in its stead. Knotting the yellow string to secure the laminated notification to the post, he didn't feel dejected. Irene's salon would suit a more modest site.

He recalled passing by as a young man, the prams berthed outside like boats in a harbour. He'd hoped for a wife to wheel his baby there to be weighed. He'd imagined Tilly taking *him* there too, albeit improbable in those black-and-white days before Mr Bevin's National Health. Testing his knots, he felt heartened at the prospect of new housing. Right to Buy had depleted the council's stock.

Uncoiling his body, Henry rubbed his spine. He should have positioned the signs further up, to save people having to crouch. Bending again, he picked at the knots, but his nails were too blunt. He'd come back later with a pair of scissors.

"It's an absolute liberty!" He turned to see a woman in a green waxed jacket, and a furious expression framed by a tangle of mousey hair. He'd misheard her harrumphing as traffic noise but, with no-one else within earshot, he deduced she was speaking to him.

"Sorry they're so low, but I'll fix them later."

The woman flapped his apology away. "You can tell them from me, we won't stand for it. This is a respectable neighbourhood."

Did his new role include placating irate members of the public? Although more proficient with numerical figures than flesh-and-blood ones, he was willing to try. "A terrace of three new homes isn't in keeping with the area?"

"Not if they're housing a horde of nutters!" The woman thrust out her jaw. "I've no problem with them personally but kiddies walk to school along here. If Ghyllside is closing they've got to go somewhere, but this is a busy thoroughfare. What if they ran out into the road?"

"Ghyllside's closing?" No mention of this when his letter to Tilly ricocheted onto his doormat, marked

ADDRESSEE UNKNOWN.

"Haven't you read your own notice? We'll fight it, you see if we don't!" With that, the woman stormed off.

Henry squatted to examine the sign. Ghyllside wasn't mentioned but his vision snagged on *supported housing*. He'd inferred it was planning-department lingo for connection to the utilities.

Sweat lapped his armpits, his groin. Could his letter to Ghyllside have provoked this? Could it heck! No-one would mistake his query for an invitation to come and *live* in the patch. Besides, the government had threatened care in the community since Enoch Powell's water-tower speech, three decades ago.

Crazies a stone's throw from The Willows? He wouldn't know who was who. And Irene would have a razzie. She might have imagined herself broadminded when nagging him to write to the hospital, but only because pleasing *my lady* kept her business afloat. She wouldn't be so sanguine about having them as neighbours.

But Irene wouldn't *have* mental patients as neighbours. She'd rejected his proposition, fearing she'd be under Tilly's shadow. This new development scuppered his chances of persuading her otherwise.

It was cruel enough losing Irene's salon to new homes. But to a bunch of psychiatric cases? Perhaps he'd join the waxed-jacket woman behind the barricades.

———————

HENRY SLEPT POORLY, plagued by dreams in which he was a boy again, hanging on the arm of a woman carrying a suitcase twice his size. He awoke equally badly, with a skull like a stuffed sock drawer. His first cigarette of the day, instead of clearing his sinuses, increased the congestion, as if cramming in another half-dozen un-partnered socks. As with the contents of The Willows' various wardrobes, bureaux and cupboards, he would someday have to subject his thoughts to a spring clean, dumping the dilapidated and dysfunctional to make space for the new. But not yet.

Lying in a hot bath, not even a sprinkling of Radox crystals could relax him as he scrutinised the room as Irene might. The basin, large enough to shampoo his hair in, would be condemned on account of the rust stains and tarnished taps. The black and white tiles, with the comforting regularity of a chess board, deemed obsolete. The bathtub, balanced on four King-of-the-Jungle paws, should be relegated to a museum. Ripping it out would be akin to amputation, but Irene would demand a fully-fitted kitchen, separate shower unit, central heating, and a melamine bedroom suite.

He pulled the plug and reached for a threadbare towel. Even the notion of replacing that worn strip of fabric induced palpitations. All the towels, linen, crockery and cutlery had been fondly selected – or so Henry assumed – by his mother aeons ago. Save for the television and a few odds and ends, neither Henry nor his father had sought to augment or update them.

Dressing, as normal, in trousers, shirt and tie – although renouncing his tweed jacket for a round-necked jersey – Henry telephoned the Town Hall. In the past, nothing bar tuberculosis would have kept him at home on a weekday, but local government wouldn't collapse because the Senior Assistant Clerical Officer without Portfolio called in sick.

Nevertheless, Henry was no skiver. He assigned himself a job. Rationalising the sideboard's gubbins would be a step towards The Willows' modernisation; blitzing the cupboards might also benefit his head.

He emptied the drawers onto the dining table. His father's fob watch, forever at twenty-five to five; a jumble of till receipts; a book of Green Shield stamps with stiffened pages; another conker; a jam spoon embossed with Kitchener's head. Where Irene would see clutter, Henry detected fragile artefacts.

By lunchtime, he had three heaps, stretching and shrinking in volume as items seesawed between them. Retain was the largest, closely followed by defer the decision to some hypothetical future when his mind and body were in finer fettle. Discard was the runt, despite comprising two sub-piles: private papers, like bank statements and payslips, for burning in the grate distinguished from genuine rubbish, such as bunged-up biros and callused rubber bands.

The conker was a definite keeper: could *this* stony lump be the one Tilly had entrusted to him?

Henry blew his nose, unblocking his head for one blissful moment until his nostrils leaked again. His handkerchief was sodden and his septum raw. Irene would impose a regime of paper tissues.

Why would a grown woman give a boy a conker? Didn't he have plenty of his own? When, seeing her suitcase in the hallway, his father chastised him for crying, he'd stanched the tears the only way he could.

He'd plunged his fist into the pocket of his short trousers. Offered her whatever was there. But if *he'd* gifted the conker, what did Tilly give *him*?

Chapter 20

"THANK YOU, GRAHAM. Please reassure the board that the clinicians share their concerns." Parveen Shakir, the consultant psychiatrist, smiled. When Graham Scott, the general manager, remained seated, she smiled wider. "We'll discuss her case next."

Graham tugged at his shirt-cuffs. "They'll expect a report on the structures you've put in place to prevent a recurrence."

"Absolutely! Heather is about to instigate a new group therapy programme."

"Not on my own." Heather Cooper, the occupational therapist, straightened her skirt. "Other team members are mucking in."

"Baffles me how she *got* to Tuke," said Graham. "Matty Osborne was the last person *I'd* have had down for the community ..."

"Excuse me," squeaked the psychologist, Norman Willis, "but you don't understand how she got here? Weren't you *at* my roadshows?"

Not again! Must Janice dedicate her career to deflecting discussion from Matty's controversial transfer from Ward 24? Or would circumstances push her to come clean? Three months on, she hardly recognised the zealous new social worker who'd meddled with the selection process, prioritising her personal values above her colleagues' experience. Could it be that Norman's cherished assessment didn't *only* reward conformity? Might it *genuinely* have the power to predict who could safely move on? But, rescued from Sister Henderson, Matty had blossomed. Frantically, she turned to Clive Musgrove, the charge nurse. "I thought you were impressed with her progress?"

"We were. Till yesterday."

"Maybe it's the aftershock from yesterday's meeting," said Heather.

"I wouldn't be surprised," said Graham. "She's lived here fifty years."

Like unlocking the door to a cage that, rather than *confining* the occupants, defended them against the dangers outside? Matty might have *enjoyed* reciting comic rhymes. Especially if, as Violet intimated, performance had brightened a dismal childhood. Yet she deserved better. "Matty was the most optimistic of the lot."

"Yes, but what was she optimistic *about*?" said Graham. "*She* thinks we're still at war with Germany."

Janice *knew* Matty had flashes of insight. Now, her stiffening jaw and damp palms threatened to defeat her *own* battle to stay positive. It wasn't a question of *whether* to confess, but *how* and *when*. Total disaster! Matty would lose the opportunity of an ordinary life. Janice would lose her job.

JANICE'S INDUCTION BACK in October included a morning with the psychologist, Norman Willis, in a narrow office made narrower by a wall of box files. His desk and a trio of grey metallic filing cabinets occupied the opposite wall. They sat face-to-face on office chairs squeezed into the alley between these bulwarks of psychological paraphernalia. Norman assured Janice that, when seeing patients, he used a less intimidating room. Only colleagues would be intermittently interrupted by Norman springing to his feet to disgorge the contents of a box file, as if his worth were gauged by forestry destruction.

The first patients to be discharged would be those who no longer required round-the-clock attention but lacked the potential to live alone, identified not by brand of psychiatric disorder, but a systematic assessment of their skills. Janice approved: diagnosis didn't dictate whether people could distinguish clean clothes from dirty or make a hot drink without scalding themselves.

After extensive research, Norman had recommended a measuring tool encompassing myriad behaviours from sociability to handling cash. Assessors marked a point on a line to denote a person's performance throughout the preceding week. Norman had trained the nurses in the assessment and collated the results. The project demanded so much time, Janice imagined he'd previously devoted his days to rearranging his boxes.

All patients had been assessed when Janice arrived, but some assessments remained unscored, enabling Norman to demonstrate the scoring procedure for real. This entailed positioning a Perspex key, marked like a ruler, on the assessment form to reveal into which section the assessor's cross fell, and inscribing the number on a scoresheet.

It seemed tedious for someone with a master's degree. "Wouldn't it have been simpler for the ward staff to assign the numbers?"

Stroking his beard, Norman launched into a lecture on the validity and reliability of rating scales, from which Janice deduced the simpler method was the less accurate. "Why don't you score some?" said Norman. "Get a feel for it." Before she could demur, he was on his feet, extracting a sheaf of orange forms from the filing cabinet.

Janice was groping for a polite way to refuse when she noticed '24' scrawled in the box after 'Ward'. "Okay." Would any of Sister Henderson's old ladies pass muster?

Norman asked if she'd mind him popping out to collect an urgent letter from his secretary. With him gone, she could colonise the whole desk.

Positioning the Perspex over the first form, she entered the figures on the scoresheet. Sadly, the patient was deficient in all areas except speech productivity, a feat rendered redundant by her zero rating for speech comprehensibility. The next was similarly dispiriting. And the one after that. Lives ruined by drugs and segregation, without even a retirement package. At least pit ponies were put out to pasture.

One more and she was leaving. Whether or not Norman deigned to show his face. But her gloom evaporated when she came upon a familiar name.

Matty Osborne! A swift glance at the numbers as she aligned the corners indicated they wouldn't amount to Matty's release. She was curious to see how far the Perspex would have to slip to secure Matty a fresh start.

If Norman had returned then, Janice might have abandoned the scoresheet to elicit his opinion on pensioners prattling poetry to order and tea served with milk and sugar irrespective of individual taste. But he didn't. By the time he got back, Janice had allotted Matty the grades she needed and buried her form in the sling of the filing cabinet marked "reserve".

Her fingers left sweaty prints on the Perspex. But the risks were negligible. A human being couldn't be reduced to a number. Even psychologists, who measured anything that moved and a fair amount that didn't, would agree with that.

———————

SHE'D HAVE TO tell David Pargeter first. There'd be an investigation, with a union rep at her side. But the conclusion would be clear from the outset: Janice would be sacked. David might suspend her the moment she spilled the beans: this could be her final team meeting. Just as she was finding her niche. And she'd looked forward to co-facilitating the choices group with Heather.

"There wouldn't *be* any aftershock from yesterday's meeting if you'd had a plan for managing the anxieties the news of the move would raise." Norman scowled at Graham until he crept from the room.

Janice blinked back tears. She'd miss Norman too. He might be a sourpuss, but he fought for his beliefs.

Regardless of how her colleagues might condemn her, she hoped they'd remember her positivity, and compassion for the underdog. "She helped herself to a few sprigs of dried-out lavender. It's not breaking and entering."

Clive squirmed. "It wasn't pinching the lavender, Janice. It was going off site without telling anyone. In her slippers. With no coat."

"She *is* vulnerable," said Heather. "Has she said why she absconded?"

"Not to me," said Clive, "and her primary nurse is on the sick."

Parveen turned to Mervyn Yates, the psychiatric registrar. "Have you been able to get anything from her?"

"I thought I'd try after the ward round."

"Multidisciplinary team clinical meeting," Norman corrected.

Waggling her spectacles, Parveen turned to Clive. "Could the nurses get her to provide a urine sample?"

"That's taken care of," Mervyn interjected. "Sent it to the lab this morning. Should have the results in a couple of days."

The doctors hijacking the meeting again: Janice anticipated Norman's protest. But he'd swapped sides. "A UTI could be at the bottom of it. Extremely befuddling in older people."

Janice perked up. "Makes them behave out of

character?"

"Sometimes," said Mervyn. "But it's easy to treat."

"So there might be a *medical* explanation for her wandering?" Any older person could have an infection. No reason for demotion to Ward 24. No reason for Janice to confess. "Can I report back on my meeting with Matty's school friend? I've discovered why the gentleman at The Willows didn't recognise her name."

Chapter 21

OH, FOR A lie down! Leaving the cups and saucers in the press office for the maid to attend to, Matty hurries to her bedroom. On the threshold, she havers. Which is her bed? It would be amusing if a guest found her, like Goldilocks, asleep in the wrong one.

In the past, she shared a room as big as a ballroom, where a person chatted to an invisible admirer from dusk to dawn. Now, with the main house requisitioned as a military hospital, Matty need never return. She laughs at the notion of soldiers commandeering a boudoir designed for society ladies. Albeit men who have forfeited the defining parts of their bodies to bombs.

Matty locates her bed, the farthest from the door, near a window with bobbled glass admitting light but fending off the view. Given the estate's contraction, this is a blessing. The farm with its pigs and sheep has surrendered to housing.

The cricket pitch, so evocative of English summers, a car park. An unhappy consequence of inheritance tax but these straitened circumstances do not deter the guests.

Stooping to sniff the lavender in the purple pot on her bedside table, Matty feels a rush of gratitude for the servants, in preserving her mother's favourite scent. Other items are more puzzling: a cube of paper tissues, a water glass and a framed photograph of a lady with a small boy.

Resting her rump against the bed, she picks up the photograph in its filigree surround. The lady wears a spotted dress with puffed sleeves, white collar and a flared skirt belted at the waist. One hand cleaves to the child, the other to a cloche hat, as the breeze bites at the brim.

Matty lumbers onto the bed and plumps up the pillow. Even if those portrayed were film stars, the photograph would not merit the ostentatious silver frame. The photographer has captured the location, and the boy's gaiety, but Matty herself would not open her purse for a picture of someone with the Eiffel Tower protruding from his head. From the ragged left edge, Matty infers that the other member, or members, of the party were also clumsily depicted. Yet someone deemed this worth conserving. There is no accounting for taste.

Depleted by this recent interview, Matty rests her eyes. The journalists' curiosity is insatiable and their questions, on occasion, impertinent. A nap should restore her customary bonhomie.

She dozes, all too briefly and, when she awakes, she is hugging that dratted photograph. Sweeping her hand across her torso, the glass splinters musically on the floor tiles, jingling xylophone keys.

Today's journalist was a charlatan, a scallywag suitor, courting Matty as a conduit to a different girl. A girl who resembles her, speaks like her, answers to her name, but is vice to her virtue. Unless apprehended, this other Matty will besmirch her reputation and trample on all she reveres.

Of course! How could she be so remiss? The lady in the photograph is the *other* Matty.

Not Matty, *Matilda*. Matilda told such dreadful lies it made one gasp and stretch one's eyes. A dissembler will get her comeuppance eventually, but Matty must distance herself lest *she* be punished for her doppelgänger's crimes. Otherwise, when Matilda shouts *Fire!* Matty would be mocked by *Little liar!*

Oh, but she is fatigued, and the private place between her legs stings. The gumption of the journalist to enquire about her waterworks! Or did she dream that?

A fine home with a doting mother: she should rejoice in her assets and say puff to matters beyond her control. Journalists will print what they please whatever she tells them. But as her musings fade to slumber, a warning sounds. Matilda would have no qualms about dragging the boy into a blazing building. Matty must sever the connection before he burns to ash.

Chapter 22

JANICE PARKED ACROSS the road and a few doors along the Victorian terrace from Number 44. By ducking in her seat and contorting her neck she could peer up at the third-floor window under the gabled roof, its history cloaked in darkness. On her first visit she'd thought Matty's family might have lodged a servant in the attic. Violet Osborne had turned that idea inside out.

Although Violet couldn't confirm or deny it, it made sense for Matty to have worked as a maid. Where Sister Henderson diagnosed delusions of grandeur, Janice perceived a bastion against despair. In TV period dramas, young women slaved in ordinary homes, rising at five to light fires in every room but theirs, only to be out on their ears for having sex. It was easy to imagine her employers forgetting her surname, referring to her as *the girl*. Could she nudge the current occupant of The Willows to bring her to mind?

She'd counted on finding inspiration during the drive from Ghyllside. But the engine had cooled before she'd thought of what to say. In her fantasy, he'd do a volte face the moment she mentioned the name: *Matty Osborne! I exchange Christmas cards with her cousin. Come in and I'll get you her address.* Reality would be different, especially if Matty had left in disgrace.

The windscreen clouded. Janice wiggled her toes. She'd freeze if she stayed in the car, procrastinating. But the grumpy geezer she recalled from November would slam the door on her if she hummed and hawed. How old *was* he? Too young for Matty's partner, too old to be her child. Old enough to recollect the cheerful teenager who made the beds and cooked the meals?

She couldn't convey the importance without breaking confidentiality. The evidence Matty had lived there was in a locked filing cabinet at Ghyllside.

Bollocks! Janice was becoming as institutionalised as her colleagues, viewing the world through psychiatry's prism. She inserted the key in the ignition. If Matty had lived at The Willows she'd appear on the electoral roll.

———————

"FIND HER?"

Leaning back to acknowledge the librarian, Janice's neck and shoulders felt the strain of hunching over the microfiche viewer, seeking assurance Matty had been more than a schizophrenic.

At least the librarian was on the case. Earlier, when

Janice asked to consult the electoral register, her response was disheartening. "The thirties? I don't think our records stretch *that* far back. I could check the archives …" Luckily, after a ten-minute wait, the librarian produced a brown envelope of microfiche, and demonstrated how to position it in the reader. Now, eyes smarting from inspecting not only the record for 1938, but for the two years either side of it, Janice shook her head. What would David Pargeter say if he knew she'd squandered an afternoon searching? "Did *they* have the poll tax too?"

The new system of local government funding, scheduled for implementation in April, was so unpopular, Janice dreamt of it bringing the Tories down. Like the contemporary poor, Matty might have refused to pay the financial price of voting. Or her employer omitted her name from the household return, lest she vote for reform. Were servants *entitled* to vote in those days? When women won the vote wasn't it limited to those with property?

"How old was your lady?"

"Nineteen or twenty."

"That'll be it then," said the librarian. "The voting age didn't come down to eighteen until the seventies."

Janice groaned. Why didn't she think of that? Matty wouldn't feature on the electoral register until sequestered in Ghyllside, if then. "But she'd be recorded on the census, wouldn't she?" Janice braced herself for extra eyestrain. Much more of this and she'd be prescribed reading glasses before she turned thirty.

"Presumably," said the librarian, "but that won't help you."

"You don't keep those records here?"

"We don't."

"Of course!" Convinced of a happy ending, she'd forgotten that access to individual census data was barred until death.

Chapter 23

P EGGED IN PLACE by the heft of it, the breath choked from her lungs. Invaded top and bottom, she cannot tell where the creature ends and she begins. She wriggles and claws, fights for air, for dignity, for life. Until she remembers: winning here means losing what she most cherishes. She has no choice but to succumb.

"Bad dream, Matty?"

A splash of sunlight on tobacco-washed walls. "Am I in prison?"

The girl grins. "Do I look like a jailer?"

Riddles upon riddles. Is she auditioning for the Sphinx?

"It's Karen!"

The face favours her maid but the body is too trim. Matty will smile until the disparate particles realign with their apposite slots.

"Janice has come to collect you for the group."

Scrambling to a sitting position, Matty sees the circus girl in the dormitory's open doorway, her hair a vibrant sunset. How blessed she is to occupy the finest house in England! A little lightheaded, she could stay merrily in bed for the rest of the afternoon rummaging through her mental store of patriotic poems. But her guests will have assembled at the card tables, awaiting her say-so to shuffle the packs. "My mother will not countenance gambling," she warns.

"I wouldn't worry about that."

In no haste to resume her public duties, Matty spots an empty glass on the bedside cabinet. "I am a tad dry, dear. Could you fetch me some water?"

"You'll be having tea in the group," says the maid.

Alongside the glass, the abomination! She *knew* something untoward was afoot! What minx positioned that impostor by her bed?

"Oops a daisy!" The maid catches her arm before Matty takes a tumble. Reclining against the pillows, the blasted photograph persists in her line of sight.

The circus girl breezes in with a glass of water, screening the picture from view. "Should we give your apologies this time, Matty? You can join us next week when you're feeling better."

"We'll get Dr Yates to examine you," says the maid.

"That will not be necessary." Such a pother over a dizzy spell. "I cannot detain them further." But what could they do? Mutiny? She chuckles: the guests would not have the oomph.

"If you're sure," says the maid.

"Quite sure." She must set an example. Having servants

is no excuse for idleness. Although not in *paid* employment, ladies must make themselves useful.

Resting her posterior on the edge of the bed as her feet slide into her slippers, Matty's gaze lingers on the photograph. Someone seems to have tampered with it and returned it to its silver frame. Unfortunately, they have removed the glass, enabling Matilda to hither and thither unrestrained. Fortunately the boy has escaped her, but where is he hiding and is he safe?

MATTY OWES HER repertoire of parlour games to her mother, who was partial to Snakes and Ladders, gin rummy and whist, while the boy enjoyed Beggar My Neighbour, Snap and draughts. Nowadays, with the butler's assistance, she hosts general knowledge quizzes for the guests, but a game based on tea is an intriguing innovation. She would have taken it for a gypsy ritual save that the circus girl's accomplice is as exotic as a schoolmistress, in an extremely dour skirt and blouse.

"Effie, can you ask Billy if he fancies tea or coffee?"

Naturally, the schoolmistress gets no sense from the shrimp-woman, who directs her reply at the baby. "We have tea at three o'clock."

"So you do, Effie. But this afternoon we agreed to try something different. We're exploring individual preferences and tastes. So, could you ask Billy if he would like coffee or tea?"

"I'll have a coffee if it's going."

"That's lovely, Billy. We'll get you a coffee once we've found out about everyone else. But did anyone notice Billy answered Effie's question before she asked it? Let's see if you can ask each other …"

"Of course," says Matty. "Happy Families."

"Not exactly," says the circus girl.

"Because there aren't any cards," says the man with illustrated arms.

"It's like social skills," the shrimp-woman tells her baby.

"It is indeed like social skills. In fact, it *is* a social skill, isn't it, when we ask another person what they prefer?"

The boy would adore this game. Matty wishes he were here to explain it.

"So, Billy, could you ask Matty whether she'd rather have tea or coffee?" continues the schoolmistress.

"Matty, do you want tea or coffee?"

"Fabulous, Billy. Can you ask again, making it clear you're interested?"

"Not really. Anyroad, she drinks tea."

"It's great you've noticed what she has generally, Billy. How can you find out what she'd like this afternoon?"

"My baby drinks milk," says the shrimp-woman.

"Okay. Billy would like coffee and Matty would like tea. Is there anything else we should ask?"

"Have we got a bottle for the baby?"

"Are there any biscuits?"

Everyone turns to the tea trolley, parked between the fish tank and the television. Miracles do happen when that chatterbox is muted.

"As we're learning the ropes, should Janice and I ask what everyone wants?"

"What a good idea," says the circus girl. "Shall I start?

Heather, would you like tea or coffee?"

"Hey, that's for us. You have coffee in your offices."

"That's true, Billy. But in this group we'll all have a hot drink together."

Oh, deary me! The fellow is incensed. Although uncouth, he *is* a guest. But she cannot reproach the circus girl and her associate as she would a scullery maid or gardener. How would her mother make peace between them? Matty gets a sniff of smoky tea. "My mother takes Lapsang souchong with a lemon slice."

———————————

JANICE TUCKED THE folder under her arm to slide the key into the lock. She stumbled into the interview room and flopped onto the nearest chair. A mug in each hand, Heather followed, closing the door with her backside. She took the seat opposite and passed Janice one of the mugs. "It seemed less complicated on the course."

"They've had so many decisions taken away from them. From the colour of their toothbrush to when to go to bed. Did you see how they looked at us? As if we had a screw loose."

"You think it's pointless?"

"Put it this way, Sister Henderson's death mask would crack if she got wind of what we were up to."

High on the wall, the clock clicked onto the next minute. As Heather straightened her already straight skirt, Janice held her breath. For all she knew, the occupational therapist might be related to the sister of Ward 24. David assured her the structures were changing but some sections of the hospital had a whiff of Cumbrian mafia.

Heather pursed her lips; not, as Janice first feared, in disdain but in a futile attempt to stem the laughter bubbling behind them.

Janice laughed too. "You must admit, there's a warped logic in adding the milk and sugar to the pot."

"If you're too lazy to *work* for your pay cheque," said Heather.

Initially, Janice welcomed co-working with Heather because of her clinical know-how. Dare she hope that, despite her prim presentation, she'd found an ally? "Today a hot beverage! Tomorrow …?"

"Opportunity Knocks!"

"The Palace of Westminster!"

"Mmm, I'd be glad if they'd exercise their democratic right to vote." Heather slumped. "I couldn't get any of them to the polling station last year."

"They're registered, then?"

Heather bristled. "That goes without saying."

"They might be more motivated when they get to Briarwood. There's a thought! What if they could vote there *this* time around?"

"I don't know how we'd wangle it," said Heather. "But it's worth a try."

Chapter 24

HENRY'S COLD WAS no reason to cancel Irene's night class. Besides, he'd no way of contacting her except in dire emergency. So, at his regular clocking-off time, he left his nest for Mr Patel's.

At the door to the minimart, Henry almost collided with a frizzy-haired woman in a waxed jacket. Recalling their altercation outside the baby clinic, he was relieved when she tutted and barged past.

Wandering the aisles, Henry opted for a frozen lasagne, raspberry Pavlova and a bottle of chilled Chardonnay. At the till, Mr Patel registered the price and stowed his purchases in a plastic carrier. Ringing up the total, he drew Henry's attention to a pink sheet sellotaped to the counter.

A grid half-filled with scribble. Henry wasn't tempted to add *his* autograph. Nor to read the small print. Blocked sinuses – and the sense of dislocation on escaping solitary confinement – played havoc with his vision. Some teenager, no doubt, begging the gullible to finance an exotic holiday disguised as a charity challenge: climbing Kilimanjaro to train Guide Dogs; trekking the Great Wall of China to cure childhood leukaemia. Producing a ten-pound note, he muttered something about the resourcefulness of youth.

"Mrs Marshall's fuming." Mr Patel doled out his change. "She's organising a protest march or somesuch."

"Isn't that a bit extreme?" Sponsorship forms were irritating, but no-one was pressganged into parting with their dosh.

"People are scared it'll affect house prices."

Henry stashed away his change. He wasn't inclined to support a homelessness charity.

"How come you're so laid-back? Doesn't your house back onto the site?"

The lettering crystallised: *We, the undersigned, reject the proposal to situate a home for psychiatric patients on Corporation Road …*

"I suppose it's different if you're not moving," said Mr Patel. "But folks see a house as an investment, a stepping-stone to bigger and better."

Wouldn't it be worse for those who *stayed*? But, with his tenure so iffy, he didn't dare castigate the council. The waxed-jacket woman looked fierce enough to fight it singlehanded.

A TUG ON his scalp as Irene teased a lock of hair between her fingers and snipped the ends. "Tell me why you're agin' it."

Henry resisted shaking his head; a reckless response when she had charge of a potential weapon. He sat facing the fire in the dining room, knees roasting and his nape plummeting from cool to icy. "Isn't it obvious?"

"Not to me," said Irene. "Or I wouldn't have asked."

"You think it would be okay?"

Her scissors clunked dangerously close to his scalp. "Could be a goldmine for me."

"How's that, then?"

"All those old biddies, too frail to go up-street."

"You'd offer to do their hair?"

"I'd expect to be paid."

"They won't be docile grannies wanting a blue rinse. You need special skills."

The scissors dropped into his lap. Henry flinched.

"I don't have special skills? Try cutting your own hair!"

He leant back and stroked her forearm. "You know that's not what I meant. I've said it time and time again, you're a brilliant hairdresser." He had, too, although it was years since there'd been anyone to compare her with. Had he not said it enough? Passing her the scissors, he ratched in his pocket for his hankie, blowing his nose while Irene selected another batch of hair for the chop. "Think of the safety angle. What if they nabbed the scissors? I couldn't let you expose yourself to that risk."

"I wasn't planning on exposing myself," she said. "Not there, anyroad."

"I'm not making funnies, Irene. I won't have you working somewhere like that."

Irene bent to kiss him. "I love it when you act

domineering."

HENRY FOCUSED ON pouring the tea while Irene examined the photograph. He'd thought she'd be amused to see a small boy clad in collar and tie for a trip to the beach. She'd wanted him to share more, but sharing Tilly made him nauseous. Or was that from the hair smouldering in the grate?

"What a stunner! Pity she didn't pass those looks on to you."

"Mind your manners, madam, or you'll not get a tip."

"You're the spit of your father, but."

"You reckon?"

"Carbon copy." Irene laughed. "Same mush, same clobber, same haircut."

Henry scratched his neck. Some of the clippings had worked their way beneath his collar. "That's your doing."

"Your mam seems dead young, but. I thought she had you late?"

He'd assumed she'd rib him about the tower jutting from his head. But Irene stopped joshing to appraise him in an extraordinary fashion. Not as the apprentice hairdresser dazzled by his three-storey property. Not as the modish woman who mocked his fuddy-duddy style. Not as the entrepreneur with an eye on his assets. Not even as the adulteress who fucked without shame. Irene observed him now from a position of infinite acumen. She beheld him as a mother.

His father to the left of the photograph, his sister in the middle. Radiant in a summer dress, right hand on her hat, the left clutching his. There was something magical about that frock, red with white spots like a fairy-tale toadstool. "It's Tilly."

Irene slapped her palm over her mouth. "Oh, Henry, I'm sorry. How could I forget?"

Chapter 25

MATTY NIBBLES A slice of toast, unable to decide whether, after smearing butter and marmalade to the edges, it would be rude to return it to the rack, when the maid asks if she cares to go to church.

"The one with the flying lion?"

"This isn't Disneyland, Matty," the maid laughs, and Matty laughs also, but reservedly. A servant should not make jokes at her mistress's expense.

Matty follows the maid to the window, more to dodge the dilemma presented by the toast than from curiosity. The girl points out the chapel beyond the tarmac drive and patch of grass. Too small to support a spire, not even one the size of a dunce's cap or an upturned ice cream cone, it does possess a stumpy turret, above which the Union Jack flaps in the breeze. "Oh, that one."

"Would you like to go to the service?"

Is that where the guests have scurried off to? "Will my mother be there?"

The maid pats her arm. "You knew it was Mother's Day?"

Something fidgets inside her. A tapeworm. Assailed by an urge to empty herself, she pulls away. Reaching the door, the discomfort fades.

The maid chases after her. "Shall I walk you across?"

"No thank you!" It pains her to speak so sharply, but only a papist would be so persistent. Matty dashes down the corridor into the lavatories, chuckling at her cunning in evading the nuns.

To her right, a row of three stalls; to her left three white sinks, each with a mirror above. No-one there, apart from a naked baby in the far basin, damp from its bath. Matty puts it to her shoulder while she assesses her options.

Oh, deary me! Whether Mother's Day or Christmas, she will have to dispose of it. Selecting the middle cubicle, she peers into the bowl, although she is not so foolish as to flush it down the lavatory. Even dismembered, it would choke the drains. She shoves the baby under her blouse, referring to the mirror to ensure it does not show. If she clasps her hands below her belly, it ought to stay in place.

By good luck or God's grace, no-one intercepts her as she waddles to her bedroom. At the bed nearest the door, she shakes the cotton slip from the pillow and stuffs the baby inside. Then she opens the bedside cupboard and secretes the bagged baby within. The door closed on the evidence, she sashays to her own bed and stretches out on the counterpane.

JANICE HAD GONE out for lunch with her parents and sister. Her mother smiled stoically between bouts of coughing, and praised the food she couldn't taste. The pub heaved with sons and daughters of all ages, from chain-smoking pensioners to screaming babies, but it would have been no more peaceful had they cancelled the reservation and stayed at home. Ignoring a dizzying temperature, her mother would have shooed them from the kitchen, single-handedly conjuring up a roast. Although *her* appetite was so small she declared herself full after the prawn cocktail, it was a treat to be out with her daughters on Mother's Day.

Janice's father, on such occasions, was relegated to cheque signatory and chauffeur. With his bleached skin and freckles, he even *looked* separate from the female side of the family. The thick dark locks and skin that turned bronze at the mere mention of the sun made mother and daughters a set, the pink in Janice's hair notwithstanding.

After coffee, their mother admitted that, despite having had *a smashing time*, she needed a rest, and their father asked for the bill. When Rosalind announced that she would walk back to the house, Janice offered to keep her company. Their mother nodded enthusiastically – while cautioning Roz to keep track of time so she wouldn't miss her train – either because she thought they'd appreciate a sisterly chat or she wanted Janice to watch over her elder sister. Janice hadn't forgotten the awful period in her early teens when Rosalind would sneak out to gorge on chocolate bars and sick them up.

Their route meandered through a park as crowded with

families honouring mothering as the pub. When Roz slid her arm through hers, Janice might have been ten again, plotting a concert for their parents featuring Abba's latest hits. Perhaps, by sharing a secret, she could recapture their childhood intimacy.

Although suffering no physical repercussions from her recklessness at New Year, emotionally it had launched her into alien territory. Her sister could help her work out how far she wanted to explore. "Can I tell you something personal …?"

It could have been the unevenness of the path, but she felt Roz shrink back. Undoubtedly the what-have-you-done-now expression was deliberate. "Sure."

"Promise you won't tell Mum!"

Roz slowed her pace. "As long as it's legal."

"It's legal. But a big step." She paused until they passed a couple on a tandem with a baby strapped in between. "I'm thinking of tracing my real mother … my biological mother, that is."

"Oh, Janice!"

"What? You're telling me *you've* never considered it?"

"Today of all days!"

Janice unhooked her arm from her sister's. "Mum would understand."

"She'd think she'd failed you."

"I don't see why. Lots of people do it."

"And lots of people *don't*. Where's this come from? Is it your job?"

"What makes you say that?"

"You know! Digging up dirt."

Until Roz reached her teens, their personalities were so aligned that Janice believed they were genetically related. Now it was hard to credit they'd been brought up in the same town, never mind the same household with the same loving parents. She gritted her teeth. "It's not dirty to wonder about the woman who gave birth to me. Or to do a job making life better for those who've drawn the short straw. What makes you so touchy?"

"Sorry, Jan. I can't take it in at the minute. Heavy shit at work."

Janice threaded her arm through her sister's. "Want to talk about it?"

"Like to a social worker?"

What was the matter with her? "Like to a sister, wombat!"

———

HE SHOULD HAVE brought a gardening fork. He should've worn an old pair of trousers, his slate-coloured cords now clarty at the knees. He should have chosen a time when the sound of children singing would not have filtered through the church walls. But, when Henry had set out for a stroll that afternoon, he hadn't known his legs would take him to his mother's grave.

FLORENCE WINDSOR, BELOVED WIFE OF GEORGE WINDSOR, BORN 1896 DIED 1933. As a child, he'd resented the omission of BELOVED MOTHER OF TILLY AND HENRY, and vowed to rectify it when the task of briefing the stonemason fell to him. But on his father's death he'd kept it simple: GEORGE WINDSOR, BORN 1890 DIED 1971.

Moss crumbled in his fingers as he rubbed it from the digits etched in granite. Both parents born in the nineteenth century: stiff-upper-lipped Victorians. But *his* childhood was ancient history relative to Irene's, a mother dying in childbirth having a Dickensian ring. It wasn't uncommon in the Depression years prior to the National Health. Infant mortality was high then too; there must have been other children in the thirteen years between Tilly's birth and his, although he'd never seen any tiny Windsor graves.

Tugging at a dandelion, the root snapped, the oppositional force propelling him onto his backside. He should never have started meddling. Unless you exhume the whole root, the weed is resurrected with renewed vigour, like a rat adapting to warfarin. Brushing down his trousers as he rose to his feet, Henry decided to return another day with proper tools. Smother the weeds with low-growing annuals. Transplant some shrubs from the garden; he'd enough lavender for a perfumery.

At the murmur of families spilling from the church, Henry scuttled off. What was so special about mothers, anyroad? Henry didn't miss his. He imagined his *actual* mother as an elderly matron decked in black, hair in a severe bun. Young, beautiful, and full of fun, Tilly was the better bargain. But Henry's gain had cost his sister dearly. Leaving school at thirteen, she'd tendered her teenage years to him. He couldn't abandon her. Irene would have to like it or lump it.

———————

JANICE THUMPED THE horn as a van cut in, compelling her

to brake and giving the Snoopy dangling from the rear-view mirror a seizure. Roz should've been pleased she'd taken her into her confidence, but she'd responded as if Janice had sought her approval, or permission, which she stubbornly withheld. Whatever relationship Janice developed with her birth mother had no bearing on Roz's relationship with hers. Two years' seniority did *not* give her privileged access to their adoptive mother's emotions. Bloody banker lecturing *her* about feelings!

The irony was that, for the moment, it was only the seed of an idea. She hadn't acted on it yet, hadn't applied for a copy of her original birth certificate. Instead of helping her speculate on what that seed might grow into, Rosalind had tried to abort it.

Her birth mother had sat unobtrusively in a corner of her mind for as long as she'd known she was adopted. Janice presumed she'd approach her in the far-flung future after she'd exhausted all the *interesting* people. Beyond biology, they'd be poorly matched.

In fact, she'd regarded her as pathetic. Bird-brained, lackadaisical, shambolic. Now she knew that even careful, educated and organised women were fallible. The sole difference between Janice and her birth mother was the morning-after pill.

Who *was* the woman in the corner? Wouldn't it be a hoot if she wore harem trousers and dyed her hair pink? Busy with work, and the struggle to forge a social life beyond monthly Labour Party meetings, it wasn't a priority to find out. But it should have been fun to ponder the possibilities with her sister.

Despite the warm air blowing from the heater, Janice shivered. Roz had always been tetchy, but she'd mellowed since her traumatic teens. A recurrence of the eating distress that blighted those years would certainly upset their mother. Hurt by her rebuff, had Janice been fobbed off too readily by *work pressures*? Maybe Roz had planned to confide in *her* when Janice stole the limelight. Time to stop playing the pesky little sister and grow up.

Chapter 26

NORMAN GLARED AT the clock, as if *it* were responsible for frittering his time. "We'd better begin."

Mervyn glanced at the door. "She shouldn't be long."

The men eyeballed each other across the table. The psychologist, Norman Willis, was the elder and more experienced, but the tower of case notes in front of Mervyn Yates, the psychiatric registrar, was taller. Norman surrendered his gaze to the ordinary ring binder in front of the occupational therapist. "Heather, could you talk us through the groups programme?"

Heather Cooper picked up her folder and put it down again. "Let's hang on for Dr Shakir."

Janice broke the silence by asking Clive Musgrove whether Effie Atkinson's doll had turned up. Clive laughed. "It was in Betty Fogarty's locker."

"Betty?" said Heather. "I'm surprised *she'd* make off

with it."

"Effie shouldn't be playing with a doll at her age," said Norman. "You were supposed to wean her off it with a handbag."

"We're working on it," Clive insisted.

"You can't rock a handbag," said Janice.

"A middle-aged woman carting a doll around with her," said Norman. "How's anyone going to take her seriously? I'd better review that care plan."

"Maybe Effie doesn't *want* to be taken seriously," said Janice. "Maybe she *enjoys* being eccentric."

Norman groaned. "Who knows? But she won't enjoy kids hurling abuse at her for it."

"There's plenty of time to get it sorted before the move," said Clive.

"It's so unfair," said Janice. "They've got to be more normal than normal."

"Welcome to the real world," said Norman.

"Anyroad," said Clive, "we've a feeling *Matty* took the doll."

"That would make sense." Mervyn ransacked the pile of case files. Opening Matty's at a fresh page, he primed his fountain pen.

"You're not going to record her nicking a doll?" said Norman.

"It's useful information," said Mervyn. "If she's getting broody, she might need her meds upped."

"A *seventy*-year-old broody?" said Heather.

"It's a *toy*," said Janice. "Not a proxy child."

"Have we any *evidence* it was Matty?" said Norman.

Sucking his teeth, Mervyn capped and pocketed his pen. The door opened and Parveen Shakir bustled in. "Sorry, folks. I hope you started already."

––––––––––––––

"COME OUT, MATTY, that's the *men's* dormitory!"

"I know that." She isn't so foolish as to hunt for him in the *ladies'* quarters.

The maid takes her arm. "Let's go and have a cup of tea."

Tea and more tea; the staff are obsessed. Yet Matty allows herself to be led. After some refreshment, she might feel better equipped to resume her search.

Hal is not the only absentee; her lady in waiting, Kitty, has also gone astray. *She* can look after herself, but it is churlish of her maid to leave without a thank you or farewell. Her rough edges notwithstanding, Matty had grown fond of the girl.

Kitty's replacement – Karen, who now ushers her into the kitchen – lacks the substance, intelligence and verve of her previous maid. When she asked what became of Kitty, the new girl claimed *she* had been with Matty from the start. Matty did not press the matter, but she does not care to be duped.

Karen pulls a lever on the boiler and steaming water belches into an ugly white mug. "Do you fancy your tea with a slice of lemon?"

The new girl *must* be a relative to be so well briefed. Substitutions benefit both higher and lower orders: employers assured of the new girl's character; servants finding situations for their kin. Nevertheless, if wantonness caused Kitty's departure, she ought to be notified. "Did Kitty get herself in the family way?"

"I'm Karen, and I'm sorry I had to take a few weeks off."

It pains Matty to see her shoulders droop, as if sharing Kitty's shame. "No-one would judge you for it, dear." She resolves to forget Kitty and take Karen under her wing.

———————

FOR ONE GLORIOUS moment, Janice heard Matty on the line, but it was purely the product of childhood elocution lessons and wishful thinking. She nudged her disappointment aside to greet the woman who'd lived the life Matty was denied. "Lovely to hear from you, Violet. Are you coming to visit?"

"I'm afraid not. I literally haven't a spare minute. I'm meeting myself coming back, what with orders for spring flower arrangements and the grandchildren due for Easter …"

My heart bleeds! She should swap with Matty for a couple of weeks. No grandkids or even old friends preying on *her* time.

"But I owe you an apology …"

"An apology?"

"I wasn't as helpful the other week as I might have been."

"Not at all, I appreciate you fitting me in. Obviously, I hoped you'd want to visit …"

"If only I could! But I wanted to bring up a *psychiatric*

issue."

"If you're uncomfortable coming to Ghyllside, we could meet at your house. Or in a café. Neutral territory."

"This concerns Matilda's *diagnosis.*"

Did Violet need reassurance Matty wouldn't attack her? Those horror movies with axe-wielding madmen had a lot to answer for. "She *can* get confused. But she wouldn't hurt a fly. And it would do her good to meet an old friend." But would it? Would Matty remember Violet and, if so, would those memories be positive? Would Matty be intimidated by someone so groomed and glamorous, the personification of everything she'd missed?

"I wasn't totally straight with you regarding Matilda's father."

"He didn't die in the war?" So he *might* have had her committed?

"Her mother kept it quiet, on account of the stigma. Never let on to Matilda. But *her* father was no hero. He didn't die *in* the war, but afterwards. Suicide. That's why her mother didn't qualify for a pension."

"That's outrageous!" Such injustice, a social worker wouldn't know where to start.

"Indeed! Abandoning his wife and child. Must have been wrong in the head."

What passing-bells for these who die as cattle? Janice had studied Wilfred Owen at school. "Shellshock? From the trenches?" She'd met an elderly patient on the male equivalent of Ward 24. Even among men with movement disorders from tardive dyskinesia, he'd stood out, hugging the wall as he sidled along the corridor. He might have preferred death to seventy years of torture.

"Lack of moral fibre. I thought the doctors should be aware. Seeing as Matilda went the same."

The same? By demonstrating that *anyone* could crack under stress? Janice recalled Norman's opposition to *family history of psychosis* reverberating through the notes: a genetic disposition inferred from what might have been bad luck. "Thanks for that, then. Feel free to ring me if you think of anything else." Anything *useful*.

"Incidentally," said Violet, "will Matilda be at the mayor's At Home?"

"What's that?"

"The mayor hosts an annual tea party for the senior citizens. It's a jolly good bash."

"Really?" Meeting Violet wouldn't help Matty. But tea with the mayor would be right up her street.

Chapter 27

ONE OF THE plusses of payroll – as with every branch of personnel – was being a step removed from the public. Henry had lost that protection when Linda Quinn confiscated his old ID. Now, manning the helpline for the forthcoming local election, Henry despaired of the pettiness. Callers blamed *him* that registering to vote made them liable for the community charge – or poll tax according to the dissenters – as if they should have the benefits of the franchise without the responsibilities. Services had to be funded somehow and they'd whinge if their bins weren't emptied or the libraries closed. The riots against the new system had been shameful; watching the footage on the news, Henry was glad he lived in the sticks.

To top it all, Linda had rostered him as a poll clerk. He wouldn't have minded transferring his regular nine-to-five to the polling station, but the hours were seven till ten. How could the union sanction a fifteen-hour shift when they quibbled about five minutes off the tea break? *What a palaver!* said Linda when he queried the hours. *Sitting at a desk in a church hall won't break your back.* But it clashed with Irene's evening class, when he should be on his back in *bed*.

Now he had some jester asking if she could use *any* polling station. "Didn't you receive a card informing you where to vote? Give me your postcode and I'll check where you're registered."

"I know where I'm registered," said the woman, "but I'd prefer to vote elsewhere."

"Voting's a privilege, not a pick'n'mix." Linda had assured *him* he could do his stint at his local station and, once the ballot boxes were collected, be home before the end of the ten o'clock news. But there'd be chaos if the electorate tried to shop around. "If you can't get to your allocated station between seven in the morning and ten at night, you should've applied for a postal vote."

"To be honest, it's not *for* me. It's for the people I work with."

"Makes no difference." *Troublemaker, passing the buck onto an imaginary friend.* "Prince to pauper, the same rules apply."

The woman tittered. "These people aren't fussed about voting where they are right now. But they're moving soon. If they could vote where they're *going* to live …"

Henry flicked through the photocopied handbook. "Will they be there on May the third?"

"It's not for another year."

"Is this a hoax?" As the line went dead, Henry concluded it was.

WHILST TIDYING CUPBOARDS a couple of months earlier, Henry had unearthed a roll of glossy paper, red with silver stars, and set it aside for Irene's birthday. Of course he'd forgotten where. Would she mind if he wrapped her gift in plain brown paper? He had masses of that.

So tricky choosing for Irene. The frilly fripperies she favoured were alien to him, not to mention the risk of arousing her husband's suspicions. Furthermore, even if he'd brazened the ladies' underwear aisle at M&S, why would she don silky lingerie for her evening class, to strip it off for bed?

Neither shiny nor frilly, Henry had nevertheless hit the jackpot with this year's gift. No fretting about keeping *my lady* waiting when she was stuck behind a tractor. No turning up for appointments to find *my lady* had cried off. The new-fangled phone would let her make and take calls in her van.

A special present warranted special packaging. Henry scratched his head, but he couldn't scratch his brain. He plodded upstairs for one last look in Tilly's room.

Well! There it was, in the drawer of her vanity table, albeit the background wasn't red but purple and the silver stars were gold. To extract the paper without rumpling it, he eased the drawer off its runners and placed it on the bed. As he did so, his gaze hobbled on a black disc. A button, an ordinary coat button, except it wasn't ordinary at all.

Taking it between finger and thumb, Henry was six

again. Patterned with concentric rings, it resembled a miniature gramophone record, with two holes to a record's one. He sniffed the Bakelite, but he couldn't smell Tilly. He smoothed the underside across his cheek, but he couldn't touch her. Tilly left *this* in his custody half a century ago?

Memory was fickle. For years he believed she'd given him a conker. Then it flipped to *him* giving the conker to *her*. Now he could feel her folding his fingers around this button as it covered his palm.

Henry flagged. A button was more credible than a conker, but it was a shabby gift. If she'd loved him, wouldn't she have selected something suitable for a young boy? Put herself in his shoes, as he'd done with Irene's phone?

Yet he trusted this version more than the others. Tilly crouching to his level, her brown suitcase beside her, burrowing the button in his hand.

Chapter 28

M OST PEOPLE SCUTTLED past, eyes averted, hiding their identities along with how they'd cast their vote. They probably got off on activists knocking on the doors of those who'd already voted, as if the last few weeks of campaigning weren't gruelling enough. But this woman strode towards her with so broad a smile, Janice felt she should know her. An off-duty nurse? A relative she'd consoled over cups of treacle-thick tea?

"Splendotint three-two-five?"

A drug? One of those toxins pumped into the patients, never the elixir the reps proclaimed. In clinical meetings, Janice zoned out as the doctors tossed neologisms to and fro. But she wasn't at work now.

When she'd failed to register Tuke House residents at their future address on Corporation Road, and Heather pooh-poohed her proposal to bring them anyway, Janice volunteered her services to the local Labour Party. Assisting with the exit poll at this *specific* polling station would serve as a naturalistic sociological study of Briarwood. Even the journey proved useful. Until setting out to find the Methodist Church – an ugly low-rise modern building which she might have taken for a GP surgery if not for the crucifix rising, like a chimney, from the side of the pitched roof – she hadn't realised the site of the new-build was so close to Sheepwash Lane. Once she lived in the community, *something* would remind Matty of her last address.

That was for the future. For now Janice was a Labour Party minion puzzled by *Splendotint three-two-five*. She hadn't noticed the names of all the smaller parties, guaranteed to lose their deposits yet fielding candidates for the sheer hell of it. Although professionally compelled to frown on the Monster Raving Loony Party, they added a humorous touch to the proceedings. But *Something three-two-five* echoed the neo-Nazi group *Something one-eight* after the alphabetical order of Hitler's initials. She stepped back.

The woman appeared unperturbed. "Have you tried the Marveleen range, but? Six-three-nine would complement your skin tone."

Clasping the clipboard to her chest, Janice patted her hair, dampened by the recent downpour. At the first spot of rain, the Tory Man, whom she'd assiduously ignored since a curt *Good evening*, had unfurled his golfing umbrella. Despite being big enough for two Janice wouldn't have shared it if he'd *offered*, which he didn't. The Liberal Democrat woman must have had a tipoff from the Met office as, five minutes before the clouds erupted, she'd toddled off and hadn't resumed her post.

When Janice could no longer pretend that an upturned collar supplied adequate, or *any*, protection, she'd made for the porch. But a sour-faced election clerk barked that no-one was allowed inside unless to vote. Although tempted to contest it – the building being a church the other three hundred and sixty-four days of the year, she might have come to worship – the red rosette pinned to her lapel gave her away. So, shielding the clipboard with her jacket, she'd raced to the side street where she'd parked her Polo. Soggy trousers glued to her legs, she might have driven home except for her determination not to let Tory Man beat her. When the sky brightened, she'd returned, defiant, albeit dank and dishevelled, hair plastered to her head.

Now this woman was fixating on the formula staining it pink. Janice was accustomed to the stares, to young men in old cars beeping. But only children and, as David had warned her, some psychiatric patients, ever *mentioned* her hair. Such directness, from one who was neither, suggested a tolerance of difference rarely encountered outside the major cities. "You're interested in colour?"

"I'm *passionate* about colour." The woman fumbled with the fastenings of a boxy vanity case. "My hands aren't, but. Here, take my card. I'm Irene. If you fancy trying Marveleen, give me a bell."

A hairdresser touting for clients; not the advocate of diversity who would help discharged psychiatric patients feel at home. Averting her gaze from the rash, Janice scrutinised the matchbox-sized card. "Is that a local number? I don't recognise the code."

Grinning, the woman dipped into her bag and brought out a gadget resembling a police walkie-talkie with an antenna poking from the top. "It's one of those car phones. Champion for a mobile business like mine."

A mobile business? She'd never use it, but Janice shoved the card in her pocket. No room for a hairdo in her flat, unless she squatted on the toilet seat while Irene stood in the shower.

———————————

"GOOD GOD, WHAT are you doing here?" It was fine and dandy people bringing their children, but otherwise the polling station was more sacrosanct than the church that lodged it. It was impossible for the ballot to proceed without prejudice or interference if people used the building as a drop-in. Or a drying room, as someone had tried earlier. (Or some*thing* had tried: the interloper was so bedraggled, he, she or it might have emerged from the ocean floor.)

"Nice to see you too, Mr Windsor," simpered Irene. "I happened to be passing and thought you'd welcome a bit of bait." Diving into her purple vanity case, she retrieved a packet of Jammie Dodgers and a tube of Pringles. "I could swear I had a bag of Hula Hoops." Installing the case on the table, she ratched through the contents.

The election clerk to Henry's left twitched. A pimply youth by the unfortunate name of Horatio, he was probably tapped. If he'd been animated at the sight of the snacks, he was whizzing when Irene produced her phone. "Is that one of them car phones? They must cost a mint."

"I wouldn't know." Irene passed Henry the Hula

Hoops. "It was a present. From a very dear friend." She held it out to Horatio. "Have a go!"

The youth stroked the frill of fuzz gracing his upper lip. "I couldn't."

"Away, it won't bite."

What game was she playing? Henry was as embarrassed as the red-faced youth. Much as he relished *a very dear friend*, this was no place for flirtation. "Mrs Lonsdale, you're most generous …" Henry ripped into the packet of biscuits and skimmed them to the third election clerk, a middle-aged librarian with the no-nonsense name of Joan. "But you can't stay. This space is reserved for the electorate."

Joan brandished a biscuit at the empty booths. "She's all right for a wee while."

"Five minutes, then." Irene was an enigma, rebuffing him one minute, cosying up the next. Fortunately, the table obscured the spike in his underpants, but it would get bally uncomfortable if she hung about.

"Mam, Mam, I'm on one of them new mobiles," Horatio whooped into the phone.

Had his gift softened Irene's attitude? Upgraded him? He'd long been suspicious of her mercenary side.

Horatio finished his call. Irene slipped the phone in her bag. Oh, her poor hands, so raw and blistered they might be rinsed in acid. Henry wanted to kiss them, soothe them, absorb her pain. Let her use him and confuse him, he loved her.

———————

WHILE THERE WERE punters exiting the polling station,

Janice needn't acknowledge Tory man beyond his role as counterpart to hers. Yet as the shadows lengthened, and the intervals between departures lengthened too, the charade became increasingly brittle. So she felt relieved when a woman approached with a clipboard. The LibDem activist had taken an extended break.

But the new arrival wasn't sporting a yellow rosette. In fact, she wasn't wearing any party colours. Her green waxed jacket and poodle perm denoted country-club Tory. "Would you sign my petition regarding a threat to our neighbourhood?"

"Sorry, I'm not local."

"You can still lend your support." The woman slid her clipboard on top of Janice's own.

Scanning the text, she nearly dropped it. "This is appalling!"

"Isn't it!"

Pages and pages of signatures. A welcoming community? Janice thrust it at her. "You're asking the wrong person."

"I see, so long as it's not in *your* backyard."

"On the contrary. It's bigots like *you* I'd hate to have for neighbours."

"Leave it, Janice!"

She'd clocked Tory Man earwigging on her exchange with the hairdresser. But she was damned if she'd provide *his* evening entertainment. "Nobody asked *your* opinion."

The woman pounced on the potential ally. "Perhaps *you'd* sympathise with our concerns about property prices."

"I might if you had proof they'd suffer," he said. "Even then, it's a lame excuse for locking people up."

Typical bloke! As if Janice hadn't the wit to argue her case. But she might have overdone it calling the woman *a bigot*! In their student days, he'd labelled her a firebrand; now the burn crept from her cheeks to her neck and the tips of her ears. How far would she have gone tonight if Stuart hadn't intervened?

"It's not entirely a matter of house prices …"

"You betcha," said Stuart. "It's about gauging a society by its compassion."

Janice laughed. "You could be excommunicated for using the S-word." She'd been personally affronted when the Prime Minister declared *There's no such thing as society.*

"Community care is conservative party policy. First mooted by Enoch Powell."

"I can see I'm wasting my time here," said the woman.

With the retreat of the common enemy, the awkwardness resumed. Stuart cut through it. "Let's ditch this and go to the pub."

Chapter 29

MATTY SETS DOWN her brush and waits for the artist to inspect her watercolour. Although *her* talents lie elsewhere, Matty is willing to patronise the visual arts. Through this afternoon's tutorial, she can salvage two stones with one bird: assisting an impoverished artist while entertaining her guests.

She havered when the girl ushered them into the *dining* room; but what harm could it do? The tables, which only in the softest light could pass for teak, can be wiped clean before the maids serve tea.

"That's marvellous, Matty. Would you talk me through it?" With her frumpy skirt and blouse and tight ponytail, she does not resemble an artist, a calling more in keeping with the circus girl's flamboyance. A caution against banking on first impressions.

"Is this the palace? Are these the fountains?"

Invited to depict where she used to live, Matty did not intend to paint the shrubbery blue. The artist is unaware that the shrimp-woman hogged the green and yellow.

The artist points to the boy. "Is this a hen? Did they lay eggs for your breakfast?"

Given the instability of the artistic temperament, Matty does not contradict the unorthodox interpretation. Besides, *she* might discern pattern inaccessible to the less gifted.

"Is there anything you'd like to add, Matty, or are you happy with it as it is?"

How to answer? She cannot be *happy* with something that, to her untutored eye, suggests the daubs of a child. Yet one cannot resuscitate a sunken soufflé.

The artist takes a strip of the tacky stuff the butler uses to secure his *Do Not Disturb* sign to the office door. Sculpting four blue pearls, she squashes one in each corner of the paper. "Okay, let's hang it on the wall."

Transforming the dining room into an art gallery? Matty will have indigestion if confronted with that ignominy at breakfast, luncheon and tea. As will the guests.

Vivacity drains out of her, as if Karen has syringed it from her veins. How many times has she beseeched them? How many times have they blocked their ears? Misconstruing the character of princes, they take it for a fairy story or accuse her of putting on airs. Sitting at the paint-smattered table, Matty wishes she had included a tower, with a princess at the top, crying *Fire, fire!*

The artist has moved on to admire the shrimp-woman's contribution. Pah! Despite having the best colours, her sheet is a turd-coloured splurge. She must be a fraud to deem *that* praiseworthy.

A fraud or a secret agent. How droll that the estate should shelter a spy. Is she ally or enemy of the Belgian detective with the floppy fringe? Matty's spirits revive as the purpose of the girl's probing clarifies. The artist is a War Office envoy commissioned to protect her from the prince.

Chapter 30

"MY SCHIZOPHRENIA MOMENT. You'd have loved it, Janice. One inner voice going, *Call social services!* and another going, *But you* are *social services!*"

Janice laughed, albeit not as freely as the others. Phil's description of a disastrous home visit as a fledging social worker had her former course-mates in stitches, despite having heard it before. But it demolished the cosy homecoming feeling she'd harboured since parking her Polo outside her old house in Nottingham earlier that evening.

Sheena had invited some of the old crowd over for a catch up, pizza and beers. Greeting some she hadn't seen since graduation, it struck Janice that she wasn't on hugging terms with any new friends in Cumbria.

The conversation flowed from Sheena's early impressions of the HIV/AIDS post to regaling each other with their most embarrassing, hilarious or agonising incidents at work. Her friends were suitably indignant at Sister Henderson's treatment of her charges and cheered that one had relocated to a more respectful regime; Janice edited out the fine detail of the deception underpinning Matty's transfer.

As Phil took the limelight, Janice's gaze swept across the debris of their meal. In the grease-smeared delivery boxes, the glasses marbled with burst beer-bubbles and the cigarette butts shipwrecked in the oil from the olives, she discerned not the cost of camaraderie but the hollowness of junk food. Should she tell Phil that, while schizophrenia might involve hearing voices, it didn't mean being in two minds? Or was that an overly literal and pompous comeback to a figure of speech? Like him saying she'd *have loved it* when, in his shoes, she'd have felt inclined to slap the woman and kidnap her child.

A wailing baby, a washed-out mother, a blaring TV. Initially, the scenario sounded run-of-the-mill. Phil had been on the brink of asking the mother if he could turn the volume down, when she got up and screeched into the pram, *Stop crying! It's your fucking programme!* Then he noticed that the infant, barely two months old, was propped up with cushions and pillows, unshielded from the assault of the TV. "Guess what the poor brat was supposed to be watching!"

Janice squirmed. "How would I know?" She spoke more sharply than she should have, but the others would be too tanked-up to notice.

"Guess! You couldn't make it up!" He paused an extra second for effect. "*Tom and Jerry.* A baby howling her eyes out while a cartoon cat takes a mallet to a mouse."

Janice nibbled a shard of pizza crust. In an alternative universe where babies were born with armour plating, Phil's anecdote would satisfy a stand-up comic. She didn't begrudge her friends their gallows humour, but that baby was a *case* to them. Elbows bent, she raised her arms to massage the knots of tension in her shoulders. Were she in her flat in Cumbria, she could've retired to bed.

Conscious she owed her friends a response, she blurted out what she'd been pondering on the journey south. "I'm considering tracing my birth mother."

"Shit!" said Phil. "*Tom and Jerry* hasn't set this off?"

Now she could smile. "Probably the client I mentioned earlier. Imagine being incarcerated for having sex! At least *my* mother was spared *that*, but she'd have had it tough at antenatals without a wedding ring."

"You feel bad for her?" said Sheena. "Is that why you're doing it?"

"I'm intrigued! She could be a sex worker. She could be an aristocrat."

"She could be both."

"Let's hope she isn't a Tory."

Like Stuart. How quickly they'd forgotten him. Janice wouldn't allude to being back on speaking terms since their meeting outside the polling station. On hugging terms, too. It would be insane to let it go further.

───────────

"THAT'S EXACTLY THE reaction I'd expect from you," said Roz. "Why do you think I didn't tell you earlier?"

"What? I haven't said anything."

"It's that social worker silence. The way you breathe."

She mustn't lose control. Not here at the payphone where her neighbours could listen at the doors to their flats. Due to the lack of privacy, Janice had been less persistent in attempting to contact her sister since Mothers' Day. "I'm trying to take it in."

"Don't fuss. It's dealt with."

She looped the cable around her knuckles and then let go, smoothing out the curves to watch it spring into coils. Reverting to its natural state. Was this calculated coldness natural to her sister? "Dealt?"

"Yes, as any woman would if she hasn't the resources to bring up a baby. As our mothers would've if they had the option."

"That's not true …" The stammer of the pips stalled her. Janice fed coins into the slot. "They would've kept us if it wasn't for the stigma." A quarter-century on, there remained sectors of society where the words *single mother* were uttered with a sneer.

"Only in fairy-tales. We were their worst nightmare."

Their parents insisted they were *loved*. Released for adoption *because* of that love. When did Roz stop believing? "You can't say for definite."

"Getting caught has given me a bloody good idea."

"Do Mum and Dad know?"

"I'd rather they didn't have to. Can you back me up on that?"

Janice had waited for a whisper of vulnerability since the beginning of the call. "If you want."

Once more, the spitting pips splintered the connection.

Janice's gaze settled on the stunted stack of ten-pence coins on the console. The conversation was far from finished. *Did you tell the father? Was the clinic gruesome? Did anyone go with you? Did it hurt?* Janice felt vulnerable too, defenceless against whatever myths her sister might debunk next. "Sorry, Roz, I'm out of cash." She didn't want to hear that, in Roz's mind, their mothers were no different to Phil's crazed client. The woman whose neediness swamped her child's.

Chapter 31

THIS TIME, WHEN Linda Quinn summoned Henry to her office, there was no suggestion of a union rep. Catching her perched on the edge of her desk, fondling a metal ball from the Newton's cradle, chin up as if offering her neck to a vampire, Henry felt he should have brought one anyway. But before he'd eased the door into its frame, she was behind the desk thumbing through a pile of papers, a studied frown snuffing out flirtation. "Getting to grips with your new role?"

Henry nodded. Linda had undone one too many buttons of her blouse. A silver chain cut through where the collar should have been, a crucifix resting on her sternum.

"You'll be pleased to hear I've had excellent feedback on your performance." Linda paused, perhaps for one of her gofers to rush in with a medal. She seemed irked when nothing materialised, obliging her to move on. "I've had a request from the mayor's office."

Henry had met the mayor in the lavatories that morning; couldn't he have mentioned the job while drying his hands? "Geoff Boyne?" Had Linda assumed a seductive pose for that upstart?

"Not Councillor Boyne personally," said Linda. "Although he's a hundred percent behind the idea."

"Which is?"

"An opportunity to project manage one strand of the strategic plan."

At last, a job he could get his teeth into. "So I'll be working in the mayor's office?"

"You can't escape me that easily, Henry!" Linda giggled, eyelashes aflutter. Was the woman on heat?

"And the project?"

Linda produced a ring binder from a drawer in her desk. "It's a division of the Care of the Elderly strategy under the Creating Healthy and Harmonious Communities banner within the Commissioning Quality programme."

"I'm to go around care homes?" Henry was reconciled to picking oakum until released by his pension, but Linda, and even Geoff Boyne, would appreciate he had neither the skills nor the temperament to inspect old folks' homes.

"Something more modest." Linda pushed the folder across the desk. "But crucial to the broader mission."

On opening the binder, Henry soon gauged the project's modesty. "I'm to organise an old ladies' tea party?"

"A social event for senior citizens of both genders. The mayor's At Home in early June."

HER PENCIL HOVERED over the page. "Shall I draft an announcement for *The Times and Star*, Mr Windsor?"

Her name was Nancy or Nora; a secretary who knew her place but had the wit to rise above it. She was a gem. "Thank you, N –."

"It's Nina." She displayed no malice as she added another squiggle to her shorthand notepad. "And flyers for the care homes and luncheon clubs?"

"Of course." Actually, there was no *of course* for Henry, but Nina had it sussed, apparently unperturbed that she would do the work and he would take the credit. Like Irene at that age, channelling her ambition towards the twins inside her. He couldn't ask when Nina's was due, but he prayed it would be *after* the mayor's At Home.

She closed her notebook. "I'll get on with it then."

Nearing the multi-use office, Henry found himself humming. Nina was an angel: his first piece of luck that year. How did they bear it, these capable women in lowly positions? Was it hormonal or that, by bearing children, they occupied a nobler plane? His thoughts drifted to Tilly: did thwarted ambition drive her away? If he'd shown more gratitude, would she have stayed?

―――――――

HE'D SHAVED THAT morning but now, stroking his chops as he dashed to the door, Henry was ready for another. Irene's skin was becoming increasingly sensitive and he'd hate to aggravate her rash.

On opening his front door, he stepped aside to let her enter. Yet it wasn't Irene, but a pinched-looking woman with frizzy hair falling to the shoulders of her green waxed jacket. "Ursula Marshall." Pausing only to shake his hand, she was over the threshold before he could blink. "From The Laburnums." What could he do but close the door and follow her into the dining room?

It was as if the Prime Minister herself had commandeered the table. "Pardon the intrusion, but you haven't signed my little petition."

"Ah, yes, this business with the baby clinic. I gather you're not happy."

"Not happy is an understatement. Social housing is completely incompatible with the area."

Finding himself fingering an unfamiliar ballpoint, he cast about for a copy of the *Radio Times* to slip under the paper to avoid marking the table. Once he'd added his autograph, the woman would leave him in peace to get ready for Irene. But Irene supported the home for the mental patients. Perhaps the mayor – or the mayor's office – was also in favour. His neighbours, however, might retaliate if he didn't side with them. Dogs fouling his garden would be the least of it. "Do you think a petition's likely to change anything?"

"I couldn't live with myself if I didn't try. I'm thinking of the kiddies. The old folk."

"That's fine, but there's a *process*. The council puts forward their plans and the community submits their objections."

Mrs Marshall jabbed at the petition. "I've got eighty-four objections. Eighty-five with yours."

Henry felt no compulsion to help her, but it wasn't her

fault she'd got it back to front. *He* found the procedure perplexing, and he *worked* at the council. "They'll want your *reasons*. Not a list of names."

"And addresses."

"You could have eighty-five thousand names and addresses …"

"And all they'd be good for is to wrap their fish and chips?" Ursula Marshall slumped onto a chair. "We need a credible counterargument. We need a *committee* …" She sprang to her feet. "Can I rely on you, Mr …?"

"Windsor. Henry Windsor." *Can you take your petition and go?*

But the woman had acquired a fascination for his net curtains. She scurried to the window. "Isn't the clinic directly opposite you?"

IRENE DROPPED A package on Henry's lap.

"What's this in aid of? It's another five months till my birthday."

"Open it and see." Parcelled in paper patterned with vintage cars – a curious choice for a non-driver – it was the size of a Penguin paperback. Henry swithered. Would Irene pick one he'd want to read?

In his hands, it hadn't the feel of a book. But he pretended, throwing out guesses to amuse her. A whodunnit? Crosswords? A compendium of witticisms for the ageing bachelor? "Brilliant!" A photo frame, painted plastic masquerading as silver. He might have preferred Irene's choice of book.

"If this house is a shrine, you could jolly it up a bit. Where's that photo?" Before he could answer she was out of the room and in again bearing a monochrome print.

"Not that one with Blackpool tower growing out of my head! I'm a miniature alien."

"Give over! You're a cutie." Irene removed the back of the frame and positioned the photograph under the glass. "This isn't *about* you, but. It's remembering your sister."

"*You* said I should forget her."

"I never said *forget* her. Face the fact she's gone for good." Irene looked wistful. "I do sympathise, but. I'm gutted our Angela's upped sticks to Spain." She secured the back and turned the frame around. "Wasn't she smart? I'd sell my bairns for that dress. If I had a cat in hell's chance of squeezing into it. They had dead slim waists in them days. Corsets, I suppose?"

"I haven't the foggiest about my sister's underwear!" Now he considered it, Tilly couldn't have worn a corset when she gave him that button.

Arranging the photograph on the mantelpiece, Irene stood back for a better view. "Funny I took her for your mam, but. She's yonks younger than your dad. Have you got one of *them* together?"

"My mam and dad?"

"Don't look so scunnered! I'll bet there's a wedding photo."

Henry couldn't recollect seeing any kind of picture of his mother. "It was different in those days. Folks didn't have cameras. Getting your photograph taken was a major to-do."

"They must've had the money, but. This house. Your

dad's shop. Don't you think it's odd?"

"What are you insinuating?"

"Mebbe there was no mother who died in childbirth. Mebbe the woman you thought was your sister was your mother."

Irene's fantasies! Although, as a boy, he'd imagined that exact scenario. "Tilly was thirteen when I was born." Besides, he'd seen Florence Windsor's grave.

"It's not impossible, but. If you want to find her, you've got to start searching with fresh eyes."

"Like writing to Ghyllside?"

"So nowt came of it! No harm done."

Apart from bruised emotions. Irene meant well, but her diversions down blind alleys ended in *his* nose bloodied on a brick wall. "You'll be telling me my father isn't my father next."

"It's clear who your father is." Irene gestured towards the photograph. "Didn't I say so already? You're the spit of that man."

Chapter 32

"WELL DONE, EVERYONE!" Parveen's smile settled on each team member in turn. "You couldn't have better results if you'd made them up!"

Janice wasn't alone in startling at the psychiatrist's comment. Norman squared his shoulders. "The board wouldn't tolerate that."

Janice flicked through her copy of the report. Collectively, the residents had improved since moving to Tuke House. Had no-one else noticed that one person's scores had plummeted?

"Who fancies helping present it to the board?" said Graham.

Janice rubbed an imaginary itch on her ankle. Maybe she should be thankful she'd survived in post so long.

"I think Clive should," said Parveen. "The nursing team have worked like slaves."

"Everyone has," said Clive.

"Any ideas why Matty Osborne's ratings have dipped?" said Norman.

Was it her imagination or did the psychologist fasten his gaze on her? Janice stared at the graph, already smudged with her sweaty fingerprints. "Isn't that weird?"

"She's come on dramatically," said Heather. "They all have."

"Yet she's scored lower here than she did on Ward 24," said Norman.

"There's bound to be a *margin of error*." Graham puffed out the phrase as he did *socially valued lives* and *statistical significance*, the lexicon of a sacred order he was desperate to rule.

"Not when the raters are properly trained," said Norman.

Muggins thinking she'd got away with it! Norman could revisit the original forms any time, the Perspex sheet perfectly aligned on top. *He* wouldn't care that she'd made the adjustments for the right reasons.

"It's still subjective," Heather insisted. "Maybe the Tuke House nurses marked her down."

"Or Ward 24 nurses rated her artificially high," said Clive.

"That would mean she shouldn't *be* here." Heather cupped her mouth.

Norman scratched his beard. "We can delude ourselves she's coping, but data don't lie. She's floundering."

"Wandering off and nicking lavender," said Graham.

"Owing to a UTI, no?" With a lacquered nail, Parveen

picked at a staple. She detached the front two sheets, with the results for Tuke House overall, from the four with the separate breakdowns. "They'll be delighted with the patients' progress. But they won't want to scrutinise the individual data."

"It's not appropriate anyway." Norman prised apart his copy, folding the redundant sheets in half and stashing them in his diary. "Individual scores are confidential."

"Let's make *these* our baseline," said Parveen. "Monitor the ups and downs from here."

Clive nodded. "No disrespect to Sister Henderson, but her lot *are* old-school."

Graham chuckled. "Some fresh blood should stir them up when she retires. If any of your staff nurses are ready for promotion, Clive, give them the nod."

———

"I SHALL WEAR my polka-dot dress."

"The one in your photo, Matty?" The picture with a double jagged edge glimpsed on Matty's locker. Janice shot the occupational therapist an apologetic glance. Heather had a knack of maintaining task focus without spoiling the fun. Earlier, she'd convinced Ronnie Bloomsburg to extinguish his cigarette until time for tea – or coffee, if they preferred – and Effie Atkinson to leave her doll on another chair, out of sight. Heather inspired trust in the group's potential to transform people who were hardly aware of themselves, let alone each other, into sociable decision-makers.

Today, discussing what members might wear for afternoon tea with the mayor, Janice felt inspired on her *own* account. It wouldn't be happening if Violet Osborne hadn't replied to her newspaper ad.

An obliging woman at the Town Hall had taken down the names of all group members, including those not yet OAPs, promising them personal invitations within the week. When, after a fortnight, they hadn't materialised, Heather joked about sweet-talking Norman into a suit and a tinfoil chain. But it wouldn't come to that. If necessary, Janice would collect the invitations herself.

Matty scowled. "That's *Matilda* in the photograph."

Go for it, Ms Osborne! When Janice had griped about patients being addressed by diminutives, like children or pets, David had counselled her to choose her battles wisely. Janice turned to Billy Dewhirst, "Billy, would you ask Matty if she prefers Matty or Matilda?"

"*I'm* not Matilda," said Matty. "Matilda tells lies."

"Let's review what we've established so far," said Heather. "Matty wants to wear a polka-dot dress. How will we find out what everyone else is going to wear?"

"Have a deek in their wardrobes," said Ronnie Bloomsburg.

"Have you *got* a polka-dot dress?" said Betty Fogarty.

"Very good, Betty," said Heather. "In this group we get to know each other by asking *questions*. But let's see what everybody *wants* to wear before we check on the practicalities. Can you ask someone else what they fancy wearing?"

"Janice," said Betty, "what will you wear for the mayor's reception?"

A couple of the men tittered. Janice beamed. "I suppose

I'll go as I am."

"Are you sure that's *appropriate?*" Betty mimicked a nurse asking a resident if he *really* wanted to leave the ward with soup stains on his shirt.

Laughing, Janice tugged at her cotton trousers. "You don't think so, Betty?"

"She grew up in the circus," said Matty.

"If *I'm* wearing a suit," said Ronnie Bloomsburg, "you should look smart too."

"Well, isn't this interesting," said Heather. "We began with *individual* preferences, but we've discovered that some of our choices reflect on us as a *group*."

"She dresses like a *clown*," said Effie Atkinson.

Go, Effie! While doubtful they'd criticise Dr Shakir's sartorial style so bluntly, Janice was thrilled they felt empowered to speak their minds. *This* was social work making a difference! She'd enjoy telling David about the breakthrough in her next supervision. "Ronnie, can you ask Effie what *she* thinks I should wear?"

THE STENCH OF sizzling bacon wafting up the corridor turns Matty's stomach, although she would never complain to the cook. Presently, the rest of the pigs would be butchered and boxed for the soldiers overseas. Men fight better with flesh in their bellies.

One of the last to reach the dining room, her seating options are drastically reduced. The minute she sits, she regrets it: the fellow opposite has egg yolk on his grizzled beard. Unable to snub him by leaving the table, she peers beyond him to the artwork affixed to the wall.

A series of faux-naive paintings of country houses from across the globe, unframed and clumsily arranged; is this the latest fad or is there a shortage of glass? As the guests are indifferent, she gazes around with a benign smile.

"Admiring the paintings, Matty?" As the maid sets a dish of cereal before her, she gasps, accidentally jogging the girl's arm. Milk pools on the tabletop. Unflustered, the maid mops up the slops.

When she raises her eyes from her bowl, the maid has gone but bits of breakfast still nestle in her companion's beard. The scandalous painting still adorns the wall.

She can forgive the weeping willows: creativity is a stranger to constraint. But to depict the boy without permission? Then exhibited so openly, where anyone might ogle him? Even men who use facial hair as napkins! She pushes back her chair, strides to the wall and tears at the paper. Soon, she has rescued the boy, and a lavender bush to boot.

"Aw," says a maid, "what did that cute little chicken do to offend you, Matty?"

"I think that one's hers," says another.

Matty detects an edge of insolence. "My dear, they are *all* mine." *Or my mother's.*

The guests begin to agitate. One claims ownership of a picture of a fishwife's cottage. The bearded chap asserts his entitlement to the castle on the hill. Matty has been charitable, but this smacks of communism. "Is that how you repay my hospitality?"

The beard laughs. "I'm not flait by your lady of the

manor hystericals!"

"You will pack your bag and leave this house by luncheon."

Instead of surrendering to her authority, he repeats her words in a mocking squeaky voice. What can she do? Commencing with the hilltop castle, Matty rips through the paintings until the floor is awash with paper and all that remains of the gallery is a plasticine-studded wall.

Chapter 33

HENRY HAD NEVER seen such a crowd at the dining table. There weren't enough chairs for the eight of them, so he and Mr Patel, as the only gentlemen, perched slightly lower on stools. Mr Patel, being the guest, had the cushioned version from Tilly's vanity table, leaving Henry the cork-topped talc-dusted bathroom stool.

Ursula Marshall called them to order. "I'm delighted to welcome you to the inaugural meeting of the Sheepwash Lane Residents Opposition Committee. Any items for the agenda?"

Henry snaffled a digestive. Generous of Mr Patel to bring biscuits, albeit past their sell-by date. "Shouldn't we draw up a constitution?"

Jacqueline Ferriss – her name a perfect match for her ferret face – seemed to startle herself when she spoke. "Let's not jump the gun. We ought to agree the name first."

"We've got a name," said Zoe Johnson, fluttering eyelashes so clogged with mascara she should have had a crane to lift them. "Sheepwash Residents Opposition Committee."

"Yes," said Jacqueline, "but where's it come from?"

"It hasn't come from anywhere," said Ursula. "It's simply a statement of intent."

"I'm sorry," said Jacqueline, "but at the book group we put it to the vote."

"This isn't your book group," grumbled Zoe. "If you want to vote on every dot and comma, we'll be here all night. Some of us have babysitters and it's double ackers after ten."

Henry took another biscuit. He'd bargained on them being gone by nine.

"Jacqueline's got a point." Susanna Nixon palmed her hair, coiled in a doughnut on her crown. "Sheepwash Residents Opposition sounds like opposing *ourselves*, not the patients. Makes us out to be as daft as them."

Ursula grimaced. "What do you suggest instead?"

Henry squirmed. "Shouldn't we settle tonight's agenda?"

"We can't *have* an agenda until we have a name," said Jacqueline.

"We'd address that through the constitution," mumbled Henry.

"How about Sheepwash Residents against Psychiatric Invasion?" Susanna offered.

Zoe nodded. "SRAPI for short."

"Oh, yes," said Ursula, "what's it called when the initials

184

form a word? Like NATO?"

"An anachronism," said Susanna.

"An acronym," said Henry, but nobody heard.

"We can't have Sheepwash *Residents* anything if we want a snappy abbreviation," said Jacqueline. "I prefer SLAPI – Sheepwash Lane against Psychiatric Invasion."

"Pardon me, ladies," said Mr Patel. "What's this psychiatric invasion?"

"I suppose it *is* a little Aliens Have Landed," said Zoe. "What about Sheepwash Lane against Psychiatric Patients in Our Midst."

"SLAPPIOM?" said Jacqueline.

"Doesn't the Neighbourhood Watch discuss crime prevention?" said Mr Patel. "I had two break-ins last year."

WHEN MR PATEL resigned from the as yet unnamed and unconstituted committee because he could not oppose a development with the potential to boost his profits (the incomers unlikely to have the wherewithal to patronise to the edge-of-town superstore), Mrs Marshall proposed they adjourn for tea. Zoe said that after all that argy-bargy she needed something stronger, while Jacqueline unearthed some cut-glass goblets from Henry's sideboard. When Susanna bemoaned the fact that Mr Patel had shut up shop early to attend the meeting – his drinks aisle might be rudimentary, she said, but it *was* cheap – Henry succumbed and opened a couple of bottles.

The women reconvened around the table, Henry requisitioning the padded stool vacated by Mr Patel. Ursula having abandoned all semblance of steering the debate, the women swapped recommendations of plumbers and cleaners as much as opposition group names. Henry was nodding off when Ursula asked if they might peek upstairs.

"Upstairs?"

"Sharpen our perspective with a bird's eye view of the site."

"Exactly," chirped Zoe. "A jury visiting a crime scene."

The women were out of their seats and into the hall before Henry could protest. With a guilty glance at Tilly's photograph on the mantelpiece, he tagged along.

Not even Irene was allowed into Tilly's bedroom. Now his neighbours swarmed in, elbowing through to the window like a bunch of tipsy schoolgirls, raucously complimenting the "vintage" homemade quilt and the "antique" iron bedstead and admiring their reflections in the triptych mirror of the "Edwardian" vanity table.

"Was this your daughter's room?" said Ursula. Despite it being her idea, she had hung back, a mother observing her children capture a playground.

"My sister's."

"The woman with the mobile hairdressing van? I thought she was …"

"Put the light out, would you?" someone hollered from the window. "It's getting dark out there and we can't see a thing."

———

ON COLLECTING THE invitations from the printers, Henry made for the typing pool. Nina had assured him she'd copy out the individual names and pop them in the post as soon as the cards arrived. She'd make it her priority.

Her seat being empty, Henry hovered by her desk, feigning nonchalance. The other typists eyed him suspiciously as he hummed beneath the clatter of their machines. Eventually, an older woman with a beehive hairdo even Henry knew was outdated, piped up, "If it's Nina you're wanting, you'll have a fair wait."

"Isn't she in today?"

"Not today, not tomorrow, not the next."

Shouldn't she have informed him she was taking leave? "When is she back?" Would it matter if the invitations were delayed another week?

"Six months, we reckon," said Beehive. "His Lordship was premature."

Had the mayor twigged she was wasted in the typing pool and commandeered her services for himself? "Pardon?"

"They've taken her in."

"Lay off him," another secretary interrupted. "She was rushed to hospital at the weekend, Mr Windsor. The baby's in an incubator, but he's doing fine."

He ought to show relief she hadn't been taken hostage. Or joy at the emergence of new life. But he blushed as if they'd dragged him into the ladies' lavatories, his stomach twisting about the job left undone.

The kinder secretary opened the upper drawer of an aluminium filing cabinet. "Was it the mayor's At Home you were after?" She furnished a manila file.

"Thanks, but I don't read shorthand."

"Neither do we. We don't read Nina's, anyroad."

RETURNING TO HIS desk in the multi-use office, Henry extracted the papers from the file. No scribbly shorthand: at the top of the heap were several addressed envelopes and lists of names in the Latin alphabet. Draping his jacket on the back of his chair, he rolled up his shirt sleeves. Placing the stack of cards to his left, the guest lists to his right, and the blotter slap in the middle, Henry prepared to cruise through the invitations.

Unfortunately, Nina's handwriting proved as tortuous as Pitman's script. He could verify some of the names against the typed envelopes but others, in batches for care homes, had him stumped. At school in the 1940s, he'd practised both copperplate and italic. Nina's shapeshifting letters implied a sloppier education: her 'u' indistinguishable from 'o', both presenting as a closed circle or extremely shallow bowl; her 'e' morphing from a reversed figure 3 into a long-tailed tadpole within a single word. Undaunted, he copied the outlines without regard for meaning; the eye perceives what's predicted, not what's there.

It was gone five o'clock when he began the final bunch. Although he did his best, Henry doubted the recipients – *Roma Bloomsbury, Bunty Coventry, Hatty Usburn, Fifi Atkins, Bilty Dowhouse* – would decry any errors. Inmates of Ghyllside would be past caring about such niceties as names.

Chapter 34

"WHAT DID *SHE* have to say about it?" Dr Shakir looked peeved, as if the patients' antics were tangential to her job.

"You know Matty," said Clive. "Evasive as ever."

"Something in the paintings must have disturbed her," said Norman.

"I can't imagine how," said Heather. "It was a really relaxed session. Matty did a super house with fountains and a chicken in the garden."

Janice sympathised: something she'd done, from the best intentions, had sent a patient off the rails. The nurses said Matty had *run amok*.

Norman crossed his legs at the ankle. "It might not have hit her till later."

"Chickens," said Mervyn. "She must've lived on a farm."

"People kept hens in their backyards during the Depression," said Norman.

"There'd have been a farm here at Ghyllside when she was admitted," said Clive.

"Chickens can't explain her volatility," Dr Shakir interjected. "Should we have her in?"

Norman stiffened. "Do we *have* to see her en masse? It must feel like a summons to the magistrates' court."

Clive was already at the door. "Not for Matty. She was *born* to perform."

"COME AND SIT by me," said Parveen, when Matty shuffled into the room. "What's this I hear about you tearing up some paintings?"

"I would never do that."

"Did you have *any* problems at the art group?"

"None whatsoever." Matty beamed at Heather. "That lady is a genius."

"Did anything there upset you?"

"Oh, no," said Matty. "I never get upset."

"Don't you get fed up with the other residents?"

"Not at all. Everyone is most pleasant."

"Frustrating sometimes, no? Having to share?"

Janice nodded. That was the nub of it, not only for Matty, and one Briarwood wouldn't solve. There, they'd sleep in individual bedrooms, but jostle for jurisdiction of the bathroom and lounge.

"Not when I remind myself of their suffering."

Janice caught Heather's gaze. *Their suffering*: could the group take credit for Matty's spark of empathy?

"How have they suffered?" said Parveen.

"Oh, I thought you'd know," said Matty. "Being Jewish."

Dr Shakir swallowed a smile. "I'm Muslim, actually."

"Ah." Matty laid her palm on the psychiatrist's arm. "Then you need not fear the death camps, my dear."

———————

A TIDY MIND: everything in its place and anything without a place donated to the poor. As is written in the Scriptures. Proverbs or the Sermon on the Mount? Her mother will inform her in due course.

Alas, a socialite's mind is not her own. Guests, journalists and even the staff employed to *lighten* her burden can intrude. The shrimp-woman and her mewling baby. The fellow with food deposits in his beard. The flotsam they leave in their wake! A duster. A trail of footprints. A bowl of puke.

So tempting to close the door on it, to drink tea and play parlour games or assemble a posy of spring flowers. But that road soon spirals into chaos. Unrestricted, trifling irregularities multiply, breeding monsters too savage to tidy or tame. The mind that results is so muddled, it is worse than having no mind at all.

Matty steels herself to unpack her thoughts, scour through shapes and scents and sounds to root out the culprit. Eyes clenched, she plunges deep within herself to pluck it, like a hair from her chin.

A delegation from the guests. She listened, as is her Christian duty. A minor misapprehension eventually revealed. Matty thought only of their welfare when she stripped the walls of some crude artwork. Alas, she had not appreciated that the pictures, albeit shabby and vulgar, were heirlooms from their native land.

Matty apologised profusely. Indeed, she could have wept. As irksome as the guests might be, Matty hates to intensify their torment. Her house should be a safe haven where they can pursue their peculiar religion unmolested. She did not mean to offend.

How can she make amends? Although she had *those* paintings incinerated, they could produce new ones. Better ones. Rising to her feet, clasping the bedside cabinet for balance, she spies a scrap of painted paper curled against the photo frame. A hen! It could not come at a more opportune moment: she can nurse her houseguests back to health with fluffy scrambled eggs.

Chapter 35

J ANICE WASN'T PRONE to getting wound up about parties, but she'd never before wangled invitations for a posse of patients to tea with the mayor. She desperately wanted them to enjoy the outing, and to do so without attracting adverse attention. A trip out for the *members* of the choices group was, for the *facilitators*, a test.

Waiting for the others in Tuke House dining room, Janice paced between the tables, wobbling slightly in her wedge-heeled espadrilles. Stooping to tighten the canvas bindings, and almost tripping on the ruffled hem of her tiered cotton skirt as she got up again, she wondered if the residents would approve of her outfit. Or of Heather swapping her crisp blouses and pencil skirts for a vintage summer dress. But she couldn't pin her discomfiture on the unfamiliar gear.

With the late arrival of the invitations, every name

misspelt, Janice worried they'd be there on sufferance. Yet the woman she'd spoken to initially was exceptionally accommodating, even agreeing to issue invitations to those below retirement age. But Janice might have been wrong to strive for preferential treatment, positioning the residents as people to be pitied. Wrong to pitch up as a group, blanketing their unique personalities in the commonality of mental disability.

It wasn't the first time she'd got carried away with her ambitions for Matty Osborne. She'd never have proposed the outing if she hadn't thought Matty would get a kick out of meeting the mayor and, potentially, her childhood friend. Now, despite several aborted phone calls, Janice still didn't know whether Violet would be there. If she was, would a crowded function room be the place to renew their friendship? Other group members might also encounter old acquaintances, not necessarily for the good. People didn't stop being rivals, bullies, or abusers on attaining pensionable age.

Unlike doctoring Matty's assessment, Janice didn't bear the risk alone. Her colleagues were unanimously in favour, although there'd been a question mark over Matty due to her outburst after Heather's art group. But she'd redeemed herself, graduating from tantrumming toddler to assistant tutor within a week.

Killing time, Janice perused the new display. Reporting back to the clinical meeting, Heather had expressed the hope that Matty, having helped arrange the pictures, might leave *these* on the wall. Apparently, she'd been uncharacteristically helpful to Effie Atkinson, praising each brushstroke and fetching the colours she lacked.

"What's *your* ideal home, Janice? A gypsy caravan?"

Betty Fogarty's quip dragged her attention from the makeshift gallery. Turning, Janice gulped at the sight of the residents spruced up in their finery: they'd easily blend in.

"Okay, ladies and gentlemen, let's get you lined up outside!" Clive ushered them towards the door.

Lined up, like at nursery school? Institutional attitudes might be diminishing, but the dregs lingered on. Janice tried to catch Heather's gaze, but she was mincing out the door. "Clive, we're not *going* in the minibus." Thanks to the Round Table logo on the side, the vehicle screamed *objects of charity*.

"I know when I'm not wanted," chuckled Clive. "But I'm having a photo of you in your glad rags whether you like it or not."

———

ALTHOUGH HIS REBELLION wouldn't register on the radar of the narcissist who provoked it, Henry relished standing alongside Councillor Boyne in his *second*-best suit. The taut waistband of the trousers might induce a hernia, but the shiny knees and elbows, and the missing button from the right cuff, signalled defiance. He wanted the bash to succeed for the sake of the old folks now taking their seats at tables draped with white linen. And for Nina who, despite abandoning the job before despatching the invitations, had been meticulous about everything else. Nevertheless, he refused to flatter the mayor by playing pageboy.

Henry had expected to remain in the background, ready

to remedy any last-minute hitch. A wilting carnation on one of the tables. An old dear rejecting both coffee and tea. A wheelchair stalled by a wrinkle in the carpet. A waitress taking a sickie. Fantasy crises kept him awake the previous night until he realised the function room staff would deal with them, event management being their defining role.

So he'd be surplus to requirements. Perhaps he'd be redeployed to some other *any other duties*. But he hadn't factored in Geoff Boyne's vanity. The mayor aped the protocol of Royal Variety Performance broadcasts, where musicians, actors and comedians queued to be presented to the Queen and Duke of Edinburgh. In today's re-enactment, Henry would portray the arse-licking flunky, while the mayor would substitute for both Their Majesties, eliciting guests' opinions on a new bus route or littering in the centre of town. "Let's make them feel important for once, Henry!" Let the dustman's son feel more important still.

Couldn't an apple-cheeked girl from catering assume Henry's part? In a frilly apron and silly hairband-cum-hat *she* could have winkled out the punters' names and passed them on to the mayor. But Councillor Boyne delighted in Henry's degradation. The absurdity of introducing individuals he didn't actually *know* was exacerbated by sloppy articulation, some mumbling and others whispering their names. After a few filthy stares when the mayor greeted a Jane as Jean, and a Mick as Dick, Henry had resorted to asking for their invitation cards, where the only challenge was deciphering his own scrawl. Any responsibility for their bungled completion could be deflected onto some anonymous scribe in the basement of the Town Hall. Unfortunately, this too caused consternation, guests foraging in bags and pockets for the piece of scalloped card they'd left at home.

With roughly half the tables unoccupied, the line dwindled to nothing. The mayor indicated banks of sandwiches, cakes and scones. "Crafty move, Henry, if you appreciate a custard slice. Criminal to let good grub finish up as pig swill."

Henry was about to retort that no haberdasher's son would appropriate public funds and if he wanted a custard slice, he'd *buy* one, when the door opened to an influx of visitors. As they bunched together at the edge of the room, Henry tried to appear approachable. A portly chap in a dark three-piece suit detached himself from his companions and bounded across, his wide grin exposing a shelf of rotten teeth. Henry accepted the brandished invitation, but he never got to read the name. The borders of his vision blurred, his ears buzzed as a female figure loomed into view. Henry hadn't given Tilly a thought during the half-hour he'd played handmaid to the mayor, but now five decades of separation crushed his heart. Her devotion, his debt. Her love, his loss. Her absence, his agony. The sister who sacrificed her teenage years for him. His sister whose unfulfilled promise defined his life.

Chapter 36

1931–1932

I GO OVER and over my story, keeping it alive as much for myself as for you. Its peaks and valleys the geography of my girlhood, it is my lodestar, my very self. My hope: if there was a *Before*, there will be an *After*. They have stolen my treasures; they cannot take my truth.

MOTHER'S DECISION ALTERED my life in ways I could not have imagined. I began breathing a superior kind of air.

One Saturday, she announced we were going to get new clothes for my interview. My performance-cum-Sunday frock being too flouncy, I needed a grown-up costume comprised of jacket and skirt.

When she told me to get ready, I thought we'd visit the pawnshop. Or see if Mildred Doherty might lend me something of hers. But Mother aimed higher. We took the bus into town.

How gay she was loading my arms with hangers. She even fetched some slacks, but I dared not try them, nervous the shop-girl would guess we were larking about.

We chose a chic, belted jacket with padded shoulders and a skirt that flared between knee and calf. The girl didn't bat an eyelid when Mother requested my initials to be sewn into the lining. "Certainly, madam. We can have that ready for you to collect by half past three."

I froze when the shop-girl asked Mother for her account number. Would the manager send us packing?

But Mother gave Mr Windsor's name and rattled off a string of digits. The shop-girl checked her ledger and wrote out a receipt. It didn't matter that my initials were MO not MW. Perhaps she read it as OW standing on its head.

THAT FRIDAY, WHEN Mother said she couldn't accompany us to the slipper baths, I didn't argue. I welcomed the opportunity to seek Mrs Braithwaite's advice. Since Violet tended to wallow in the water for the full half-hour, I could catch Mrs B alone if I was sharp. My stockings snagged on my damp legs as I dressed, but I could forfeit my comfort to safeguard Mother's future, and mine.

We stood side by side at the mirrors, combing our wet hair. When I told her, Mrs B tugged her towel tighter to her neck. "It's not easy on your own," she told my reflection.

"She isn't on her own. She's got me."

"That's not the same, Matilda. She wants a husband."

"It's not Father's fault he's dead."

"He left her in a pickle. A woman has to make ends

meet."

I recalled Mother's *If I don't work, you don't eat.* As if I couldn't comprehend basic economics. "*You* get by." Or did she? She'd blenched when she mistook Mr Windsor for the rent man.

"*I've* got a war widow's pension."

My blood chilled, cancelling the benefit of steeping in a hot bath.

"Anyroad, Matilda, you're old enough to twig a woman's after more than money from a man."

The heat reclaimed my cheeks. To recover my dignity, I remembered my costume, and the reason we bought it. "I've got an interview for Stainburn."

"Have you now?" She regarded me like I was a bearded lady from the circus.

As Violet came lumbering down the corridor, Mrs B and I huddled closer to deliver our parting shots. Me – "I don't *want* to go and live among the posh folk in Briarwood." Mrs B – "Be a good lass for your mother, Matilda. It's not every day a widow the wrong side of thirty has a rich bachelor ask for her hand."

I THOUGHT IT mean to deprive our friends of a shindig, but Mother didn't want a fuss. One Saturday she sent me to the Carnegie to return our library books and, when I got back, she was perched on the edge of a bare mattress with a plywood tea chest on the floor. Father's photograph was gone from the shelf above the washstand, my rosettes from the chimney breast. "Put on your costume, Matilda. Mr Windsor is collecting us in half an hour."

"We're flitting? Today?"

"You knew it was coming. Don't take on."

It might have been the shade of her lipstick, but she wasn't the mother I cuddled up to in bed. "You're not married."

"We will be! We're exchanging vows at the registry office this afternoon, and then ..." Mother widened her eyes and honeyed her tone as if addressing a three-year-old, not a young lady on the cusp of thirteen. "Uncle George is whisking us off to Grasmere for a night in an hotel!"

"Uncle George?"

"Mr Windsor. Now, get ready to go downstairs and say cheerio to Mrs Braithwaite and Violet."

"Aren't they coming to the wedding?" I wasn't so naive as to think they'd join us at the hotel, but I'd miss them at bedtime if Mother shared with Mr Windsor, not me.

"They wouldn't feel comfortable among Mr Windsor's friends."

"*I* might not feel comfortable."

"Then you'll be glad the ceremony's quick. Now hurry and change. I won't have you making me late for my own wedding."

The wardrobe rail was empty apart from my costume and Mother's duck-egg blue blouse. Although the fabric was faded, and frayed at the cuffs, the blouse would've done for future contests when I'd developed a bust. Now, too shabby for Briarwood, she would leave it behind along with our friends and neighbours, in the only home I'd ever had. Would she discard her daughter as carelessly?

As I made for the door, she handed me an envelope.

"Take this to Mrs B, please, Matilda." The cushion of notes was more than our rent.

I found Mrs Braithwaite in the kitchen, darning the heel of Violet's school stockings. She barely acknowledged me when I entered, and Violet herself was nowhere to be seen. When I gave her the envelope, she flung it on the table like a grubby rag.

My tears touched her as fortitude could not. "It's not your fault, Matilda." She jumped to her feet and hugged me. "Your mam was *born* with her nose in the air. Now she's found her Prince Charming, she can't wait to wipe the muck from her shoes. But I'll always consider *you* a daughter. If you need me, you know where I am."

WHEN MOTHER BECAME Mrs George Windsor, I became the solitary Osborne, formally attached to no-one but myself. But there were compensations. Meat and cake every day, and no griping tummy when I brushed my teeth for bed. No queue for the lavatory and a flush to expel the dirt. Water, hot or cold, at the turn of a tap. Mr Windsor's gramophone and his collection of recordings: Glenn Miller, Louis Armstrong, Duke Ellington and Bing Crosby, as well as the classics. Best of all: my darling attic room with a window at each end, and a bed, desk, vanity table and wardrobe of my own. I adored the sloping walls papered with flowers, pears and pomegranates in blue and green against a buff background, and the view across town to the Solway and the Scottish hills beyond.

Mother joked that climbing the stairs to my eyrie brought on altitude sickness. A couple of times she covered her lips with a hankie as if she might genuinely bring something up. I said she should see a doctor. There'd been a medical man at the wedding, and Mr Windsor could afford to have him visit the house. But Mother assured me it would pass. I resolved to keep an eye on her but, with so many distractions, I didn't pay as close attention as I ought. Fortunately, she no longer went out to work; she stayed at home to help Mrs Embleton with the cooking and cleaning and, in the afternoons, she put her feet up in the parlour to read *Good Housekeeping*.

That was how I generally found her on returning from school. "Matilda," she said one afternoon, once Mrs Embleton had left us, "it's time you learnt about the birds and the bees."

I blushed; it wasn't a suitable subject for the parlour, in daylight at that. Could anything be more repulsive than a gentleman depositing saliva in a lady's mouth? I wished I *didn't* know about it. Mother should have gathered that, as a doctor, I'd be spared marriage and *relations*. She being blessed with a daughter already and he being so old, Mr Windsor wouldn't bother Mother with that malarkey either.

I grabbed the teapot. "Shall I pour your Lapsang souchong, Mother dear?"

LIVING UNDER MR Windsor's roof, and eating his food, it didn't occur to me that he would have a say in what I got up to elsewhere. That Uncle George – or the prince as I nicknamed him, a step down from the King whose name he bore – would ban the recitals. I heard him tell Mother it was vulgar to prance on stage where any Tom, Dick or Harry could ogle me, and did not hear her contradict him, or declare that not even Hilda, should she ever get past the preliminaries, would *prance*. Shortly after, she passed on his decision as if it were hers. "You're so busy with your schoolwork."

I did need extra lessons to catch up with my classmates. At Lawrence Street, there'd been no Latin or Greek. And elocution practice was superfluous in my new life; except for Mrs Embleton and the milkman, there was no-one to tempt me into Cumbrian vowels. "It's the only time I see Violet."

"You've new friends now."

"Violet's like a sister to me."

Mother winced. She patted her stomach in a peculiar fashion. "Perhaps you'll have a real sister one day."

Yuck! Mother swallowing the prince's saliva? She shouldn't debase herself for my sake. "I'm quite content with a proxy sister."

Mother brightened. "Let's invite your new friends to tea!"

"Wouldn't Mr Windsor mind?"

"Uncle George would be delighted."

I was composing a list of the cakes we'd have when I had another idea. "Might I have a birthday party? If thirteen's not too old."

Mother embraced me. "However old you are, Matilda, you're my darling girl."

MRS EMBLETON LAUGHED when I told her *I* would prepare the party food. Why shouldn't I? There was a girl no older than me on the front of the Bero book, and I'd cooked at

The Marsh since I was five.

Mrs Embleton proposed we do it together. "Mr Windsor would have a dicky fit if I left you to cater for eight hungry lasses yourself." I accepted graciously, gratefully: Mother was poorly again and in no position to help. Merely mentioning *jam tarts* and *Victoria sponge* made her retch. She couldn't stomach breakfast, and spent most of the day on the couch reading *The Lady* and sipping beef tea.

I ricocheted between relief and agitation when the prince summoned the doctor. Mother's condition must be serious. Yet Dr Glover was positively *beaming* when he came downstairs with his black bag. Was that because his patient was in fine fettle or because he envisaged repeat visits lining *his* pockets?

Mr Windsor caught me haunting the doorway of the front parlour and ushered me forward to meet the doctor. "You're a fine young lady, Miss Matilda," he said. "You'll be a boon to your mother when the time comes."

Dr Glover's allusion transported my ambition beyond a bedtime story. "I hope so, sir." Bolstered by the smiles on both men's faces, I continued, "There must be no higher calling – other than the church – than healing the sick."

Their smiles faded. Had I insulted the doctor by pitching his profession beneath a clergyman? Did I sound childish or priggish when I'd *meant* to sound mature? Was I getting above myself by voicing *any* opinion? I *did* want to be a credit to Mother, but The Willows felt foreign without her to translate. Inwardly, I crumbled, crushed by the demands of recent months. Passing required more than perfect enunciation. Sometimes, you had to purse your lips to stop any words leaking out.

I DIPPED MY pen in the ink well and took an envelope from the pile. I would distribute the invitations to the Stainburn girls in person, but my former schoolmates would be thrilled to receive a personal letter in the post. So why did I hesitate to inscribe their addresses? Mr Windsor had provided the stamps.

Would my Stainburn friends mix with my friends from Lawrence Street? Why shouldn't they, when I liked them equally? But what if Alexandra should mock Hilda's accent? What if Jessica was rude about Peggy's frock?

I put down my pen and tiptoed downstairs to Mother's bedroom. I tapped on the door and opened it a crack. With the curtains closed, I could make out the bow of her body under the counterpane. I waited, but she didn't stir.

Up in my room, I stared at the invitations splayed on my desk. In due course, Mother would rise from her bed to brush her hair and powder her nose. But she'd be too preoccupied with making herself pretty for Mr Windsor to advise me on schoolgirl rivalries. Busy confirming everything was ready for the evening meal before letting Mrs Embleton go. Besides, I was eager to catch the post.

The hooks jangled on the rail as I slid my frocks back and forth on their padded hangers. I'd acquired more in twelve weeks in Briarwood than in twelve years at The Marsh. And not a thread second-hand.

I twirled around the room as my plan took shape. If my Lawrence Street friends arrived early, the girls from Stainburn might never *see* their worn-out frocks. No-one need decline my invitation for want of anything decent to wear. My peach silk would look sublime on Hilda, my blue taffeta heavenly on Peg.

IF I HAD written a more tactful note to Violet, I wouldn't have to host a party deprived of my oldest friend. I learned too late that inviting her to borrow a frock was like lending a rival a red rosette.

> *Thank you for your charitable offer of a few hours'*
> *retreat from the slums. Unfortunately, I'm unable to*
> *take advantage of your invitation to swap my rags for*
> *your regal robes as my mother has made other*
> *arrangements to ensure I'm clothed and fed. I have*
> *obtained a situation at Holker Hall.*

When we issued orders to our make-believe servants, we never suspected I'd live somewhere with a daily woman while she'd join the staff of a mansion house. I wanted to clutch her, fight her, chain her to The Marsh. Yet not so long ago I'd have been jealous. A smart uniform. Clean country air.

MOTHER'S ABDOMEN WAS a drum. "There. Feel it?"

At first I assumed the alteration stemmed from rich food and idleness. Then I felt embarrassed strangers had discerned its cause before me. But I soon recovered. *I* would be the sister, not them.

The baby's fist or foot met my palm. "Was *I* a kicker?"

"I imagined you a dancer. Pointing your toes."

I jumped up to pirouette, arms aloft like the ballerina on

the jewellery box Mother bought me for my birthday. As I spun, nostalgia chased my cheer. Might she love the second baby more than me? I was there first, but Mother had leisure to *enjoy* the second. The Marsh meant work, work, work.

Dizzy, I sat and took up my knitting; I wanted it finished in advance of the birth. I'd chosen white yarn but, once the baby was born, the prince would bring ribbon to lace through the coat and booties. Bold pink for a brother. For a sister, delicate blue. "Do you hope it's a boy or girl?"

"Which would *you* prefer, Matilda? A brother or sister?"

"A sister. Because I could guide her. But Mother, I asked *you*!"

"I only pray that he or she is healthy."

I blushed; an aspiring doctor should have said the same. "I suppose Mr Windsor wants a son. To continue the family name."

"I couldn't give him as many children as King George."

"Why not?" If a sister shared my bed, I could tell her stories till she drifted into blissful sleep. "We've plenty of room."

"It's more precarious as you get older," said Mother. "And after those miscarriages … Dr Glover warned me to be cautious."

I dropped a stitch and had to orchestrate my needles to pick it up again. "You're not old."

"I'm nearly forty."

Sudden tears gushed out of me, huge hulking sobs as if I was a baby myself. Mother beckoned me; I cast my knitting aside and moulded my body to hers.

"Poor Matilda, you've seen such changes."

Although she no longer smelled as she should, although Mrs Embleton would burst in shortly with the tea tray and although my leg threatened to cramp, I wanted to stay curled around her bloated belly forever. Naturally, I couldn't. I beseeched God not to take Mother as he'd taken Father. To keep her safe until I had earned my black bag and stethoscope, and could care for her myself.

Chapter 37

WHEN JANICE AND Heather unlocked their cars outside Tuke House, the residents gravitated to the occupational therapist's metallic-grey Volvo. "No offence, Janice," said Jimmy Ryan. "We might not make it to the Town Hall in your heap of junk."

Nevertheless, Clive directed Jimmy, along with Ronnie, to the back seat of Janice's Polo, deaf to their gripes about two-door cars. It made a mockery of promoting choice, but there wasn't time for the rigmarole of *Betty, would you ask Effie whether she'd prefer to go in Janice's car or Heather's?* Janice had to admit it would have been simpler to travel to the mayor's At Home in the hospital minibus.

At least Clive *tried* to solicit volunteers for the front seat. Janice found being unpopular a novelty: at school, choosing teams for games, she'd always been an early pick.

"Starlet or gypsy?" said Betty.

Heather did look glamorous with her hair in victory rolls. She certainly had the figure for her pinched-waist vintage dress, but she'd have to go easy on the sandwiches. "You can swap places on the way back," said Janice.

"Seems the decision's been made." Clive rushed to hold the door as Matty clambered onto the passenger seat of the Polo.

"Well done, Matty!" said Heather.

Did Janice imagine it or did Matty curl her lip? She hadn't noticed any previous animosity towards Heather. Maybe, having proclaimed *she'd* wear a polka-dot dress but ending up in an attractive, and more age-appropriate, lightweight skirt-suit, Matty felt upstaged.

On the journey, Matty entertained herself reciting monologues, blending Lear's "The Owl and the Pussycat", Wordsworth's "Daffodils" and Samuel Taylor Coleridge's "Kubla Khan". The men grumbled, until Janice suggested taking turns. That silenced them for a few minutes, such that, when Jimmy Ryan broke into "The Raggle Taggle Gypsy", she startled, braking sharply for a zebra crossing. Adding her voice, and encouraging Matty and Ronnie to pitch in, conjured cosy memories of singsongs in the family car. Despite a clash of words and melody, or maybe because of that, it felt so *normal*, she might have kept driving until they were hoarse if Heather and the others weren't expecting them at the Town Hall. Detached from the hospital, her passengers were transformed from patients to people. This was why she championed community care. This was why she trained as a social worker. Not for the paltry pay, not for professional prestige, but for the human connection with people who were otherwise hard to reach.

As the sea came into view over the railway line, Jimmy switched to "What Shall We Do with the Drunken Sailor?" Janice could imagine him as a navy man, although Ronnie had the tattoos. It might have been the sight of the wind turbines that prompted *his* choice of Stevie Smith's "Not Waving but Drowning". Janice could've hugged him, if it wasn't unprofessional, and if he wasn't in the backseat and she in the front with her hands on the wheel. And on the indicator and the gear lever, as they came into town. Deeply moved, she continued to the Town Hall on automatic pilot, pondering the feasibility of a Tuke House poetry group. What better way to lift the lid on painful emotions? With the bonus of residents and staff engaging on an equal footing.

A warm breeze carried the stench of hops to the car park. They met the others at the entrance to the Town Hall.

"I hope there's rum butter," said Betty.

"And chocolate cake," said Billy.

"And gypsy creams," deadpanned Jimmy.

On the other side of the revolving doors, a sign pointed to the function room. "You might want to have your invitations ready," said Heather. "Don't fuss about them muddling your names."

"I'm changing mine to Bilty Dowhouse." Billy waved his card.

"And I'll be Bunty Coventry." Betty giggled like a teenager.

Janice admired their good humour. Maybe they found

respite in *someone else's* craziness, liberation in leaving their hospital identities behind. Some of that ease receded as they passed through the leather-padded door. They hovered at the edge of the room as if on their first day at school. Was it the spaciousness that intimidated them or the elegance of the decor? Was it the brightness or the buzz? Was it the mayor himself, in his glitzy chain of office?

Billy broke the inertia. From the corner of her eye, Janice saw him advance towards the mayor, but her attention flipped to Matty who was making for the door. Having tried and failed to intercept her, Janice had no choice but to follow her outside.

HENRY GRIPPED THE porcelain with both hands, grounded by its chill. Reflected in the tarnished glass above the basin, his ashen face validated his mumbled plea of nausea as he'd dumped a scalloped card on the mayor. The young lady escorting the care-home guests *couldn't* be Tilly, but she might be wearing Tilly's dress. The match was so uncanny, the colours chiming with those his brain imposed on the black-and-white print. A lead he could pursue if he discovered how she had acquired the dress.

Open your gob and ask her, Irene would say. *Don't mistake a molehill for Scafell Pike!* But he couldn't approach her looking like a chap who'd seen a ghost or was in the process of becoming one.

The door swung open and an elderly man shuffled to the urinals. Henry ran the tap while, farther along the narrow room, the man fumbled with his fly. Pushing back his sleeves, Henry coaxed a lather from a pebble of slate-veined soap, trying to ignore the stop-start dribble of the man's piss. The man himself had no such inhibitions. Heedless of the hazards of diverting his attention from ensuring the trickle met its target, he shot unwary glances Henry's way. He'd never been propositioned in a public lavatory. Shaking off the water, Henry decided he'd be safer in the function room with the spectre of his sister.

With surprising dexterity, the chap was at his elbow before Henry could locate a dry patch on the roller towel. Too quick to have buttoned his fly, although Henry wasn't tempted to check.

"I thought so," said the man, his dentures slip-sliding about his gums. "George Windsor's lad, aren't you?"

Two decades since his father's death, he'd have few surviving peers. But, if any *had* hung on, this was where they'd be. "Yes, I'm Henry." To compensate for not extending his hand – his own was clean, albeit damp, whereas *his* had recently held his cordy – Henry stretched a smile broader than warranted.

The old chap's grin spread to his bushy eyebrows. "Windsor's Haberdashery. A treasure trove. Our Vera's second home. You never fancied taking it on?"

Henry had *yearned* for it, but the ready-made career was not to be. His father retired and sold the shop while Henry was off doing national service. Now he dodged both question and questioner, yanking the towel around its wooden roller in search of a section marginally less soggy than the rest. "There was no future in it. Women haven't the patience for sewing and knitting nowadays. They go for ready-made." He transferred the remaining moisture from his mitts to his trousers.

"Could've been a nice side-line for your sister."

Two leads in one afternoon! He could kiss Geoff Boyne. By God, he could marry him! "You knew my sister?"

"Not in the biblical sense, marra!" The man bashed him on the forearm. "But our kid came close."

Bile fouled his throat but, unsavoury as the link might be, Henry was loath to lose it. "What's his name? Is he here?"

"Walter died at El Alamein."

"I'm sorry."

Walter's brother flapped his condolences away. "Can't keep the mayor waiting." He pulled open the door and ushered Henry into the portion of no man's land between the function room and the toilets.

Reluctant either to grab the handle – his interlocutor had bypassed the basins – or to leave a fellow thirty or forty years his senior to bear the weight of the door, Henry stepped into the lobby, his mind abuzz. If Tilly left to wed this Walter, why keep it secret? Then, when she was widowed, why not come home? Unless their relationship existed only in the men's imaginations. Tilly would have attracted numerous admirers, their father's business increasing her worth beyond her pretty face and personality.

"Pity what occurred," said the man.

What occurred? Henry turned from the outer door precisely as it was thrust open. Almost simultaneously, Walter's brother – perhaps tired of holding it, perhaps remembering to wash – released the inner door. Dizzy with spiralling thoughts of his sister, Henry didn't have a chance. The outer door having thrown him off balance, on colliding with the inner door Henry fell and struck his nut on the tiles. Geoff Boyne, swooping in to investigate what had delayed his meet-and-greet assistant, deftly rolled him into the recovery position before shouting out for someone to call 999.

———————

MATTY HAD PREPARED for the Palladium but found herself at the Folies Bergère. Those lords and ladies seated sedately at their tables did not fool her, little fingers angled as they sipped their tea. They might gentrify their bathrooms, but no amount of hot water would flush the filth from their heads. Demanding more than a recital, their smutty paws would be all over her the minute she left the stage.

Although brown, the circus girl's hands on the wheel are spotless. But are her thoughts clean? Not all gypsies fly the high trapeze. Some trudge door-to-door selling dolly-pegs and cursing anyone without the means or inclination to buy.

"Feeling better, Matty?" How could this sweet girl take her to that place? Presumably its bawdy reputation never entered her head.

Matilda is not so innocent. Matty tried to evade her by travelling in the other car. But the hussy caught up with them at the Folies Bergère. Matty marked her winking at the men, even if no-one else did. Matilda, Madam to the prince.

"Can you say what upset you? Did you recognise someone?"

Matty assumes a banal expression as it comes through to

her that caution is of the essence. She cannot rely on anyone but herself. And if they take her mind away, she will not be able to rely on herself.

"Was Violet there, Matty?"

Parma Violets, Matty has not tasted them for years. Why was that? She used to purchase them from the estate shop: jelly babies for the boy and Parma Violets for herself. As the car turns onto the familiar avenue, she tells the circus girl that she will ascertain, by closing time, whether they have any in stock.

"I'm sorry I can't come with you, Matty. Heather will be wondering where I've got to."

"Do be careful, dear." *She* would never wear slacks, but a lady *is* more exposed in a skirt.

HENRY LOITERED UNTIL a thickish crowd had gathered before creeping past the triage nurse's window. They couldn't prevent him going, but he didn't want to appear ungrateful to the NHS. In conveying him to A&E, the ambulance crew had salvaged the remnants of his dignity. Nevertheless, he imagined the catering staff relishing the irony: *We were primed for an accident among the old folk. We didn't reckon on seeing the project manager stretchered out.*

Keen to put his first aid training into action, Geoff Boyne had seemed miffed to find neither bleeding nor broken bones. The light-headedness Henry felt in the ambulance might have stemmed from concussion, or from school-boy jubilation at a legitimate escape.

Henry's status took a nose-dive at the hospital. At the

Town Hall he'd been the focus of compassion and concern. Even the stick, Zimmer frame and wheelchair brigade acknowledged his temporary incapacity trumped theirs. In Casualty he was reduced to one among many, and less deserving than most.

Waiting to be examined by a doctor, the end-of-term sense of deliverance dissipated, leaving Henry feeling a fraud. And frustrated he'd be home later than if he'd stuck out his stint at the Town Hall. Screened by the queue at the triage nurse's window, Henry crept out.

The instant the late afternoon sun stroked his face, his head began to pulse. For safety's sake, he crossed the hospital forecourt and re-entered the building at the WRVS café.

No cream came with his scone; those served at the mayor's tea party would be lighter than the one he now hacked at with a plastic knife. With his first bite, a rock formed in his stomach. His sole lead on Tilly in years, and he'd done a runner?

Chapter 38

ONCE THE DATE was confirmed for the public consultation meeting, Janice decided to write to the patients' relatives, chewing over the right words to flag it was happening, while stressing they needn't attend. She implied they'd find it tedious, although fearing the opposite, an airing court for prejudice, if the woman with the petition was typical of those it would attract.

As a junior social worker, Janice didn't expect to be there herself. But she'd hoped to be involved in preparatory discussions or, failing that, receive regular updates. Yet, scouring the minutes of the Resettlement Steering Group meetings, there was never any advance on *Progress on consultation meeting with local residents proceeding according to plan.*

So she was taken aback when Graham phoned the office less than thirty-six hours before the meeting. "Tomorrow evening? I'll check my diary." Not that she had a social life but she'd have to consult her manager. "Have you asked David?"

"David doesn't know the patients like you do. Besides, he's on leave."

If David wanted her to deputise, he'd have mentioned it in supervision. Either it had slipped his mind or he considered the task beyond her. She felt torn between colluding with Graham's attempt to circumvent local authority reporting structures and the meeting going ahead without *any* representation from the lead agency for community care. "It'll be fine." She'd run it past David's manager, Yvonne Conway, if she could get hold of her.

"It starts at seven thirty, so if you're there around seven fifteen …"

"Okay, but I assume we'll get together here to iron out tactics first?"

"Great idea in principle, Janice, but we'd struggle to find a window. Diaries are chocka with holidays coming up." Had Graham forgotten it was him – or his superefficient secretary – who'd set the date?

"How about a breakfast meeting tomorrow? That often works for Parveen."

"Dr Shakir's sent her apologies, so it's you, me and Clive. Oh, and Norman."

"That's it?"

"Don't worry, I'll do most of the talking."

She pursed her lips, reining in bitter laughter until the receiver clunked in its cradle.

———————

HENRY HADN'T *INVITED* the opposition committee to congregate in his front parlour before processing to the consultation meeting. Unless it were on one of those dizzy days following his visit to A&E. When his neighbours came with their homemade placards, he couldn't turn them away. But he wasn't obliged to *encourage* them. "It's not some hippy protest march. You can't troop in singing 'We Shall Not Be Moved'."

He found an ally in ferret-faced Jacqueline. "Henry's right. They won't take us seriously if we're too strident."

The women left the placards under Henry's bay window and walked unencumbered to the school hall. Posters for the Green Cross Code and Cycling Proficiency Test adorned the walls, but the chairs were adult sized. A dozen rows faced a small stage where three men and a woman sat in a line, like masters at assembly. Henry and his neighbours had scarcely sat down when a chap in a brown suit sprang to his feet and welcomed everyone to the meeting. As he introduced himself and his colleagues, Henry registered that the girl who'd accosted him outside The Willows last November was a bona fide social worker. Perspiring, he wriggled out of his jacket and hung it on the back of his chair.

Brown Suit was a gabber. Even by local government standards, he was fluent in jargonese. Had the occasion been less dire, Henry would have enjoyed the spectacle of the man's colleagues twitching, powerless to intervene. Ursula Marshall didn't let good manners deter her while, on stage, Pink Hair looked fit to bowk. Divine retribution for snooping that day, with her phoney excuse of a child needing statutory protection. Gathering intelligence more like, ammunition for tonight.

Brown Suit's jaw dropped as the social worker stood up. The tops of Henry's ears blazed as she directed her sob story not at Ursula but at him. Defence or prosecution? Or a threat to release a file on him to the *Times and Star*? To shame him about his liaison with another man's wife? But hippies *invented* free love. Besides, she couldn't *possibly* know.

THE SEATING SEEMED designed to alienate the audience, with the team from Ghyllside above them on the stage. Janice would've argued for rearranging themselves at floor level were it achievable without inconveniencing those who had bagsied front-row seats. The atmosphere soured further when Graham opened his mouth, addressing the prospective neighbours how he ought to have spoken at Tuke House. No reference to Acts of Parliament, the changing cultural climate or enlightened perspectives on mental health. He simply stated that the authorities thought psychiatric patients should move to the community, and said so again and again. It sounded patronising, arbitrary and frankly ridiculous from a man in a Donald Duck tie.

"That's beside the point," a frizzy-haired woman interrupted him midsentence. "This is a respectable neighbourhood. Some of us have children! Mortgages!" It was the bigot who'd brandished the petition on polling day.

Instead of responding to her reservations, Graham reiterated his manifesto.

"We've heard that. But have you listened to us? We've

nothing against psychiatric patients, but this is the wrong place for them."

"I'm sorry you feel that way," said Graham. "Our planning department did a thorough site survey."

"That's supposed to reassure us?"

Sweat snaked down Janice's back as the audience applauded.

"Well yes." Graham looked flabbergasted that anyone *wouldn't* be appeased by an in-house option appraisal. Laughter erupted from the floor.

Someone had to speak for the patients. Even the woman with the petition would warm to Betty Fogarty and Jimmy Ryan if she met them in congenial circumstances. If she'd sung along with them on the drive to tea with the mayor.

Janice rose to her feet. "It's not easy if you've never met a psychiatric patient. But they're not monsters. These are ordinary people, with the same desires as you and me."

"If they're *ordinary*, what's kept them in Ghyllside?"

"A good question." Janice inhaled deeply. "Let me tell you about one of our residents. A real character …"

"Obviously, we can't disclose confidential information," quipped Norman.

Janice harrumphed. *What did he take her for?* "She's lived in Ghyllside for half a century, since she was younger than me. Could be somebody's grandmother. Probably is, although she wouldn't know it. Because she couldn't keep *her* baby. An unmarried mother, locked up and left to rot! We can't undo past damage but doesn't she deserve something better for her remaining years?"

"Thank you, Miss Lowry," said Graham.

Janice flopped onto her seat. Had she been overly emotional? No, she'd given the dispossessed a voice.

"Time served isn't the issue," said the petition-woman. "It's whether you can promise she's cured."

———

WHY DID SHE persist in pitching her lecture at him? Ursula had raised the objection. Henry tried to make his face reflect his indifference, but the young social worker kept prodding. As if he were a letterbox and she had a sack of junk mail to offload.

The misdirected letter and the wide-open gate. *Could* this fallen woman have some *genuine* association with The Willows? Henry couldn't say who watched him once Tilly disappeared. But there must have been *someone* for those few weeks prior to his departure for boarding school. His father couldn't have left him unsupervised until he shut up shop.

He would have a quiet word with the young social worker when the meeting finished. Some additional detail might jog his memory and resolve the riddle in the paperwork. His good deed for the day helping them tie up loose ends.

———

GRAHAM AND CLIVE dashed off after the meeting, but Janice found herself collared by Norman. "You were out of order back there."

Pigs would fly before he'd congratulate her on an impassioned defence of patient rights. "Pardon?"

Norman leant in so close his beard scraped her cheek.

"There might be more to Matty's story than getting pregnant."

"You don't think she was?"

"Oh, *that's* well documented. But we can't guarantee it got her admitted. She could've been unstable already. In fact, that might be how she got pregnant."

"I see, because you'd have to be *unstable* to have sex with a wanker who won't take his share of the consequences. Now you mention it, you'd have to be unstable to have sex with *anyone* when there's no contraception and the world will condemn you for having a fully functional uterus."

"Steady on!" Norman stepped back. "I only meant it's stretching the evidence to say she was hospitalised for having a child."

"Sister Henderson said she was." She called it moral something or other.

"I wouldn't bank on Sister Henderson's testimony. Where are the *other* unmarried mothers? They weren't *all* certified insane."

Janice had asked the same on Ward 24. Before she'd had a solid sense of Matty's qualities and imbibed the injustice as if it were hers. She shivered in the wake of Norman's icy logic. She looked around for a sympathetic shoulder; Graham would be useless but Clive might understand. But the hall was virtually empty, apart from the grumpy-faced man who'd been sitting beside the frizzy-haired woman and would be as intolerant as she was. "I reckon *the others* were the abnormal ones. Women who could give up their babies *without* losing their minds."

———

TO AVOID TELLING his neighbours he was holding back to speak to the social worker, Henry veered into the lavatories, saying he'd catch them up. The knee-level urinals reminded him uncomfortably of when he was the height to use them, of when his defining feature was an ache where his sister used to be.

In the hall, the social worker debated with her bearded colleague. Henry kept a polite distance, nodding now and then in her direction. How long should he wait?

His father must have been at his wit's end when Tilly left. Grateful for whatever assistance he could get. Did other parents try to dump their recalcitrant daughters on the widower with the big house and small son? The Willows a rubbish tip for the wayward girls, the black sheep, the ever-so-slightly deranged? Girls too busy flirting with delivery boys to attend to him.

Nothing about her to hang a memory on, but she might remember him. Even if she didn't, the social worker might argue her claim. He refused to be bullied into befriending a lunatic. Certainly not one who'd endangered him as a child. She could've attacked him with a carving knife. Turned on the oven without lighting the gas. Waltzed off to a dance hall leaving him alone. No wonder his father never mentioned the madwoman.

Thank God for the bearded chap! He absorbed the social worker's attention while Henry slipped from the hall.

Chapter 39

S HE DIDN'T SAY how she squared it with Eric, but Irene
continued her evening classes into the summer. On
account of her new bikini, she renounced stodgy ready-meals
and insisted Henry prepare a salad, albeit with a side-serving
of Jersey Royals glistening with butter. Her conversion to
rabbit food required a trip to the market in his lunch break;
Mr Patel's lettuces turning slimy when rinsed under the cold
tap, and his tomatoes being prone to spewing their seedy
innards on the kitchen cabinet at the nip of a knife.

Irene informed him classes *would* be cancelled during
the first week of August for the Lonsdale family holiday. The
twins being otherwise engaged this year, she seemed more
excited about visiting her sister than having time with her
spouse. Nursing a mug of milkless, sugarless tea, she showed
him photo after photo of an ice-white apartment block, a
sunburnt couple clinking glasses on the balcony, a sandy

beach, the sea. A shopfront adorned with Union Jacks and a signboard announcing *Full English breakfasts*. A woman with Irene's chin pulling pints. "It's paradise, Henry. Come with me next time!"

"Eric would love that."

"Give over! Me and you on our own. I can tell Eric I'm taking a friend. He wouldn't mind, he hates the heat. We could go in October for your birthday."

It was as if the path ahead had been shrouded in darkness and now, in the distance, a candle glowed. Could he become the type of bloke who patrols the promenade in T-shirt, shorts and flip-flops? Could he order paella at a pavement restaurant, and a ceramic jug of sangria with floaters of fresh fruit? Could a siesta divide his day into two easy episodes of food, booze and relaxation? Could he heck! "You know I can't leave The Willows."

Irene returned the photographs to the paper wallet. "Well, thank you, darling, for your generous offer. And at such personal risk!"

"Don't be like that. I'd jump at the chance of more time with you."

"You won't jump high enough, but, that's *your* problem!" Irene rose from the table and grabbed her handbag from the fireside chair. Retrieving her mobile phone, she jabbed at the keypad. "It's just me! Shall I get some fish and chips on the way home?"

Chapter 40

"CAN I BUY you young ladies a drink?"

Stifling her laughter, Sheena showered the table with droplets of beer. At uni, she and Janice relished dismissing men who assumed their evening incomplete without an injection of testosterone. With no riposte suitable for someone she'd see at work on the Monday, Janice introduced her colleague to her friend.

Mervyn Yates appeared more human in the pub than at Ghyllside. It might have been the subdued lighting softening his cropped hair and jug ears, or his off-duty gear of crew-neck cotton sweater and stonewashed jeans. Or, as conversation with Sheena limped along so badly, that there was nothing to interrupt.

After a string of scorching days, Janice had eagerly anticipated Sheena's visit. A hike up Cat Bells or a gentler stroll around Derwent Water, with a picnic at Friar's Crag, compensating for a working week traversing picture-postcard scenery in an oven on wheels. With sun-kissed skin and tingling calf muscles, they'd spend the evenings at the flat with a bottle of wine, expanding on events edited out of their brief and infrequent letters and phone calls. Accustomed to swapping opinions on everything from child abuse inquiries to the shade of a lecturer's lippy, Janice envisaged nattering until their throats seized up. The weather had other plans.

On the Friday evening, as Sheena motored up the M6 and Janice prepared a salad Niçoise in her tiny kitchen, the heatwave broke. A thunderstorm brought perilous conditions to the motorway. Then an accident slowed the traffic to a crawl. Sheena pitched up three hours late, and frazzled. Eating dinner on the sofa, Janice wished she'd made soup. "I hope you brought your waterproofs."

"I don't *possess* any waterproofs. Besides, it was wall-to-wall sunshine in Nottingham."

Grievances too minor to name, let alone argue out of existence, left a sense that their friendship, like the Lake District's charm, was provisional. The cramped flat couldn't contain what went unsaid. Janice couldn't admit her resentment at having to conjure up indoor activities in a corner of the country famous for its alfresco attractions. Couldn't protest that, if she'd been interested in the minutiae of the AIDS post, she wouldn't have flung *her* application in the bin. Outdoors, amid the splendour of the fells, they might have talked themselves back to their former intimacy. Instead, they eked out the morning at the Pencil Museum and the afternoon dipping in and out of gift shops in Keswick. Now live music at The Matador would provide the illusion of a fabulous conclusion to a fabulous day.

So when Mervyn approached their table, instead of grappling for a polite way to get rid of him, Janice told him they were drinking Jennings bitter. As he took their glasses to the bar, Sheena looked askance.

"We wouldn't be able to hear ourselves anyhow," said Janice. "Not once the band comes on."

Fingers circling three pint glasses, Mervyn seemed so grateful, Janice pitied the men she'd chased off in the past. Maybe it wasn't only arrogance that drove them to barge in on women's tête-à-têtes. She pictured Mervyn at work, his tower of case notes a paltry defence against Norman's belligerence and Parveen's no-shows. The registrar was the perpetual new kid, moving jobs every twelve months. A recipe for loneliness. While Janice beamed cordiality, Sheena asked if he'd come alone.

"I'm afraid so," said Mervyn. "I can never tell if it's me or R&B my flatmates can't stick."

Sheena nudged Janice. "You didn't tell me you were dragging me to an R&B night."

Janice bristled at *dragging*, but ghosted a smile.

"It's not very fashionable," said Mervyn. "But I've seen these before and they're ace. If you don't agree, I'll stand you another pint."

Fortunately, Sheena concurred with his verdict, as far as Janice could tell from her fervent applause at the end of each number. At the interval, Mervyn volunteered to queue for drinks, accepting a fiver from Janice since it was her round. She thought him considerate in giving them some privacy, but Sheena strode off to the toilet. Janice couldn't join her in case they lost their seats.

At the end of the evening, Mervyn thanked them for their company. "Maybe I'll see you here again, Janice. I come most Saturdays unless I'm rostered to work."

"Okay. Give me a nod when there's something worth seeing."

Back at the flat, Sheena turned down Janice's offer of a nightcap. "I'd rather hit the sack."

It wasn't yet midnight. "Is something wrong?"

"Did you know he'd be there?"

"Mervyn? No!"

"It's …" Sheena brushed her fringe from her forehead. "I'd be thrilled if you'd found someone, but you might have warned me I'd been invited to play gooseberry."

"Found someone? He's the junior psychiatrist on our team."

"Your non-verbals didn't strike me as professional."

"Bloody hell, Sheena. I'm not that desperate."

Had the atmosphere been different, Janice might have elaborated. Explained how, even if she'd fancied Mervyn, she'd have held back. At least until she knew where things stood with Stuart. But she was embarrassed to let on they'd drifted into something less than *being a couple again* but closer than *venom-spitting exes*. A few drinks. Rambles at weekends or in the snatched daylight hours after work. And, always with protection, shagging like they were the last two people on earth.

Chapter 41

PARMA VIOLETS. SUCH sophisticated confectionery, small sweets resembling purple pills. Ever since the circus girl mentioned their medicinal properties, she treats herself to a packet when she draws her pocket money from the bank. Her maid might scoff, but gypsies are schooled in herbalism. There is more to pharmaceuticals than a doctor's pens and folders. With so many depending upon her, Matty must safeguard her health.

The speediest route to the market square is across the cobbled courtyard and down the main corridor. The most charming route, especially when the weather is benign, is to pass in front of the annexe, and saunter down the driveway with its borders of flowers and shrubs. When she mounts the steps to the grand entrance, Matty recalls being a debutante off to a ball.

Today, although high summer, the sun is a faded

thumbprint, the sky bath-water grey. She is barely beyond the annexe when the heavens open. As if a nun had pulled the chain of God's lavatory, drenching her from hair to heels.

In the entrance lobby, her slippers leave a track on the parquet floor: a new style of signage to direct guests to the shop.

"Matty! Where have you been? You'll catch your death!"

Not having *been* anywhere, Matty cannot reply. Yet her heart sings. Kitty! Darling Kitty, how she has missed her! Wiping the water from her eyebrows with her cardigan sleeve, she notices her former maid is admirably turned out, in a navy blazer with gold buttons and matching knee-length skirt. Matty is delighted she has found her feet again and hopes a genuine Christian family took the infant in.

"You'd better hurry back to Tuke and change into some dry togs." Kitty pouts. "I'd go with you only …"

Matty admires the girl's costume. *Uniform.* It comes through to her that Kitty aspires to serve her country as a Wren. "Only you must wait here for your interview."

"How did you …? It's supposed to be confidential!"

"I will not breathe a word."

"Listen, Matty." Kitty casts furtive glances around her but there is no-one to eavesdrop in the wood-panelled vestibule, save for the telephonist in her closet, and Matty has it on good authority the poor dear is deaf. "I didn't tell you because I didn't want you getting het up. But it's a brilliant opportunity."

"Brilliant indeed." The ocean. The adventure. The saucy sailors. Should she counsel her to be careful or has the girl learnt her lesson?

"Thanks, Matty, it's nice of you to take it that way. But we'll have ages to discuss it if I'm appointed. And Clive will find another primary nurse who'll move out with you next year."

"Mrs Gilmore?" The chap in the brown suit startles them both.

Plucking a briefcase from the bench, Kitty makes to follow him. Before she does, she urges Matty to make haste to Tuke House to change her clothes.

She cannot deny her summer frock and cardigan is somewhat casual attire. But Matty is not after a position in the royal armed forces. Chortling, she continues up the corridor to the shop. Imagine the Belgian detective recruiting Kitty as a spy!

Chapter 42

URSULA DALLIED AT the door to the attic bedroom. "Your sister won't mind?"

She meant Irene, but Henry's response applied equally to Tilly. "She's away."

He'd answered the door to Mrs Marshall ten minutes earlier. She arrived with a bottle of red, which, judging by its dusty shoulders, she'd bought from Mr Patel. "Oh, Mr Windsor, where were you?" Without waiting for an invitation, she'd pushed past him to the dining room, plonked the wine on the table and ratched in the sideboard for glassware. "Don't imagine we're celebrating. Drowning our sorrows more like."

Henry felt reassured her anger wasn't *totally* directed at him. His training – years of appeasing Irene – kicked in. Ferreting in the drawer, he found a corkscrew and unsheathed the wine.

He was wiping his fingers on his hankie when Ursula emptied her glass and signalled for a top-up. Only then did she shed her waxed jacket and flop onto a chair.

Generally adrift when Irene was on holiday, he'd never felt as perplexed as now. Had he missed an opposition group meeting? Or was it the state of his front garden? "Are you going to tell me what this is about?"

"The *fucking* planning meeting. You were our spokesman." Ursula's language had been more refined when she'd first sat at Henry's dining table.

Henry brought the heel of his hand to his forehead. "Was it tonight?" He hoped he hadn't overdone the theatricals, but he couldn't confess his relief at being spared portraying the public face of NIMBYism. No entreaty, however eloquent, would persuade the council to refuse a planning application from the National Health. "How did it go?"

"It was dreadful. All that work down the drain! How would *they* cope with a load of loonies living next door?"

"So they passed the plans?"

"In favour of Ghyllside." Ursula wiped her eyes, blacking her cheeks with mascara. "I should warn you, Henry, your name's mud on Sheepwash Lane."

Unacquainted with his neighbours until the brouhaha erupted, Henry was shocked his unpopularity hurt. "I'm sorry. But any of you could have presented our case."

"We *couldn't*! It wasn't a free-for-all like the Ghyllside meeting. The Chair wouldn't let us say a word unless our name was on his list."

Henry refreshed Ursula's glass. "What now?" A formal appeal would drag, a repeat of national service: weeks of tedium pepped by days of humiliating defeat.

"Let's go upstairs."

"Pardon?"

"Call me sentimental but I want a last glimpse of the clinic before it's ruined."

Having disappointed her once already that evening, Henry felt compelled to follow her to the attic. On entering Tilly's bedroom, instead of going directly to the back window, Ursula stationed herself beside the bed. "That quilt is exquisite. All hand sewn, by the looks of it. I'm in awe of your sister."

Henry had assumed his mother made it, but what did that matter now? He watched her smooth her palm across the quilt, fondle the edge.

Ursula yanked off her shoes. "I'm tempted to lie down to get the measure of it. Would that be terribly naughty?" Without pause for permission, she dived under the quilt. "It's so cosy. A cut above our modern duvets." The bed creaked as she wriggled into the wall. "Why don't you join me?"

In forty-odd years of sexual fantasy, Henry had never been propositioned in Tilly's room. So when Ursula invited him into bed with her, he froze. But rejection might cause further offence.

Undoing his laces, he scanned her face for a hint of her intent. When he eased his feet out of his brogues and slipped off his jacket, she grinned like a child. What did Henry know of children? His concept, even of his childhood self, misty as an autumn fell top.

Helpless against a force far superior to his own, Henry shut his eyes and puckered his lips.

Chapter 43

J ANICE HAD TO bob about for a clear view of the road beyond the flies smudged to trails of blackberry jam on her windscreen. Having forgotten her sunglasses, each turn of the wheel necessitated shifting position to dodge the glare. As for her supposedly stylish espadrilles, she felt safer driving barefoot. Nevertheless, singing along with Elton John in the cassette deck, Janice felt happy, and happier still to pitch up at the B&B with ten minutes to spare.

She found her parents drinking coffee in the guest lounge. Her dad was as expected, spruced up in his linen suit, but her mother was country-set incarnate in a flowery summer dress with a scooped neckline that accentuated her cleavage. "Very Laura Ashley." Her wide-brimmed hat precisely matched her bag and shoes, in a similar shade to Janice's hair. Most astonishing in a woman normally *au naturel* was that the get-up coordinated with her lipstick.

Under the hat, her ebony hair cascaded with curls.

"I thought I'd make an effort."

Janice had also made an effort, braving The Lanes at Carlisle. In Monsoon, the viscose top and trouser ensemble attested smart yet funky; in her bedroom mirror that morning they'd become pyjamas. The trousers were perfect with a plain white T-shirt, but she couldn't wear a T-shirt to a wedding. She reverted to the flared skirt and peasant blouse she'd worn for the mayor's tea party, and neither hat nor handbag had crossed her mind. "Am I underdressed, do you reckon?" Her parents said she looked fantastic. As they would. She left her car keys at the B&B and slipped her purse into her pocket.

Fields of custard-yellow rapeseed flowers surrendered to megastores as they approached the city. Her father steered through one-way streets to the station.

Janice had been both relieved and peeved to discover Roz had rejected a shared room in the B&B, opting instead for a day-return train ticket, and bringing a friend. What kind of friend would Farouk be? As he slid onto the backseat beside her, Janice wondered whether this was the bloke who'd got Roz pregnant or her strategy for evading sibling tête-à-têtes.

Conversation was sparse as, between *her* struggles to read the directions and *his* to follow them, her parents navigated to the church. It freed Janice to notice the sharpness of Farouk's suit and the sweetness of his smile and the tender way he held her sister's hand. Like their mother, Roz had the matching hat, bag, shoes and lipstick, accessorising a strapless satin dress. As couples and families streamed into the church, Janice noticed that most of the women were kitted out as elegantly – or fussily – as Roz and her mother. If she'd brought Stuart, he'd have accused her, as had Billy Dewhirst, of lowering the tone. She hoped she wouldn't embarrass her mother in front of her Italian kin.

As far back as Janice could remember, the Lowry branch had tottered on the edge of the Camilleri clan. Had her mother *always* been the odd one out, even behind the counter of the ice cream parlour? Or did it start when the Irishman to whom she'd pledged her future had no allegiance to the Pope? Or when they failed to furnish the batch of *bambini* other marriages produced with ease? Was it when, shopping for *bambini*, they picked one with skin on the darker side of beige? When they had the audacity to repeat the process two years later? Or maybe it was when the Irishman, having consented to his daughters' baptisms, vetoed Catholic schools. Or when she shirked Mass except at Christmas? Fortunately, given that four people relied on her example today, her mum retained the muscle memory of when to stand, sit and kneel.

The organist changed tempo; the congregation arose. As her cousin dawdled down the aisle on her dad's arm, Janice's eyes prickled. Against her better judgement. The virginal robe, the impossible promises, transferring the woman from one man to another: no feminist could agree to a traditional wedding. Yet it might be worse never to have the option.

Did Matty dream of parading before family and friends in a white veil? Did pregnancy block that avenue or did she attach herself to the wrong man? Someone as alien to *her* family as an Irish Protestant to Italian Catholics? Janice's mother, in sterner times, would have been ostracised for her choice.

Now, turning to her mother, Janice felt confused to see her grimace. But it was simply the signal to kneel.

JANICE *APPEARED* TO be enjoying herself – chatting and laughing with relatives, praising the food and the bride's gown– but she *felt* offbeat, and not only from dancing at the disco with her dad. Sitting with her parents, she'd unpeeled her identity as a skilled professional to reveal a gawky adolescent underneath. During the journey back to the B&B, she couldn't shake off a sense of estrangement. From the celebrations. From her self.

Despite Roz's two years' seniority, Janice had been the more outgoing of the two. Now her sister had overtaken her, with a mortgage and a partner – although Farouk's *exact* role remained undefined – and careering through a to-do list of grown-up dilemmas. While Janice sat tight in some metaphorical sandpit, renting a poky flat, sleeping with a man whose politics appalled her, dyeing her hair and fantasising about her birth mother. Why hadn't she gone further? Was she afraid of finding someone who parked her baby in front of *Tom and Jerry*? Or someone as deluded as Matty?

Time to act. And, whatever Rosalind might think, there was no reason to keep it from her parents. She'd swim in their support.

THE NEXT MORNING, she found her parents seated side-by-side at a wrought-iron table on the patio of the B&B.

They'd positioned themselves with their backs to the building, gazing across the garden to the patchwork of fields with woodland beyond. Janice paused to admire them admiring the vista of ripening crops and sheep-mown meadows, until a girl barrelled from the house bearing a breakfast tray.

"Isn't it glorious?" said her mother, after sitting down from their good-morning hugs.

It was another balmy day, wisps of cloud and a murmur of breeze tempering the sun's severity. Bees hummed in the herb bed and chirruping swallows swept the sky above the fields. On the table, summer fruits in jewelled colours tempted her taste buds. "Fabulous," said Janice, but she couldn't *feel* it, not how she should.

She'd taken a seat adjacent to her mother where they could see both each other and the view. Her parents looked more themselves in shorts and T-shirts, her mother's face unadorned. "Everything okay?"

Janice reached for the coffee pot. An ache in her temples rebuked her: if she was going to binge on booze, she should remember her sunglasses for the morning after. "Haven't woken up yet."

"You need a holiday," said her mother. "You're working too hard."

Janice chatted about a planned trip to Sicily with her Nottingham friends, until the waitress had replaced their bowls with plates of eggs, bacon, sausages and mushrooms. As they ate, they watched a kestrel hover and swoop down to snatch *its* breakfast from the grass.

"I wondered if you felt awkward about Rosalind," said

her mother.

Awkward was putting it mildly! But Roz's abortion was meant to be secret. "I'd have liked to have seen more of her this weekend. But Farouk seemed nice."

"He's very attractive," said her mother. "I've never met a Tunisian before."

"That's London for you," said her dad. "She's mixing with a cosmopolitan crowd."

While I'm in a backwater, regressing to a relationship from my student days. "What did you think of him?"

Her mother set down her knife and fork. "To be frank, I thought he was flashy."

Janice laughed. "We were all flashy yesterday. *You* were anyhow."

"Brash, then. But if Rosalind likes him …"

Her mother's tone surprised her. Maybe Roz *had* told them about the abortion. Maybe they blamed Farouk. "You think it's serious?"

"I've no idea. We thought she might have confided in you."

"We hardly spoke yesterday."

"She's too *young* to settle down."

"Mum! She brought a *friend* to a family gathering." Why was her mother so flustered? What were yesterday's cosmetics intended to hide?

Her father leaned in, although the other tables were unoccupied and no staff were around to hear. "A *Tunisian* friend." His Fred Flintstone T-shirt belied the solemnity of his tone.

So? Janice wished his intention *was* cartoonish. The sun

shot arrows at her eyes. How could *her* parents be racist?

"She's always been fragile," continued her mother. "We'll back her up regardless, but she might not realise what she's getting into."

"Getting into?"

"Oh dear," said her mother, "I've made a pig's ear of this. I wanted to protect *your* feelings and I've got you in a tizz about Roz."

"I don't see the problem." Except in exposing their murky attitudes. It *had* to be down to Farouk being a dark-skinned North African. They'd never been weird about boyfriends in the past.

"Well, I'm glad," said her mother. "We *hoped* you wouldn't feel pressured to copy her. Which would be fine if you *genuinely* ..."

As alcoholic residue colonised her skull, Janice didn't know whether to slap her mother, collapse in hysterics or jump in her car and burn rubber all the way to Cumbria. "I might feel pressured to get myself a Tunisian boyfriend?" The passion with which she'd challenged a lecturer's stance on interracial adoption! Why had she stuck up for these renegades?

"To trace your birth parents!"

"Rosalind's tracing her birth parents?"

"You didn't know?" Her mother grabbed her hand. "I presumed she'd told you. You used to be so close."

"It's a big step for Rosalind," said her father. "It'll take some adjusting as a family, too."

"It shouldn't make a scrap of difference to what *you* do," said her mother. "You should feel at liberty to choose what's right for you."

Roz had *chosen* to have an abortion. She'd *chosen* to tell Janice what she'd done. But *chose* to keep quiet about a matter affecting her more. In fact, she'd *chosen* to go behind her back and follow the path she'd reproached Janice for even considering. *Chose* to tell their parents, having previously insisted they'd be hurt if Janice researched *her* heritage.

In the group at Tuke House, Janice and Heather presented themselves as people comfortable with choice. Relative to the patients, they were. But the world beyond the institution imposed knottier decisions than how to take their tea. Janice's identity had been shaped by *her parents'* choice to pluck her from the orphanage. *Janice* hadn't chosen her family, she hadn't chosen Roz. "You're our *real* parents. Why chase after a stranger?"

Chapter 44

THE END OF the holiday period brought Graham Scott to the clinical meeting once again. This time, he came with good news. The formal consultation now complete, and the objections dissected and dismissed, the chief executive had sanctioned the closure of Tuke House. With the plans approved by the local authority, Briarwood's baby clinic would be demolished within the week. As the clinicians raised their mugs, the tea and coffee might have been champagne.

Janice turned to Heather. "Let's take the choices group to see the site."

"We've beaten you to it and booked the minibus," said Clive. "They'd *all* benefit from a trip."

Herded like sheep. Doubling the stigma. But the mayor's tea party had revealed the complications of smaller-scale transport arrangements.

"You'd better liaise with Estates over safety," said Graham.

"We shouldn't take anyone out there until we're certain they're moving," said Norman.

"Didn't I make it clear?" said Graham. "The board's rubberstamped it."

"The project as a whole," said Norman. "But not for the individuals within it."

Parveen tapped the wing of her spectacles. "Because that's a *clinical* decision."

"Haven't they *all* been assessed as right for the scheme?" said Janice.

"We agreed to reassess them," said Norman.

"I have sleepless nights about Matty Osborne," said Graham.

"I have sleepless nights about them all," said Parveen.

"We can't subject them to a twenty-one item behavioural assessment for a *bus* trip," said Janice.

Before Norman could respond, Parveen cut across him. "That *would* be disproportionate. Let's set aside a morning to review whether everyone's on track. Our priority is their mental state, no?" She smiled at Heather. "And whether they understand what moving to the community means."

JANICE CONCURRED WITH Heather that, with minor changes, the choices group could segue from *conversation skills* to *psychoeducation*. If they recorded the participants' ideas on a flipchart, they could share the group's progress with their colleagues.

"Suppose you were moving house," said Heather. "What

would you need to consider?"

"What would you be thinking about?" Janice added. A tricky concept even for those with more organised minds. "What would you have to *do*?"

Ronnie gazed around the room. "Write stuff on a flipchart."

"It definitely helps to make a list," said Heather. "And the flipchart's perfect for *our* list, so everyone can see it."

"Would you like to scribe, Ronnie?" said Janice. It would be a huge achievement if members could assume leadership roles.

Dolefully, Ronnie shook his head. Janice was on the verge of grabbing the board marker herself and etching *Make a list* on the chart, when Heather rephrased the invitation. "Would you write down what people say, Ronnie?"

Ronnie jumped to his feet and took up position at the flipchart.

"Can anyone remember moving house in the past?" asked Heather.

Matty Osborne sat up straight. "Oh my dears, what a trial! What to take, what to leave behind? Will it fit in your suitcase?"

"Thank you, Matty," said Heather. "So, you're saying that when you move house you'd pack a case with the things you want to take with you? Ronnie, would you write that down please?"

After selecting a pen from the ledge of the A-stand, removing its cap and sniffing the tip, Ronnie scrawled the word THINGS in green.

"That's fabulous," said Janice. "Let's think about what

kind of things. What would you put in your case, Matty?"

"I would take my beautiful clothes."

Unprompted, Ronnie scribbled BUTIFULL below the word THINGS.

"Would you pack what you're wearing today?" said Heather.

Matty studied her cotton blouse and skirt in disgust. Then she laughed. "As if I gave a fig for fashion! Those hideous smocks I stitched myself, and I was no seamstress. But for afterwards … Afterwards I dabbed rouge on my cheeks and looked them firmly in the eye."

"That's the spirit, Matty," said Billy.

Both Heather and Janice nodded vigorously, but Matty didn't blink. "The prince bought me that dress for our holiday …"

When Ronnie wrote PRINSE on the flipchart, Effie sprang to her feet, snatched a marker and blotted the word with frenzied black zigzags. "That woman never is, never was and never will be a princess!"

Heather and Janice exchanged glances, partly enthused by the energy, partly anxious where it might lead. But the flare fizzled out as abruptly as it began. Effie picked up her doll and settled back into her seat.

Oblivious, Matty rambled on. "A beautiful frock. Red with white spots. I counted the days until I could cast off those ghastly smocks to the nuns."

As Ronnie wrote GASTLY SMOKS on the chart, Janice no longer cared whether it would be comprehensible to their colleagues. Matty was emerging from her secluded sanctuary and, except for Effie's outburst, the other residents were rapt. Janice didn't dare make a sound, not even to praise Ronnie for scribing, lest she break the spell. Eyes wide and statue-still, Heather must have felt the same. This was more poignant than the singsong en route to the mayor's tea party. No longer sheltering behind grandiose delusions, Matty was connecting with her loss. The group's empathic attention would help her bear it.

"But I was duped." Sombrely, Matty brushed imaginary crumbs from her skirt. "Had I not been punished enough?" The proud aristocrat unmasked, Matty dribbled her words, a wounded child. "I thought they were taking me home, but they flung me in prison. Purgatory."

Janice shivered as the pieces came together. The picture might be bleak, but it refuted Norman's contention that her disturbance predated the pregnancy. Matty was a victim, pure and simple, the asylum compounding the iniquity that brought her to its doors.

Like her friend Violet, Matty *must* have been a domestic servant. Gruelling hours, denied a life beyond work. Friends – male friends especially – discouraged. Hiding her pregnancy to keep her job. Banished when it became too advanced to hide.

As for the father, he could walk off scot free. Who was he? Another servant? The master of the house who'd coerced into performing functions outside her contract? If she had one. A vinegary slick of nausea tickled Janice's throat.

But it was Janice's job, and privilege, to bear witness. How many times had Matty been chivvied out of telling her story? How often branded a liar like her namesake in the poem? Her experience validated, Matty might tunnel through her grief to surface into sanity.

Janice slipped from her chair to crouch beside Matty's. "Is that how you came to be here, Matty?"

Matty stared at Janice transfixed. Then she grinned. "Ah, you're a cheeky one. You know how I came here – or shall I explain about the birds and the bees?"

HEATHER SIPPED FROM her mug. "That's Ronnie, Effie, and Billy written up. What shall we put for Matty Osborne?"

Janice enjoyed their debriefing sessions in the small interview room. Although frequently drained by the intensity of the work, she valued the camaraderie. Of all the resettlement team members, Heather was the one with whom she felt most attuned. Yet she hesitated to acknowledge how near Matty had come to the edge. "She was very cooperative ..."

Heather nodded. "And focused on the task ..."

"She seemed to grasp it better than any of them."

"Ronnie's scribing didn't do it justice."

"She was amazing on personal disclosure," continued Janice.

"Eight out of ten?"

"Cool." When Heather recommended a rating system for group contributions, Janice had the same sinking sensation as when Norman outlined the hospital-wide assessment. You could measure a person's height or weight, record the length of their hospital stay, but could you rate their input to a discussion? She'd bowed to the occupational therapist's expertise but nevertheless felt it inadequate to the marvellous messiness of human behaviour. Until today. Today she welcomed the safety net. In the midst of Matty's reminiscence, Janice had begun to panic. "And eight or nine for engagement?"

Heather twirled the pen between her fingers. "Or a seven, given her drifting off towards the end?"

Drifting off was an understatement, but Matty had washed up on dry land. "I'm fine with that. What about relating to peers? Not her strongest suit."

"No, but she didn't rise to the bait when Effie said she wasn't a princess. That shows a degree of self-control."

Self-control or indifference to other people's existence? Totally detached from the here and now? "Six?"

Heather flicked back the pages in the ring binder. "We gave her a six last week when she sang *Rock-A-Bye Baby* every time Effie opened her mouth."

"Stretch it to a seven?" said Janice.

"Fantastic. Now, how about Jimmy Ryan?"

Chapter 45

MATTY HAS ALMOST reached the shores of sleep when whispering assaults her ear. "None of your lies, Matilda, or I'll have you locked up."

Her eyes snap open but the prince has cloaked himself in shadow. "No, you will not. My mother would forbid it."

His breath warms her cheek. "Your mother cannot help you now."

"I wish she had never married you." Matty pursues a cooler place on the pillow.

His breath catches her other ear. "I do too, until I remember the boy."

His sole weakness. Her sole weapon. "Hal would perish without me."

"He will soon forget you. When he leaves for prep school, I can send you anywhere."

"You cannot decide my future. You are not my father."

"For which I thank the Lord every Sunday. However, I am your guardian. Respected county-wide as a Master Mason. People listen to me."

"Then they are fools! You are not fit to fasten my father's shoes."

"Your father was a certified lunatic."

"My father was a war hero!"

"Lies, lies, lies, Matilda!"

"I speak the truth! Ask my mother!"

"Your mother's dead, and your father."

"I will run away. You cannot stop me."

"Let's see how far you get with no money, and no skills except lifting your skirt."

A tap on her hand. Matty screams.

"You're all right now, Matty. Just a nasty dream." A girl, one of the maids.

Matty hauls herself to a sitting position. "The prince was here. He must not escape!" She will have him shackled and thrown in the dungeon.

The girl looks alarmed initially, before breaking into a broad smile. "Ah, the prince! Your knight in shining armour. Does he have a brother for me?"

Matty's shoulders droop. Her spine softens from the base of her skull to her rump. Her heart contracts and the blood stalls in her veins. Matilda has told so many lies the authorities are befuddled. Unless she distances herself, Matty will be tarred with the same brush. She forces a laugh. "Indeed, a nightmare. Would you get me something for my head?"

"A headache? Poor Matty! I suppose you're written up

for paracetamol, but you'll have to wait until the night charge brings the keys for the medicine trolley. Let me make you a nice cup of tea."

———————

A BANK OF plywood panels shielded the front of the site from the road, but Henry had an unobstructed view of the back from Tilly's bedroom window. Yet on entering the attic, Henry's stomach cramped. He hadn't seen Ursula Marshall in the six weeks or so since she'd seduced him, and he didn't want to. He preferred to pretend it hadn't happened. It certainly shouldn't have.

He wouldn't recognise her husband if he collided with him in the street, but she must've had one. Didn't most women? He imagined a burly brute who would strike first and ask questions later, or dispense with questions altogether. That Ursula had initiated it would be no defence. A court would decree he'd taken advantage of a woman when she was plastered.

Then there was Irene. He'd badly let her down. That their relationship limped along from year to year with no official status was immaterial. If he was serious about their future, he ought to be able to stay celibate for a week.

But his biggest betrayal was of Tilly. He'd defiled her sacred space. Although he'd sponged the quilt and washed the rest of the bedding, the room reeked of spunk. He wished he could keep away, but he was addicted to the view.

Until they demolished the clinic, Henry could hope for a reprieve. Fear drew him to the window whenever he was at home. Again and again, throughout the evening, postponing bedtime, taking a peek if he got up for the toilet in the night. His relief on finding the building intact rapidly lapsed into anxiety, compelling him to climb the stairs again. His brain had no compassion for his calf muscles.

It was nigh on a year since his demotion. Bereft of its foundations, his life began to crumble; the future would be bleaker still. How long before Irene dumped him? Before a deranged old woman knocked at the door?

THE SAME FORMULA for each new dance: "ladies" on one side of the hall, "gentlemen" – including women deputising for men, gentle or not – on the other. The teacher demonstrated their respective steps, and they copied. Hilda – a diminutive, shrunken figure even in spangled five-inch stilettos – appeared, at first glance, as if she belonged in an old folks' home, watching TV with a crocheted blanket over her knees. But she swayed with such energy and style – the male part as nimble as the female – Janice was in awe of her. Especially from the back, as she modelled the steps, her sun-and-cigarette ravaged face out of sight. Someone said Hilda was seventy. Matty's age!

Bopping to the beat of the cha-cha-cha, Janice couldn't quite believe she'd signed up for a ballroom dancing class. Sheena and the rest would be in stitches. But she loved it, from the rumba to the foot-tangling foxtrot, those old-fashioned dances made her feel graceful in a manner inconceivable in the stomps and jerks of disco. It helped that she'd landed a talented partner, who steered her smoothly around the floor even when her feet fought to rebel. While she balked at gender dictating who would lead and who would follow, when she surrendered, they glided like the couples on *Come Dancing*. Now, as they merged in a ballroom hold, her right hand clasping his left, her left hand resting on his shoulder, she registered the other women's envy. Like Hilda, Mervyn was uninspiring when immobile but, in movement, pure poetry.

When he'd invited her to go dancing, she took it for granted Mervyn had a nightclub in mind. But ballroom brought fewer complications: no mistaking an evening class for a date. Janice name-dropped Stuart as an extra safeguard, implying a stronger tie than was the case. In the improbable event of Mervyn's hands straying beyond where Hilda had taught the gentlemen to put them, she could do a DNA. He'd easily find another partner and, now he'd completed his year in rehabilitation and graduated to primary care, there'd be no embarrassment at work.

The cha-cha-cha had to be her favourite. As they sashayed through the steps, melding together, dividing and reuniting, twirling under Mervyn's raised arm, she thought of Matty. Janice blamed the music: "Tea for Two" chiming with both the choices group and the nauseating milked and sugared concoction on Ward 24. From what Hilda told the class about its origins, Matty would have been in Ghyllside by the time the cha-cha-cha migrated from Cuba. But she must have caught the quickstep and the waltz, maybe the tango, until robbed of her dancing shoes at twenty. She might have done the chlorpromazine shuffle at Ghyllside, in the theatre now used for the mind-numbing packaging work that constituted industrial therapy, but where was the joy in that?

Chapter 46

FIFTY-EIGHT! ALREADY? HIS father had a business and two sprogs well in advance of *his* sixth decade, while Henry was stranded on the starting blocks of life. Unfortunately, his knees, like his attitudes, were antique, unfit for two more years' enslavement to the council. In contrast, his girlfriend – partner? paramour? bit on the side? – had yet to turn forty, young enough for another kiddie, for another career. Would retirement accentuate the age difference? Would she trade him in for a man with fewer miles on the clock?

Don't get so maudlin, you divvy! It must be worth something that she'd persuaded him to take the day off, and cleared her diary, to spend his birthday as a couple.

Although she hadn't *completely* cleared her diary. Fetching his present at breakfast time, she'd admitted there was one client she couldn't cancel. Feeling floored, he attempted to lift his mood with humour, but Irene didn't appreciate his joke that the denim jeans and loud chequered shirt meant she fancied courting a cowboy.

"Not a cowboy, Henry, but someone in tune with the nineties. Not a pre-war clone of your dad." Irene gulped down her coffee and grabbed her bag. "I want to see you in that clobber." At the door, she paused. "So I'll have the pleasure of ripping it off."

Rinsing the cups and plates, Henry tried to shed his sense of abandonment. She'd be back sharpish. But the intervening hour would be hollow with nothing to fill it. Wheeling the Ewbank across the carpet, his spirits sank deeper. Cleaning had no purpose if Irene wouldn't move in. For her evening class he simply sprinkled Ajax down the lav and spread fresh sheets on the bed.

October: cementing his inadequacies, his birthday tainted the entire month. He didn't know *how* to celebrate, being deficient in some mystery ingredient that rendered life fun. He'd *never* had it. At school, he'd cashed in his birthday postal orders for balsawood model-kits and sherbet lemons, neither of which lasted beyond his Sunday thank-you letter home.

Tilly had the flair, but she left when he'd barely begun measuring his years on two hands. A cake with six candles, his sister prompting him to make a wish before blowing them out. A memory or a dream?

A chemical smell caught his throat after peeling back the cellophane from his new shirt, a milder version of Irene's lotions and potions, hairsprays and shampoos. Would Tilly have chosen something more subtle? Plain white, or a blue stripe he could wear with a suit?

He stowed the pins in an ashtray and extracted the ring of plastic from under the collar. Shaking out the shirt, the folds persisted from where it had been packed around the cardboard sheet. Should he give it a once-over with the iron? Henry chuckled. If she kept her word, Irene wouldn't notice the creases.

THE GUESTS BECOME fractious if cooped up indoors, so the ever-resourceful circus girl has arranged a charabanc excursion. Assembled at the majestic frontage at two o'clock, they pose as sleuths in their outdoor apparel, hatted and coated and hand-bagged. The shrimp-woman sulks about leaving her baby, but otherwise the group is in good cheer.

When the bus circles the rose bed, Matty is astonished to see the butler at the wheel. Regrettably, her mother has had to let the chauffeur go, but he ought to have passed on his peaked cap to his replacement.

The motor is also galling initially. Matty anticipated a full-length coach but this is no bigger than a delivery van. However, an Arthurian emblem on the side redeems the vehicle; what it lacks in size it remedies in gravitas.

As they troop aboard, it proves adequate for their party of a dozen. In wartime, even the grandest families must economise.

All the window seats are taken when Matty clambers up from the kerb. She asks a gentleman to give up his seat so she might wave to the estate workers as they cruise by but, unable to make herself heard above the rumble of the engine, she makes do with an aisle seat.

They are chugging down the drive when the circus girl gets up to ask if anyone has guessed where they are going. The person obstructing her view of the window wears a dark three-piece suit; are they destined for the cemetery? But everyone else is so jolly.

Excitement mounts as the circus girl confirms they are to inspect the site of their new accommodation. Matty turns to her neighbour. "It might be somewhat modest. These are straitened times."

At the word *modest*, the man pets his groin and counts the buttons on his fly. Matty ponders the enigma of trousers, whether they would be less bother than stockings and a suspender belt. Shifting her skirt to check hers remain attached, she discovers a unified garment from toes to waist. She resolves to bestow an award on the inventor.

The funeral man puts a paw on the nylon at the top of her leg while undoing his fly with the other. Matty informs him she has enough money, having cashed in a chit this morning at the bank. Lowering her skirt fails to disengage his left hand from her leg. With his right he ferrets in the opening in his trousers and digs out his joey. The giant slug amuses her but, loath to offend him by sniggering, she bites her lip.

Her flesh squashed between his finger and thumb, Matty endures the discomfort by inhaling through her mouth. He must have suffered some calamity, his wife dead in childbirth. Yet her sympathetic smile goes unnoticed, his faraway eyes half-closed as he jigs his joey.

Matty wants to retrieve her bag from the floor. She

might need money after all. But she dare not disturb the widower. As with waking a sleep-walker, it is dangerous to interrupt.

As the man huffs, and his hand abandons her leg, Matty feels another on her shoulder. "Come and sit at the front!" The circus girl looks seasick.

Trundling down the aisle, the rocking tosses her into the seats at either side. Thinking to take the circus girl's arm for ballast, Matty turns, but the girl is consoling the widower.

An enormous thump! A wallop on her head.

Matty is horizontal. The butler squats beside her. Who is at the wheel?

———————

IRENE WAS FOND of taking a catnap afterwards, and Henry was fond of watching her, admiring her ability to let go. Yet her slumber seemed less peaceful today, her breathing laboured, snuffling and squeaking like a baby and its toy. Her face, mottled and swollen, looked as if setting the scene for a cold. After her appointment, she'd been strangely subdued, and Henry was reduced to undressing himself.

His stomach rumbled. Would they get to Ennerdale in time for lunch? Under the bed clothes, Irene scraped at her arms and torso. When he called her name, she stopped agitating but didn't wake up.

Then she did: spluttering, hands to her throat, eyes wide. "I can't breathe!" When she batted back the duvet, her skin was inflamed. As if she'd scrubbed herself with a cheese grater.

Henry bashed her between the shoulder blades,

struggling to dredge up what little he'd absorbed from the basic first aid training at work. Irene continued wheezing, biting at the air.

"Don't worry!" *Don't die on me!* Yelling reassurance and whispering a plea. "I'll get help. Where's your phone?"

Irene flapped her wrists; sounds leaked from her lips but they couldn't pass for words. The mobile would be in her bag, no nearer than the house phone. Henry raced downstairs to dial 999.

NOT BEING A relative, Henry was refused a ride in the ambulance. Their roles reversed, Irene would've smashed such fuddy-duddy prohibitions, but Henry caved in. A wretched little boy, watching the woman he loved leave without him.

But this time he could follow. He dressed and rang for a taxi. It didn't take the driver long to coax the story out of him. "Exact same thing happened to me, marra. Flight frey Tenerife. Packet of salted peanuts. Throat seized up in a flash."

"But you're fine now? No after-effects?"

"A right maff they made cutting into her windpipe and poking a biro through it. Jammy we had a doctor on board."

"How's the wife now? She recovered okay?" Better to hear about a woman. Their throats might be different to men's.

"She was at yam, touch wood. Golfing trip with the lads. Lucky she missed it. Faints at the sight of blood."

"But the woman on the plane? *She* survived?"

"Couldn't tell you, marra! Last I saw they carted her off

on a stretcher. You a golfing man yourself?"

AWAITING PERMISSION TO see Irene, Henry petitioned the Great Architect of the Universe to spare her. He'd parade in jeans and cowboy shirts Monday to Sunday. Get a passport and visit her sister in Spain. Sell The Willows. Set her up in a shop with her name over the window and a youngster for the dyes.

He was relieved no biro had been inserted into Irene's windpipe; no artificial airway of any kind. An antihistamine injection had stopped the swelling before it sealed her throat. He found her beached on a couch in a curtained cubicle, an advert for home baking, her eyes two currants above doughy cheeks. Seeing Henry, she began to sob, splodged mascara adding bramble smears to a face stippled raspberry pink. "Oh, Henry!" Her voice dubbed by a lesser woman, prone to panic and doubt.

Irene was no cry-baby. *Her* tears couldn't be ignored. Piercing his heart, they begged something from him. Something, as with the capacity to delight in birthdays, he didn't have to give.

But he could try. He rushed forward and, one buttock balanced on the edge of the examination table, wrapped his arm around her shoulders. With his free hand he squeezed hers. "It's all right now. I'm here." He had to stand on tiptoe to get close enough to hug her; after a while, his shoulder nagged and his thigh began to twitch. Yet he felt ennobled that a woman wept in his embrace.

Bent on being the man she needed, Henry didn't budge when the curtain rings clinked. But he loosened his hold and turned his head when the fellow growled. A beast of a man, the type to bare his biceps in the bitterest winter, paws like bricks at the end of brawny arms. "Well, you've surpassed yourself, Irene. I never thought you'd two-time me with such a feckless waste of skin!"

Chapter 47

MATTY GLARES AT the drapes. Who in the Lord's infinite wisdom chose grey? Had they consulted her, she would have recommended yellow. Even black would be preferable, it being a jelly-baby colour.

The hangings depress her, drabness secluding her tiny cell. The nuns preach acquiescence, but Matty yearns for a life beyond these diminished horizons. Yet, for all the sense she can make of the bovine mumbles and intermittent squeals breaking through the barrier, it might be on Mars.

Do not succumb to despair, Matty! Entrust yourself to the Almighty! Or His loyal servant, the butler who will shortly present his report. But, oh, these aching bones! How could he leave her undefended?

The butler had set off to use the telephone, promising to return in two minutes. Two minutes precisely: fusing his middle and index fingers into the starting pistol at a sack race and firing them at the ceiling. More than two minutes have passed since then.

She was ill-advised to lie down, like Goldilocks, on an unfamiliar bed. But raising her head as a prelude to deserting it, the room spins. If only she knew what lay behind the drapes. When the boy conjured monsters from the gloom, Matty would carry him to the window and show him the stars. Explain the sky was full of fairies, the twinkling lights their wands. But there are no good fairies behind *these* miserable curtains. No windows. No sky.

Damn that squeaky wheel! Has the butler gone for a can of oil? If so, he ought to have clarified his intentions, with another finger to indicate he required a minute more. Or has he gone to procure a bottle of aspirin? He would have gathered before she did that her head is sore.

The bed is so firm, she is bound to bruise. No bedding, not even the basics of sheets and blankets, let alone a counterpane or a quilt. Is that a clue? The air is tinged with antiseptic. The rumblings she took for Martians or cattle are the groans of injured men.

Now she really *must* get about her business. *Her* condition is trifling compared to theirs. Her mother would be mortified to see Matty lying on her back feeling sorry for herself with genuine invalids a hop, skip and jump away. The butler cannot pander to *her* when there are yawning wounds to be plugged, raging thirsts to be slaked.

Inch by inch, she shuffles her legs to the edge of the couch. Cupping her chin in case of spillage, she rolls onto her side. Gingerly, she pushes up on her arms and lowers her feet to the floor. She stands, clinging to the couch and panting, waiting for the universe to realign.

Her home has been transformed so swiftly. She was forewarned of the *possibility*, but she should have been updated in advance of the soldiers' influx. Matty has done her best to prepare her guests for the disruption but, due to Hitler's tortures, the poor souls are slow to adapt.

Matty laughs. She *can* be pompous: the butler is correct to tease her. Important as she might be in society circles, the generals' priorities lie elsewhere. They must have engineered the outing in the charabanc to evacuate the premises for the conversion.

Some misfortune intercepted the excursion. The bomb! Matty would never forgive herself if a guest was maimed. Or killed. But if anyone *was* so unfortunate, let it be the shrimp-woman. It would be an abomination to see the circus girl's life curtailed.

With work to be done, she will have no truck with self-pity. Braced by the couch, Matty lumbers along to the end. Her public expects her to display some initiative. If she cannot assist with bandaging and brow-mopping, she would willingly recite.

She measures the steps to the curtain by eye. She must not forsake the couch until she has established whether she can walk unaided. Tasting bile, she queries whether she has the stomach for the task. As a girl, the schoolyard frothed with stories of soldiers with gaping holes where their noses and other protrusions had been. Feeling with her fingers, *her* nose is unimpaired.

She must trust that duty will conquer squeamishness. The young Princess Elizabeth does not shirk *her* responsibilities. Nevertheless, Matty steals another moment to compose herself.

It comes through to her that her father is among the casualties. Will she recognise a man she has never met? How splendid if she could whittle out the shrapnel. If Matty saves him, her mother need not marry the prince.

Hope propels her across two feet of linoleum, between the flaps of sombre curtain and into a corridor. A wall confronts her, painted an insipid porridge colour barely brighter than the drapes. Both left and right, cloth partitions shield the men. She must breach the barricade and enquire how she can be of use.

Matty turns to her left, prodding the material until she discovers where the edges meet. She titters: a feeble defence against the enemy, yet it deters the volunteer aides.

Etiquette demands she announce herself before barging in. With nothing to knock against, Matty coughs. In a chamber identical to the one she vacated, a man snores. Garbed in checked shirt and workmen's trousers, he makes a more credible labourer than soldier. Excepting a puffy jawline, he appears in finer fettle than she is. Malingerer! She will have him court marshalled and shot.

Matty will go and shake him. Treat him to the lash of her tongue. But a sudden movement stalls her. The tiniest alteration in the angle of his head. Or a flicker of the ceiling light fiddling with the shadows. She *knows* this man, but he is not an estate employee. She came for her father and found this charlatan instead.

She must act, but she fears she will faint. A tiny yelp, more animal than human, escapes her lips. She gazes around for a weapon, but there is only a hefty tubular chair. She cannot deal with him without assistance. If she visits another closet, will she find a soldier with a gun? Would he believe her story?

She has no option but to try. If *he* catches her, she is ruined. Turning, she barges through the drapes, but the fabric snarls her, enveloping her in its folds. Gasping for air, she brushes her body, but cannot locate her skirt.

Hands, strong but kindly, lift her from the floor. "What are you like, Matty? I leave you for two minutes ..." The butler escorts her to a vacant cubicle and helps her onto the couch.

———————

HENRY HADN'T REALISED he'd nodded off until a commotion in the corridor rattled his jaw. From cheeks to chin his face felt distended: Desperate Dan minus the comic hero's strength. He'd be mincemeat if Eric showed up again.

Not a cuckold on the warpath; behind the screen of cinder-coloured curtains, Henry heard someone fall. He ought to investigate, but any activity beyond a blink might antagonise his jaw.

The ruckus paused, migrated to the compartment to his right. Supine on an examination table, neither his pain nor the speckled ceiling-tiles could distract him from the jabber. Two baritones and a shrill soprano. The man with the cultured accent asked if this hurt, or that. The other bloke, a local, deferred to the female, who whimpered more than spoke. Henry discerned the medic's frustration.

Unable either to make sense of the conversation or to

switch it off, Henry registered a similar impatience. Like tuning into a radio play halfway through. The female – child or imbecile – fought shy of the simplest question. The Cumbrian, instead of collaborating with the medic, proved a cruddy go-between.

A foretaste of Ghyllside graduates as neighbours? A sprint to Mr Patel's for a bottle of Valpolicella and a frozen lasagne would stretch to a marathon if one of them headed the queue, counting out the price of a packet of fags in two-pence pieces while the attendant perused the top-shelf magazines. One of *them* could be in the next cubicle. Perhaps the old biddy the social worker yattered on about at the meeting. The girl who went doolally instead of watching him.

Hurry up! Henry's jaw throbbed so violently it might have been preparing for take-off. What a day! Irene's allergic reaction put the fear of God into the pair of them, drew them closer until Eric fetched up. Henry's leg going into cramp as he unravelled himself from Irene. His offer to sit down and discuss it amicably answered by Eric's fist.

That wouldn't be the end of it. Could he rise to the occasion? As a boy, he'd been a magnet for bullies; could he protect himself from Eric? And Irene too?

At last, the voices were silenced, the radio dead. The curtains by his feet divided and a young chap slipped through the gap. His white coat hung on his weedy frame like a school blazer he'd yet to grow into, so Henry was taken aback when he boomed: "Henry Windsor? Seems you've been in the wars."

His father believed warfare the making of a man; no

wonder Henry, born too late for that developmental milestone, felt incomplete. But Henry had taken a blow for Irene, albeit an involuntary one. Even conscripts could be heroic; could he summon the courage to battle on?

He might not need to. Her affair out in the open, Irene's marriage would be defunct. Besides, she couldn't stay with a thug.

Henry fixed his thoughts on the future, as the doctor manoeuvred his jaw. When he'd finished, he picked up the case notes and guffawed. "Not much of a birthday, Mr Windsor."

On the contrary, it was perfect: the pain a path to conjugal bliss. Irene would move into The Willows. She had nowhere else to go.

Chapter 48

1932–1936

WHEN WE MEET, you will judge me. I cannot blame you for that. But you must agree I made a fair crack at mothering, for a lass of thirteen with her own mother gone.

I will never forget that October night when Mr Windsor knocked on my bedroom door to inform me I had a brother. But I couldn't bring myself to thread pink ribbon through his knitted jackets. The only ribbon in the house was black.

Week after week, I dragged myself to school, a charcoal armband rupturing mustard and maroon. I'd arrive home to a wailing baby in a soiled napkin while the nurse chatted with the butcher's boy at the back door. Even so, the prince refused to issue her marching orders, although he could have replaced her ten times over. I think he appreciated someone cheerful and attractive in the house, the rest of us mired in grief.

Then, one morning in the run-up to Easter, I came downstairs to the scent of burnt porridge and the bagpipe drone of a mewling babe. A frazzled Mrs Embleton stabbed my brother's lips with the rubber teat of a bottle while he averted his head. As soon as I took him, he settled – Mrs Embleton too. "Is Nurse still abed?" I assumed she had taken bad.

"You didn't hear owt, up in that attic? According to Mr Windsor, she done a flit in the night."

My brother smiled, as if glad to be shot of her. "Who'll look after Hal?"

Mrs Embleton wiped her palms on her apron. "He's asked me to do it. Till he finds another girl."

She could barely cope with the cooking and cleaning. She could watch the baby for an hour, but full-time duties would be the death of them both. Mr Windsor, having left for work, could not prevent me swapping my uniform for a house dress. Before long, I had exchanged the rule of the school bell for the pulse of my brother's cry.

Nevertheless, I imagined it a temporary solution. Mr Windsor clearly agreed. Approaching my brother's first birthday, and the anniversary of Mother's death, he suggested I resume my studies. He had found a woman who would care for Hal in the daytime amongst her own brood.

I could not bear to leave him. His demands might sap my energy, but his love more than replenished it. With him I felt so close to Mother I almost forgot her passing: wheeling his perambulator to the cemetery and doing for him as she had done for me. It was as if I had become her, but I could not share so strange a sentiment with Mr Windsor. I had to tell him something: to ease *his* conscience and for his cronies at the Masonic Lodge. "Thank you, but I've had all the education I need."

"I thought you had ambitions. Fancied yourself a doctor."

Now it seemed childish whimsy, but my hope to be of service remained intact. "I wish to train as a nanny." Even untutored, I had fared better than the wastrel *he'd* recruited.

"I believe a nanny can command a sizeable salary." Mr Windsor looked aggrieved, but, as a businessman, he sniffed the benefit to him. "If that's what you want, then staying at home with Henry will stand you in good stead."

HENRY'S SECOND BIRTHDAY: I baked a cake and cut it into the shape of a bear. Mr Windsor shut the shop early to have tea with us, shed his coat and dived into the spirit of it, applauding when Henry blew out his candles and striking a match to reignite them so he could do it again.

After Mrs Embleton had left, and I'd put the birthday boy to bed, I joined the prince in the sitting room and poured him a sherry.

"It doesn't get any easier, does it?"

"Hal's no bother."

Mr Windsor shook his head. "I'm a husk without her, Matilda. A man might not show it, but our emotions run deep."

Not knowing how to reply, I sat in silence. Presently, he would ask me to refill his glass from the decanter or turn on the wireless or read from *Verse Worth Remembering*.

"You're becoming increasingly like her." His voice quavered. "Prettier by the day."

Squirming in my seat, I joked that my nose was sharper than Mother's, my deportment less composed.

He scarcely noticed, as if I was a waxwork, not a flesh-and-blood girl. "Such a beauty. Lucky the lad who lights on *you* at the altar."

"I'll never marry."

"So young, yet so cruel."

I did not ask whom he deemed the victim of this cruelty: me or mankind. Then, as suddenly as it had begun, the spell was broken and he was himself again. I was relieved when he took his drink to his room.

Alone in my attic, released from the pressure of his gaze, I chided myself for my coldness. My own anguish should not stem my sympathy for *his*. What it must cost him to flatter the girl who magnified his sorrow with reminders of his loss.

Old as he was, it sent my girlish heart aflutter that he regarded my looks equal to Mother's. I *would* be amenable to marriage, eventually, if I could bypass *relations*. I might relish ingesting compliments along with my breakfast egg and toast.

I WAS DRESSING my brother in his suit when a letter came to say Violet had succumbed to scarlatina and been sent home to recuperate. My immediate thought was not *whether* to go to her that day, but *when*. Mr Windsor could not object to my leaving his son in his custody on a Sunday, but would God excuse me from church? I decided He wouldn't miss *one* less voice raised in worship, whereas a visit would make a genuine difference to Violet and allow me to atone for my wounding party invitation all those years ago.

"If they've sent her home she must be contagious," said Mr Windsor. "Can you afford to jeopardise your own health? And Henry just over the mumps."

Ambling to church, swinging the boy by the arms, I felt grateful for his guidance. "I'll write to her after luncheon. Henry can draw her a picture."

"And tomorrow you should ring Browne's and order a hamper."

"On your account?" I stopped, causing the boy's arms to stretch so widely he squealed.

"We're no better than heathens if we can't offer a neighbour Christian fellowship."

He accepted the folks of The Marsh as his neighbours? I'd presumed he felt contempt for my humble roots. I'd lived nigh on four years in his house and still confused his character. Nor did I admit his kindness in keeping me on.

Sitting on the hard pew, focused less on the pulpit than on curbing my brother's fidgeting, I realised his father *was* fond of me after a fashion. I'd thought him aloof, but perhaps he found *me* remote. I resolved to show more respect. I'd start by discarding that nickname; it was childish to refer to him, even in private, as the prince. But what to call him? Mr Windsor was too formal and Uncle George made Henry both brother and cousin.

I patted his knee to steady his leg. Although he lacked a mother, his sister's love was abundant. How did Henry perceive it? Was I merely a nursemaid to him?

Our family might defy convention, but Henry needn't suffer for it. Would he feel more secure if we shared the same father? If we three connected like points on a triangle, not a line with a child linking unrelated ends?

I would avoid mentioning I wasn't a Windsor and call Mr Windsor Father if it eased the boy's mind. We already had unofficial names for each other: me Tilly, he Hal.

"WHAT MESSAGE DO you want with it, madam?"

Oh, the joy of the telephone! The clerk couldn't see I was no madam, but a girl masquerading as an adult. But I could picture Violet's face when the hamper arrived. Mrs Braithwaite's too. "*Wishing you a speedy recovery.*"

"And?" The clerk's pause made me feel an impostor. But Father reiterated before setting off that morning I should not stint. *Wishing you a speedy recovery from Mr Windsor? Wishing you a speedy recovery, kind regards, George?*

"*Wishing you a speedy recovery.* Full stop."

"You'd like it sent anonymously?"

I would not repeat the blunder of those party invitations. Philanthropy does not flaunt its generosity. Violet would know who sent it – who else could meet the expense of a basket from Browne's? – and know she owed nothing in return.

HENRY'S THIRD BIRTHDAY. Father bought him a train set and we all had fun assembling the track and sending the engines on a tour of his bedroom. We could have played with it until midnight but even big boys of three need a regular bedtime – not easy to enforce when the person responsible for getting him into his pyjamas and brushing his teeth and telling him a story is as reluctant as he is for his special day to end. I knew that once his son had settled down to sleep, Father would flag. I didn't so much fear his sadness as his mode of expressing it. I hadn't forgotten how oddly he behaved the previous year.

When I slipped into the parlour, I found the curtains drawn and the lamps lit on the bureau. Father slouched in his usual chair, hands hidden in his trouser pockets. "Sit down, Matilda."

I felt his gaze on my breasts as I took the seat opposite, spreading the skirt of my frock so it would not crumple. Mr Windsor liked us looking tidy even if we rarely ventured further than church but I might have chosen something with a higher neckline. Or changed into a plain house dress after the celebrations.

Mr Windsor cleared his throat. "I have a friend coming for tea on Sunday."

"A visitor!" We hadn't received anyone socially since Mother was alive. "I'll bake a Battenberg. Or Madeira cake if you prefer." I couldn't trust Mrs Embleton to do it. She was becoming more scatter-brained by the day.

"A cake would be most appreciated." Father nipped at the creases down his trousers. "But you might make yourself scarce."

"I could take Hal to the park."

"Mrs Penrose is eager to meet my son."

But not your daughter? "All right. I'll stay in my room."

"I'd rather you left the house entirely. Otherwise it confuses the boy."

It confused *me*. "Is it about school?" But a schoolmistress wouldn't come on a Sunday and Henry wasn't due to start infants' for a couple of years.

Mr Windsor seemed unwilling to enlighten me. He twisted the rebuff into an indulgence. "You work so hard, Matilda. Take some time for yourself."

I couldn't tell if the thundering in my chest was excitement or anxiety. I hadn't left the house unaccompanied since I wore mustard and maroon.

"You should visit your friends at The Marsh. Take them a basket of fruit."

FATHER WOULD HAVE paid for a bigger one, but I bought a basket I could manage on the bus. Yet it looked colossal on Mrs Braithwaite's kitchen table. The colours too fierce. Nursing my teacup as I sat beside the range, I felt equally misplaced.

Violet had been back at Holker Hall for several weeks, apparently. Neither of us mentioned the hamper, but Mrs Braithwaite let me know they were both offended I'd failed to visit. I explained I'd wanted to, but couldn't chance passing on the infection to Hal.

Mrs Braithwaite sniggered, revealing a chain of rotten molars. "When Mildred Doherty had the measles, your mam left you tucked up in bed with her to get them over and done with. You're doing that bairn no favours cosseting him like a china doll. Mumps and measles and scarlatina are what childhood's about."

Since she was in no mood to be cordial, I drained my cup, made my excuses and left. Outside, the sun bounced off the pavement, blinding me momentarily after the inner gloom. So I didn't notice Hilda until she hailed me, didn't hear her at first above the squeals of the seagulls and bairns running riot in the street.

Hilda embraced me as Mrs Braithwaite ought to have done, albeit with an odour of stale tobacco and carbolic soap. "Away and sit down." She dragged me to the doorstep as if it was a throne. A chap in shirtsleeves without a collar rose to make space for me. Breathlessly, Hilda introduced us.

"You're not from round here, then?" said the man, Bert Crenshaw, in response to my *Pleased to meet you.* I couldn't recall any Crenshaws at Lawrence Street, so he couldn't have been local himself.

Hilda giggled. "It's the elocution lessons."

Bert nodded. "Lady Violet's better half."

Hilda dismissed him to fetch some tea. When I protested I'd slaked my thirst at Mrs Braithwaite's, she didn't shout him back. "Us lasses have some catching up to do." From her proprietary manner and his obedience, I deduced they were courting. While the only young men *I* spoke to were delivering groceries to the door! I felt as gauche as a schoolgirl meeting a starlet. How had I been left behind?

With her hair in pin curls and her fashionable frock – although, up close, I could see the fabric was shoddy – and the practised insouciance with which she exhaled cigarette smoke, Hilda had style. Shy initially, as the cigarette she thrust upon me had me gasping like a tubercular, Hilda was so friendly, I couldn't *not* relax. I swiftly adapted to the stench of the docks and the – cosy or claustrophobic? –

proximity of the houses opposite.

Describing her job at the West Cumberland Laundry, Hilda made it sound an eternal party; some of the girls had formed a dance troupe. As for romance, it was a game: she let Bert feel her bits through her brassiere and bloomers but wouldn't allow him *inside* her clothing until they were engaged. When she suggested we make up a foursome to go to the Stanley Hall one evening, I was tempted. But my first duty was to Hal.

"Add a tot of rum to his bedtime cocoa and he won't know you're gone."

I would never stoop to that. But leaving my brother was simpler than soliciting Father's permission. If he disapproved, could he prevent me? Could a young lady from Briarwood visit a dance hall with her reputation intact? I had no-one to ask.

"Do give it a go, Matilda. For all I said about roving hands, Bert's a gentleman and his friend Walter's a saint. I could do your hair and make-up and you could lend me one of your frocks."

"Let me see what I can do." If Mrs Penrose came to tea again, I'd be looking for somewhere to go. And Hilda, now *she'd* matured, was a less complicated friend than Violet had ever been.

FATHER STOPPED FIDDLING with his cufflinks and stared at me sternly. "We need to discuss a topic of some delicacy."

Defiantly, I met his gaze. Only in my imagination had I been on a foursome with Hilda. Only in my dreams had Walter acquired sufficient substance to hold me in his arms.

"In due course, I expect to have a new wife."

Was he fishing for congratulations? "Mrs Penrose?"

"I'm not yet in a position to propose. So not a word to Henry or Mrs Embleton. Especially not to Mrs Embleton."

So why take me into his confidence? I hadn't even met her.

"If I do remarry," he continued, "my wife would not want another woman in the house."

"Mrs Embleton?" With so many jobs now beyond her we'd barely mark her absence.

Father glowered. "I'm talking about you, Matilda. I thought it fair to warn you in time to make alternative arrangements."

"You're asking me to leave The Willows? To leave my brother?"

"You can't have anticipated staying here permanently?"

"No, but ..."

"You wished to train as a nanny."

"After Henry goes to boarding school." At nine or ten, with a few years at Briarwood Juniors behind him.

"You might have the opportunity to begin that process earlier. I must know your intentions before making further enquiries."

"My intentions?" Wasn't that what a father should ask a suitor?

"Whether that's still in your sights. I believe the most prestigious training college is in London. I'm willing to pay your fees but the best isn't cheap. I'd want assurance of your commitment."

From The Marsh to London, like one of my stories.

Perhaps I'd meet a real prince there. But living three hundred miles from my brother? Bereft of his cuddles, his cheeky grin? "Henry needs me. I'm the nearest to a mother he has."

"And I'm indebted to you for plugging the gap. You've done a superb job for one so young. Hopefully, he'll have a stepmother soon, and you'll be free to pursue your own interests."

"You can't make him switch affections at the drop of a hat."

"Which is why I'm acquainting him with the future Mrs Windsor in advance. But while we're on the subject, your mollycoddling is unhelpful. It poisons his attitude to anyone else. I was ashamed of his sullenness on Sunday."

"He'd be wondering where I was." He'd clamped his arms around my legs the instant I got home. "We've barely been separated in his life."

"Which is making him soft. But let's say no more on the matter. It's my fault you've spoilt him. I let you muddle through alone."

"I wasn't muddling." I wasn't alone. Mother's spirit showed me what to do.

"I've no desire to argue. As I say, the error is mine. I've been preoccupied, neglectful, but that's about to change. The future Mrs Windsor will take him under her wing."

"While I'm out in the cold?"

"Oh, stop being so theatrical! I saw you for a dramatist the minute we met. Those ridiculous public speaking contests! No, sending you to train as a Norland nanny is not exposing you to the elements. Nor is retaining your room for visits. I'm trying to do what's best for everyone. A little cooperation wouldn't go amiss."

I DID NOT *ask* Mr Windsor, I *informed* him. His child, his responsibility. He could take Henry from me and give him to a stranger. He could take my home, but he would not take my love for that child.

I savoured the rage he fired in me. I hadn't felt more driven since Mother was alive. I woke up singing, my voice soaring heavenward as my feet descended to my brother's room. As I reached his door, Henry joined in. "All Things Bright and Beautiful." Mr Windsor wouldn't intrude on a hymn.

I refused to pine, to grovel. The red rosette was his, mine the moral victory. I'd make him suffer for the prize. But I'd do it subtly. Keep my comforts as long as I could. I'd burn the prince's coal, eat his food and wear the cloth he'd paid for. But I would not submit to his rule.

I told him I'd be out until late on Friday. That he must read his son a story and put him to bed. I did not mention I was going to the Stanley Hall with Hilda. And two handsome men.

If I took to Walter and he took to me, anything could happen. Before Mrs Penrose issued my marching orders, I might be married myself.

THROUGH NIGH ON four years as my brother's nursemaid, I never felt deprived. But, on discovering dancing, I lived for Friday nights. For all the heartache of leaving Henry, when the front door closed behind me, I skipped down Sheepwash

Lane.

Walter was not as handsome as I'd imagined. To tell the truth, he wasn't handsome at all, with tombstone teeth and receding hair. But I didn't notice his teeth on the dancefloor where, with the slightest pressure on my back, he twirled me around the room.

I relished the ritual of getting ready with Hilda in her bedroom at The Marsh. The stories she told about the girls at the laundry. The way her tongue parted her lips as she powdered my cheeks. I thought we'd carry on indefinitely, so I was brought up short when I arrived one Friday to find a jug of ale on the dresser and a half-empty glass alongside. As I removed my coat, Hilda quaffed its remaining contents, refilled it and offered it to me. I demurred.

"Don't be an old maid!"

I'd never been within spitting distance of beer before and, although not as disagreeable as the pea-soup bouquet of the brewery, it did smell sour.

"The glass is clean if that's what you're bothered about."

Cautious not to appear uppity, I took a swig. Swallowed. Scowled.

Hilda laughed. "You'll get used to it. Same as smoking."

I still hadn't taken to smoking and doubted I would. "What's the grand occasion?"

"It's Bert's birthday. Nineteen today."

"I wish I'd known. I'd have baked a cake."

"I've got a better treat in store for him. If all goes well, I'm giving him my cherry." Hilda tilted her head, like an actress in a magazine.

Her cherry? But she'd vetoed cake. Cocktails? Bubbly

drinks in conical glasses with a piece of glacé fruit skewered across the rim?

"You don't think I'm fast? It isn't fair to make him wait till we're married and Da won't consent till I'm eighteen."

"You're considering *relations*?"

"Keep your voice down. My da's downstairs."

Despite her veneer of sophistication, she needed a wiser friend. "Do take care of your reputation, Hilda."

"Give over, Matilda. Everybody knows you can't get caught if you do it standing up."

THE BEER HAD left me wobbly when we met up with the boys. But I'd be right as rain once the Savana Band struck up. When Bert insisted on a kiss for his birthday, it occurred to me I should protect my own reputation. But I couldn't deny a friend.

For a few hours, I forgot Hilda's foolishness as I tangoed, foxtrotted, quickstepped and waltzed. Nor did I give a thought to The Willows. Afterwards, hot and pleasantly tired, I strolled on Walter's arm towards the bus station, Hilda and Bert slightly ahead.

We were almost there when Bert ushered Hilda into a ginnel. Some of the sparkle ebbed from the evening. Should I hang on to wish Hilda goodnight? As I shilly-shallied, Walter indicated the next alley along. When I declined, he looked hurt. "A kiss and a cuddle, Matilda. Is that too much to ask?"

"I'm worn out, Walter. I'm ready for home."

"I should've known you weren't serious." Sulky, like Henry told to tidy his toys. "What would a smart lass from

Briarwood want with a gowk such as me?"

"Don't say that." I stroked his cheek. I wasn't a snob.

Before I knew it, I was in the ginnel with his lips locked onto mine. If I ignored the press of the wall against my back and my feet's fatigue, it was bearable, as cocoa might be bearable when you'd requested tea. Walter expressed his gratitude in low moans and fluttering eyelids. Even as he thrust his pelvis against mine, squashing my buttocks on the alley wall, I deemed it a minor inconvenience. A small price for hours on the dancefloor. He'd get bored eventually and let me go.

Chapter 49

October 1990

HEATHER LOOKED AGHAST. "Did she notice?"

"Thankfully," said Janice, "she was oblivious. Lost in her own little world."

After Matty's fall, Clive had driven the minibus to the West Cumberland to take Matty to Casualty. Although not insured to do so, Janice would have been willing to drive the rest back to Ghyllside, but Clive advised taking taxis. The residents didn't appear unduly upset that their excursion had ended in a hospital car park, and crashed out in the lounge on returning to Tuke House. Uncertain what to do about Billy Dewhirst, Janice had bleeped Graham Scott, who dashed from his budgetary control meeting as if from the hobs of hell. Having guided her through a critical incident form, Graham delegated the task of engaging with Billy directly to the medics.

To be fair on Graham, he'd urged her to vent her feelings once the paperwork was complete. But Janice couldn't open up to a man whose gut response to the name 'Rogers', was not Carl, the founding father of humanistic psychotherapy, but Buck, the hero of a fictional space opera. She'd been ready to leave the ward when Heather pitched up. They'd settled themselves in the nurses' office, huddled over cups of tea like refugees of some freak-weather catastrophe. Now approaching five o'clock, neither could envisage going home until they heard from Clive.

"Makes you wonder how she'll manage in Briarwood," said Heather.

"Isn't she at greater risk here?"

"From Billy Dewhirst? He wouldn't know where to put it."

"I'm starting to see the sense of single-sex wards."

"Separating men and women as if they were alien species? It's not *normal*."

"At least old dears like Matty would be safe."

"We could keep everyone safe in cages. Accidents happen in psychiatry, Janice. Once she's installed in Briarwood, we'll joke about today."

"I hope so. Maybe I need another trip to Ward 24 to remind me how awful things *can* be."

"Even that's changing, now Sister Henderson's retired."

"Karen's got her work cut out turning *that* regime around."

"So long as she stops the care assistants serving the tea with the milk and sugar …"

Duly prompted, Janice took a sip. "Urgh, you've done a

Sister Henderson on me!"

"Sorry!" Heather swapped Janice's mug for hers. "Or shall I make you a fresh one?"

Widening her eyes, Janice adopted a pedagogical tone. "Heather, would you ask Janice if she prefers her tea with sugar, or without?"

They were giggling unprofessionally when a key turned in the lock and the door opened. "Glad you two are enjoying yourselves," said Clive.

"How's Matty?"

Clive flopped onto the nearest chair. "Fucking general nurses! *Haven't you got doctors at Ghyllside?* As if you can't have medical *and* mental health problems."

"They didn't see her?"

"Oh, they *saw* her! Had to threaten them with the GNC."

Janice had never seen Clive so agitated. Although devoted to the patients, she thought of him as Graham's yes-man. In her first year at Ghyllside, she'd been disappointed in her colleagues' dispassion. Yet here was Heather reassuring her that, despite the blip, they were heading in the right direction; here was Clive fighting for Matty to receive the same community services as any other citizen.

"I'd better write up the notes. Either of you fancy a refill?"

Conscious of his weariness, Janice rose from her seat. "Stay where you are, Clive. I'll make you a cuppa."

WHAT AN EVENTFUL day! Little wonder Matty is weary.

After the evening meal, she leaves her guests to entertain themselves in the drawing room and prepares for bed. She could sleep standing up.

And yet. She lies on her back. She lies on her side. She screws up her eyes. She opens them wide. Her thoughts are racing, jumping, spinning, as if her skull is hosting the Berlin Olympics. But *these* games are less orderly than Hitler's. As soon as she packs a thought away, another springs up jack-in-the-box style.

She is still awake when the guests retire. Now she must contend not only with her own disarray but the snuffling and snoring that manifests theirs. Has she the strength to smother them one by one with a pillow? Simpler to step outside.

Never one to dwell on misfortune, Matty feels instantly cheered. Although her carcass aches from her fall, she casts off the covers and slides out of bed. She dons her dressing gown and shoves her feet into her tartan slippers.

Slinking down the corridor, she recalls playing hide and seek with the boy, inventing variations to occupy him when his father was peevish. Now, letting the outside door close quietly behind her, she feels electrified at the thought of outwitting the prince.

Out in the cobbled courtyard, she cinches her gown at the waist and tugs the lapels to her throat. The night might be cold, but the navy-blue sky is shot through with diamonds. The firmament soothes her, as it soothed the boy when demons stirred his sleep.

When she has had her fill of stars, Matty turns back, confident she will swiftly nod off. But when she tries the handle, the door to Tuke House is locked.

———————

IT WAS MIDNIGHT by the time Henry was released. He'd sat in draughty corridors queuing for an x-ray, then in the cubicle for the results. Although his jaw wasn't broken, the staff recommended he press charges. Terms like "zero tolerance" and "environmental safety" tempted him to shed his self-image as a wimp. But not for long. The police would mark him as a cry baby and what would Irene think?

No sign of her since that vicious punch. Why hadn't she looked in on him? She was partly responsible: he wouldn't have been assaulted if she'd chosen a civilised spouse. Perhaps she'd relapsed and was languishing in intensive care. But, when he found someone to ask, he was informed she'd left.

"Did her husband take her?"

The nurse shrugged. With such a rapid turnover, the staff probably wiped the patients from their memory banks the moment they passed them their coats. He didn't begrudge them. Henry had no complaints about his treatment.

Waiting to be demobbed, Henry dozed, roused intermittently by the hum of activity beyond his cubicle. The examination table was no substitute for his bed. Thank heavens for small mercies, there wasn't a peep from the next compartment.

As luck would have it, he was deep in dreamland when they peeled back the curtain to say he could go. Henry wiped away a trail of drool, suddenly afraid to surrender the sanctuary. Might Eric be lurking outside, ready to finish him off?

Fortunately, the staff ordered a taxi, and the driver parked at the door. Henry felt relieved it wasn't the chap who had brought him to the hospital several hours ago. He hadn't the energy to explain how he was leaving in worse shape than he'd arrived.

––––––––––––

MATTY HAS NEVER been locked out of her bedroom before. She has been locked *in*, on numerous occasions, but being locked *out* is different. Is it worse? Naturally, she regrets the faff of foraging for food and water, but it is exhilarating to be outdoors when everyone thinks she is in. She can stroll through the grounds studying the constellations. If she can smash the window, she can raid the shop for jelly babies and Parma Violets.

Shivering in her nightclothes, she decides to pop back for a scarf. She pushes at the door, and rattles the handle, to no effect. Matty hesitates to ring the doorbell. With a skeleton staff on duty at night-time, she is loath to add to their load. Furthermore, once disturbed, they might encourage her back to bed.

She will perish, however, if she stays outside. She will have cross the cobbles and break into the main house. Fortunately, she finds an unlocked door and ambles through, blinking at the fluorescent light. She sets off down the corridor.

A board suspended from the ceiling reads Wards 23 & 24: an invitation to visit the boudoir where she slept in her youth. They will be honoured to receive her. Matty mounts the stairs.

Hearing footsteps descending towards her, Matty composes her features into an openhearted smile. A man appears on the tiny landing where the staircase doubles back. "Matty Osborne! You could give a bloke a coronary snooping in the middle of the night."

Matty's smile falters, but only slightly. *Her* fame precedes her, but who is he? His white tunic suggests a dentist or a greengrocer, but he carries neither forceps nor fruit. In the dim light of the staircase, she cannot make out the name on the badge clipped to his breast pocket. She sweeps her body, inadvertently loosening the belt of her peignoir, which swings open to reveal her nightgown.

"Up to your tricks?"

How dare he? Although Matty respects the Magic Circle, she would never dissemble. Or has she misjudged him? Presumably he meant to compliment her on the ease with which she Houdinied from her bedroom.

"Everything rosy on Tuke House?" The man snorts. "Think yourself too good for *us*?"

Having no sensible answer, Matty makes to continue up the stairs. The fellow bars her path. "How about a kiss for your old chum?"

So *that's* his game! Matty tilts her head. Scrunching her eyes, she waits. Instead of lips smacking hers, a thumb smooths her cheek. Like a lullaby. Until the devil grabs her flesh between his fingers and twists. The pain shoos her wanderlust away.

"Go on, you old goat." With a tap on her derrière, he

trots down the stairs. "They'll make you a cup of cocoa if you ask nicely. Or if you rattle off one of your poems."

On reaching the corridor, he turns to the right. A door opens with a sigh and closes with a bang. Her cheek stinging, Matty lacks the oomph to mount the remaining stairs. She can forsake cocoa. Wrapped in her robe, she settles herself on the floor.

Chapter 50

GROGGY AFTER A night of physical and mental anguish, Henry was battling with his breakfast when he heard the doorbell. His hand froze between the table and his mouth, then began to tremble, splattering his tie with oxtail soup – not his standard morning repast but all his aching jaw could tolerate. The bell chimed once more. Irene? It could as easily be her husband calling to skelp him again.

Creeping down the hall, the clatter of the letterbox warned him to keep back. A firework posted through the slot could set the house ablaze before he could scribble a farewell note to Irene. He hovered by the hallstand, eyes and ears primed for incursion, but nothing dropped onto the doormat.

"Let me in! It's perishing out here."

Henry rushed to the door. It didn't matter that smiling felt excruciating. It didn't matter that his cheek stung on meeting hers. Irene was safe! Grabbing her suitcase, he ushered her indoors.

"That's a right bobby dazzler you've got there."

Henry tried not to wince as Irene's fingertips caressed his jawline. "Never mind me. Let's get you warmed up."

Irene glanced at her case, a new-fangled pull-along with a purple carapace. A lightweight mac was looped through the strap.

"Of course you can stay here." Registering her wrinkled brow, Henry pressed on, "We'll modernise. A total refit from top to bottom."

"Oh, Henry!"

He took her blistered hands as gently as he could. "Money no object – I'll apply for a mortgage if need be."

"I'm not stopping, Henry."

"Okay." His cheek throbbed, but he should have anticipated it wouldn't be so straightforward. "A trial period? See how we get on first?"

Irene yanked her hands from his. "A taxi's picking me up any minute."

"Don't let him win!"

"*Him* happens to be my husband. My bairns' father."

"He's not blackmailing you?"

For the first time, Irene laughed. "He wouldn't have the foggiest how to begin. Eric's all action, he doesn't do words."

"He hasn't lamped you?" Although her face was swollen, he couldn't detect any bruises. But her turquoise shell-suit could have hidden other marks.

"Eric wouldn't clout me. And he's sorry he thumped

you. *He's* prepared to fight for me. I'm not convinced *you* would."

"What else can I say? Please don't go back to him."

"I'm not *going* back to him."

"There's *another* man?"

"What do you take me for? I've enough on my plate with you and Eric."

"So where are you going?"

"Spain. To help our Angela run the bar."

"You'd abandon your precious ladies?"

"My ladies nearly killed me yesterday. Over there they bleach their hair naturally. In the sun."

"So you'll be gone a while?" Talking tortured his jaw, but the words bubbled from his throat, pleading for a reprieve. "What about us?"

"That's up to you, Henry."

They'd come full circle. Had anaphylaxis stolen her faculties, or had the shock spraffed his? "It's up to me? Then don't go. Live at The Willows. Pack in work. Let me look after you."

"Playing second fiddle to your sister?"

"Don't be daft! It's not like that."

"Can you prove it, Henry? Can you put me first and sell this house?"

A tossed coin, Tilly one side and Irene the other. How could he choose? In his mind, he'd keep it airborne forever, but in real life, even the flimsy ha'penny would fall. "Hang on a couple of days till you're stronger. You can't travel in that condition."

"If you were fussed I was bad fettle, you'd come with

me." Irene's shell-suit crackled as she tilted her case onto its tiny wheels and dragged it towards the front door. As she paused, hope surged up his gullet like heartburn, until she extracted her mac and eased her arms through the sleeves.

Henry watched helpless as, one by one, she did up the buttons of her coat. Commencing below the collar and working downwards, beyond her breasts, beyond her belly, feeding the discs to the holes. The coat taut across her tummy. When did she get so fat?

He should give her something to remember him by, to guarantee her return. But the taxi was waiting, there wasn't time to fetch anything from his bedroom, even if he ran like the wind. Fumbling in the pocket of his shorts, Henry retrieved an object hard and knobbly, almost a sphere. A conker, brown and shiny, threaded with grubby string. "It's a twelver, but you can borrow it. Then you'll *have* to come back."

She laughed, or perhaps she cried, but she squirrelled it away. "Oh, darling, why *wouldn't* I come home?" In the hall with her suitcase alongside her, she crouched to wipe a tear from his cheek. Wobbling on her heels, or from the weight she carried awkwardly in front of her, which tested the fastenings of her coat. Squatting to his level, her coat stretching until the bottom button tiddlywinked to land on the tiles at his feet. When it stopped spinning, he offered it to her, but she closed his fingers around it. "Hold onto it for me, Henry. I'll be back for it soon."

Chapter 51

GRAHAM WORE HIS usual brown suit and an unusually serious expression. Janice wished someone else could represent the management position. Someone who understood that this latest incident, although disturbing, was trivial compared to the injustice of being deprived of her baby and the best years of her life.

All team members had juggled their diaries to attend the emergency meeting. Apart from Norman. Janice resented his refusal to reschedule a regular outpatient: prioritising people with homes, families and jobs.

"The ball's in your court," said Graham, for the second or third time. "Only you clinicians can decide whether Matty should go back to Ward 24."

"Do they have a vacancy?" asked Heather.

"Not currently," said Graham. "But Sister Gilmour might do a swap."

Moving patients like pieces on a chess board! Janice noticed how pragmatism often trounced Norman's assessments; it was a weird system, accounting not for people but beds.

"And what does Matty have to say for herself?" said Parveen.

"I spoke to her this morning," said Clive. "She denies leaving the ward."

"With respect," said Graham, "she might not tell the charge nurse she's unhappy here."

Clive bristled. "Matty's not too shy to voice her complaints."

"Shouldn't you be thinking less about what she *wants*," said Graham, "but where she's safe? Not just now, but long term. We can't have a vulnerable old woman roaming the streets."

"There'll be twenty-four-hour cover at Briarwood," said Clive.

"You've got twenty-four-hour cover here," said Graham.

"And the lapse is being investigated," Clive insisted.

"Has she absconded at night before?" said Heather.

"There's no record of it," said Clive.

"She did have a head injury," said Janice. "Couldn't that make *anyone* act strangely?"

"The West Cumberland gave her the all clear, no?" asked Parveen.

"They did," said Clive.

"How's she been otherwise?"

"She was brilliant in the art group," said Heather.

Parveen frowned. "She ruined the paintings, no?"

"She did the first time," said Clive. "But she was a reformed character after we had her in here."

"Sounds like you need to speak to her again," said Graham.

"That's no problem, but what am I telling her? Is she going or staying?" Parveen gazed around vaguely. "Where's Norman?"

Clive explained he had a suicidal patient he couldn't cancel. Graham nodded.

"We can't send her back without a detailed psychological assessment." Parveen stroked the arm of her glasses. "But let's see what she can tell us. Clive, could you go and get her? And Graham, I imagine you can leave this to us?"

ANOTHER PRESS CONFERENCE. A roomful of journalists hanging on her every word. This time, they expect her to hold forth on her recent adventure.

Matty does not know how or why she woke up on a staircase. Nor does she believe it is anyone's business. But she might capitalise on their inquisitiveness to enlighten the public on the phenomenon of sleepwalking. One of the defining factors being that the person affected is unaware of having left her bed.

"The boy used to sleepwalk. Sometimes he would wake up in my bed."

Ah, she has captured their attention! They bombard her with feverish questions, albeit unrelated to the original topic. *Do you mean one of the men here, Matty? Has one of the men come into your bed? Or is this about your baby? Did you dream you had him with you here?*

"Oh, let me tell you, I had *such* a peculiar dream!" Matty chortles as she recollects it, although it was decidedly unpleasant at the time. She was climbing a rickety ladder when the devil put in an appearance. Trapped on the middle rung, she was terrified of losing her grip and falling to her death. And then, when she thought she was done for, an angel tapped her on the shoulder and carried her home.

"Would you like to go back to Ward 24?"

A ward is part of a hospital; Matty is not sick. "No, thank you." However, if Florence Nightingale requested her assistance, she would reconsider.

"Are you sure, Matty? You might find it less stressful."

A shiver ripples through her. But she must keep calm. It would benefit no-one to tell the journalists whom she *found* on her hospital visit. She swipes the edge of her hand across her lap. Mollified, she does it again. It is then that she marks, among the journalists, various members of her staff. The butler. The artist. The circus girl with her charming smile. Matty smiles back. "I am quite content here."

"Did you go looking for Karen?" asks the circus girl.

"Karen?"

"Karen Gilmour," says the butler. "Your primary nurse when you first moved here."

The maid who got herself in the family way. Or her sister. If Matty had been firmer in her guidance, would the girl have strayed so far? "I did go looking for her." She must have done. And the boy, too.

"We could easily arrange a visit," says the butler. "You

only have to ask."

"I could not put you to any trouble," says Matty.

"It's no bother," says the butler. "That's why we're here."

Matty smiles. The butler smiles. The artist and the circus girl smile, and everyone else in the room. Splendid! What a jolly crew.

Chapter 52

S TANDING AT A lectern outside her front door, the lady is serenity personified. In a claret-coloured costume, with subtle make-up and sculpted hair, she defies her undoubted sorrow. Her cultured vowels evoke the aristocracy; her regal posture, the finest finishing school. She speaks with such authority, no-one would dare butt in.

In accordance with its educational remit, the BBC transmits her speech repeatedly throughout the day. Matty feels an affinity with ladies in other country houses also studying her technique. Chancing upon a newspaper and pen, Matty jots down some aides-mémoires for her own press conferences: S-M-I-L-E and T-A-L-K N-I-C-E, one letter in each white square of the crossword puzzle grid.

Unfortunately, her guests are unimpressed. Some jeer, and even curse, *Good riddance, you old witch!* and *Fuck off out of it, hoor!* It is testament to her breeding that the lady preserves her poise, heedless of this pasting. Nevertheless, Matty feels beholden to defend her. "Shush, let her speak!"

"Do you know what's going on, Matty?" says the butler.

"Indeed I do. That lady is being evicted from her home. People should show some respect."

"Don't worry about her, Matty," says the butler. "She's tough as old boots."

Taking the newspaper from her, he shuffles to the front page where the lady waves solemnly from the backseat of a taxi-cab, biting her lip.

"She could come here! We have oodles of room."

The butler laughs. "Some might say it's the best place for her."

"Put her in a padded cell," says one of the guests.

Matty hoots. The house is not old enough for dungeons. But, as she now recalls, it is destined for a higher purpose. "We will all be moving in due course."

The butler looks delighted. "That's right, Matty, we will. They're going to start building before Christmas."

"I don't want to move to Briarwood," whines the shrimp-woman.

"That lady does not want to move either," says Matty. "But *she* does her duty with panache."

———

THE MEMO QUIVERED in his hand as he marched down the corridor to Linda Quinn's office. For a full year, Henry had undertaken his revised responsibilities without complaint. But this was a travesty.

Was it payback for his swift exit from the old folks' tea

party? How could Henry be criticised when the mayor summoned the ambulance himself? Besides, Henry had tried to make amends, proving his commitment to the Care of the Elderly strategy under the Creating Healthy and Harmonious Communities banner within the Commissioning Quality programme by proposing an innovation of his own. The mayor was chuffed to send each centenarian in the district a signed birthday card, as the Queen did on a larger scale, so long as Henry did the donkey work. Councillor Boyne must've harboured a grudge since June, biding his time for the golden opportunity to humiliate him. The dustman's son was probably a bully from birth.

Henry had scarcely scanned the memo when he was out of his seat in the multi-use office. His courage a leaky vessel at the best of times, he seized the moment. Acquiescing to his prescribed role in the *Christmas Cheer for Senior Citizens in Residential Care* project would burst the dam, drowning him in degradation. With Irene abroad for the foreseeable future, and Tilly an increasingly lost cause, life would be unbearable.

Henry had been tightly strung already that morning when the porter tossed the orange internal envelope onto his desk. The finest Prime Minister since the war had been ejected from her post. Even from the fringes of local government, Henry could see that politics was an ugly game, but Margaret Thatcher had been extraordinarily shabbily treated, betrayed by her ministers. They said she'd outdone herself with the poll tax, but Henry couldn't see the problem with asking everyone to pay the same. *People* used parks and public libraries, not *houses* as the rates system implied. The worst of it was when *women* slated her; sour grapes among those lacking the talent to spear the glass ceiling themselves.

Linda's door was closed, but Henry didn't let that deter him. He barged in, belatedly recollecting the time he'd found her perched seductively against the desk. Fortunately, she was behind it today. "I didn't hear you knock."

"Sorry, Linda, but it's urgent." Henry dropped onto the seat opposite, flinging down the memo like a gauntlet.

Linda pushed it back. "So Councillor Boyne's been in touch."

"You knew?"

"I *am* your manager."

"You realise what he's asking? It's outrageous."

"What part of bringing Christmas cheer to senior citizens offends you? Or is it a general aversion to the season of goodwill?"

Henry began to wilt. "I've no objection to helping the mayor dole out presents –"

"Ah, you're miffed you're not Santa? You don't have the physique."

"There's no mention of fancy dress in my job description."

"So? *Any other duties*, remember?"

"You're kidding!"

"Can I remind you that you're here because you couldn't meet the demands of your previous post. I *fought* to keep you on."

"But an elf, Linda. It's three steps down from court jester."

"Loosen up, Henry. It'll be fun."

"It's no fun being made to look a fool."

"Think how dull life must be in those care homes. Or on a long-stay hospital ward. Cut off from the community. Every day the same routine. Wouldn't it be an honour to light up those empty lives?"

"By letting them laugh at me?"

"It won't come to that." Linda reached across her desk to set the Newton's cradle in motion. "But if that's what it takes, then yes."

"Seems I've no choice." Henry prepared to bow out before things got worse.

"I hope you'll enter into the spirit of the thing." Henry was practically at the door when she called him. "Ever had any doings with Ghyllside?"

"The loony bin?"

"*Psychiatric hospital* I think you mean. Anyway, you'll know the government's shutting them down and transferring the patients to more up-to-date facilities."

The metal balls ticked back and forth. "I've heard something to that effect."

"The mayor is beyond thrilled about the group who'll be moving into Briarwood. Unfortunately, not everyone shares his liberal views."

Henry rocked on his heels. "I don't see where I come in."

"He's establishing a task force to give them a warm welcome. He's asked managers to identify local authority staff with relevant experience. He thought you'd be eligible."

"Me? I was on the cricket team that played the staff

twenty years ago, but I didn't get to bat."

"That might not count," said Linda. "But no matter, you can begin building bridges when you take them their gifts. In fact, didn't some of them attend the mayor's afternoon tea?"

Shame engulfed his armpits at the memory of the polka-dot dress. But no-one would wear a cotton frock in December and, if they did, he'd be prepared. "Why's Geoff Boyne so interested? Got a mad wife in the attic?"

Linda grabbed the executive toy at both ends, bringing the swinging balls to an abrupt halt. "I suppose he's serious about serving the *entire* community. Isn't that why we're here?"

———————

THE IRON LADY ousted from Downing Street: nothing so momentous had occurred since springing Matty from Ward 24. Watching her farewell speech on the evening news, those plummy vowels and the royal *we* grated as much as ever. Stabbed in the back by her colleagues, she couldn't hide her tears from the photographers as she was whisked away. That didn't earn her Janice's sympathy; this was the woman who'd stolen morning milk from children, humiliated the miners, imposed the poll tax, sold off council houses and attacked the welfare state. The woman who'd scorned society as she dismantled it brick by brick.

There were cream cakes in the social work department and, down on Tuke House, the nurses had taped the teary photo, reproduced in all the papers, to the office door. According to Clive, Graham Scott questioned the propriety, but he'd argued that keeping abreast of current affairs was integral to rehabilitation, and it took a monumental news story to lance the residents' apathy. How unfortunate Thatcher hadn't resigned before the local elections. The drama might have inspired the residents to use their votes.

Janice called in at the off-licence on her way home and stocked up on silver in her change. After a baked potato in front of the TV news, she took a glass of wine to the payphone downstairs. After chatting with her parents and a couple of friends, she didn't try her sister. Rosalind's politics had shunted to the right since she'd sold her soul to corporate banking. Janice couldn't face hearing her protest she should be proud the country's first female prime minister had *coglioni*, regardless how she used them.

Saturday morning entailed a trip to the supermarket and launderette. In the afternoon, she tried to discharge her surplus energy with an hour's run. Reaching her front door, slick with sweat and high on endorphins, it wasn't enough. She was too young to let housework and virtuous exercise consume her weekends. She wanted to go *out*.

She couldn't phone Stuart for the same reason she'd avoided Rosalind. Even a noisy nightclub demanded *some* dialogue. Mervyn might have obliged, but she didn't have his number. Despite the intimacy of the ballroom hold, they remained casual acquaintances.

Fuck it, she'd go to The Matador. If she didn't bump into Mervyn, she'd appreciate the beer and the band. She might recognise faces from Labour Party meetings, people who didn't work in health or social services who might morph into *friends*.

THEY STARTED AS soon as they were through the door to her flat, peeling off each other's jackets and collapsing onto the couch before she'd offered him a drink. His tongue interrogated her body along with his hands. Janice had felt randy in the pub, but it wasn't until his erection pressed against her thigh that she was confident they had a common goal. It would be embarrassing to misinterpret her dance partner's intentions.

When she withdrew, whispering she'd fetch a condom from the bedroom, a frown puckered his brow. What? She shouldn't have to explain to a medical man that it wasn't worth playing Russian roulette with HIV. Or to explain she'd come off the pill after breaking up with her boyfriend. Suddenly she felt sober enough for a job interview.

"Don't move!" His weight shifted as he groped on the floor for his jacket.

Janice laughed when he produced a condom and tore at the wrapper with his teeth. "So you don't only go there for the music!"

"If you were ever a Boy Scout, you'd know it pays to be prepared."

"Sadly they wouldn't have me. Maybe you can show me why."

"My pleasure."

She eased him into her. "It'd better be my pleasure too."

"I'll make sure of that." True to his word, Mervyn fucked as deftly as he danced. Janice didn't mind letting him take the lead when he was so attentive. When she came the first time, she asked herself why she'd thought him unattractive. When she came the second, she reproached herself for making do with Stuart.

Wanting time to think, she didn't invite him to stay the night. Instead she lay awake, musing on her luck in coming of age in an era when women enjoyed the same sexual freedoms as men. Unlike Matty Osborne. Unlike her biological mother.

She still hadn't begun to trace her birth mother. She felt curious, but not curious enough. Now she envisaged her as an innocent waylaid by passion, too besotted to realise she'd gone too far. At least, Janice hoped so. The sex being as gruesome as its consequences was too grisly to contemplate.

Chapter 53

MATTY IS AT pains to avoid being taken unawares like the lady on the television. It is all well and good to demonstrate dignity in adversity, but it is preferable for life to proceed so smoothly the need does not arise.

She cannot badger the Prime Minister for a moving date; Churchill has bigger fish to fry. Nor should she alarm the guests with repeated warnings that she is unable to host them permanently on the estate. The servants are even less informed, so Matty bears the anxiety alone. Nevertheless, relative to the men weighed down by battledress, her burden is feather-light chiffon.

It would be premature to pack up the bedding and crockery, committing her guests to shivering on the floor and, as in the ghetto, eating from the pot. But she can cache the inessentials. Whatever she does now will save time when the order comes to depart.

Matty gathers bits and pieces as she does her rounds. Cutlery from the kitchen, ashtrays from the parlour, slivers of soap from the bathroom, hymnals from the chapel: small items that will not be missed. Unable to locate a suitcase, she stuffs them in her bedside cabinet and, when she cannot close the door without a fight, in the lockers by the beds of the guests. Where necessary, she creates extra space by transferring *their* knickknacks to the waste-bin.

Believing herself to be discreet, Matty is astounded when a journalist probes into her strategy. Who has let the cat out of the bag? But, once it *is* out, she accepts his inquisitiveness as an opportunity to instruct her public. It cannot *kill* anyone, not even a kitten. "Some individuals resent change," she says, sipping an under-sugared cup of tea, "but, as my mother counselled, forewarned is forearmed."

The journalist lacks the manners to acknowledge her advice, never mind follow it. "What they *resent* is your having got rid of their personal belongings."

"They will perish if we roll up at our billet with nary a jam jar or a Primus stove to make tea."

"Are you nervous about moving, Matty?"

"One tries to keep cheerful."

"What would make it easier to stay cheerful?"

"A little more sugar would be tickety-boo." If the butler had left the bowl, she could have helped herself.

"Would you like to see where you're going to live?"

"I have no desire to inconvenience the authorities."

"It would be no trouble."

About to remark that the journalist cannot know either

way, Matty bites her tongue. Kindness costs nothing and pays dividends. "When I *do* visit the new premises, I will reserve you a place in my retinue. You could bring a photographer. What a scoop!"

The journalist inscribes her words in his notepad. Matty sups her tea. It has a refreshing sharpness, as if tinged with lemon. But by the time the young man caps his pen, Matty's interest in both reportage and refreshment has waned. She is planning the speech she will deliver on relinquishing the estate, and the handsome outfit she will wear.

JANICE HUMPED THE bags over the threshold and shut the door with her bum. En route to the staircase, her gaze swept automatically across the wall-mounted shelving, the three wooden pigeonholes where the mail was stowed for each flat by whoever got to it first. Often, that was Janice but today she was home later than usual, having called at Safeway's to buy the ingredients for dinner. She hoped Mervyn liked *pasta marinara*.

An envelope lay face down in her slot. Someone sending Christmas cards before she'd *bought* hers? She dumped the plastic carriers on the lino and, her leather work-bag dragging on her shoulder, slid the envelope out. When she saw Roz's writing, along with a pictorial stamp in sentimental Victoriana – a boy and girl building a snowman against the backdrop of a village church – she put down her shoulder bag too.

It was out of character for Roz to send religious cards, not even in a contemporary style. Or was there another message behind the mosaic of Madonna and Child?

Pity I can't phone you, but wanted to let you know ASAP I won't be home for Christmas. Off to Tunisia to explore my "roots"!!! Wishing you a fab time with Mum and Dad.

The card flopped to the floor and, when she picked it up, her hand shook. She dived into her bag for her purse. *Bloody traitor!* Roz could do as she chose, change her mind and change it back again but, if she'd wanted to tell her, she could've shown some sensitivity. A trip to Tunisia to meet her father. Had she met her mother already but thought it too trivial to say?

A stack of coins on the console, Janice keyed in her sister's number. Listening to the ring tone, she steadied her thoughts. She mustn't succumb to anger, or whine like a kid abandoned while her big sister played with her friends. *Janice's* feelings were irrelevant. Ploughing ahead with inadequate reflection, Roz could get hurt.

On hearing a voice, Janice assumed that, in her frazzled state, she'd pressed an incorrect digit on the panel. Yet, after an embarrassing to and fro, she established that she *had* reached her sister's flat. The last time they'd spoken, Roz lived alone.

"Ah, Janice!" Farouk pronounced her name the French way, with a soft initial and an extended 'ee' sound on the second syllable. "She will be sorry to have missed you. Could you ring again in one hour?"

She shoved back her sleeve to check her watch, although it wasn't necessary. "I can't. I'm cooking for a friend. Could you tell her …" What, exactly? Even if Farouk lived with Roz now – and answering her phone wasn't *proof* – she couldn't discuss it with him. "Tell her thanks for the card."

"Ah, you received it! So I must apologise for stealing her from you. But in our work, it's so difficult. Christmas was the only time we are free."

"You're going with her? To Tunisia?"

"I am. She could not meet my family else. My mother is not educated. Her English is weak."

Janice re-read her sister's words. "I thought she was exploring her roots."

"Exactly. She thinks her father came from North Africa. It makes her curious to see my country."

"So she hasn't arranged to *meet* her father?"

"How could she? She does not know who he is."

Chapter 54

"COME ON, HENRY, take them off."

Not content to deprive him of his dignity with the grass-green suit and pointy hat modelled on a picture in a children's book, the mayor wanted to sabotage his sight. "How can I? I'm blind as a beetle without them."

"Whoever heard of Santa's elves in specs?"

Both men looked to the chaplain, who had volunteered his tiny office as a changing room. The pelt of cotton wool serving as eyebrows, moustache and beard obscured Reverend Vincent's expression. "I doubt it matters either way."

Following the reverend's lead, Henry shouldered a sack of presents. The bell tinkled on the tip of his hat as they aimed for the door. He thought himself safe until, beaming broadly, Councillor Boyne whipped Henry's glasses from his face. "That's better."

He felt the frame scrape the bridge of his nose, yet the chaplain's office door had locked behind them before Henry cottoned on to why the corridor had lost its edges. "Give them here, Geoff. It's not funny."

"Stop twining! No-one's gonna chaff them from the chaplain's desk!"

A fuzzy red-suited figure retreated into the distance, the sole shreds of sanity buried in his pack. "Reverend Vincent! Fred!" Henry's voice was a squeak.

"We're coming!" cooed the mayor. Gripping Henry's arm, he dragged him forward. "Let's not keep the old fogeys waiting."

Hampered by the heavy sack, blurred vision and the curled toes of his green felt overshoes, Henry barely registered the route: down some stairs, along a putty-coloured corridor and across a cobbled yard to a two-storey building, all to the accompaniment of a jingling bell. He couldn't trust he'd find his way back, even *with* his glasses. Not since waking up in a wet bed at boarding school had he felt so vulnerable. Not since national service was he so mindful of his dependence on a bully.

Geoff Boyne abandoned Henry beside a Christmas tree in a stuffy room, fortunately with Santa seated in front. Henry couldn't make out whether an additional chair had been provided for the elf. Dumping his load, he poked a finger under his hat to dab at the sweat. With a list of names and the mayoral cheque-book, Henry had purged Woolworths' shelves of initialled hankies and soap-and-bath-cube gift-packs. On revisiting his list, and realising that some of the names to which he'd assigned smellies were male, he'd had to reallocate them. He'd taken pride in managing the task unaided, with secretary Nina still on maternity leave. Now he removed a parcel from the sack and passed it to Santa.

The chaplain consulted the tag. "Jenny Ryan! Is there anyone here called Jenny Ryan?"

One of the ladies he'd saved from man-style handkerchiefs. Even with imperfect vision, Henry could see *she* wasn't coming forward. Instead, a chap too normal in demeanour for a patient, in jeans too scruffy for staff, whispered in Santa's ear.

"Mea culpa," said Santa. "Is there a *Jimmy* Ryan in the room?"

As a man collected his gift, Henry hoped *he* hadn't cocked it up. There'd been so many names – not just at Ghyllside but at all the old-folk facilities – the Jenny he'd rescued might have been elsewhere and it mere coincidence Reverend Vincent had misread *this* label. Henry's vision was insufficiently acute to make out whether the shape of the parcel indicated bath salts or monogrammed nose-rags. But, as Santa amended Renée Bloomsbury to Ronnie Bloomsburg after the intervention of the chap in jeans, Henry cringed. A man, in what Henry first took for a shirt with paisley-patterned sleeves and revised, as he drew nearer, to heavily tattooed arms, grabbed a poorly-disguised presentation box of lavender soap and talcum powder. Above the groans and titters, Henry sniffed the mayor's spleen.

"VICTOR LORTON!"

Janice swallowed a giggle as Clive inspected another gift tag and whispered in Fred Vincent's ear.

"Correction – Vicky Logan!"

The first time, Janice assumed it was deliberate. As a comedian himself, Jimmy Ryan lapped it up. While Clive scowled and the relatives squirmed and Billy Dewhirst threw his bath cubes on the floor, Janice continued to smile. How cheekily subversive to highlight the hypocrisy of pseudo-personalised presents. More effective than lectures on *depersonalisation, group treatment* and *objects of pity*. But the game had grown stale.

"Matt Ousburn!"

Of course no-one moved. "Matty!" Janice yelled.

"Damned elves," said the mayor. "Can't get the staff."

Had she been in the room, Matty might have concurred. While Janice applauded her snubbing Santa, she couldn't have intended to miss the mayor. Unless, with her talk of princes, she considered a trumped-up councillor beneath her.

When the chaplain called her name again, a care assistant said Matty was in her room. As he made a display of placing her present under the tree before moving on to the next misnomer, Janice had a sense of déjà vu. As last year, Matty was absent from the party. As last year, Janice's attempt to find guests for her had failed. In fact, it was worse than last year: back then she'd convinced herself she'd soon be introducing Matty to her sister. Bloody woman! Although she'd sent Violet an invitation, Janice hadn't expected her to turn up.

Janice scooted from the lounge to check the dormitory,

but Matty wasn't there. Should she see if she'd gone to visit Karen on Ward 24? Her whereabouts weren't Janice's specific responsibility, but it would get her out of the party.

The music resumed in the lounge. The door opened and Santa stepped out, the mayor and the elf on his heels. Annoyed at herself, annoyed at the pantomime of the party, annoyed at her complicity with the crazy system, Reverend Vincent made a convenient scapegoat. *His* church had punished women for sex unsanctified by marriage. "Matty Osborne's disappeared." Said with enough of a snarl to pin the blame on his cruel comedy; not so much to disconcert the visitors.

Reverend Vincent peeled off his beard. "I've an idea where she might be." He handed the mayor his keys. "See you at my office? I'll be as quick as I can."

———————

WITH THE SHINDIG in full fling, Matty slopes away. So long as the Yuletide punch keeps flowing, the guests will not notice she has deserted them. According to her mother, a well-prepared knees-up runs itself.

Her mother. Festivities of any kind rekindle Matty's loss. She knew the reins would pass to her eventually, yet her mother bowed out before her time.

As she traverses the drive towards the estate chapel, the sky pivots between day and night. Bushes and buildings retain their contours but not their colours. The naked trees are skeletons, their lost leaves churned underfoot to mash, dampening her toes through her slippers. The groundsman ought to have swept them up once they passed the delightful crackly stage. She will have words.

Oops a daisy! Sliding on the sludge, she evades a tumble by grasping the limb of a tree. When she steadies herself, she wipes her palms, tacky with mildew, on her skirt.

A brass bell hangs above the chapel door. When did she last hear it ring? Her mother's funeral? Shocked at this reference to her mother's passing, she clutches her cardigan to her chest. She cocks her head, listening for further revelations, but there is only her rasping breath.

Her mother dead? The pain now consuming her testifies to the truth. Loneliness shadowing her every movement, she must have been orphaned with Adam and Eve.

"Your mother has birthed your baby brother but, sad to say, she did not survive the ordeal." Matty swings towards the voice, but the prince hides in the gloom.

Still seeking her mother, she shuffles around the perimeter. A second lap cannot conjure a gravestone. Thievery or another casualty of war? Would the prince defile hallowed ground?

Her legs cannot bear the weight of her sorrow. She will go inside and rest her posterior. Rattling the wrought-iron handle at the chapel entrance, the door is jammed shut. No matter, the porch affords some shelter.

If her mother has no grave, might she still be living? Her cheeks tingle at the thought. But dare she believe it? There is no virtue in clothing oneself in falsehood because the fabric is more agreeable. If the Belgian detective visits again, she will set him the task of finding out.

———————

RAISING HIS WRIST to within an inch of his eyes, Henry squinted at the phosphorescent dial of his watch. In the half-hour or so they were inside, plus almost as long idling outside, the sky had begun the nightshift, but office hours weren't done. Officially, he remained indentured to the mayor, although by now Councillor Boyne would've returned to the Town Hall alone. Shivering in the chill air, he tried to maintain the veneer of decorum appropriate to a local government officer; not easy with less than twenty-twenty vision and masquerading as an elf.

Exiting the party, Henry had looked forward to having his sight restored, even if, once out of the vicar's earshot, Geoff Boyne would harangue him about the jumbled names. When a woman accosted the reverend, Henry discerned her pink hair through the haze. He'd hung back, although it was unlikely the social worker would recognise him in this get-up months on from the public consultation meeting.

He'd been unnerved when the chaplain gave the mayor a jangling bunch of keys and marched off, while the mayor hared in the opposite direction. Henry was tempted to stick with the cleric, as the less deranged, and because *his* attire sanctioned Henry's. It wasn't only the pink-haired woman's presence that made him dither. Had she summoned the reverend to bestow Last Rites on one of the chronic cases in an area off-limits to visitors? The mixed-up names notwithstanding, he'd got off lightly at Ghyllside. No straitjackets or eerie sound effects; even the protests at the presents were subdued.

Doffing his hat, Henry set off in pursuit of the mayor. Recalling a door opening from the hospital corridor onto a cobbled courtyard, he braced himself to negotiate that journey in reverse. When he reached the wall, he navigated by touch until rough stone surrendered to glossed wood and a metal lever.

The door was locked. Henry shook the handle, pulled it towards him and pushed it away, to no avail. Geoff Boyne's mischief? Was the chaplain aware he'd given a psychopath his keys?

Keep calm, Henry, there's bound to be a simple solution. Yet shuffling ten paces to the left and then back to the door, followed by ten to the right, did not magic another portal into existence. Could he trace the perimeter to the grand entrance where the taxi dropped them off? The chaplain's office wasn't far from there. But Henry didn't dare attack the darkness minus his glasses.

His best bet would be to wait outside the ward for someone to find him. While Councillor Boyne wouldn't exert himself to search, the reverend would be more charitable. If he realised Henry needed rescuing.

The breeze cut through his thin jacket as he lurched to the annexe. In the light cast by a lamp above the door, curious green moths flitted about the asphalt. Henry had watched them for some time before it dawned on him they weren't glow-worms but scraps of the sloughed soles of the elf's overshoes.

He was trying to collect the debris when the door opened. "Lost something?"

Henry stood up, swaying between relief and embarrassment. "My colleague."

"Are you sure that's where you last saw him?"

Henry mumbled about the mayor, the mysterious moths and his missing glasses.

"Fred Vincent's office? Don't worry, I can take you there."

Henry had to resist the urge to kiss the young woman, so deep was his gratitude. He hoped she was a genuine member of staff.

"Talk of the devil!" Henry's saviour clapped a hand to her mouth. "Don't tell him I said that."

It certainly seemed a monster of some kind that now approached through the darkness. As it neared, it split into three, hinged at mid-height. Was the chaplain among these spectres? Henry was veering towards the larger one on the left when the middle one let out a bloodcurdling cry. Spooky as it was, the noise confirmed his theory that mental patients were unpredictable and should be given a wide berth.

IT WAS PITIFUL: Matty shivering coatless on the bench in the church porch. She must've found the party excruciating to seek such a lonely refuge. Her face had lit up when she heard them, although it was unclear whom Matty was most pleased to see.

Janice took her icy hand to escort her back to the ward. Would Matty's wandering lead to another disciplinary for the nurses? Not if Janice forgot to mention finding her improperly clad.

They shambled three abreast, Fred and Janice each hooking an arm through one of Matty's. Granting Matty the tarred path, Janice and Fred trod either side on the grass.

She'd claimed to be looking for her mother's grave, but the hospital chapel had no graveyard and presumably never had. It did make Janice wonder where Matty's parents were buried, but it wasn't the place to pursue it. "Santa left you a present under the tree," said the reverend.

Through their linked arms, Janice felt Matty's shudder of rage and revulsion at being treated as a child. Janice scrabbled for a suitably empathic response. "You don't have to …"

The lamp above the door shed its light on one of the nurses chatting with the chap who'd played the elf. Matty stalled.

"Let's get you into the warmth," said the chaplain.

Despite their combined efforts to propel her forward, Matty wouldn't budge. Janice was amazed at the strength contained in so small a package. "And we can forget about your present."

As Matty screamed, the nurse hurried towards them. "What are you like, Matty Osborne? It's nowt but a man in fancy dress!" Taking charge, she gestured to the chaplain to let go of Matty's arm so that she could lead her indoors. As Santa walked off with the elf, Janice recalled how her case-hardened social work colleagues teased her for drawing meaning from the meaningless. *Sometimes*, they insisted, *patients are simply nuts*.

Chapter 55

SOME YOB HAD put a match to the blue touch-paper and ignited a firework in his skull. It screeched, thumped, crashed from one side of his cranium to the other, generating heat enough to roast his carcass. When it burnt itself out, Henry had less than a second's release before a different hoodlum doused him with water and shoved him in a freezer, detaining him among shanks, hams and haunches until icicles hung from his nose and frost filigreed his pubic hair. Convulsions threatened to break his bones or, at the very least, a tooth. Another brief respite and lobbed back on the bonfire. Some holiday!

Even his thoughts taunted him. Half-baked ideas wrote themselves on scraps of tissue paper, Christmas cracker mottos of schoolboy puns sloppily translated from Chinese. WISHING YOU A PROSPEROUS AND ELFY NEW YEAR! GOD ELFS THOSE WHO ELF THEMSELVES! They fluttered about his head, contemptuous, until consumed by the fire.

In his lucid moments, the stench of sweaty sheets urged him to bathe, or phone Irene, but the fever left him energy for neither. Once, he edged downstairs, tread by tread on his backside, on a mission for soup. He woke up with his spectacles askew, his cheek squished against the hallway tile, conjuring copy for the *Times and Star*. STRANGE STINK ALERTS NEIGHBOURS TO FESTERING BODY OF LOCAL AUTHORITY FORMER DEPUTY-HEAD OF PAYROLL. A quote from Ursula Marshall: *He was a quiet chap, lived with his sister. Inoffensive, kept to himself.*

He'd thought Irene would return for Christmas. For her children if not for him. But, as she explained in one of her rare and precious phone calls, the twins jumped at trading Cumbrian blizzards for cut-price booze and beach barbecues. Unlike some.

"It's an open invitation." Her stock reply whenever he voiced his discontent. Otherwise, *she* policed their contact. She'd ditched the mobile phone he'd bought her, and was never available when he rang her sister's bar.

SOMEONE IS PLAYING GAMES WITH YOUR EMOTIONS announced the latest cracker fallout. WHAT IS SHE HIDING FROM YOU?

Tentatively, he lifted his head to a less searing spot on the pillow. He'd read that a human head weighs the same as a bowling ball but, never having sampled tenpin bowling, the analogy was redundant. Perhaps a slip of paper would glide past with more details; until then, Henry tried to relax and let it go.

How *could* he relax when his body spiked from hot to cold and back again, as rockets and Catherine wheels exploded in his brain? Although exhausted, sleep eluded him, as if his role – nay, the primary purpose of his being – were to monitor the slightest shift in the pattern of his symptoms. If this was a tenth of the agony of childbirth, it intensified his respect for super-secretary Nina. Previously, together with admiration, had been resentment she hadn't rushed back to work. DON'T TAKE OTHERS FOR GRANTED! declared the newly-minted dictum. THINK OF OTHERS BEFORE YOURS-ELF! Had the fever come, like Marley's ghost, to recalibrate his character?

A fresh insight, sharp enough to shear an artery: YOU MURDERED YOUR MOTHER! RIPPING HER APART IN YOUR HASTE TO EXIT THE WOMB! No excuse that he was a baby and couldn't help it. Guilt's penance: his miserable life.

Then another unfurling, stealing the crown for The Year's Most Outrageous Hypothesis. IRENE LEFT TO HAVE A BABY. It explained everything or, at a minimum, her keeping away.

Golden-haired cherubim trumpeted from the bed posts and alabaster statues of the infant Jesus balanced on the architrave above the door. With *his* father such a paragon, Henry hadn't dared apply for the job himself. He'd have had to grow another personality first.

Instead of muddying the waters, however, this wiped the slate clean. Farewell conflicted loyalties; Henry would be redeemed via service to his child. He'd set aside his own desires to perform his moral duty. The child would make him young again. The child would make him brave.

His mind cleared of paper, Henry scrambled out of bed. In the hall, he donned his overcoat, scarf and trilby to confront the kitchen cold. No dillydallying, he'd install central heating for the baby. The child would want for nothing, but the expectant father made do with canned tomato soup heated on the hob. Unfortunately, there was no bread to crumble into it; his head might be stable but his legs couldn't power him to Mr Patel's.

Afterwards, he settled easily into sleep, awakening to darkness and the peal of church bells. The shriek of fireworks, outside now, where they belonged. He crept to the window and drew back the curtain. Fountains of coloured light flashed hope across the sky. Out with the old, in with the new: 1991 would be the year he'd relinquish illusion and honour his father's legacy. Become a real man.

"GO TO BED, Matty, if you're tired."

She cannot. Everyone is drowsy – or bored, or squiffy – but determined to greet the New Year. The BBC is a letdown: instead of the Hogmanay special from north of the border they broadcast middling quiz shows tarted up with a string of tinsel and a kilted piper in the corner of the screen. The butler's card games degenerate as sherry and beer pickle the guests' brains. Yet Matty feels too washed-out to fret about tonight's shoddy entertainment.

They say she has been off-colour. Her nose is raw and her ribs ache, and her head, topped by a paper party hat, feels encumbered by a hefty crown. Fortunately, the messages get through unhindered. Having received a troubling tip-off, she cannot give up and retire to bed.

When darkness falls, the prince takes position outside

the annexe door. His cloak of evil cossets him through violent weather and he never feels fatigue. He will wait as long as necessary to sneak inside. On ordinary nights, both guests and staff are too vigilant to allow a stranger through the door. But this is no ordinary night. Tonight any visitor is welcome, especially a swarthy stranger knocking at the stroke of midnight with a lump of coal. The prince being cunning, Matty must be extra shrewd. Weary as she is, she cannot lower her guard.

She looks around for a weapon. A fireside poker would do. But someone has removed the fire tools – the shovel, the brush, the tongs as well as the poker – and taken the fireplace too. Without a hearth, where will she stow the coal? Without coal, do they *require* a first footer? Alas, his absence cannot be guaranteed.

The bells! She must have dozed.

"Away, Matty! On your feet!"

The butler escorts her to the floor. Where are her dancing shoes? Can she remember the steps? But this needs no rehearsal. Crossed at the chest, hands in a circle, only their arms dance.

Matty scrutinises the faces, but none fits the prince. Finally, she can relax. The words are mournful, but the melody bubbles with promise.

When the song is done, the butler fills their glasses to toast 1991. "You know what's happening this year? We're moving to Corporation Road."

Someone has summoned a lifeboat. Matty will sail to shores beyond the prince's reach. Sadly, her guests cannot accompany her in a single-berthed boat. She prays they will find their harbour; her duty now is to herself. She must even leave the boy behind, entrusted to his father's supervision.

"Where's that come from?"

Although edging towards sixty, Henry felt like a six-year-old, with a six-year-old's concept of procreation. "I thought you looked …" Never refer to a woman's weight gain! "… different."

"Of course I looked different. I was badly. Puffed up with an allergic reaction, not a bairn."

Henry wiped his nose on his pyjama sleeve. "When are you coming back, Irene?"

"I'm champion where I am."

Despite the chill in the hall, sweat flooded every fold and furrow of his skin. "I miss you!" She shouldn't make him spell it out.

"That's not a good enough reason."

Her words made his eyes sting. He dug behind the lens of his glasses to rub a corner with his fingertip. "When does your visa run out?"

"The Common Market's scrapped visas. I can stop here for ever if I want."

Why hadn't he searched for Tilly in Europe? It hadn't occurred to him to get his letters translated into Spanish, German or French. "When will I see you?"

"When you get your arse on a plane." Her tone was as stiff as a backcombed hairdo with a lacquer shell. "Don't waste my time phoning until you've got your act together."

"That's harsh."

"It's no picnic for me, either. You're an addict. The more I support you, the deeper you dig into your rut."

"You've been reading them self-help books."

"It's not me who needs help. *You* should get yourself to the doctor's for a tonic."

If she hadn't cut the call, he'd have maintained it was barmy to bother the doctor with a virus. Medicine was impotent in that regard. As the receiver clicked into its cradle, Henry heard the strangest sound. Not a throat clearing, not a gargle, but an aborted sob.

NEVERTHELESS, HENRY WAS obliged to visit his GP. The prospect of asking for a sick note shamed him, but it was less daunting than resuming his job. His fever had retreated, taking his vitality with it. His work ethic, too.

It wasn't as if he hadn't tried. He'd set his alarm and bullied himself from bed as soon as it burst into his brain. He'd even turned off the hot tap early to avoid the temptation to wallow in the bath. Yet, unable to dodge his reflection in the shaving mirror, his red-rimmed eyes betrayed his lack of verve.

No-one enjoyed getting up for work in winter, leaving home in artificial light. Life entailed doing what you had to do, not what you chose. But Henry couldn't force himself anymore. His body refused to submit to his will.

Stooping to tie his laces, his head swam and his vision blurred, transforming his brown brogues into felt slippers curling at the toe. He didn't need to don the guise to be rendered a fool. However attired, Henry was an elf.

SETTING OUT FOR the surgery, Henry pulled his trilby down to his eyebrows. He didn't want any neighbours wishing him a happy new year. With any luck, they'd be at work.

Brash sunshine mocked his mood without warming the air. His hair had grown over his ears since Irene left, but they still burned with cold, bringing nostalgia for the balaclavas he'd worn as a boy. Who knitted his hats when Tilly left?

The thought, so innocent and automatic, angered him now. Why did everything revert to Tilly? Irene was right. He was obsessed. A fat lot of good it did him.

Turning onto Corporation Road, the ground rocked beneath his feet. He'd been at sea and hadn't recovered his land-legs. Henry thrust his fists into the pockets of his herringbone coat. As a minibus braked at the site of the old baby clinic, he steeled himself for imminent invasion. Patients spilled out onto the pavement and loitered there, ridiculous in fluorescent vests and hardhats. A nursery class playing at builders.

He tilted the brim of his hat against them, although they were too preoccupied with posing for photographs to notice him. Or care. Observing them from across the road, Henry was riveted. Appalled. Preening by the plywood panels enclosing the building site, they seemed unaware of the spectacle they created.

One of them, a shrunken crone who could have been any age from forty to seventy, cradled a doll as big as a baby. A doll! The attendants should never have allowed it. But what could you expect from a custodian with pink hair? There she was, that hippy social worker, whispering to the woman with the doll.

Mindful of his appointment, Henry pressed on. Something fluttered past his eyes. He'd have sworn it was an out-of-season butterfly, were it not so sapped of colour. It flew away, then floated back again. Henry caught it between finger and thumb. A slogan from a Christmas cracker, like in his fever dream. He opened it out, but the words were indecipherable: a faded bus-ticket, dappled green print on slate. He'd examine it later, killing time in the doctor's waiting room or with his reading glasses at home. But a gust of wind snatched it from his fingers. Where it went, he couldn't see.

He stopped, one hand at his thumping heart, the other leaning on a lamppost. He was going mad. If he didn't watch out, they'd have him in Ghyllside. It must be Christmas leftovers, but his head proclaimed it a message from the pink-haired social worker. THIS IS THE WOMAN I MENTIONED AT THE MEETING. Bereft at giving up her baby, she'd mothered a doll. THIS IS WHO LOOKED AFTER YOU AS A BOY. There wasn't a freckle he recognised. But why *would* he half a century on? PUT THE KETTLE ON, SHE'S CALLING ROUND FOR TEA.

Chapter 56

MACARONI CHEESE WITH green beans: stodge Janice could get at Ghyllside canteen any day, and at a conventional mealtime, instead of eleven in the morning. The beans, fresh from a tin, lacked the bite and colour of those she picked in summer from her dad's allotment, and the pasta sloshed on the plate. But Janice relished every mouthful. From a cook who, until recently, couldn't make a cup of tea, it was haute cuisine.

Meals were dispatched to Tuke House from the hospital kitchen in a toy-train of heated catering-trolleys. Although the main meal would be delivered by a catering service in Briarwood, at other times of the day residents would have the freedom – or hassle according to Jimmy Ryan – to fend for themselves. The occupational therapist determined that even those who scoffed at "women's work" would acquire some basic cooking skills prior to discharge.

Miserly budgets, institutional bureaucracy and the residents' apathy had scaled down Heather's original ambition from producing a week's worth of menus to one simple meal, plus shopping for ingredients and clearing up. Decision-making, navigating the supermarket, managing money, following a recipe, hygiene, time-keeping, using equipment safely: skills others performed automatically, the residents of Tuke House had to rediscover or learn from scratch. Mastering them – or making a tentative bumbling acquaintance – upped their scores on Norman's assessment. Janice equated the challenge to her rustling up a banquet in Japan.

Matty was one of the last to benefit from Heather's one-to-one sessions, delayed by a bad cold at New Year. Recuperation had revamped Matty's mental state, improving her orientation to reality, with no mention of her mother's marriage. Despite being too unwell to join the trip to view the foundations, she seemed in favour of the move.

Janice was delighted when Matty invited her to share her macaroni cheese. Might she open up more over a meal? Feigning fascination in the pepper-pot, Janice tiptoed around her forgotten history in Sheepwash Lane. "Did you cook much before you came here?" Would Matty admit she'd *had* a *before*?

"Breakfast, dinner *and* luncheon. Baking too – they liked cakes and biscuits for afternoon tea."

Bullseye! "You must've worked your fingers to the bone!"

"First up and last to bed." Matty looked wistful, as if reliving her days as a teenage skivvy. "Needs must. They relied on me."

"They? Can you remember their names?"

Her meal half eaten, Matty flanked her plate with her cutlery. Janice coughed as a slimy bean slipped down her throat. She should've approached both food and conversation at a more leisurely pace.

"Drink some water, dear!" said Matty.

Inwardly whooping, Janice sipped from her glass. She *hadn't* flunked it! Nor was she at risk of choking. She swallowed another forkful of soggy pasta. "This is scrumptious."

"Nursery pap," said Matty.

Nursery pap for the curmudgeon from The Willows who denied her existence? Or grown-up meals as Janice cooked for Mervyn? "Did you get to cook for someone special?"

"Indeed I did."

"Were you fond of him?" *Don't rush it, Janice!*

"I loved him."

Why didn't he love you back? "What was he like?"

"He was partial to jelly babies. Yellow ones."

"Any idea what happened to him?"

"They would have sent him away."

"Sent *him* away?" Some scandal? Or the war? If circumstance *forced* them apart, might he still care? "Do you dream of meeting up again?" *Get real, Janice! No man would mothball his life for fifty years until his princess returns. The chronic schizophrenia story isn't a fairy-tale.*

"We will," said Matty.

"You will?"

"Meet up again. When I leave here."

MATTY HAS BEEN ill, gravely ill. For months, possibly years. Like the plague of influenza that almost snatched her from the cradle, a hurricane has blown through her brain. It has smashed memories as if they were balsawood models, creating crevasses to plug with rags and papier mâché, which a *child* knows is no defence against a tempest. But, the storm abated, she floats. An interlude to take stock, before relaunching her life.

Despite having little in common with the geriatrics in the sanatorium, their sluggishness conjures a tranquil climate conducive to healing. The wardens are considerate, although their advice can be misguided. She does not admonish them for their ignorance, since her ailment is not in any textbook, and their intentions are pure. But she must beware of their excitement: at this delicate stage in her convalescence, relapse is a constant peril.

Her recovery has been hard-won, nine tenths drudgery with a smidgen of repose. Learning to walk again. To talk. To bathe and launder her clothes. The experience will stand in good stead for her vocation, however; a bedside manner finely tuned. Amid the hours she will devote to her medical studies, Matty will not neglect her family and friends. She will assist her mother with the chores and tell her stories in bed. She will read to the boy, and play draughts and marbles, and kick through leaves for conkers. She will dance with Hilda, recite with Violet and rejoice in a red rosette whoever wins.

"Matty, you're holding your breath again!"

See? The superintendent is so solicitous, he observes the ins and outs of her lungs. An ordinary establishment provides nutrition, fresh air and injections; here at Ghyllside an extra layer of attentiveness displays God's grandeur. She laughs. "At last I am cured and can bid this place farewell!"

"Glad to hear it, Matty. But it'll be a while yet. You don't want to peak too soon."

Her career has schooled her in pleasing an audience. But some things are private. However spick, however span, she would no more expose the contents of her head as reveal her hand at cards.

Chapter 57

A FORTNIGHT'S REST should have scotched the virus. But when that expired, Henry remained unfit and, as the gap lengthened, it felt harder to return. A rookie demobbed from national service bewildered by the language of policies and procedures. Unfortunately, the one that now came to mind proved cold comfort. If this dragged on, Linda Quinn would call him in for interview under the Managing Sickness and Absence Policy. He'd have to crawl to the Town Hall on his knees.

Until then, the doctors signed him off in fortnightly chunks. They didn't have time for preamble. Apart from this youngster, newly spawned from medical school by the look of him. A skinny specimen with prominent ears, a mutant, perfect prey for bullies. That might be why Henry came clean with him; Dr Yates presented no threat.

It seeped like pus from an infected blister: Irene; Tilly;

the job casting him Geoff Boyne's Fool. Now, awaiting his diagnosis, scanning the desk to avoid his gaze, the tools of the doctor's trade had blurred. The sphygmomanometer fused with the narrow box that housed it, the gauge a solid line. A flask of lollipop-stick tongue-depressors melded into a log. The telephone a squatting toad. Henry wiped his glasses on his tie.

"No-one prescribed antidepressants?"

Henry fumbled in his pocket for Tilly's button. Rubbed his thumb across the grooves. "You think I'm mental?" The doctor hadn't heard half his story. He'd have Henry committed if he described his dread of the new neighbours. How his thoughts took physical form. It was happening now, a tickertape ribbon running along the bottom of the image on his retina, the tele-printer announcing the football results on TV. THAT'S NOT TILLY'S BUTTON. IT'S FROM THE NANNY WHO LEFT IN DISGRACE.

"A mild reactive depression. Given sufficient stress, any of us could snap."

HE THINKS YOU'RE BONKERS. "It's this virus. Knocked the stuffing out of me."

Dr Yates grabbed his prescription pad and pen. "We could try you on Prozac."

ONCE YOU START ON DRUGS, YOU'RE HOOKED. END UP AS FUCKED AS THE NANNY. SERVES YOU RIGHT FOR TELLING HIM YOUR SOB STORY. LESSON ONE OF BOARDING SCHOOL: DON'T SNITCH.

"Or if you're not keen on pills …"

The youngster would have the latest treatments on tap; methods unfathomed by his older colleagues. The subtitles faded from Henry's inner screen. "What's the alternative?"

"A winter break might help."

"A holiday? On the national health?"

Dr Yates fiddled with his pen. "We can't *prescribe* a holiday. But in your situation, after all this pressure …"

Impossible! He had to stay for Tilly, and besides. "I'd have to be at work to qualify for holiday."

"Not necessarily. Not if the environment's toxic." The doctor shuffled the paperback-sized cards constituting Henry's medical record. "You're what, twenty months off sixty? They might grant you early retirement to get you off their books."

Blimey! "It would be that simple?" The doctor began to resemble a human being.

"I'm not au fait with council policies. And we'd have to *try* to get you fit for employment first."

"So I'll *have* to go on medication?" He needn't *take* the tablets.

"Or I could refer you to a psychologist."

"A shrink?"

"A psychologist's not the same as a psychiatrist. He'd explore *why* you're depressed and what *you* can do to alleviate it."

"Haven't we covered that?" His father would be aghast how much he'd disclosed.

"Mr Willis would delve deeper. Your conflicting feelings about your girlfriend. The struggle to separate from your sister."

His sister? Rather than a punch to the gut, it took a weight from his shoulders. Like floaters in his eye, another parade of cracker mottos filled him in. DON'T WAIT FOR

TILLY. It breezed away before the next. TILLY ISN'T COMING HOME. Then: TILLY NEVER EXISTED. The figment whipped off to clear the stage for the clincher: TILLY WAS YOUR IMAGINARY FRIEND.

———————

"GOOD DAY AT the office, dear?" When Mervyn called at her flat after evening surgery, Janice's flippant suburban-housewife greeting masked an attack. Pouring his glass of Shiraz, she figured she'd become complacent. Ought she find other friends, or a lover she didn't only connect with on the dancefloor or in bed? As he flopped onto the sofa, she emptied a packet of salted nuts into a bowl and slid it across the coffee table.

"The usual coughs and colds, and old folks slipping on the ice. And I referred a chap to Norman Willis."

As he palmed some nuts, raised his chin and tossed them into his mouth, Janice resolved to stop serving Mervyn salted snacks. "Poor sod won't know what's hit him when Norman starts measuring his daily living skills."

"Very drole! I don't know what you've got against him."

"I don't know what you've got *for* him. You bickered relentlessly in the MDT."

"I've a lot of respect for Norman. He's got a sharp brain."

"Maybe he should apply it more."

"He's great with outpatients. Even the suicide risks."

"Pity Tuke House hasn't seen the benefit. Effie Atkinson still drags that doll around and if anyone can get underneath Matty Osborne's story it's a psychologist."

"Matty's too fragile for psychotherapy."

"Why shouldn't she have the same opportunities as the bloke you referred today?"

"I would've thought it was obvious." Mervyn glared at her over his wine glass.

Janice glared back. The first argument of their non-romance. "Not to me." Was she furious with Mervyn her non-boyfriend, Mervyn the biological psychiatrist or at the stifling institution through which they'd met? Or was she most furious with herself?

"Dicing with her mental state. She must've buried her past for a reason."

"Because no-one would listen."

"I don't want to argue with you, Janice."

"Isn't *my* brain big enough?"

"I've had a busy day and I'm knackered."

And the little woman's busy day doesn't count? Something saved her from verbalising the thought, and it wasn't Mervyn's sensitivities. The topic was different, as was the setting and they were having pre-dinner drinks, not breakfast. But the mood was exactly as it had been on the morning of her interview. When she'd said goodbye to the idea of a slate cottage on an untarred road with Stuart and a couple of dogs. "Sorry." Twice she'd fallen for men whose ideology alarmed her. Maybe *she* should consult a psychologist.

"Me too." He drained his glass. "Can we go to bed so I can show you how sorry I am?"

Chapter 58

AFTER BREAKFAST, HENRY donned his coat and a fleece hat and headed for the attic. Since Dr Yates had extolled the health benefits of routine, Henry had reported to Tilly's window with the same discipline he'd sat at his desk at the council for nigh on forty years.

He no longer felt guilty about watching other men work. Monitoring the growth of the houses opposite was no more outlandish than his job. His vigilance did not *totally* allay his anxieties, but it was preferable to being ambushed by a fait accompli.

Whether from the chilled air or the monotony, standing sentinel at Tilly's window anesthetised his brain. His thoughts slowed from the speed of a racing car to a horse and cart, then clip-clopped to a powwow with the psychologist he hadn't yet met.

Clocking Ghyllside in the header as he extracted the

letter from the manila envelope, he'd almost dropped it. But, reading on, the euphemism *referral to this department for help with your current difficulties*, having first elicited a cynical snort, brought tears to his eyes. *Current difficulties*: portmanteau for anything from an ingrown toenail to a burst pipe. Had the postman accidentally – or deliberately – delivered it to the wrong address no-one need know the new doctor had diagnosed a mental collapse.

Your name has been placed on our waiting list and we will contact you regarding an assessment appointment as soon as one becomes available. Henry was content to idle in the administrative queue. His name on a list signalled progress without the embarrassment of confessing his woes to an actual person. Or attending Ghyllside. Like happy-pills minus the side effects, it had given him the impetus to apply for a passport. He could defer the decision of whether to use it until he felt more robust.

Henry's imaginary psychologist was an older version of Dr Yates, with a little of the no-nonsense crispness employed by the matron at his prep school fifty years before. Although a mere figment, the psychologist berated Henry for referring to the attic as Tilly's bedroom: *Haven't we established Tilly isn't real?*

Hard to accept when the room screamed of his sister: the patchwork quilt; the pear and pomegranate wallpaper; the vanity table with its triptych mirrors. But it could equally have been the abode of a succession of young women employed to look after him. It didn't take an expert to envisage a motherless boy blending them into a single person who'd love him unconditionally. An *imaginary* sister explained Tilly's absence from their parents' gravestone; the thirteen-year gap in their birthdates; their father's reticence after she'd gone. It explained the failure of his twenty-year letter-writing crusade.

And yet. The memory of her suitcase in the hallway was so vivid. Her crouching down and vowing to return. The button concrete evidence. *We agreed that wasn't Tilly*, scolded the psychologist. *The button broke off because her coat was too tight and her coat was too tight because ...* That was the madwoman the social worker jabbered about. She'd stuck in his mind because she was the last. After her, his father sent him to boarding school for safety's sake.

The rough paper between his thumb and fingertips wasn't another phantom slogan. While the builders raised the dwellings, and his fantasy psychologist dismantled his dreams, Henry scratched at the corner of wallpaper beneath the window ledge. He tugged until he had a piece large enough to take in both hands and rip to the skirting board, lacerating pomegranates and pears.

Henry shed his coat and dashed downstairs for a brush, sponge and enamel pail, and the kitchen spatula as proxy scraper. Back in the attic, he rolled up his sleeves and set to stripping the walls.

His nanny must have *known* she couldn't return to The Willows. Cruel to make a promise she couldn't keep. Simply to stanch his sobbing.

The dampened paper wrinkled and span in concertina curls to the floor. Neither the sour smell, nor his aching knees, nor the white flakes dusting his fingers could dent his determination. Henry had confined himself in a stranger's story. Was he finally ready to write his own?

———————

SEATED AT A dining table with one of the assistants, Matty turns the pages of a book. As thick and hefty as an encyclopaedia, this is an anthology of *wall*paper. Walls made of paper one could spit through? Paper *for* walls? At first, it made her giggle. A new parlour game to join other recent acquisitions: a catalogue of bedroom furniture; carpet squares bound in a book even bulkier than this; colour charts of paints with extravagant titles as if from one of Mrs Christie's novels. Why so many names?

Matty does not object to making a meal occasionally; Cook deserves an afternoon off. Nor to depositing her laundry in the belly of a fancy machine. But she has never had to hang wallpaper. "Would a lick of paint or distemper not suffice?" Paint has come up trumps here in the dining room, a plain background complementing the art.

"There's no rush," says the shop-girl. "The decorators can't start until the plaster's dried out."

Fortified by the reference to *decorators*, Matty riffles the pages. Nevertheless, she is dizzy with choice.

"That's nice," says the shop-girl. "Kind of William Morris."

Matty would merrily delegate the decision to the shop-girl, except that she would not sleep a wink within an orchard of pomegranates and pears. Letting her gaze linger as if considering, the fruit starts to rot. And the pong! As if the milkman's Shire has opened its bowels onto the page. Acting fast to prevent the putrid flesh liquefying and flooding the table, Matty shuts the book.

"Had enough for today?" says the shop-girl. "It might be easier once you've seen the new place and got a feel for your room."

Her room can be papered with newsprint for all Matty cares. She has no doubt who has contrived the fruit's decay. He poisons everything he touches. How sly of him, after all her vigilance, to access the sanatorium through a book. She must make haste. "I could go tomorrow."

Grinning, the shop-girl pats her hand. "That's the spirit, Matty! Two fingers to the sceptics who said you wouldn't make it."

SCISSORING AROUND TEMPLATES of Easter eggs and bunnies, Janice envied her mother. Teaching might be stressful – the aggressive or indifferent parents; the unpaid hours preparing classroom materials; the dreaded OFSTED – but the mission was clear. Whereas Janice, eighteen months post-qualification, didn't know what social work was *about* anymore. So how could she decide whether to jack it in?

The confusion wasn't restricted to work. Her entire life was off kilter. She had no outside interests other than politics (which, even with the end of the Gulf War and the resignation of Margaret Thatcher, didn't meet the criterion for leisure), drinking (which, being unhealthy, didn't count) and dancing (entwined in a doomed relationship). And despite having disentangled herself from Stuart, her sex life was a mess. "I used to be so certain. But the older I get, the more flummoxed I feel."

"Welcome to adulthood, Jan!"

"A great help you are, Mum! Every grown-up's as mixed up as me?"

"You're not mixed up. You're adjusting to a new phase. Things'll settle down for you soon."

"What if they don't? What if I keep making the wrong choice?"

"That implies there's a *right* one."

"Isn't there?"

"There must be *hundreds* of options. All leading somewhere worthwhile! If your path comes to a dead-end, retrace your steps and begin again. There's ample time to figure yourself out."

"You were married at my age."

"Your Nonna would've disowned me if I'd lived in sin."

"But *you'd* found your soulmate. Whereas *I* go for men whose attitudes give me the creeps."

"Twice is a pattern set in stone?" Her mother's voice hardened. "If you're not happy, find someone more compatible and be thankful you can."

Her mother hid her face, rummaging through a box labelled EASTER. Janice chewed on the inside of her cheek. Snug in the nest her mother had made for the family, it hadn't occurred to Janice she might have dreamt of a different life. Even the trauma of infertility put Janice and her sister centre stage. She'd taken her parents' mutual love for granted. Was she mistaken? Egotistic and naive? Was her adoptive mum as constrained by time and culture as her biological mother had been? Janice cringed at the thought of her bed-hopping. She cringed at the infantile part of herself that couldn't allow this woman any roles other than teacher, wife and mum.

Brandishing a plastic silhouette of a basket of eggs, her mother beamed. As if *that* was why she'd turned her back. "But don't get too picky. No-one's perfect. Not even you."

Catholic versus Protestant; Italian versus Irish; teacher versus car mechanic with oil-stained hands: her parents patched their differences so neatly, Janice hardly noticed the seams. Could *she* learn to compromise? Did she want to?

Chapter 59

HENRY'S SUITCASE PERCHED on the bed, the yawning lid with its scarlet lining the maw of a hungry hatchling. The beach towel and dookers, the T-shirts and underwear, gathered on the counterpane alongside. Ludicrous to get rigged out for summer when snowdrops lingered on. The crinkly shell-suit, like coveralls at crime scenes, affirmed the distance he was travelling from who he thought he was.

Suck it and see, said Irene, *no need to commit yourself till you're sure*. But even a taste of a different lifestyle would modify the flavour of the old one. A Henry with a passport, suitcase and nylon leisurewear might never find his way home.

With luck, the flight would be cancelled. The train to the airport delayed. A sudden snowstorm might foul the roads and runways. As Henry half-closed his eyes to sneak a cellophane packet of rainbow-coloured briefs into his case, he hoped some catastrophe would leave his roots undisturbed.

But, truth to tell, the house already spurned him. Mouse manure in the kitchen cabinet. Shelves and sills filmed with dust. At night, on that borderland between sanity and slumber, the bed springs creaked in the attic room above.

———————

A SPLENDID DAY for an excursion. Thrusting through the minibus windows, the sun makes a halo of the circus girl's hair. Seated directly behind the chauffeur, Matty has an excellent view of the bookmakers and charity shops flanking the route.

The circus girl asks Matty to enlighten the passengers as to their precise location. Squinting at a signboard on the redbrick wall, Matty croons, "High Street." She is glad to be of service to the refugees, as they are illiterate. "Sheepwash Lane." Matty giggles. "What an amusing name!"

"I suppose in olden times they'd dip the sheep there," says the circus girl.

In her mind, Matty substitutes the buildings for fields of bleating ewes. If she were to count them, would she fall asleep? To remain alert, she bites off the head of a jelly baby, a green one, like the grass, and sets aside the yellow for the boy.

At the end of the road, the driver stops to let a lorry pass. Reading the sign a second time, the three syllables glide off her tongue, as if she were a shepherdess who regularly bathed her flock in this street. Or perhaps the name *seems* familiar because of a poem. She could recite "Little Miss Muffet" for the circus girl, but *she* is leaning forward to advise the driver on parking protocol.

"Coming, Matty?" A redbrick house, two storeys capped by a pitched tiled roof. From the bare windows, she deduces it is uninhabited, but it is prized above its neighbours, which are mere cement platforms waiting on walls. The unfenced garden is a muddy rectangle but the path to the glass-panelled door has been scrubbed.

The guests huddle on the pavement while the butler secures the van. He cautions them that the house, unfurnished and undecorated, is not yet a home. "I trust you have your tape to measure up for curtains." The butler attests he has it under control.

Progressing single file to the door, Matty feels giddy, as if the path is a tightrope. Fortunately the circus girl is at her heels to steady her if she wobbles.

As the butler fiddles for a key, a guest requests a hot drink. Matty is about to assert that her hospitality can stretch to tea, with a slice of lemon if he wishes, when the circus girl cuts in. "I'm afraid there's no electricity. But we can go to a cafe when we're done." It is the first sour note of the day.

The second follows shortly after. Craning her neck toward the roof, she detects no window in the wall framed by the inverted V. Her room will be a fire-trap: no means of summoning help.

––––––––––––

AS FAR AS Janice was aware, this was Matty's first visit to the new-build on Corporation Road. Asking her to name the streets was an inspired experiment, sadly yielding uninspiring results. Announcing Sheepwash Lane, Matty betrayed no hint of recognition. She'd have to make do with Effie, Ronnie and Jimmy for family now.

Janice could taste the anxiety as Clive parked the minibus and led them to the front door. Her own veneer of optimism was paper thin. Despite Clive warning the residents the house was a husk, Ronnie demanded a cup of tea and stomped around the rooms in a funk when told it wasn't possible. Of the four, Matty seemed most at ease, tolerating the absence of heating or refreshment, albeit attributing the deficiencies to wartime rationing. When Clive invited them upstairs to view the bedrooms, Matty led the way.

Later, Janice would struggle to recall the exact sequence. But the outcome could not have been foreseen. Effie treading on her shoelace as she raced from room to room, grazing her knee on the concrete floor, and wailing at the dribble of blood. Clive unable to attend to it because of Jimmy using the toilet when there was no water to flush. Effie bravely accepting a tissue in lieu of a bandage but requiring reassurance she wouldn't lose her leg. Clive pottering in the kitchen cupboards for a first aid kit. Effie insisting on replacing the tissue with a plaster, with another for her doll.

WHAT BROUGHT HER to this hovel? There is tea in abundance at the estate, and a bed on which to rest her derrière. Once again, she has been hoodwinked into acting on others' interests. In consequence, her mind is a maze.

Who invited *that* silly article? Like the shrimp she resembles, she delights in disrupting Matty's thoughts. While everyone else joined in the game – a variation on charades involving imagining the tiny house with carpets and pictures on the wall – *she* tossed the baby into the air. Naturally, Matty caught it, but what was she to do next? Nobody said.

The shrimp-woman sprawled on the floor, bawling as if an ogre had killed her mother, whining for the circus girl. Now Matty must seek a quiet corner to reorganise her head. But where?

Downstairs, the butler squats to fix the taps beneath the kitchen sink. Butler, chauffeur, master of ceremonies and now plumber! A small establishment cannot accommodate multiple specialists, but it pains Matty to witness him so reduced.

Someone should supervise the seating arrangements. The peculiar house is devoid of chairs. A guest has bunked on the windowsill, but Matty's legs are too short for a similar pose. Opening the front door, she lowers herself onto the step. Although the air is chill, the sun is cheery. The baby coos contentedly when she puts it to her shoulder and pats its back.

None of your lies, Matilda! The baby falls from her arms. *I'll have you sent to the asylum!* How had he found her here?

She places the baby on the step. The nuns will find it a Christian home. She must wipe it from her mind, as if it never existed. If only she could forget the prince as easily. If only he would leave her alone.

She marches down the path to the estate van, admiring the wheel-patterned livery on the side panel as she tries the door. Locked! It does not matter, as she is not qualified to drive. She will *walk* to the cafe. A cup of tea never fails to raise her spirits.

The street sign reads Sheepwash Lane. She imagines a queue of bleating sheep, and Christ the Good Shepherd pointing his staff towards a salon scented with lavender. If she meets Him, Matty will be honoured to assist. She will work with her mother, soaping and combing and drying the fleece.

Every gate bears the name of the wood that made it. Pine, walnut, acacia; no mention of washrooms for sheep. No mention of ladies, or laundry.

Her legs complain of boredom. Her throat of neglect. She will knock on a door and ask for tea, and rest her rump on the step.

WHY PRIORITISE A first-aid kit over running water? Janice was mired in a reverie of psychiatry's absurdities, when she realised she hadn't seen Matty for a while. Abandoning Effie to her whimpering, she rushed to the next room, where Ronnie was attempting to open a sealed window. "Have you seen Matty?" Nothing to get wound up about at that stage. If Matty had strayed from the group, she wouldn't have gone far.

Clive hadn't seen Matty either. "I'll have a look outside." The note of concern ignited Janice's own. The risk of harm was miniscule, but management would take a dim view of their charges going AWOL. If Matty couldn't stay put with a ratio of one staff member to two patients, how could she live safely with three staff for twelve residents in three separate homes?

Janice had already scanned the gardens front and back from the upper windows. "I'll go. I've an inkling where she might be."

Racing from the house, Janice hoped her hunch was correct. Could it be that, at a level too deep to articulate, Matty *had* sensed her history with Sheepwash Lane? If she met the occupier of The Willows, she just might charm him. The incident needn't culminate in tragedy. Matty might secure her future by reconnecting with the past.

WITH HIS SUITCASE packed, the water turned off at the mains and the pipes drained, Henry was set to go. He paced the hallway, patting his coat to confirm his ticket, passport and wallet were where they ought to be. But his taxi was not.

He grabbed the phone and dialled the number. By the time the receptionist picked up and cottoned on his taxi was tardy, it was by ten minutes, not five.

"He must've come and got no answer." He almost heard her shrug. "Shall I send another?"

Sweat trickled from his armpits into the fabric of his cowboy shirt, but what could he do? It was too late to trek to the station on foot, dragging a wheeled suitcase like a ball and chain.

When he opened the front door and hefted said case

onto the step, the sun drove daggers into his eyes. Would he swelter in his overcoat? English weather could turn on a knife edge. Checking his pockets again, he pulled the door shut.

What the …? An old woman stood smack in the middle of his shrubbery, snaffling his lavender. "What in hell's name …"

The intruder gawped. It was obvious she was tapped, although someone had dressed her smartly in an old-lady style tweed suit. Henry swapped his scowl for a smile. "Can I be of any assistance?" Had she wandered from an old folks' home or an expedition from Ghyllside?

Up close, she didn't look menacing. If anything, she was more scared of him. Her jaw dropped, as did the lavender from her hand. He'd have to phone someone to collect her. As he fumbled for his key, his taxi drew up at the gate.

Henry was tempted to hop in and leave the crone to her own devices. Had the cab come on time, she could have harvested as much lavender as she wanted; even in its summer glory he never gave it a second glance. She could've stripped the shrubbery bare and he'd have been none the wiser. But, having found her on his property, he was obliged to help.

The driver hooted. Henry gestured he was on his way. He'd give his visitor a ride to the retirement home at the back of the grammar school. They'd sort her out, whether she was one of theirs or not. Lugging his case along the path, he offered her his hand. "Got yourself lost, have you?" He couldn't hang about coaxing an address out of her if he was to catch his train.

The woman only gaped. But the cavalry was coming! Above the hedge, Henry discerned a shock of dyed-pink hair. How pleasant to pass on the responsibility. How comical to learn that mental patients, if this gormless creature was typical, were as meek as lambs. Henry could embark on his first foreign holiday without fear of Armageddon. Ursula Marshall was a meddling misanthropist: the prospective new neighbours posed no threat. By the end of the afternoon, he'd be airborne; by evening, he'd be reacquainting himself with Irene's curves.

ENTERING A SMALL garden, Matty immediately feels at home. Behind the verdure, shrubs battle for supremacy, with a lavender bush bearing the jungle's crown. Matty snaps off a sprig and sniffs it. It is coy, refusing to surrender its bouquet. She rolls the brittle flowers between her fingertips and lets them fall. Drawing closer, the stems scraping her ankles, she ferrets around for a specimen worthy of her mother.

Your mother married a prince, did she? Trembling, Matty spins towards the voice.

Standing on the path in a heavy coat, the prince leers. Would he take her, here in the open? Would he lift her skirt and wield his joey, trusting she will hold her tongue for the sake of the boy?

There is no boy now. No baby. Can Matty conjure the courage to confront her tormentor? Give her rage free rein? *He ruined you, Matty. Stole your future, and your past. But you can crush him to rubble. Are you ready to seize your revenge?*

For her mother who died in childbirth. For the brother she loved as a son. For Matilda whose honesty branded her a liar.

The air is electric with anticipation. Stirring from half a century of hibernation, Matty is reborn. Her mother married, not a prince, but a roof over their heads, food on the table and babies in both their bellies. Truth is a monster roused from torpor, too wild to be tidied away. Truth makes mountains of her muscles, spears of her vertebrae, a powerhouse of her brain. After eons of incarceration, her life is set to resume.

Chapter 60

1936–1938

WOULD YOU HAVE made do with Walter, if you didn't inherit his teeth? I might have been able to keep you if I'd let him have his way. But, back then, I had no thought of children. Except for our brother.

In the alley, I let Walter lean into me, tolerating if not savouring his canoodling until a pistol-shaped lump pressed against my pelvis. When I wedged my fingers between us to nudge it aside, Walter must have assumed I wanted to *coddle* the thing. Before I could protest, it was in my hand.

It wasn't a pistol. It was part of his anatomy, yet more akin to Henry's arm than the worm between his legs. Lacking the vocabulary, we christened Hal's his joey; too tender a term for Walter's appendage.

What was I to do with it? Did he need to wee? Disgusted, I slapped him and raced for the bus.

Trundling uphill to Briarwood, I lamented the loss of my dance partner. But I was glad I had learned his character before committing my heart. Walter was as limited in his manners as in his looks.

The gas lamps flickered as I approached The Willows, weary in body and spirit, desperate for bed. I thought the worst was over. I thought I'd had a lucky escape.

I'D TAKEN A gamble in setting out for The Marsh before Mr Windsor arrived home. A gamble I came to repent. No-one could fault me for expecting the boy's own father to supervise him for a few hours, but I shouldn't have burdened a daily woman who was floundering already.

Hal couldn't give a coherent account of the incident. According to Father, Mrs Embleton was no more precise. As he said, if she *was* responsible, she'd be in no hurry to admit it. The extent of the burn suggested he hadn't merely brushed against the range. Yet, regardless how boisterous his behaviour, I was loath to believe Mrs Embleton would have *pushed* him. Regrettably, her remedy doubled the damage. The doctor said butter doesn't *cool* a burn, it *fries* it.

All was calm by the time I got home. Mrs Embleton dismissed. My brother asleep, thanks to a sedative, both for the physical pain, and for the wretchedness his Tilly wasn't there to soothe it. Mr Windsor listening to Mozart in the sitting room with a decanter of sherry at his side.

AS I ROSE from my seat to retire to bed, relieved Father hadn't admonished me as I deserved, he asked me to fetch a towel from the airing cupboard. Although I couldn't see any spillages, and a hankie should suffice to absorb anyone's tears, I didn't quibble. My mind was still in shock.

Returning with the towel, I froze. Father's trousers girdled his ankles, his hand on a hummock in his underpants.

His three-year-old son could control his bladder. Yet I braced myself to assist him, wondering if we'd need to re-upholster the chair.

Father gestured for me to pass him the towel and shut the door. "Sit across from me, Matilda. There's no cause for alarm."

Mechanically, I obeyed, averting my gaze as he draped the towel over his groin and wriggled out of his drawers like a bather at the shore. Muttering *You're a good lass, Matilda. You're a pretty lass. A kind lass. You understand, don't you, Matilda? You won't deny me this.*

I wanted to insist I *didn't* understand and I *would* deny him, but the words perished in my throat. His arm jerked up and down beneath the towel, his face a mask, his eyes glazed. "Wet your lips, Matilda." I pretended not to hear until he repeated himself with extra punch.

I whimpered, my traitorous tongue abrading my lips. Trapped, cemented to the chair, I bore my penance for disappointing Walter. For neglecting the boy.

With a macabre grimace, his body convulsed as if in the throes of a fit. What would become of Henry and me if he died?

When he stopped, he seemed enraptured. A moment later he was sobbing. "I'm sorry. I'm sorry. I'm sorry. It's because I miss her so."

Mrs Penrose? Mother? Did *his* grief outweigh mine? I stayed in my seat, pummelled by a tide of nausea. There had to be some flaw in me to glimpse two gentlemen's joeys in one night.

THE FOLLOWING MORNING it seemed incredible. Walter's peculiar behaviour in the ginnel. Mr Windsor's stranger antics at home. But Henry's injury was palpable enough. Ditto Mrs Embleton's absence. Between them they consumed every atom of my energy, filled every chamber of my mind.

Weeks passed with no talk of me flitting. Nor of Mrs Penrose moving in. As Henry's burn healed and scarred, fibrous tissue formed around our family of three. Binding us together. Keeping others out.

On Friday nights I remained at home, Father at the Lodge. The ballroom seemed as distant as the landscapes in the bedtime stories I'd told Mother at Mrs Braithwaite's. Hilda and Walter, people I'd invented to add a pinch of spice.

No-one spoke of finding a replacement for Mrs Embleton. I assumed her workload without complaint. Too busy to hanker after a life beyond The Willows. Too busy to face the guilt of harming Hal.

FOR HENRY'S FOURTH birthday, Father booked us a week in a Blackpool boarding house. Although October was late for a coastal holiday, we could catch the famous illuminations, with six miles of coloured tableaux comprised of electric light. Father was unusually jolly, laughing on the rides at the Pleasure Beach and rolling up his trousers to paddle in the sea. None of us wanted to come home again. The boy was in tears as he clambered into the car.

I brought back two souvenirs: one to hold in my hands, the other in my heart. A photographer snapped us on the promenade and, when we viewed the prints at his studio the next day, Father bought two copies, despite the tower sprouting from Henry's head. He didn't say as much, but I imagined he wanted me to have an amusing memento of our threesome when I eventually left The Willows.

My second souvenir went by the name Reginald Morgan. I wouldn't have met him if I hadn't paired up with a girl from the guesthouse. Iris, paid companion to a crotchety aunt in an antique bath chair, was more constrained than I, but more adept at escaping her shackles. Even without the romantic element she enabled, I'd have been delighted to make the connection. She made me realise how much I had missed having a friend.

When I mentioned I liked dancing, Iris suggested a trip to the Tower Ballroom. She didn't have to take the gentleman's part for long. We'd barely stepped onto the floor when I felt a tap on my back.

As a dancer, Reginald was Walter's equal, and his superior in teeth and hair. And in the music of his accent: a lilting Welsh where Walter's Cumbrian scraped the ears like a truculent violin.

I didn't get to confer with Iris until we caught the tram to South Shore. Fortunately she was as pleased with *her* partner as I was with Reginald. Twice we left Father playing cards with the aunt and, armed with buckets and spades, took Henry to the beach. The boy didn't grumble when two fine fellows chanced to picnic beside us; not when they feigned more interest in him than in us girls.

We also wheedled another two evenings at the ballroom, Reginald's appeal mounting with every dance. I'd planned to let him kiss me on our last night. Fondle my breast, although only through my blouse.

Then Father announced, over high tea of tripe and onions, *he* was also coming. "You'd enjoy that, wouldn't you, Henry. Your sister gliding across the dance floor. The ornate ceiling. The band."

"It's awfully late for him. He'll be cranky on the drive home."

"He'll sleep on the backseat, won't you, son?" Mr Windsor actually winked. "It's not a proper holiday until you bend the rules."

I found myself smirking as the landlady set down a plate of bread and butter. Seaview Lodge was girded with rules.

A true gentleman, Reginald talked business with Father and waltzed with the boy. But with no dark corners in the ballroom, how would I grant him that kiss?

Then, with half an hour until the final number, Father shook Reginald's hand, scooped up Henry and warned me to return to our digs before the landlady locked the door. He gave us his blessing? Conceivably he foresaw marriage to Reginald as a means of shedding the burden of his deceased wife's daughter.

In advance of the national anthem, I led Reginald outside and away from the glow of the prom. If Reginald thought me brazen, he didn't show it. He melted into me, his joey swelling as it pressed against my pelvis. A loving metamorphosis; unlike Walter, Reginald kept his joey in his pants.

We exchanged addresses, swore to write. I imagined our letters becoming progressively more intimate, a proposal within a year. I began to imagine a whitewashed cottage in the Welsh valleys, with room for a child or three. We would find a bed for my brother if his father agreed to let him go.

IN A FEW short weeks it was as if the holiday hadn't happened. As if Blackpool's beaches and glamour didn't exist. Not a word from Reginald, although I wrote to him each afternoon while Henry was napping.

All that remained was that silly photograph, the tower on Hal's head not an innocuous optical illusion but a taunt. A reminder I'd been foolish to pin my hopes on the man I met in the ballroom in its base. Yet I had to believe in someone. I couldn't succumb to despair. Thrice a day I sent the boy to watch for the postman. Thrice a day I hid my dejection when my brother reported the postie had passed us by.

I regretted not thinking to ask Iris for *her* address, although I'd be lost if she abandoned me too. If she blamed me, as Reginald must have done, I'd feel even more alone.

I thought Mother's death the worst I'd sustain. But God had chosen me for heavier trials. I was a girl hastened into womanhood, never imagining a woman's lot could be so harsh. Powerless to save myself, I resolved to dedicate myself to Hal's salvation. *He* would not follow his father to hell's inferno.

THE FIRST TIME I thought I was dreaming. The second I realised I'd been naive. Saliva and cherries would be paradise compared with this.

His weight crushed my chest. His arms pegged mine to my sides. His rock-solid joey thrusting into a cavity I hadn't known existed, shattering the lock. I couldn't stop myself screeching, forgetting my fears of waking the boy. "It won't hurt if you don't fight it." I dug my nails into my palms, prayed for it to finish, but it didn't prevent the sting of his limb chafing the walls of that private passageway, the force fit to spark a fire.

At breakfast, his conduct did not alter: he unfurled the newspaper, joked Henry had shot up an inch overnight and thanked me for his perfectly boiled egg. Not a whisper of change in him. Not a shadow of shame.

In my room at night, he was beyond reason. So I mustered the courage to confront him in the sitting room one evening, my brother snug in bed. Discounting *my* feelings, he polluted the air between us with a litany of justifications.

"My house, my rules." and "You're the double of your mother, how could I resist?" and "You're not a child, Matilda. There are lasses younger than you with a brood of bairns." and "I know what you got up to at Blackpool. You've been gagging for it since." and "What choice do I have after you chased off Mrs Penrose?" and "Sing it from the rooftops if you want folk knowing you're a slut," and "Go if you're not happy. I'm not keeping you in chains."

I WAS TRAPPED. My brother would languish if I left him but

I would continue to suffer if I stayed. Besides, I had nowhere to go. I was willing to sacrifice my own happiness for Henry's but, the more I endured the prince's nocturnal visits, the more degraded I became. When I looked in the mirror, my skin, hair and eyes still shone but underneath I was tarnished. The prince had blackened my soul.

Disguising my disgrace exhausted my patience: I penalised Henry for his father's sins. I pushed him away when he came for a cuddle. I spanked him for refusing to tidy his toys. I sent him to bed without a story. I shook him for dawdling on the way home from the park.

How could I guide and protect him if I became as cruel to Henry as his father was to me? I had to control myself before I did him some serious damage.

Then, one night, as he knelt by his bed, his palms pressed together and his eyes screwed shut, I heard him ask God to make him a good boy tomorrow. "So I won't make Tilly sad."

The next day, I tried harder. Perhaps my brother did too. But it couldn't prevent me shouting at him for clumsiness. As I mopped up spilt milk, we were both in tears.

I would go to Wales and throw myself on Reginald's mercy. Even if he didn't care for me romantically, he was enough of a gentleman to help me get back on my feet. Find me a refuge, a job to pay for my room and board. A space to recuperate, to gather my strength and plan how to deal with things differently on returning home.

I racked my brains for a way of disappearing without hurting Henry, but he was too young to keep a secret and

I'd no notion of what Mr Windsor would do if he learnt of my plan. Would he try to thwart me or be glad to see me go? I couldn't risk finding out.

Who could I turn to? Almost at my wit's end, I remembered Violet's mother. She'd promised to be there if I needed her the day we left The Marsh.

"YOU MUST HAVE egged him on."

"How? I didn't *know* about relations until he took advantage."

"Don't act the innocent with me, Matilda Osborne. I've seen you and Hilda trooping to Stanley Hall like a pair of hoors."

Her tone made clear what a hoor was. Fortunately, my brother was outside. When I shooed him off to play, his eyes widened. "In the street? On my own?" Mrs Braithwaite sneered.

Now I sipped my tea, although it had gone as cold as Mrs B's welcome. "It's debauched."

Mrs Braithwaite barked into her fist. She'd been hacking and wheezing since she opened the door to us but I'd paid it no heed. Now it wrung her whole body, as if she'd swallowed a hare and it was boxing an exit. Bending forward, she took a rag from the pocket of her pinafore and showered it with blood-spangled phlegm. "Aye, there's worse fates than a bit of how's your father with the man who feeds and clothes you and puts coal in the grate."

Setting down my cup, I prepared to go. But something made me pause. "I'll go to the vicar. He'll tell Mr Windsor to mend his ways."

When Mrs Braithwaite began to shake, I took it for another coughing fit. I thought she was insane when it shifted to laughter – but she thought *I* was. "Tell the vicar, tell the world if you're after a ticket to Ghyllside."

"The asylum?"

"Think on it, Matilda." For a moment, I glimpsed the old Mrs B. The woman who considered me a second daughter. "Who would *you* trust, a master mason or the orphaned daughter of a lunatic without a penny to her name?"

"How dare you call Mother a lunatic! Just because she married the wrong man!"

"I mean your father, you barmpot."

Her nonsense made my head spin, but I jumped to his defence. "He was a war hero. Fought for his country in the Flanders Fields which is more than Mr Windsor did."

"That's as maybe, but he didn't come through it a hero. You know how he died?"

Mother said it was *of* the war but not *in* the war. And it wasn't Spanish flu. "How could I? I was a baby."

"It's time you twigged you're from tainted stock, Matilda Osborne. Bring you down a peg. Rid you of your airs and graces."

Should I have left there and then? Reminded her God creates all men equal? Proclaimed I was proud of my father, and didn't care a fig what others thought? Too stubborn for my own good, I read his epitaph in her eyes. "Suicide?"

"Don't take *my* word for it. Ask anyone hereabouts." Mrs Braithwaite cast red clots onto her rag again. "Your mam should have told you. It's cruel, folk knowing the crack and you're in the dark."

My father not a hero but a mental case? A criminal. A moral coward. Something perished inside me, such that when Mrs Braithwaite reached out, I flinched. She gloated, as if taking pleasure from my debasement, as if she'd filched the last red rosette. I'd never been fairly matched against Violet, with the main prize beyond my reach. Violet's mother qualified for a war widow's pension. Mine didn't. *That's* why she married the prince.

The boy's jacket lay rumpled on the doorstep. With his shirt sleeves rolled up and his socks sagging at his ankles, he was playing hopscotch with a gang of ruffians. He didn't come when I shouted, so I marched down the street and wrenched him by the ear.

Chapter 61

April 1991

IN SOME FARAWAY future, it might make a story to tickle her Nottingham friends. When she can distil the humour as Phil did with the baby propped up to watch *Tom and Jerry* on TV. Life on social work's frontier: if you couldn't laugh, you'd cry.

Stunned, as if *she* had been assaulted, Janice evinced neither laughter nor tears as she relived the moment for both Health and Social Services reporting systems, and for colleagues with the time and sympathy to listen. Apart from the taxi driver – and the victim himself – she was the key witness, for all she wished she *hadn't* seen Matty act the stereotypical psychotic, *hadn't* heard her blood-curdling shriek. As she told Graham Scott at The Willows, and David Pargeter at Ghyllside, the attack was unprovoked. Although she'd trespassed into his garden, the man approached her patiently, as if offering an apple to a wild pony. When Matty lashed out, he staggered, stumbling over a suitcase to land on his back. By the time Janice got there, Matty was clawing at his face. It was the driver who pulled her off and bundled the man into the taxi, while Janice hovered, kicking at the crumbling concrete path.

Matty swiftly reverted to her brand of normal, prattling about her mother marrying a prince; what was once endearingly quirky, now a trailer for a horror film. Waiting together in the frowzy shrubbery – the taxi driver having radioed his base to summon reinforcements – Janice could hardly look at her. Nauseous from unruly hormones, she concentrated on avoiding spewing up.

The relief when Graham arrived! He'd quizzed Matty gently – and surprisingly skilfully – but couldn't fathom why she'd gone berserk. Then he drove Matty to Ghyllside, and sent Janice back to Corporation Road, where Clive was freaking out. Amid whinging they'd been promised tea at a cafe, he drove the rest of the group to Tuke House.

Everyone treated Janice kindly. Far kinder than she deserved, given she'd scuppered Matty's chances. She'd mismanaged the case from the get-go, convinced she knew better than Norman with his metaphorical measuring stick, than Graham with his conservatism, than Mervyn with his biological reductionism. She'd learned a painful lesson about environmental influence: put a woman in a madhouse and she'll behave as a madwoman, but putting her in an ordinary house wouldn't necessarily reverse the process.

It could have done if Janice had intervened before she laid into Mr Windsor. If she hadn't been distracted, not only by Effie, but by the environment within herself.

A feminist wasn't *allowed* to believe pregnancy turned a woman's mind to mush. Much as Janice admired those whose brains stayed sharp while their bodies softened, it struck her that *her* transition to motherhood might take a different trajectory. Her beginnings in the belly of a woman for whom she was at best an inconvenience, at worst an incursion, crystallised a determination to reassure the embryo that she'd nurture it and shelter it, protect its life with hers.

It wasn't rational to keep it. The timing and circumstances were abysmal. Her career barely launched and the father a virtual stranger, not even her type. She hadn't a clue what part Mervyn would want in their future, if any. It didn't matter. With or without him, this child would thrive.

Her parents would support her. Her real parents, the pair who shaped her personality, not her DNA. *They* – or the prospect of them – could linger in limbo to be resurrected if and when their grandchild raised questions she couldn't answer. She had other priorities now.

Somehow the day's debacle gave her focus. Janice had travelled miles from the girl who'd moaned to her mother that her life was unravelling. If they agreed, she'd go home to have the baby, and get a job with a more varied caseload in a locality team.

No point staying in Cumbria when she'd exhausted the options for Matty. Or so she'd thought, until Graham Scott phoned to invite her to accompany him on a visit to The Willows. "The Chief Exec wants me to patch things up. Keep it out of the press."

"DON'T WORRY, MATTY, you'll soon settle in."

"My name is Matilda. And I'll never settle here. Never."

The nice nurses laugh; the nasty ones tell her to *mind your manners* and bustle her so roughly in and out of the bath that, undressing for bed, her arms are blotted with bruises. When she protests, they threaten her with the psychiatrist.

At first she treasures these interviews with clever men in three-piece suits. They will acknowledge their blunder and release her. From the defendant's side of the desk, she watches them convert her plea into luscious copperplate. Until she mentions her stepfather, and the nibs cease scratching at the page.

Each night in her narrow bed, denied sleep by the chorus of grunts from her fellow detainees, she repeats the journey from the convent. When the taxi swept up the tree-lined drive and stopped at the imposing building, she resigned herself to servitude in a country house. Although Briarwood had raised her expectations above Violet's, she would have adapted. It wouldn't be forever: war would bring peace and new horizons to pariah girls like her.

She drew solace from seeing Mr Windsor in the teak-clad entrance lobby. If she lodged here, she'd be free from further violation; if she forgave his past offences, he might let her meet her brother on her day off.

Mr Windsor hadn't come for reconciliation. He'd come to destroy her, to see her buried alive. With the force of a biblical stoning, each loss and betrayal of the last few years rained down on her again. But she rallied. Roared and spat.

"You're not my father!" He laughed, said her father was tapped, and had bequeathed his madness to her. When her rage turned physical, they trussed her up in a jacket that tied at the back and pinioned her arms across her chest.

Matilda will never submit, but she hides her vexation from the staff. Except when swamped by despair. "I'm twenty years old and my life is over."

The nurse chuckles. "If *you're* twenty, Matty Osborne, *I* must be in nappies."

Matilda examines the woman's face anew, its crags, caked but not concealed, with cosmetics. "Have I been here before?"

"You're home on Ward 24, my love. Safe and sound. You're done with the pressures of Tuke House."

"Can I get jelly babies?"

"Of course you can, sweetheart. I'll write you a chit in the morning and one of the care assistants will escort you to the shop."

The nurse stows her belongings in a bedside cabinet, its top refreshingly free of photographs and potted plants. No trinkets to tidy. No knickknacks gathering dust. Nothing to clutter her mind.

"Remember that poem," says the nurse.

"I don't know any poetry."

"Nonsense. You kept the entire ward entertained. Away, we'll say it together: *Matilda told such dreadful lies it made one gasp and stretch one's eyes …*"

———

"THE CHIEF EXECUTIVE will be writing to apologise, but is

there anything *else* we could do to smooth the waters?"

Mr Scott proved more accommodating in the front parlour of The Willows than at the consultation meeting in the school hall. Henry had been braced to defend himself against accusations of harassment; the man's air of appeasement had him stumped. Not so Irene.

He'd been touched when, having missed his flight, she'd boarded the next plane, but her aversion to The Willows was as fierce as ever. Yet he didn't contradict her when she informed Mr Scott that the house was no refuge. "But how's he gonna get shot of it with care-in-the-community for neighbours?"

"It would do for a mental health centre," said Mr Scott. "If you get an estate agent to valuate it, I'll see about taking it off your hands."

Henry pictured Ursula Marshall's face when she discovered there'd not just be loonies around the corner but comings and goings all along Sheepwash Lane. Parking spots clogged with social workers and psychiatrists. "I *can't* move, though, can I?"

He watched Irene's gaze flit to the mantelpiece where, earlier that morning, she'd dusted a photograph of him as a boy with Blackpool tower perched on his head. Before she could side-track the conversation, Henry outlined the position regarding his sick leave and the doctor's intimation a psychology report might grant him an early pension. "But the waiting list's nigh on a year."

"I can escalate that for you." Mr Scott seemed so pleased to play Mr Fix-it, Henry felt bad they'd run out of problems.

But the social worker had another trick up her sleeve. Apart from a bizarre exchange with Irene about her hair, she'd sat like a dummy until then. "Does the name Matilda Osborne ring a bell? Please keep it confidential, but that's who attacked you. If she had some connection to this house, it would help her rehabilitation."

Irene gasped. "Matilda?"

When the doorbell rang earlier, Henry had nipped into the sitting room while Irene met the visitors at the door. He had roughly a minute to decide what to do with the photo on the mantelpiece of the seaside holiday he couldn't recall. Three figures: how someone divides them into a pair plus one could reveal the essence of his personality. Like the optical illusion of the young woman and the old crone.

For years, Henry perceived it as a picture of brother and sister, their father out on a limb. Yet Irene had mistaken his father and Tilly for the primary couple, Henry the only child. Today it seemed different again. Grouping by gender: the boy splitting off from the girl to stand by the man he would become. Hearing voices in the hallway, Henry stashed the photograph in a drawer.

Does the name ring a bell? Henry directed his reply, not to the woman who'd posed the question, but to nice Mr Scott. "Osborne?"

Perpetual sunshine. Irene in her element. Never seeing Linda Quinn or Geoff Boyne again.

Chapter 62

1938–1939

D OUBTLESS YOU WOULD have preferred a better father.
But Mr Windsor took care of you. In accordance with
his idiosyncratic style. Not as an aggrieved guardian. Not as
the guilty party. But as a businessman, practical to the core.

YOU COULD SAY the nuns took in fallen women out of
charity. Or you could say saints need sinners more than
sinners need saints. Our labour was the lifeblood of the
convent, our toil the bedrock of the sisters' leisured prayer.
Their virtue glistened against our depravity, their voluntary
abstinence sanctified by our abhorrence of the regime foisted
upon us.

I refused to dwell on the spitefulness. I refused to
crumble. I ignored the cold corridors, the sound of sobbing
in the dormitory, skin cracked and flaky from the laundry.

The first day I pushed away my plate of grey stew but a growling stomach taught me to wolf down whatever was offered the instant grace was said. I almost wept when they swapped my pretty frock for a shapeless gown of coarse cotton and hid my hair with a scarf. But, with no mirror to disabuse me, I imagined myself modelling for *Vogue*. When children's voices rang out from the adjacent schoolyard my innards curdled, until I pictured Hal playing among them, secure in the sense of his Tilly nearby.

The chapel, where we assembled twice a day, was an art gallery and concert hall. I sloughed off my woes to contemplate the stained-glass windows, the exquisite carvings on wood and stone. The choir so angelic I couldn't believe it comprised the nuns who cawed at us like crows.

We might have trembled at the nuns' chastisements, but we didn't do so alone. United in affliction, the camaraderie echoed my childhood on The Marsh. The sisters might decree when we ate and slept, and even when we might move our bowels, but they could not order our thoughts. They controlled our tongues in the daytime, but the night was ours.

At sixteen, Gladys was pleased to find a situation as a priest's housekeeper, until she discovered her duties included warming his bed. Agatha, now eighteen, was sent to charm a gentleman every Saturday for five years, to redeem her father's debts. A bank-manager, with bowler hat and furled umbrella, dragged Nelly, at fourteen, into the shrubbery in a public park. When she limped home in the gaslight, her father thrashed her for staying out late.

These girls sobbed as they told their stories, and

sometimes we who listened joined in. "It wasn't your fault," we chorused. "It wasn't your fault." If their bellies allowed, another girl would climb into their bed and embrace them until drained of guilt and shame.

A different kind of story made *me* cry.

"It was divine," Beryl said, of her secret rendezvous with a married man. "I've no regrets, for all the trouble it's brung me."

"He made me feel like a lady," said Winifred, of the postman's visits while her employer was out.

"You forgot you hadn't two pennies to rub together," said Doreen, about summer evenings in a meadow with an amorous farmhand. "Small wonder the church is agin' it. It takes you to heaven, and it's free."

Your father robbed me of more than I realised. Might Reginald have taken *me* to heaven too? Might Walter, with his buck teeth and thinning hair, have shown me relations could bring joy?

The new knowledge awoke me from my stupor. It fuels my anger, sharpens my resolve. To survive. To shine. The prince might think he's broken me, and the nuns might try to mill those shards to dust, but I will triumph. I'll fetch you from the family who adopts you. I'll make a home for you and my brother. I'll fulfil my ambition to become a lady doctor. I'll dedicate myself to diverting girls from here.

"WHICH ARE YOU, Matilda, victim or vamp?"

I was drawn to Ethel from the beginning. Whether it was her lopsided grin or the riot of frizzy red hair rebelling against her cotton scarf, I can't say, but I hoped we'd be friends. So when she peeled back my blanket with a curt *Shove over, Matilda, my feet are icebergs!* I welcomed her in, although there was barely room for one girl's monstrous belly and her feet weren't chilled in the least.

We nested our heads on the single pillow, clutching hands and juggling hips and shoulders, our outer arms strapping our chests to prevent us tumbling to the floor. The whisper of her breath in my ear. "Or were you like me, penalised for loving too freely?"

I was happy for her: better another girl gain a rosette than no rosettes get awarded at all. "What's his name?"

"Promise you won't tell?"

I promised, but what did it matter? After this, we'd go our separate ways.

"Mabel."

"Mabel?" I cupped my mouth lest the others hear me laughing.

Ethel tensed. "I thought you'd be broadminded."

So it wasn't a joke. "I'm sorry. I've never heard of such a thing."

"And now you have, you're appalled."

"No! I didn't know you could."

"Oh, you can!"

Jealousy bubbled inside me as Ethel itemised Mabel's qualities, stinging my throat. I stroked her belly. "Mabel didn't do this?"

"Of course not, you oaf!" Ethel laughed but, as she related the dark side of her story, tears stanched her words. "Love made us brave, but it made us reckless." The stronger their affection, the less inhibited they became. "What chumps we were. We couldn't imagine people could hate something so pure."

But their neighbours were incensed. A band of youths – *Clean-living boys we'd been at school with!* – accosted them in the forest, threw them on the ground and thrust into them one after another. "I stopped counting after the fifth. Our only consolation was lying on a bed of pine needles, not a concrete floor."

Futile to report the incident: one of their assailants was the local bobby. "Corrective rape, they called it. After a fashion, it worked."

I filed away the term to ponder later. Right then, I burned with fury and concern, albeit the flames diminished by disappointment that someone as bold as Ethel would let others dictate whom she loved. "It worked?"

"Don't get me wrong, I'm an invert through and through. I'll die before another fellow fucks me. But it was the finish of me and Mabel. We tried, but every meeting resurrected our ordeal."

NIGHT-TIME PLEASURES TEMPERED the days' drudgery. Canoodling with Ethel abolished all pain. Even Mr Windsor's brutality seemed trifling when recast as the prologue to a genuine romance. Until a crash at evening worship fractured the sweet strains of "Ave Maria". I turned to see my friend flopped between kneeler and pew.

Sister Bernadette rushed to her assistance, but Sister Ignacia, who was conducting, urged the choir on. When the hymn ended, Mother Superior stood by the altar and instructed us to face the front while the sisters escorted her to the infirmary.

"WE GIVE THEE thanks, Almighty God, for all Thy benefits, Who lives and reigns for ever and ever. Amen." We crossed ourselves, poised to be dispatched to the laundry, but Sister Ignacia left an uncustomary gap. It transported me back to The Willows and Mr Windsor telling me he'd lost a wife but gained a son. Would Sister Ignacia's news be good, bad or a tantalising mixture? "We thank you, Heavenly Father, for the life of Ethel Jerrold, our sister in Christ." What did that mean?

Some argued Ethel must be dead because we'd never given thanks for anyone else's life as she was evacuated to the infirmary or the lying-in room. But others protested that, if she were dead, we'd be praying *for the soul of the dear departed*. When Winifred petitioned the normally kindlier Sister Bernadette for clarity, she chided her for putting earthly attachments above her trust in God.

I took comfort in Ethel's love for Mabel. I imagined them under the dryers at the beauty salon, a younger girl polishing their nails. I sent them to Browne's to purchase ballgowns on Mr Windsor's account. I took them to the Stanley Hall to make up a foursome with Hilda, and we'd foxtrot and tango to the Savana Band till twelve.

Bathed in dreams, I scarcely noticed my hand dip under my nightgown and edge around my bulky belly to explore between my legs.

THE LYING-IN ROOM is a small-scale dormitory with six beds. Four are currently occupied – me, Beryl, Gladys and dear Ethel, very much alive.

They whisked *you* away before I left the delivery room: before I held you, before I saw your face. I pray they transferred you as quickly to your new mother, before you had chance to miss the one who'd harboured you since spring.

Unlike Beryl, Gladys and me, Ethel has to nurse her son until he's robust enough to leave. No-one wants the bother of a sickly child. Not even Ethel. She groans when Sister Francis brings him from the nursery for four-hourly feeds.

When I hear his plaintive bleat, my breasts dribble milk I made for you. Ethel's indifference doubles the torment. It isn't *his* fault his father harmed her. It isn't *his* fault she's obliged to let him go.

Foolish to find romance in her story. There's nothing noble in loving another girl. Not if it renders her so unnatural she makes an enemy of her child.

FLOUNCING OUT OF bed, Winifred snatched the baby from Ethel's arms. I braced myself for wailing, but Winifred had unbuttoned her nightgown; he latched onto her breast as if she'd nursed him from birth.

The whole room was soothed. Ethel began to cry, honest tears that herald healing. I scrambled into bed beside her, steadied her shudders and told her, as we'd told the others, she wasn't to blame.

Beryl, Gladys and I became milkmaids to her nameless child. Passing him from teat to teat, he sucks the pain from our wooden breasts.

When Sister Francis takes him back to the nursery, I

creep into Ethel's bed and spoon against her. While the other two sleep, she tutors me in female love. Ethel says war is brewing, and war scoffs at certainties, recalibrates creeds. Amid the devastation, war will liberate Sapphists through friendships fostered in the Women's Royal Navy. We'll march side-by-side in our uniforms, medals pinned above our breasts. Competing and cooperating for the accolades, as with Violet for rosettes.

BLANKETS YANKED BACK, a biting chill awakes me. Blinded by torchlight, I'm wrenched to my feet. "May God have mercy on your souls!" Sister Ignatia makes a mockery of mercy: she thinks we should roast in hell.

Ethel is exiled to the laundry. I'm locked in a nun's barren cell, with a straw mattress, a prie-dieu and an agile mouse.

Sister Bernadette brings my porridge. "Your father's been notified."

"My father's dead."

"Your guardian, then. He's making arrangements."

"He'll have me home?" Even if he used my transgression to justify his night-time visits, it wouldn't be forever.

"I'm to accompany you. All that way in a taxi. Perhaps I'll get a glimpse of the Lakes."

Together in a taxi: dare I trust her with the truth? *Is* she the kindest of the nuns, or the one with the prettiest face? When Gladys reported what the priest had done, they rinsed her mouth with soap. I hear Mrs Braithwaite asking, between spells of coughing, whose version they'd believe.

As for Ethel, can I ever forgive her? If I'd been sharper,

would *I* have tried to save my skin?

"God won't condemn us," I told Sister Ignatia. "Only you think it vile." When I reached for Ethel's hand, she shook me off.

"Who is the instigator?" cried Sister Ignatia. "Ethel, did you invite Matilda into your bed?"

"No! She forced me!" God must've favoured Ethel, because the tears began to flow.

"The Lord can't abide a liar, Matilda," said Sister Ignatia. "And neither can I."

Chapter 63

Autumn 1991

ALTHOUGH THEIR LANGUAGE skills are deplorable, Henry and Irene have successfully synchronised their daily rhythms with those of their adoptive country. After a coffee and toast *desayuno* at a quarter to eight, she'll grab her tabard and he'll grab a basket as they exit their first-floor apartment. At the bottom of the steps, he'll watch her unlock the salon before meandering to the market to amuse the stallholders vis-à-vis his ineptitude with the peseta, the Castilian for garlic and how to test the freshness of a melon. At two, he'll help Irene shut up shop, serve her lunch and bed her, the order dependent on which of her appetites reigns supreme.

Afterwards, she'll draw back, separating their skin like a label from a waxed sheet. *Sorry, Henry*, she'll say. *This bedroom's an oven.* Henry will apologise, and promise to find someone to fit an air conditioning unit as fierce as the one in the salon, while relishing the petty quarrels that validate their godless coupling.

Today, when Irene complains the ceiling fan stirs the air without troubling the temperature, he strokes her cheek and reminds her it was her idea to relocate to the Costa Blanca.

"I *know* it was my idea. I can't get over *you*, but. I thought they'd have to cart you out of that crypt in a coffin. No regrets?"

At fleeing a draughty house with windows rattling his father's disapproval? At bidding farewell to the sector that swapped numeracy for a machine? At landing a May-to-September affair? His sole regret is not bailing out sooner. "I'm the luckiest guy alive."

"All those years waiting for Tilly."

The name makes him wince. It hangs between them, tangible: an office envelope with a disconcerting memo inside. Henry pulls on his shorts. "I was a stubborn old mug."

Irene picks her bra from the floor and threads her arms through the straps. "I still wonder if it was *her*."

The memo escapes the envelope, but Henry doesn't *have* to read it. He pauses in the process of putting on his T-shirt, shielding his face until he's more composed. "Who are we talking about, dear?" After a hectic morning at the salon, Irene has a tendency to ramble.

"The one who belted you. The old biddy from Ghyllside."

Henry saunters to the window. Raising a slat of the blind, the glare scorches his eyes. When he turns, Irene is wriggling into her knickers, salmon-pink lace to match her bra. "A bolt from the blue whichever way you look at it!"

The mimeographed sheet unfolds itself, insisting he inspect it. Henry gathers his defences. *If* he had a sister, she'd have had a claim on the profits from the sale of The Willows. Not half the money, of course, but Henry has made a substantial donation in her honour. To a mental health charity Irene recommended: a local outfit her daughter has hooked up with, some malarkey about getting Ghyllside inmates involved in dramatic arts. What more can he do? He scrunches the memo and hurls it at the sun.

MATTY IS PREPARING for another recital when her visitors breeze in. The words are etched on her brain but even the most eminent orators must maintain their instrument in tiptop condition. She enunciates carefully, rounding and elongating the vowels while keeping the consonants crisp. She lifts her chin, connecting with every member of the audience, including those who have sneaked in without paying.

She has been much in demand of late – comic verse is undergoing a revival among the chattering classes – and, although it can be tiring, it is never tire*some* to perform. Nevertheless, as the nuns cross the room to join her, she welcomes the prospective respite. They have not come to hear her rehearse. For such distinguished guests, her maid will say puff to rationing and offer them an unscheduled cup of tea.

As the pair approach, Matty gasps at the younger nun's

guise. The streak of pink in her hair is of no consequence – reminding her of a gypsy she once befriended – and she is fascinated neither nun wears a wimple or veil. But her shape is astounding. Matty cannot help herself. Before they have wished each other good morning, she voices her dismay. "Did the bishop do that?"

At the younger nun's blush, Matty clamps her lips together. *Silly girl!* They cautioned her about those dreadful lies.

Matty switches her gaze to the older nun. Her peculiar prawn-like features behove the cloistered life. She leans forward to hand Matty a bundle. Gripping her seat, Matty shakes her head, pressing against the upholstery as if to shelter within.

"Effie wants you to have her, Matty," says the younger nun. "She can't take her to Corporation Road."

Naturally: the corporation has no use for babies. But would not the convent give it a home? She braces herself to explore its geography, albeit only with her eyes, her body burrowing into the back of the chair. "It is beautiful." Matty expects the nun to slap her, or warn her not to get attached.

"She's yours," says the older nun.

Without command or consent, Matty's arms mould themselves into a cradle. The baby melds with her body, its wobbly head pillowed in the crook of her elbow. "My own baby?"

"Her name's Margaret," says the older nun.

The baby's nose wrinkles. Matty shares her distaste, although the name was good enough for the King's second child. Should she call her Princess? Or Georgia? No, she will stamp out all memory of her baby's father. Kitty will protect them both; ensure they thrive.

As she wipes a tear from the baby's cheek, her lady in waiting waltzes in; teacups, saucers, teapot, milk jug and lidded sugar bowl tinkling on the tray. The willow-pattern set is Matty's favourite: a memento of her dazzling Chinese tour.

"Shall I be mother?" Matty turns to the younger nun. "Janice, how do you take your tea?"

Want to know what's next for Matty?

Missing Matty already? Can't wait to find out what happens next? Then subscribe to Anne Goodwin's newsletter for an exclusive extract from her work in progress, the sequel to *Matilda Windsor is Coming Home*.
Go to bit.ly/mattyat100

You can also tell Anne what you thought of Matilda Windsor by getting in touch with her via her website or Twitter, or by leaving a review online.

Acknowledgements

Thanks to all the patients / residents / service users and colleagues, who taught me so much about mental health, and life in general. I had no thoughts of writing this novel when we worked together; I hope I have made good use of your wisdom without intruding on your privacy.

Thanks to Cumbria where I grew up (albeit not alongside Matty in the 1920s and 30s); apologies for the liberties I've taken with your history and geography. Thanks to the GonMad Cumbrian Dictionary for reminders of the rich dialect.

I'm indebted to several people who assisted in the process of transforming my thoughts into a novel through critiquing extracts and pre-submission drafts; providing factual information and advice; some generous folk fulfilling both functions. Any remaining inaccuracies, intentional or unintentional, are my own. The roll of honour includes Alan Steele, Amanda Bell, Anne de Gruchy, Anne Hudson, Charli Mills, Clare Goodwin, Eamonn Griffin, Janet McElwee, Katherine Doube, Keith Finlinson, Linda Bowes, Norah Colvin, Steffanie Edward, Terry Anderson, Trevor Jones AKA How Michael and Valerie Francis.

Special thanks to John Whalley for naming the hospital and to the members of Nottingham Writers' Studio who welcomed Matty on her first public appearance in 2015, and to Catherine Haines who organised the event.

Plaudits yet again to the small-but-perfectly-formed team at Inspired Quill, especially Sara Jayne Slack for steering the publication process and for incisive and encouraging editing. Thanks to Valeria Aguilera for the vibrant cover, melding the gloomy Victorian asylum with Matty's polkadot dress!

Finally, thanks to you, the reader, for taking a chance on my words.

About the Author

Anne Goodwin grew up in the non-touristy part of Cumbria, where this novel is set. When she went to university ninety miles away, no-one could understand her accent. After nine years as a student, her first post on qualifying as a clinical psychologist was in a longstay psychiatric hospital in the process of closing.

Her debut novel, *Sugar and Snails*, about a woman who has kept her past identity a secret for thirty years, was shortlisted for the 2016 Polari First Book Prize. Her second novel, *Underneath*, about a man who keeps a woman captive in his cellar, was published in 2017. Her short story collection, *Becoming Someone*, on the theme of identity, was published in November 2018. Anne is also a book blogger battling disreputable fictional therapists and inaccurate portrayals of mental health matters.

Find the author via her website:

annegoodwin.weebly.com

Or Twitter:

@Annecdotist

More From This Author

Sugar and Snails

At fifteen, she made a life-changing decision. Thirty years on, it's time to make another.

When Diana escaped her misfit childhood, she thought she'd chosen the easier path. But the past lingers on, etched beneath her skin, and life won't be worth living if her secret gets out.

As an adult, she's kept other people at a distance... until Simon sweeps in on a cloud of promise and possibility. But his work is taking him to Cairo, the city that transformed her life. She'll lose Simon if she doesn't join him. She'll lose herself if she does.

Sugar and Snails describes Diana's unusual journey, revealing the scars from her fight to be true to herself. A triumphant mid-life coming-of-age story about bridging the gap between who we are and who we feel we ought to be.

Shortlisted for the Polari First Book Prize, 2016

Underneath

He never intended to be a jailer …

After years of travelling, responsible to no-one but himself, Steve has resolved to settle down. He gets a job, buys a house and persuades Liesel to move in with him.

Life's perfect, until Liesel delivers her ultimatum: if he won't agree to start a family, she'll have to leave. He can't bear to lose her, but how can he face the prospect of fatherhood when he has no idea what being a father means? If he could somehow make her stay, he wouldn't have to choose … and it would be a shame not to make use of the cellar.

Will this be the solution to his problems, or the catalyst for his own unravelling?

Becoming Someone

What shapes the way we see ourselves?

An administrator is forced into early retirement; a busy doctor needs a break. A girl discovers her sexuality; an older man explores a new direction for his. An estate agent seeks adventure beyond marriage; a photojournalist retreats from an overwhelming world. A woman reduces her carbon footprint; a woman embarks on a transatlantic affair. A widow refuses to let her past trauma become public property; another marks her husband's passing in style.

Thought-provoking, playful and poignant, these 42 short stories address identity from different angles, examining the characters' sense of self at various points in their lives. What does it mean to be a partner, parent, child, sibling, friend? How important is work, culture, race, religion, nationality, class? Does our body, sexuality, gender or age determine who we are?

Is identity a given or can we choose the *someone* we become?

All titles available from all major online and offline outlets.

Lightning Source UK Ltd.
Milton Keynes UK
UKHW042136120521
383424UK00005B/29